"With her clean, sleek prose, Laurie Alice Eakes is one of the best storytellers the world has today. *A Necessary Deception* is one of her best, deftly weaving an intriguing spy chase with the elegant life of the ton in a beautiful love story that kidnaps unwitting readers and holds them hostage to the very last page."

Delle Jacobs, award-winning author of
His Majesty, the Prince of Toads

"In *A Necessary Deception*, Laurie Alice Eakes weaves the fine silk threads of historical richness, dangerous intrigue, and forbidden romance into a flawless literary tapestry. This is Georgette Heyer meets Terri Blackstock in 1812 Regency London, an adventure that will leave readers breathless."

Louise M. Gouge, award-winning author of
At the Captain's Command

"A time of romance and intrigue with characters who grip one's heart and won't let go—this is the kind of book I look forward to reading when I want to be uplifted and carried away."

Jennifer Hudson Taylor, author of *Highland Blessings*
and *Highland Sanctuary*

"Laurie Alice Eakes writes a page-turning story with an in-depth knowledge of the period, an eye for detail, and an escalating mystery that will keep readers guessing till the end."

Ruth Axtell Morren, author of *Wild Rose*
and *The Rogue's Redemption*

"Intriguing, suspenseful, masterful, and romantic—all the things you want in a great book! Add to that enchanting characters with real problems and real flaws who grow throughout the story, and a twist-and-turn plot, and I guarantee that once you dive into this book, you'll be happily lost in Regency London for the duration."

MaryLu Tyndall, Christy Award nominee and author of
the Surrender to Destiny series

"Laurie Alice Eakes's novel is a captivating combination of romance and suspense set in the glittering Regency period."

Jane Myers Perrine, author of *Second Chance Bride*

"*A Necessary Deception* will lure you into a fascinating Regency full of danger, surprises, and a romance to quicken your pulse."

Jillian Kent, author of *Secrets of the Heart*

Books by Laurie Alice Eakes

THE MIDWIVES

Lady in the Mist

THE DAUGHTERS OF BAINBRIDGE HOUSE

A Necessary Deception

A NECESSARY DECEPTION

LAURIE ALICE EAKES

A Novel

Revell

a division of Baker Publishing Group
Grand Rapids, Michigan

Published by Revell
a division of Baker Publishing Group
P.O. Box 6287, Grand Rapids, MI 49516-6287
www.revellbooks.com

Printed in the United States of America

Library of Congress Cataloging-in-Publication Data
Eakes, Laurie Alice.
    A necessary deception : a novel / Laurie Alice Eakes.
        p.   cm. — (The daughters of Bainbridge House ; bk. 1)
    ISBN 978-0-8007-3466-4 (pbk.)
    I. Title.
PS3605.A377N43 2011
813′.6—dc22   2011022823

Scripture quotations are from the King James Version of the Bible.

This book is a work of fiction. Names, characters, places, and incidents are the product of the author's imagination or are used fictitiously. Any resemblance to actual events, locales, or persons, living or dead, is coincidental.

11   12   13   14   15   16   17   7   6   5   4   3   2   1

The LORD is my strength and my shield; my heart trusted in him, and I am helped: therefore my heart greatly rejoiceth; and with my song I will praise him.

Psalm 28:7

DARTMOOR PRISON
DEVONSHIRE, ENGLAND
March 1812

Entrée into the prison proved easy for Lady Lydia Gale. As the stranger at her cottage door had assured her when he arrived at dawn to inform her of a certain French major's presence as an enemy "guest" of England, a few shillings exchanging hands had placed her in the guardhouse. She held a handkerchief sprinkled with the honey-citrus aroma of linden blossom oil beneath her nose against the prison stench, awaiting the arrival of Chef de Batallon Christophe Arnaud.

Her cousin and companion, Barbara Bainbridge, stood beside her, her lips set, her hands twisting in the folds of a cloak soaked with the rain that had begun the moment they reached the walls of Dartmoor Prison. "We're going to contract a chill or worse."

"We'll be in Plymouth with hot tea and fires sooner than you think." Lydia raised her other hand to finger the pearl and ruby bracelet that had scarcely left her wrist in the three years since Monsieur Arnaud's messenger had appeared on her doorstep at dawn, carrying her husband's last letter and gift that were somehow smuggled out of French-occupied Spain. Even with it resting between the edge of her kid glove and the sleeve of her pelisse, the bracelet's coldness of metal and stones chilled her skin. "And since this man is a major in the French Army, helping him is simple."

And her chance to be a good wife, even if she was now a widow.

"If it will cost us money, you know you don't have any to spare."

"I'll manage something, if he needs money."

That too she had worked out on the journey from her cottage in Tavistock to Dartmoor Prison. Barbara would object, but Lydia thought no price too high if it helped her to accomplish something, to succeed at fulfilling a promise—at last.

"Hush." Lydia raised one finger to her lips at the sound of voices outside the door, one the heavy burr of the Somerset militia that served as guards in the prison, the other the rich timbre of accented English.

The door opened. Rain-laden air swept into the chamber along with a fresh wave of foul air so strong it seemed to cling to Lydia's lips like poison. But she made herself lower the hand-kerchief out of courtesy for the man who had given her husband aid and managed to get a letter and valuable bracelet to her through war-torn Europe. How, she never asked. One was better off not knowing of the doings of the smugglers who traveled between France and England.

"Remember she's a lady and mind your manners, frog." The guard shoved the newcomer through the doorway with the butt of a musket.

The man staggered, caught his balance with a hand against the desk of the prison governor, then straightened to his full height—a considerable height for a Frenchman, at least half a foot taller than her own above-average height. "Madame Gale?"

"Yes." Lydia gulped down an odd tightening in her chest and looked up into eyes the color of the sea on a sunny day. "Monsieur Arnaud?"

Beside her, Barbara stiffened and drew in a sharp breath.

Lydia forced herself to release her bracelet and hold out her hand. "I'm pleased to have this opportunity to thank you in person, though not under these circumstances. *Comprenez-vous l'anglais?*"

"Yes, I speak English, but if you speak French . . ." He glanced at the guard looming behind him.

"*Oui, je parle francais.*"

Barbara didn't know much of the language, but no matter. Lydia could convey the contents of the dialogue later.

She glanced at the guard. "Please close the door."

The man obliged, then leaned against it, the tip of his bayonet poised a mere inch behind the Frenchman.

Arnaud switched to French. "Please forgive me for not shaking your hand, madame." He glanced down at Lydia's pearly gray glove, then his own bare hand, where grime circled each ragged nail and streaked the back. "We have little water for washing."

Or laundry or barbering. His dark hair hung in lank strands around a gaunt face mostly obscured by a matted beard. His clothes had once been a uniform, to judge from the epaulets on the shoulders and shining brass buttons. Now the blue wool lay behind a layer of mud and she didn't want to guess what else.

Her stomach rolled, but not from the odor of uncleanliness swirling through the office. She felt sickened that her own countrymen could let human beings live in such deprivation. No one, not even the enemies of England for nearly twenty years, should live like hogs on a farm. No, worse. Hogs were well fed.

"My husband Charles said you took care of him," Lydia blurted out. "You gave him your own room in the officers' quarters, fed him, got him a physician." Tears of outrage and grief trickled from the corners of her eyes. "And we repay you with this."

Barbara gripped her arm hard enough to hurt. "What are you saying?"

"That we're cruel." Lydia spoke the English explanation between gritted teeth.

"The frogs don't deserve no better," the guard protested.

Lydia clenched her hands into fists. "No one deserves this kind of treatment." She turned back to Arnaud and switched back to French. "How did you come to offer your enemy such kindness?"

Arnaud's shoulders lifted in an elegant shrug. "I found him after the English abandoned Spain. All the horses on the beach were wild from being left behind, and the chevalier had been knocked down. No one noticed in their scramble to escape."

"You risked your own life." Lydia blinked to clear her eyes of the tears threatening to overflow down her cheeks, afraid if she used her handkerchief to wipe them away, the scented linen would make him think his filth was offensive to her. "You didn't have to help him."

"But no, I did." Arnaud smiled all the way to the corners of his beautiful eyes. "Perhaps you can think of me as the good Samaritan."

"As the—" Lydia's eyes widened. "You know the parable of the good Samaritan? I thought—I beg your pardon."

"No need." Arnaud chuckled deep in his throat. "Most of my countrymen did abandon their faith in the Lord when the

12

revolution came, but my maman made certain I did not. She is *une Americaine. Je suis un homme de foi. Comprenez-vous?*"

"I understand," Lydia murmured as a glow of joy ignited inside her.

From the look of amazement on Barbara's face, she had gathered enough of the French dialogue to work out that, despite the broadsheets and prints declaring all Frenchmen to be godless heathens worshiping at the tree of liberty, Arnaud claimed to be a man of faith in God.

Lydia smiled and switched to English. "The Lord has honored your kindness to your enemy and sent you to where I can give you assistance. What do I have to do to procure your parole?"

"Lydia," Barbara gasped.

"Such kindness from you is welcome, but, madame—" He dropped his gaze to the muddy floorboards, and his face darkened beneath the layer of whiskers and dirt. "To obtain a parole, I must have the means for shelter and living."

Tears started in Lydia's eyes again. A man proud of his faith—a man who had used his own resources to see that a stranger, an enemy, received comfort to the end of his life and got a message to that stranger's widow—deserved better than this kind of humiliation.

"I know. I made enquiries of the governor as soon as I learned you were an officer and eligible for parole." Lydia shoved her handkerchief up the sleeve of her pelisse and traced her fingertips around the corners of a ruby in her bracelet. "Tavistock isn't far from here, and my cottage—"

"Lydia, you cannot," Barbara cried.

"I will be absent from there for several months." Lydia slid her fingers from the ruby to the clasp. "That will give you time to find work and other shelter."

"*Merci bien, mais*, madame." If possible, his face darkened further with obvious embarrassment. "Will I not be unwelcome there?"

"Tavistock is a parole town. They're used to Frenchmen there. You should be able to find work this time of year. Until you do . . ." She hesitated. "Will the guards steal from you before we can procure your release?" She worked the bracelet clasp beneath the sleeve of her pelisse.

"That is one thing they leave to us—what little wealth we have." Hope sparked in his brilliant eyes. "I will repay every franc—mmm, shilling."

"You paid me well by making my husband comfortable at the end." The bracelet slid into her fingers. "Take this to Mr. Denby on High Street in Tavistock. I have left him a letter. He is expecting you."

"Lydia, no," Barbara gasped.

"But, madame—" He shook his head and tucked his hands into his pockets. "That was your husband's gift."

"Which you ensured arrived at my door safely." She tucked the bracelet into his pocket and changed to English. "Guard, fetch the governor. This man will be free by noon."

Lydia's husband had left her little more to live on than the ownership of the cottage, but he had been knighted before his death. Whereas impoverished Mrs. Gale, widow, might have been shoved aside, Lady Gale, widow of a fallen officer, got the attention she needed to ensure Christophe Arnaud indeed left Dartmoor Prison by noon and headed west on a hired moorland pony to the parole town of Tavistock.

"You were mad to give him your bracelet," Barbara

pronounced. She and Lydia jounced along in a hired chaise bound for Plymouth, where Lady Bainbridge and Lydia's two younger sisters were spending a night on the long journey to London. "It was your last gift from dear Sir Charles."

"It was a gift with a promise attached."

Returning the bracelet was the least she could do for the man who had made her husband's last hours as comfortable as possible. Charles's letter had made clear to her what was expected of her should the occasion arise. It had arisen. It was one task she could claim as having accomplished with success.

Her cat's basket cradled on her lap, Lydia leaned back against the cushions, closed her eyes to remember the joy on Arnaud's face when he rode out of the prison gates, and waited for the peace of a task well done to sweep over her, run through her.

But all that swept over her was cold, damp air and the musty smell of the hired chaise. All that ran through her was the discomfort of knowing Mama would be worrying over why Lydia hadn't yet arrived at the George. Lydia should have sent a message, but she had spent every extra penny she possessed on the cost of traveling to Dartmoor, then on delivering a message to the local jeweler to advance whatever coin possible if a Frenchman appeared with her pearl and ruby bracelet.

Out of habit, Lydia stroked her left wrist. "I'll have to find something else to wear here or I'll forever feel as though I'm forgetting something."

"You shouldn't have trusted him." Barbara flounced on the opposite seat. "If you'd taken it to Mr. Denby yourself, you could have used some of the coin instead of letting that Frenchman have all of it."

"I doubt Mr. Denby would have been willing to engage in satisfactory business at seven o'clock in the morning." Lydia peered out the window. Gray mist swirled past the glass. She sighed. "This fog will slow us down, but we should arrive by dinner."

They arrived when the after-dinner tea was being served. In the private parlor where Mama, Cassandra, and Honore sat around a small table, one inn servant had just taken away the last of the removes, and another was about to bring in the sweets. Damp and travel-stained, Lydia stood in the doorway, feasting her eyes on the three female members of her family. Mama, too thin and with too much silver showing in her blonde hair after one more lung fever of the winter, glanced from one daughter to the other, her lips curved in a gentle smile. Cassandra, as tall and dark as Lydia but more slender in build, glowed in her pink muslin gown and velvet pelisse. Across from her, Honore, petite, blonde, and vibrant, chattered nonstop and emphasized the description of a gown she'd seen in *La Belle Assemblée* with sweeping gestures of fork and knife.

Lydia wished to rush forward and embrace all of them at the same time, hug them close to make up for the months since they'd all been together. Instead, she took the basket of sweets from the waiter and carried it to the table.

"Lydia," Cassandra and Honore cried.

The latter launched herself from her chair. The former rose with more dignity.

Mama remained seated but held out her hands. "I was so worried, Lydia. What delayed you?"

"I had some business to take care of."

Although she hadn't thought of it, Lydia decided at that moment not to mention that a Frenchman was by now residing in her cottage. If Mama didn't like the notion, it would distress her for no reason, and Honore just might get romantic ideas.

"It couldn't have been good business," Honore declared. "You look dreadful. How old is that gown?"

"As old as you, I'm quite certain." Lydia hugged her youngest sister. "I'll leave fashionable attire up to you, since you'll be the true belle of the Season."

"With my blonde hair?" Honore shook back her honey-toned curls. "You and Cassandra are far more fashionable."

"And I'm an ancient husk of a widow." Lydia turned to her middle sister. "Being engaged seems to agree with you. Will your fiancé be in town?"

"In April," Cassandra said. "He's concerned about some sort of disturbance with workers in the north." She embraced Lydia.

Something thudded against Lydia's leg.

"I'm so sorry." Cassandra blushed. "I was reading before dinner and slipped the book into my pockets . . ."

"Cassandra, you must stop doing that." Honore gave her sister a look of horror. "It ruins the line of your gown."

"I expect she'll walk down the aisle to her groom with a book in her pocket." Lydia rounded the table to clasp Mama's hands. "I do apologize for worrying you over being late. It couldn't be helped. But no scolding. Barbara has done enough of that already."

"And where is Barbara?" Mama asked. "She did come with you?"

"I wouldn't dream of leaving her behind. But she insisted on seeing that someone carried our luggage to our room. She'll get the kitchen to send us up a cold collation. I'm far too dirty to sit at the table." After all, she had brought the prison stench with her. "But before I bid you good night, how are Papa and our brother doing? Will they join us in town?"

"In April." Honore grimaced. "All the men are waiting until the Season starts to join us. And Beau must wait until his term at Oxford is over, of course, if he doesn't escape to the wilds of Scotland or someplace else instead."

"They aren't interested in shopping." Mama laughed. "Your father turned green when I suggested he come be fitted for a new coat or two."

"I understand." Lydia plucked at a frayed edge of her sleeve that she hadn't noticed with her bracelet on. "But I suppose I must get a gown or two."

"A gown or two," Honore fairly squeaked with horror. "You need a full wardrobe. No more dull widow colors. It's been three years. Indeed, you should be looking for another husband to get you out of that little cottage."

"I'd rather see you safely betrothed and Cassandra wed, thank you." Lydia tried not to let her shudder show at the idea of another marriage, another male to direct her life into emptiness. "I had my chance."

"When you were with him for only a week—"

"Honore." Mama's gentle but admonishing tone cut the youngest sister off. "Spend your energies persuading your eldest sister to let me buy her several new gowns."

"I can fetch my periodicals." Honore started to rise.

"Not tonight." Lydia waved her youngest sister back to her chair. "I've been up since dawn and have a cat that needs a walk. We'll have plenty of time in the carriage to discuss fashion." After giving them each a kiss on the cheek, Lydia trudged up to the room she shared with Barbara, where she found her cat, Hodge, staring at a knothole in the wall.

"Find a mouse?"

"Let's hope it stays in the wall." Barbara removed a sliver of chicken from a covered tray on the room's table. "I had the kitchen send up some fowl for him."

"Thank you." Lydia held the tidbit out to the cat.

Hodge's pink nose sniffed at the chicken. His whiskers quivered, and he snatched the morsel from her fingers. After a second piece, he began to purr.

She stroked the long, silky white fur. "You're such a good kitty. Would you like a walk?"

"You shouldn't go outside alone," Barbara said. "Let me fetch my cloak and I'll join you."

"I'll get one of the inn maids to go with me. You eat your supper and get yourself into bed." Lydia affixed a leash to Hodge's collar and carried him downstairs.

He didn't like the leash, but she feared losing him beyond a hedgerow, so she insisted he wear it whenever they traveled. Not that they had gone farther than her family home at Bainbridge since Charles had gifted her with the kitten seven years earlier. Lydia had used the leash on him since then, so he was used to it and only occasionally tried to bite it off.

Once on the ground floor, she saw no one to ask to accompany her. A chorus of voices from the kitchen suggested the servants enjoyed their dinner. She needn't disturb them. No one would annoy her around this respectable inn.

No one annoyed her around any of the respectable inns in which the Bainbridge ladies spent their evenings and nights over the next six days. After being holed up in one of the carriages with Mama and Barbara discussing ailments and medicaments, or with Cassandra and Honore—the former managing to read despite the bouncing vehicle, the latter ceaselessly discussing gowns and beaux—Lydia welcomed her evening strolls with Hodge. She'd spent so much time alone in the past several years that so many persons close at hand left her exhausted. Fresh air cleared her head.

Not that the air of Portsmouth smelled particularly fresh. Too many naval vessels rode at anchor in the harbor, their stench of bilges, unwashed bodies, and pea soup dinners riding on the breeze. The inn garden plants, evergreen bushes vibrant beneath a March drizzle, helped mask the odors of the harbor. Peace, aloneness . . . save for the cat happy to prowl beneath the shrubbery.

Breathing deeply of the piney scent of the garden, Lydia set Hodge on the crushed shell path—

And a man stepped into her path. "Madame Gale."

His voice was low, indistinct, as though he wore a muffler against the chill.

She retreated from the stranger. "You startled me, sir. I don't know you."

"Nor do you need to."

"Then I needn't speak to you." She tugged on Hodge's leash.

The man glided in front of her, barring her path. "You helped Christophe Arnaud get a parole from Dartmoor Prison."

"That's no one's business." Cold in the evening wet, she stooped and picked up Hodge, turning away as she straightened. "It was all quite legal."

The man closed his hand over her arm, halting her retreat. "You're not going anywhere yet, madame."

"I beg your pardon." Lydia stiffened. "Unhand me or I'll scream for help."

"And create a scene? I think not. You wouldn't want to reflect badly on your sisters."

He was right, blast his eyes.

The man laughed. "We have some business to transact."

"We do not. I fulfilled my promise. My debt is paid."

"But at too high a price, I think." The man's fingers tapped on her arm as though he played a tune on a pianoforte. "You see, Madame Gale, Christophe Arnaud never arrived in Tavistock."

"What happened to him?" Lydia focused all her attention on the stranger now. "I saw him leave. He had an escort. He had everything he needed. He—was he injured? Assaulted?" She squeezed Hodge so tightly the cat shot out of her arms with a yowl.

How could she have made amok of such a simple act of kindness?

"He eluded his guard and escaped."

"Escaped." Lydia peered through the darkness, trying to see the man's face. "What are you saying? He was paroled from Dartmoor. He didn't escape."

"Not Dartmoor, my lady, England."

"But that's not possible." She shook her head, sending half of her hair sliding from its pins and into her face. "He wouldn't have had the time or the means to get away."

"Of course he did, and you provided both. In other words, my lady, you allowed an enemy of England to return to his country. Lady Gale, you have committed an act of treason."

2

Lydia's damp cloak felt as though it were lined with lead, weighing her down from her shoulders to her heart to a sinking sickness in her belly. If this man were telling the truth, she had misread Christophe Arnaud, had looked into those beautiful blue eyes and read truth instead of the lies he'd said about his gratitude for her assistance.

No, not lies. He must be grateful. She'd given him the means to get away from his enemies.

His enemies, her countrymen. Countrymen she had betrayed by trying to make up for her failings of the past.

Her heart began to pound like the drums of approaching soldiers. She took a deep breath in an attempt to lift the pressure crushing her chest. "I would never have helped a dishonorable man, abetted the actions of an enemy. I—I thought he was—"

She stopped. She need not admit her poor judgment in character. No one need know she found Christophe Arnaud attractive as a man, appealing as a brother in Christ, touching as a man in need of help, as her husband had been when captured behind enemy lines after the Spanish disaster three years earlier.

"You gave Monsieur Arnaud a bracelet, did you not?" The man's quiet voice purred across the space between them. "A bracelet given to you after your husband somehow didn't manage to get aboard the transport ships and return to England."

"Somehow?" Lydia clenched her fists. "He was a good officer. He waited to see his men safely aboard."

"And Monsieur Arnaud just happened to help—"

"How do you know this?"

"It's my business to know." He released her arm and moved away from her.

Lydia took a step backward. "Hodge—"

No Hodge. The leash went slack in her hand. The cat no longer tugged at the end of the leather strap.

"Are you looking for your cat?" The man loomed up before her, a blackness against the rain-gray evening. He held her cat. The feline's white fur shone against his dark coat. And Hodge was purring, the traitor. Another treacherous male.

Except she was the one accused of treachery.

"Give him to me," she commanded.

"When we're done speaking."

"I have nothing to say to you."

"You have a great deal to say to me. To begin with, tell me, my lady, how would your husband, wounded and behind enemy lines, manage to send you an expensive piece of jewelry?"

"Monsieur Arnaud—"

"Out of the goodness of his heart for an enemy?" The man's laugh rumbled like Hodge's purr. "More likely it was a favor for a comrade in arms."

"But my husband was an English—" Lydia's stomach twisted. Only her will kept her from doubling over. "You're accusing my husband of working for the French."

"And the bracelet was sent to you with a coded message just for such an occasion as today—the means to get a fellow follower of Napoleon out of prison, should the worst occur."

"That's preposterous. He'd have no way of knowing I'd use it. I could have sold it, lost it, refused to help."

"Could you have refused to help?"

"I—" Lydia swallowed against the bile burning her throat.

Again that purring chuckle, echoed by her unfaithful cat. "Of course not. Even if you no longer possessed the bracelet, you would have done what you could to help Arnaud for the sake of your husband's memory."

To prove she could succeed in one of his requests as a widow, as she had failed to do as his wife. But Sir Charles Gale would never ask her to betray England. He wouldn't have betrayed England. He had returned to his regiment out of loyalty in the dark days when the war was going badly for England and fears of invasion were only minimally allayed.

"I erred in assisting Arnaud." The words barely managed to emerge, though "I erred" should have slipped out with ease. She had said them far too often in the past seven years. "But it proves nothing against my husband or me," she added with haste.

"Does it not?" He stroked Hodge's pale coat, his hand, perhaps in a glove, dark against the silvery fur. The purr grew louder. "The Home Office and War Department wouldn't agree."

"The Home Office?"

"We manage matters of domestic protection. Spies and traitors on our soil."

He might as well have thrown her feline against her middle. His words struck with the force of ten pounds of clawing cat. For a dozen heartbeats, she couldn't breathe, couldn't think.

And the man kept talking as though discussing the March drizzle soaking her hair and cloak. "Arnaud never took the road to Tavistock."

"How do you know?"

"I was waiting for him."

Cold more profound than the late winter weather ran over Lydia's skin, penetrated to her bones, her marrow. "Why?" she whispered.

"Why did you help him escape?"

"I never—" She stopped. She need not defend herself to this stranger. This enemy.

"Where is he, Lady Gale?" the man purred along with Hodge.

"I have no idea." She injected her tone with all the hauteur of a lady of quality, as she'd been raised.

"Why did you help a French prisoner escape from England?" The demand lashed out at her.

She winced but remained silent. The hair on the back of her neck felt as though it stood on end, rather like Hodge when he sensed a foe nearby—puffed-up fur and silence.

Yes, silence. He'd stopped purring.

A shiver crawled down Lydia's arms. She slid a foot back, then stopped. Even if she could leave her cat behind to an uncertain fate, she couldn't run away now. She must know what this man wanted, why he had approached her in the dark with his accusations of treason and offhand mention of the Home Office. What proof he possessed.

"You can remain as silent as you like, my lady," the man said, shifting and receiving a protesting *mrauw* from Hodge, "but I have a fisherman in Falmouth who will swear to the fact that you were there arranging transport across the Channel for him."

"I wasn't." His announcement startled the denial from her. "I couldn't have been."

"Can you prove it?"

"I was with someone all day."

"Your paid companion."

And she hadn't been with Barbara all day. She'd gone into Tavistock before leaving for the prison. Any number of urchins loitered about. She could have sent one with a message to Falmouth, Plymouth, or anywhere in between.

"I see you understand your dilemma." Self-satisfaction colored the man's tone. "But you needn't believe me. That fisherman is waiting not a dozen yards away, ready to tell you he received your message and complied."

"But—" Lydia's nostrils flared, as though she could smell the fisherman.

Something smelled like dead fish indeed, but it didn't lie in the rain-washed garden.

"And I found this in a Falmouth jewelry store." The man shifted. Gravel crunched. The light from the inn reaching the garden shimmered off metal interspersed with the dark fire of jewels. Lydia didn't need to touch or see the object to know it was her bracelet.

"You—you could have stolen it, set upon Mr. Arnaud on the road."

"He had an armed escort. And I have a statement from the jeweler besides."

The bracelet sparkled in the feeble light from the lantern above the inn door. Hodge batted at it.

The man chuckled and the bracelet disappeared. "All this evidence gathering has cost me dearly."

"Then why—?"

As though lightning streaked against the gray-black sky, illuminating the scene like day, understanding flashed into Lydia's mind.

Blackmail.

"I can pay you nothing for your silence." Now that she knew the game, she stood upright and composed. "I have no money."

"I know that. But you have something I hold of more value than money—social connections."

"I don't—"

But of course she did through her family. Everyone who was anyone would either come to Bainbridge House or invite the Bainbridges to their homes over the next four months.

"What do you want me to do?" She would go along with him, find out as much as she could.

"Introduce my friends to your connections so they get invited to the best parties."

"Why?" She didn't have to feign bewilderment. "How will that help your . . . cause?"

With every word he spoke, the more she realized he could not be from the British government. The English government didn't need to resort to blackmail for aid.

She was being blackmailed by a French agent.

"I won't do it." Despite the frozen lump in her middle that had once been her liver, she spoke her declaration with clarity and strength. "I won't betray my country."

"But you already have."

"Your evidence is false."

"Then produce Monsieur Arnaud. Otherwise you must do what I say."

"Or call your bluff."

"Do you dare?" The man shifted. A hint of lemon verbena wafted to her nostrils. "Let's see here. You have a brother who is a promising student at Oxford. You have a sister about to be married to a peer of the realm, and another sister about to make her come-out into Society. And we mustn't forget your frail mother and your father's standing in the House of Lords."

Lydia folded her arms across her middle, pressed hard against the desire to be sick or run or drop to her knees in surrender to the burden he dropped onto her shoulders. If she were a lone woman, she would take the chance of calling this man's bluff.

But she had a family she'd already let down too often as she pursued her own way in the world.

If she were allowed to succeed at something in her future, protecting her family from this villain would be it. And yet . . .

"I can't aid in your doing something to harm my country or my family," she said.

"Your country? What makes you think it's not mine too?"

"A manner of speech, is all." She made herself smile so he could hear congeniality in her voice. "I speak of England as my country. But of course a loyal Englishman would be concerned about a French officer escaping back to France."

"Indeed, I am. I have reason to believe he intends to send agents to foment trouble. You fear revolution, do you not?"

"A guillotine in Hyde Park? Y-yes." The quaver in her words was genuine.

"So I will send you someone to help ferret out these trouble-makers."

"Indeed. Well, sir, you only needed to ask. You needn't resort to blackmail."

"It is necessary." He lifted Hodge in his hands and held him toward her. "In the event you grow fearful of your role, I need a leash to keep you bound to me."

And what a leash—the potential to cost her her life and ruin her family.

"What must I do?" she asked on an exhalation of breath.

Carrying her limp and still-purring cat in her arms, the cut leash dangling from her wrist, Lydia trudged back to the inn. Warmth surrounded her inside the entryway. Aromas of roast beef and spilled ale stung her nostrils, and her stomach roiled. Her heart ached. She thought she'd been given an opportunity to make up for resenting being a wife, for driving her husband back to the battlefield and keeping him there. All she had to do was give aid to a French prisoner who had given aid to her husband. But she'd misread the man, mismanaged the release, risked the future of everyone in her family.

Feet dragging, she climbed the steps to her bedchamber. Before she shifted Hodge so she could open the door, the latch clicked and Barbara stood between jamb and panels.

"Where have you been?" her companion demanded.

"Hodge's leash broke." With the help of a knife. "I had to find him."

"And now your cloak is all muddy. You should have left him behind with that Frenchman."

"Hodge and I haven't been separated since Charles gave him to me as a betrothal gift. He would have been distressed."

"Captain Gale couldn't be distressed," Barbara pointed out. "He's dead, God rest his soul."

"If God has it," Lydia muttered.

"Lydia." Barbara's eyes widened with shock.

"Forgive me. I'm fatigued beyond reason. I can't be accountable for what I say." But of course she could. She was accountable for her words and her actions. "Where's—ah." She set Hodge in his box.

He sniffed at the now-empty bowl, flashed her an indignant glance from clear, green eyes, and snuggled into a nest of blanket strips.

His life wasn't topsy-turvy. He could sleep with a clear conscience.

Although she knew her conscience was clear as far as the stranger's accusations were concerned, Lydia couldn't sleep. She dared not toss and turn for fear of waking Barbara, who enjoyed the sleep of the innocent—or was that naive?—so she lay awake with her eyes open. That way she managed to focus on the occasional display of lights tossed across the ceiling by a passerby with a lantern. She strained to hear snatches of conversation in the street or corridor. She recited every poem she knew by heart, anything to keep herself from thinking of the accusations, the evidence— false as it was—a pair of deep blue eyes, and a melodious voice.

Lord, I only wanted to do something right on my own.

If it only affected her, she wouldn't care. She would retire to her little cottage on the edge of Dartmoor and keep drawing her sketches and painting her pictures, selling enough to keep the wolves from the door, since her husband had left her with an income of less than a hundred pounds a year. She had failed to produce the heir that would have had the Gale lands and income going to his branch of the family instead of to a distant relation.

But if she went along with the man's request, succumbed to the blackmail, let yet one more man control the order of her days, she would likely be stepping into a den of traitors. With the country at war with France and experiencing unfriendly relations with America, any number of personages wanted to bring harm to England. And not all of them surfaced from outside the realm. Unrest murmured through the cities and countryside. Parliament enacted laws many opposed, and mill owners installed power looms. And no one liked the way the Navy pressed men into service against their will.

She could never find the source of the blackmailer, how he'd gathered so much information so quickly, how he'd known to use her, how he would follow through. But surely the Home Secretary or someone in the War Department would keep her information secret if she turned herself in. They would want to do so in order to hunt down the real traitors.

If they didn't arrest her on the spot.

By the time a rooster crowed the dawn, before the light penetrated Lydia's chamber, she knew she must go to the authorities and take the risk. She could not compound her error in judgment about Christophe Arnaud by giving in to further treacherous actions.

Decision made, she rose and prepared for the next leg of the journey. Her family met her in the private parlor, where fresh rolls and coffee steamed on the table.

"You look awful," Honore announced upon Lydia's entrance.

"That's unkind," Mama scolded. She tilted her head to one side and nodded. "But you do. What's wrong? Are you ill?"

"You can't be." Honore leaped from the table. "If you're ill, we can't go to London, and Cassandra's wedding will be a disaster."

"Did someone want me?" Cassandra glanced up from the book beside her plate.

"No, dear." Mama patted Cassandra's hand, where it held her pages down. "Go back to Mr. Homer."

"Boring old Greeks." Honore curled her pretty upper lip. "I want to find all the Minerva Press novels I can in London. That's as much Greek as I want." She giggled. "Minerva? Greeks? You know, it's a fine joke."

"Minerva was the Roman goddess, not the Greek one," Cassandra said in repressive accents.

Honore giggled again. "Will you take me to the lending library, Lydia?"

"Yes, of course." If she wasn't in Newgate. Or would it be the Tower of London for a traitor? "Or Barbara can, if I'm occupied."

Occupied going to the authorities, the Admiralty there in Portsmouth, and beg for their mercy, their assistance. If the man from the garden who had called himself Mr. Lang was a faithful subject, someone in the government would provide her with better proof, assure her she was working for the right side.

If he was on the wrong side, her life and her family's lives could crumble to bits.

"I'm afraid we cannot leave as early as we planned." Lydia poured coffee for herself and Barbara, whom she heard running down the steps. "I have an errand I have to take care of first."

"But we'll be forever," Honore protested.

"Can't it wait, my dear?" Mama asked. "I was hoping we could reach London today."

"No, I'm sorry, it cannot." Lydia grasped the door handle. "I'll send word if I'll be more than an hour."

"But where are you going?" Barbara asked. "You can't go tramping about Portsmouth without an escort."

"Yes, I can. I'm no green girl. I'm a widow." Lydia opened the door.

"And pretty enough to make a sailor forget himself." Barbara slid off her chair. "I'll come with you."

Lydia held out a hand. "Please. It's business having to do with . . . with . . . my husband's military service."

That would do. It was close enough to the truth she didn't feel she'd lied to her companion or family.

"I'll be back before you finish breakfast."

Hopeful words.

Cold before she exited the warmth of the inn, Lydia strode forth into the damp morning. A brisk wind off the sea brought the odors of fish along with even less pleasant smells from the naval vessels bobbing at anchor. Her nose wrinkled. Her stomach rebelled. She shoved her hands more deeply into her fur-trimmed muff and headed for the Admiralty. The walk took her long enough to compose her speech. She hoped it didn't sound like an excuse of the guilty.

But when she reached the premises primarily occupied by the Admiralty, every word slipped from her mind. Faced with a sea of blue naval uniforms and red-coated marines carrying swords and muskets, and all of the men staring at her—a woman striding alone to the door—she faltered and bent her head as though she would find her scattered thoughts lying about the pavement.

"Don't do it, my lady."

Lydia started at the now-familiar voice murmuring behind her.

A hand pressed against the small of her back. "Don't turn around. You don't want to be able to recognize my face."

"I know your voice."

"Do you." He chuckled.

No, she didn't. Muffled, it could have been any man.

"You'll learn to know that what I say is truth," he continued, "even if you know not the voice. Believe me, my lady, you will cause more trouble for everyone—to yourself, to your family, to England—if you walk through those doors. If you try to go to the government again, you will be stopped and your family ruined. Is that clear?"

It was clear. The choice had been taken from her. She must play his game, appear to cooperate.

And try to ferret out who the true traitor was in their midst.

3

The first of the three Bainbridge carriages slowed, turned, stopped. A glance out of the window and Honore's squeals told Lydia they had arrived at Bainbridge House in Cavendish Square. The Season had begun. Her role as government agent had begun.

She wished the carriage would continue around the circle of fenced-in grass in the center of the houses and depart from London to unknown places.

The carriage didn't budge. Honore grasped the door handle.

"Wait until a footman—"

Lydia's admonition fell on deaf ears. Honore leaped from the carriage before a servant lowered the steps. One of the two men sent out to assist with the vehicles stopped and stared at the golden-haired girl racing toward the house.

"She'll have to lose those hoydenish ways if she doesn't want to ruin her chances for vouchers to Almack's," Barbara said with a sniff.

"She'll settle after she's been here a bit." Lydia rubbed her naked wrist. "We'll wear her down with shopping. Every day . . ."

Every day they would be out at the shops, buying fabrics, choosing patterns, enduring fittings, purchasing shoes and fans

34

and hats to match. Lydia needed another bracelet so her bare wrist would stop irritating her. She needed painting supplies if she wanted to get work done before Father arrived with his disapproval of her art. Cassandra would want to haunt the bookshops and libraries and would insist on visiting the museums. Honore would want to see what was left of the menagerie at the Tower.

Lydia had a list of printers and newspapers to call upon with her portfolio. She hoped to interest a printer in her work to make more income. The endless activities preceding the Season just might prove to be her savior.

If she wasn't home, she couldn't receive callers. If she didn't receive callers, she couldn't introduce anyone into Society. If she introduced no one into Society, she couldn't comply with the blackmailer's wishes.

Which might turn out to be dangerous.

"I can't do this." She clutched at her suddenly throbbing head.

Barbara patted her hand. "We'll have you into bed with a hot brick and tonic in a moment. All will look so much better with a good night's sleep and no travel in the morning."

Lydia squeezed out a smile. "I'm sure you're right."

If only Barbara were right. But too much time passed before Lydia could find out if Barbara's idea worked. First Lydia needed to oversee the unloading of the third carriage with its mounds of luggage and ensure each person's belongings reached the correct room. Those rooms needed an inspection to make certain sheets had been properly aired, grates swept, and chimneys cleaned before fires could be allowed to burn. Everyone wanted hot tea and a hasty meal.

Fires blazed in a trice, but hot tea and even the coldest of collations remained absent. Lydia promised to find out the reason after she sought out extra blankets for Mama's room, which seemed oddly absent of warm coverlets.

Lemster, the longtime butler, found her on her knees in the linen room, praying for a few moments of peace more than seeking blankets. She jumped at his cough behind her and glanced up. "I thought we kept blankets on the bottom shelf."

"We have a special box of cedar on the top shelf, Miss—er, my lady." Lemster's gaze flashed upward. "I'll lift them down for you. They might be too high for you."

"Of course."

Lydia stood three inches taller than the butler, but he'd known her since she was born and likely still thought of her as a little girl to whom he'd smuggled sweets from her parents' parties. She didn't mind the assistance in the least. A headache pounded behind her eyes.

"About tea?" she asked with a hint of desperation in her tone.

"Ah, yes, that's why I came to find you." Lemster sighed. "Cook is having histrionics because you all are here and she's not prepared."

"No, I'm sure she isn't prepared. She didn't know when we would arrive. Did you or Mrs. Pollock assure her a cold collation is acceptable?"

"It's no use. She has her pride, and sliced ham offends her sensibilities."

"I'll go down." Lydia closed her eyes. Lights flashed, and she snapped them open again. "Who is the cook these days? I believe Monsieur St. Jacques retired?"

"Ha, that's what he claimed, the lying—" Lemster closed his lips.

Lydia raised her eyebrows and waited for the enlightenment she knew was coming.

"He took the pension from Lord Bainbridge and went off to the country seat of some French family."

"In France?"

"No, my lady, émigrés who've settled in Shropshire." He spoke the last word with a curl of his upper lip.

"Now, Lemster, French émigrés are not the enemy."

Unlike French prisoners.

A shudder ran through Lydia. "So who is the current cook?"

"His daughter." Lemster looked like she'd served him nothing but lemon tarts minus the sugar.

A corner of Lydia's mouth twitched. "I'll go talk to her."

She left the blanket distribution to the butler and descended the back steps to the kitchen. She pushed through the green baize door to the aromas of cloves and garlic, onions and baking ham, the smells so strong she had to brace her hand against the door frame while she fought off a wave of dizziness. Suddenly, she couldn't recall the last time she'd eaten more than a mouthful. Probably the day she left for London.

The day she waylaid her journey at Dartmoor Prison.

She jerked her thoughts away from that Frenchman and focused on the French lady. In the center of the room, a petite female in a snowy apron and cap presided over surely every other servant in the house, including Mrs. Pollock, the housekeeper.

"Sliced ham, I am told to serve them. Me, who makes a finer pastry than even my father, expected to serve sliced ham." The accent was slight, the volume great, and the face as delicate as perhaps one of her self-acclaimed pastries. "If they had but sent a rider ahead, one little boy on a horse, I could have had the meal divine ready."

"Or wasted it if we were delayed." Lydia broke into the recital.

The cook fell silent. The servants spun on their heels and

bowed or curtsied, except for Mrs. Pollock. She wrung her hands, and it looked like tears would begin to leak from her faded blue eyes, as they did the cook's big brown ones.

"Miss Bain—I mean, m'lady, we didn't know you were here," Mrs. Pollock all but whimpered.

With her lined face, silver hair, and stooped shoulders, the housekeeper should probably be the next servant to retire with a pension. Shadows deepened the set of her eyes, and a tremor showed in her hands.

Lydia felt like crying herself. She'd known the housekeeper all her life.

"Mr. Lemster sent me down." Lydia blinked. "You have all prepared for us as well as can be expected, and I want to assure all of you, especially you, Mademoiselle St. Jacques, that we will delight in your fine pastries at another time. For now we simply wish for . . . whatever is available."

Her bed and a hot brick and Hodge. Perhaps a cup of tea and some toast.

"Ah, madame." The tiny cook rushed forward, parting the crowd of maids and footmen like a cutter parting a wave. "You are unwell. Do sit yourself down and I shall make you the remedy. It's the head, no? The megrims?"

"No. I mean, yes." Lydia found herself nudged into a chair.

A clap of hands small enough to belong to a child sent servants scurrying for this ingredient and that. A ham appeared on the table with a footman slicing it as thin as foolscap. Two maids crouched at the fire, slices of bread on toasting forks. For Madame. The chef busied herself pulling a pinch of spices from one box and a scoop of herbs from another. She poured boiling water into a pot and assembled it with a cup on a tray, which she presented to Lydia like an offering.

"This will make you well," Mademoiselle St. Jacques announced.

Lydia sniffed the steam billowing from the spout of the silver teapot. She caught a whiff of mint, chamomile, cinnamon, and . . . "Lavender?"

"*Oui. C'est tres bien.* I will pour. Unless you do not wish to partake in the kitchen?"

Lydia smiled. If only the woman knew how she'd prepared most of her own meals and eaten at the kitchen since her marriage. She would probably be scandalized.

"I'd rather not move," Lydia admitted.

"*Bon.*" The cook poured the fragrant brew into a cup. "Drink, then eat the toast and go to your bed."

Lydia took a tentative sip of the tisane. Her nostrils flared at the sharpness of the aroma. Something inside her head expanded like a sail filling with hot air, and she took a full mouthful. "It's delicious."

Beaming, the cook darted to the hearth to gather up slices of toast and add them to Lydia's tray. "Eat and drink. All is well when one has food. Tomorrow I will create the meal most special, and you must enjoy it."

Lydia suppressed the urge to say, "Yes, ma'am." Instead she said, "Where are you from, mademoiselle?"

"I am from Shropshire now, a loyal subject of poor King George." The French woman's mutinous expression dared Lydia to ask her further questions of her origins, then softened. "I've been here for twenty years, but always *mon* papa said to speak the French, that the English nobility prefer the French."

"Odd, isn't it, when we are at war with the French? For myself, I prefer English."

She doubted she would speak another word of French in her life after her last conversation in that language.

"I will endeavor to speak the English, madame." The cook went back to work on a kettle suspended over the fire, and Lydia added nibbles of toast to her swallows of tea. By the time she finished the first cup, her headache had eased and her stomach no longer rebelled. She managed to rise and direct a footman to take the tray of food to the back parlor, where her mother and sisters and Barbara awaited, and headed for her bedroom.

As she hoped, Hodge and a hot brick resided on her bed. She snuggled under the quilts, fell asleep within minutes, and dreamed of a Frenchman with deep blue eyes and a melodious voice. She kept shouting at him to speak English, but he continued to prattle on in French.

"Fool." She woke herself up with a start.

Her headache had indeed gone, but fearing she would dream of Christophe Arnaud again, she climbed from bed and pushed the curtains aside. Gray light spilled into the room. At the top of the area steps below Lydia's window, the cook berated a tradesman for doing something inferior.

"I'll have to speak to her about making so much noise this early," Lydia grumbled.

A glance at the enameled clock on her mantel told her the time was not all that early. She had slept for nearly twelve hours. And the cook's harangue explained why she'd been dreaming of a Frenchman.

Lydia hoped it wasn't because, somewhere in her brainbox, she thought of him with kindness. After he had betrayed her, no kindness toward him should remain.

Shivering in the morning chill, she pulled the bell rope and began to hunt out clothes to wear. She'd planned to take a day or two to recover from the journey before launching into shopping and sightseeing excursions, but her thoughts of the day before prompted her to drag her sisters out of the house that morning. Honore would be no trouble. Cassandra, on the other hand, was likely to rebel. The London townhouse boasted a fine library full of books collected by Bainbridges for the past fifty years.

Dressed with the assistance of a housemaid, Lydia descended to the library and found Cassandra poring over a thick volume, a quill in one hand, a cup of coffee in the other. She wore her dressing gown and spectacles, and her dark hair hung in tangled ribbons down her back.

"What will Lord Whittaker think of you looking like that in the morning?" Lydia asked.

Cassandra jumped. Her spectacles slipped down her nose and she snatched them off. "He won't. He's never seen me in spectacles. I'll take care to wear them only when—when he's not about."

"Hmm." Lydia didn't like the sound of that. "Cassandra, perhaps you should tell him first. You can't always be alone once you're married."

"You were always alone after you were married."

Lydia's face tightened. "So I was. What could I know?" She started to turn away.

"Oh, Lydia." Cassandra leaped from her chair and flew across the room, displaying a shocking amount of leg through the parting dressing gown and a too-short night rail. "I didn't mean—I never think—I'm a beast. What can I do to make it up to you?"

Lydia braced for Cassandra's hug. "Get dressed and be ready to leave the house within the hour."

"Where are we going?"

"The Pantheon Bazaar for fabric and Gunter's for ices and cakes and wherever else we must."

"We'll be out all day?" Cassandra's face registered dismay. "I really cannot go. I need to finish this canto and just discovered the answer to a phrase—"

"You are getting married in three months. You need clothes for your wedding journey and your new status. Those pale muslins won't do any longer, which is good. They make you look sallow."

"Whittaker says I have a creamy complexion."

And a fine dowry for a younger son, who hadn't expected to inherit the title and estates and cotton mills of his brother.

But she shouldn't be so cynical. She had scarcely spent an hour with the young man. For all she knew, he desperately loved Cassandra. She was a charming girl, once one got her nose out of books.

"Let's find fabrics that complement your coloring," Lydia said. "It'll take weeks to outfit the two of you."

Weeks in which Lydia hoped to avoid meeting callers with letters of introduction.

A vain hope. As London began to fill with persons preparing for the Season, many noticed that the knocker hung on the door of Number Ten Cavendish Square, and calling cards began to appear on the entryway table. Lydia wished she could sweep them up and use them for tinder in the fires, but she knew not returning the calls meant social ostracism for her sisters. As their chaperone, she needed to advance their status, not decrease it.

So on the Monday after their entry into town, she ushered the girls to the homes of ladies in their neighborhood. The day was clear and fine, and the Bainbridge ladies walked the short distance to the first house, directly next door to theirs. They stayed only long enough to leave their card and mention the date of Honore's coming-out ball, a terribly late May 11, then they proceeded to the next house.

And so March passed without a hint of anyone arriving at Bainbridge House demanding an introduction to Society on the word of Mr. Lang. Peace settled over Lydia. She even began to enjoy wearing fine clothes again, scouring bookshops, and chattering lightheartedly over cups of tea. Perhaps this would all go well after all.

Then, on Good Friday, the twenty-seventh day of March, as they readied themselves for church, Mama emerged from her usual place beside the fire in her sitting room. "We must begin to receive callers, girls. I've decided that Mondays will be our at-home days beginning with next Monday."

4

Mama's color looked better than it had since Lydia met the family in Plymouth. Lydia wondered if she could go home once the girls were outfitted.

But of course she couldn't. Mama had spent quite a lot of money on outfitting her eldest daughter too, and Lydia had given her word.

Her word given to Mama to help launch Honore. Her word given to her husband to help the Frenchman who had helped him. Her word given to a man with a nefarious purpose to help his agent. She must cease giving her word to anyone. Commitments bruised, cut, destroyed.

A commitment to the Lord didn't destroy, of course. Of course. Of course. But sitting in the pew at St. George's Hanover Square, Lydia pondered what good it had been to her lately. She'd done what she thought was her Christian duty in an attempt to make up for being a poor wife, a wife who couldn't keep her husband with her, and now she jumped at every rap of the knocker, every click of heels behind her, every shadow caught from the corner of her eye. She, the lady who had blithely resided beside Dartmoor with only a cat and a companion for company although her family begged her to return home, had turned craven. It must stop. She declared to herself that she would work for her country, even while being forced to work against it to protect her family and not let them down, as she had too many times in the past eight years. Yet she had avoided the opportunity to do so, to ferret out the real traitor who would knock on her door one day.

When the first knock sounded on the door the thirtieth day of March, the Monday after Easter, Lydia didn't hear it. She stood in the middle of her bedchamber with her hair tumbling down her back and Hodge sprawled at her feet amidst a pile of hairpins, purring as though he were laughing.

"If we had a garden," she declared, "you'd be banished to it."

Hodge batted at a hairpin. It bounced away from him and he pounced.

The gold-ended clips seemed to have caught his attention. Moments before, as Lydia had slipped the last one into her coiffure, he'd sprung from the bed and grabbed for the shiny object. It flew from Lydia's grip, taking her carefully arranged curls with it.

"Barbara, are you anywhere around?" Lydia called.

Silence.

"Cassandra? Honore?"

The upper story rang with the hollowness that spoke of no one nearby. She feared callers might be arriving two floors down, and Mama expected Lydia to pour tea and ensure that everyone received a cake or sweetmeat, enjoyed the company of someone in the room, and found her gloves before she departed.

"Help?" The request emerged in a feeble, resigned tone.

Careful not to crumple her blue muslin gown, Lydia crouched and gathered up her pins. Before she began to pile her hair atop her head again, she grabbed the playful cat and locked him in the dressing room. He commenced yowling as though she were sticking sewing pins into him instead of hairpins into her hair. Those she poked and prodded with more haste than style, gathering, twisting, anchoring the heavy black tresses and wishing she'd cut her hair when doing so had been the fashion. At the least, she needed to hire a lady's maid. Barbara knew less about hair styling than did Lydia.

Appearance presentable, she draped a paisley shawl around her shoulders and descended to the drawing room on the ground floor. The clink of china and hubbub of several conversations reached her on the first landing, warning her that their Monday at home had drawn a number of guests. All acquaintances and friends?

Her stomach in a knot tighter than her skewered hair, she rounded the corner to the final flight.

Not all acquaintances. Two strangers stood in the entryway, presenting their cards to Lemster—their cards and what looked like a folded and sealed sheet of vellum.

Lydia froze. Her fingers turned white on the banister. Her stomach rolled. She swallowed against a taste of bile, turned to go back to her bedchamber, and the step creaked.

"Ah, Lady Gale, there you are." Lemster's voice rang up the stairwell, reminding her to be brave and fight back. "I was telling these gentlemen I didn't know if you were at home, but here you are."

"Yes, I'm right here." Smile tight over her teeth, Lydia faced the butler and callers and completed her descent to the entryway. "How may I be of service, gentlemen?"

"We have a letter of introduction, my lady." The speaker was a man of average build, a bit taller than Lydia, and average looks—mousy brown hair and blue-gray eyes, regular features and pale complexion.

In contrast, his companion embodied Society's definition of an Adonis. His guinea-gold hair curled just so around a

46

well-formed scalp. Blue eyes the color of sapphires sparkled in a lightly tanned face with the classical features of a firm chin and full mouth, a strong nose that wasn't too large, and high cheekbones. His physique, clad in a fine blue coat and biscuit-colored breeches, did justice to his face.

"From Elias Lang," the first man concluded.

The silk shawl wasn't heavy enough to stave off a wave of cold seeping through Lydia's bones. She managed to keep smiling as she took the letter from the man and read Elias Lang's request that she make his dear friends George Barnaby and Gerald Frobisher welcome, as they were recently arrived in London and knew no one of any significance.

The moment of truth had arrived. She could do as the letter requested, or she could expose these men for the traitors to England they surely were. But she would only harm her family. The man calling himself Lang would declare she had aided the escape of a paroled French officer, and the war of accusations would be on. She had no proof against these men; Lang held proof against her.

She took a deep breath to settle her stomach. She reaffixed her smile. She held out her hand. "Welcome to London. Do come in and allow me to introduce you to our other guests."

"We are obliged, my lady." The younger man, the Adonis, spoke in a voice as melodious as he was handsome. "Do, I pray, stay close to me. I'm newly finished at Cambridge and am afraid I may still have some of my poor student habits."

"Are you a scholar, sir?" Lydia made herself take his arm as Lemster opened the drawing room door. If he was, she would steer him clear of Cassandra.

He laughed. "My mother wishes, but alas, I was better at rowing than learning."

They stepped into the room. Conversations ceased. A dozen

pairs of eyes swiveled toward the doorway, and ladies began to wave their fans. Especially Honore. She took one look at Mr. Frobisher and her eyes widened, her lips parted as though she were gasping for breath, and color tinged her cheeks, making her even prettier.

Not my little sister. Her throat closed to keep herself from crying out. *Honore must have nothing to do with these men.*

Honore glided forward. Her pink sprig muslin skirt swayed and floated around her like sunrise-tinted mist. The scent of lilacs drifted along with her. She smiled at Frobisher. He smiled back. He bowed. She curtsied. They stood with gazes locked. Two beautiful young people coming face-to-face set the hairs rising along Lydia's arms.

"Honore," she managed with as much calm as she could summon, "may I present Mr. Gerald Frobisher, the friend of a . . . friend back in Tavistock." The last words choked out. "Why don't you fetch Mr. Frobisher a cup of tea."

"I need nothing." He glanced at a nearby settee, woefully empty. "Perhaps Miss Honore can tell me about the best sights in town."

"I'd be happy to." Honore accepted the unspoken invitation and settled herself on the settee, which was covered in deep blue velvet that brought out the gold of her hair and rich lapis of her eyes.

"I don't think that's wise," Lydia said. "You don't know him."

"The purpose of an at home is to get to know people." Honore smiled at Lydia, then Frobisher.

Lydia wanted to scream with frustration. Beyond making a scene, she could do nothing to stop the tête-à-tête.

"I'll return in a quarter hour." It was the best she could do—remind Honore of the restriction of time spent with a single guest.

Lydia spun on her heel and stalked across the room to where Mr. Barnaby leaned on the back of a winged chair talking with Mama and another older lady. A snatch of conversation told

Lydia he amused them with an anecdote about traveling to town on the mail coach after his carriage threw a wheel. Again, she couldn't interrupt the dialogue without looking foolish, without causing trouble for her family.

Her temples began to throb. She refused to give in to the pain. She needed to think, to watch, to get to know these men and find chinks in their polished social manners, to discover what they were up to and how she could stop them.

Or be reassured that all was well after all?

She started to return to Honore and Mr. Frobisher, but a flurry of movement at the door announced the arrival of more guests. Lydia moved forward to greet them. Another group departed with promises of invitations and admonitions to call on them. Then Cassandra's fiancé slipped into the drawing room unannounced. Lydia stepped out of the group of ladies surrounding her and opened her mouth to welcome him.

He held his finger to his lips and glided up behind Cassandra. She sat with a book on her lap while she gazed at two gentlemen as though she didn't quite see them, which was probably true, nearsighted as she was. Lydia headed toward the group, not certain what Geoffrey Giles, Earl of Whittaker, was up to and wanting to be near to prevent any mishaps should his actions be unwise or Cassandra's reaction unfortunate. But yet more guests arrived, and Lydia diverted her trajectory back to the door.

"Good afternoon, Lady Jers—"

A shriek ripped through the subdued chatter. Silence fell. Lydia whirled around in time to see Whittaker drop the book Cassandra had been holding, his face stricken, and Cassandra standing in front of her chair, hands upraised as though preparing to fight.

"Dear me," Sally Jersey drawled. "And here I thought Miss Bainbridge was a quiet young lady."

"She is." Lydia struggled for words. "He must have startled her. She isn't wearing—" She snapped her teeth together.

Another secret—Cassandra and her spectacles. Lydia felt like all the secrets inside her would send her exploding and whirling in a circle like a balloon that had lost its hot air.

"She looks quite well dressed to me," a soft voice said from behind Lydia. "I love her gown." The speaker hurried forward on too many pink flounces. "Did Madame Lettice make it, Cassie?"

Lydia didn't know the young lady but loved her. Her remark and action broke the awkward moment, and the room returned to normal. Lydia sidled toward the couple and friend of Cassandra's in time to hear Whittaker stammering out an apology.

"I wanted to surprise you, not scare you."

"I—I'm sorry." Cassandra's face glowed the color of a ripe cherry. "My book just disappeared and . . . Oh, Whittaker, you're a beast."

The latter emerged with such affection and such a brilliant smile that Lady Jersey fanned herself. When Whittaker rounded Cassandra's chair to take her hands in his and return her grin, more ladies drew handkerchiefs from their reticules to dab at their eyes.

"Young love." Lady Jersey sounded a bit wistful. "When is the wedding, Lady Gale?"

"At the end of June. Whittaker will be completely out of mourning for his brother by then. May I fetch you a cup of tea, my lady?"

So Lady Jersey, as one of the foremost patronesses of the assembly rooms, would use her social powers to ensure that Cassandra and Honore, especially Honore, received their vouchers for Almack's.

"I'd prefer lemonade, my dear. Now I must go see your dear mama and meet the latest Bainbridge beauty."

"Honore is the true Bainbridge beauty." Lydia smiled at her

sister, though she wanted to scowl at the way she gazed into Frobisher's eyes.

First Lydia must fetch the lemonade. Next she would break up that interlude. Sally Jersey had given her the perfect excuse.

She fetched the fruit drink for the countess, then headed for Honore. Many ladies and gentlemen stopped her along the way. They hadn't seen her in years and wanted to know how she fared. They admired her gown. They hinted that she was on the lookout for another husband. To all comments, Lydia murmured some appropriate response—"Well, thank you"; "Thank you"; "Not while Honore is in competition"—and maintained her forward momentum toward her sister. By the time she reached the far side of the room, Frobisher had departed and two other young men had taken his place.

"May I go for a drive with Mr. Taft?" Honore asked. "He's Whittaker's cousin, you know."

"Yes, you may. Fetch a warm pelisse. The weather is still chilly." Lydia was so pleased that Frobisher had departed that she would have allowed Honore to go riding with pretty much any other gentleman.

But he and Barnaby hadn't departed. Lydia saw Honore off with a beaming Mr. Taft and found the two newcomers blocking her return to the drawing room.

"We're taking our leave now," Barnaby said with a little bow. "Thank you so much for welcoming us into your lovely home."

Lydia merely inclined her head.

"We would like a few invitations to parties," Barnaby continued. "The Tarleton Masquerade, a dinner party with your father's political cronies . . ."

"Almack's?" Frobisher asked. "And White's, of course."

"And no doubt Carlton House too." Lydia curled her upper lip.

"We'll be happy with Watier's." Barnaby didn't seem in the least put off by her sarcastic suggestion that she could get them into the residence of the prince regent. "Prinney plays there, does he not?"

"I wouldn't know." Lydia managed to sound bored. "You'll have to find a man to recommend you for the clubs. I'll see what I can do about Almack's if you stay away from my little sister."

"Oh, no, we're riding in the park tomorrow morning." With a brilliant grin and a bow, Frobisher swung away and headed for the front door.

"We'll see about that," Lydia hissed after him.

Frobisher laughed and lifted his hat onto his curls.

"Perhaps you will go riding with me in the morning, Lady Gale?" Barnaby asked. "I'm certain I can meet the right persons while in your company."

"Right for what?" Lydia demanded. "What do you want?"

Barnaby bowed. "Right for entering London Society. Is tomorrow at eleven o'clock too early? You do ride, do you not?"

"I ride." Lydia hadn't been on a horse since visiting her family the previous summer, but she could manage a gentle mount through the park. "But I need to take my sisters shopping tomorrow."

"No, I wouldn't do that if I were you, my lady." Barnaby bowed and followed Frobisher to the door.

Lydia sighed. "I'll be ready at eleven o'clock."

If she didn't find another way to avoid the men entertaining her and Honore. And if she couldn't, perhaps she should request a spirited mount like the one Cassandra preferred. A broken leg would keep her from receiving unwelcome visitors.

She smiled at her own morbid humor and returned to the drawing room. Most of the ladies and gentlemen were taking their leave. Mama glowed from her chair at one end, as some of the best ladies of the *ton* complimented her on her daughters and lovely house and promised invitations to more events than all of them could attend separately, let alone together.

At the far end of the room, Cassandra peered up at Whittaker, a beatific smile on her soft mouth as he talked and gestured and made those around him laugh.

Once again Lydia experienced that twinge of regret, of emptiness. Or was it apprehension for her younger sister? Lydia had gazed at Charles Gale that way, though not with Cassandra's nearsighted haze. Lydia had hung on his every word—words about military life, about the pleasure of travel because of his military life, about how he'd been promoted without having to buy a further commission. Not until later, not until he departed for his regiment, despite claiming he would sell out and make a home for them on his family estate, did she realize what warning signs she should have read into his speech.

He'd never talked of anyone but himself and the Army.

Don't let her make the same mistake I did. She prayed without much hope of anything changing for Cassandra. God hadn't seen fit to free Lydia from her current predicament.

And perhaps she was too jaded to see that Whittaker and Cassandra truly loved one another. People did live in happy unions. Her parents' marriage had been arranged, yet they held a great deal of respect and affection for one another.

When they saw one another.

Perhaps therein lay the secret to the Bainbridges' successful union—distance. Mama hadn't come to London for the Season for two years. With Papa in the House of Lords, that left them apart nearly half the year.

As long as Whittaker gave Cassandra a large book allowance, she would be happy. As long as he understood that his wife should have been allowed to attend a university, he would be happy too.

Lydia didn't want her sister to suffer. Yet every time she looked at the couple, she ached inside. Was it fear or envy?

She stopped looking at them. She began to gather up teacups, glasses, and plates until a small hand closed over her arm.

"We're not at home," Barbara whispered. "We have servants here."

Lydia started and glanced around. A handful of remaining guests stared at her with surprise or disapproval. She smiled at them. "Yet a little sleep, a little slumber, a little folding of the hands to sleep: so shall thy poverty come as one that travelleth, and thy want as an armed man." She quoted from the sixth chapter of Proverbs. After all, who could argue with Scripture?

"You would know about poverty," a plump matron with a plain daughter at her side murmured just loud enough for Lydia to hear.

Ah, the cat claws of the Upper Ten Thousand.

Lydia smiled. "My husband served his country. Perhaps his country should have served him better."

Just as she realized how treasonous those words could be taken in the right—or wrong—circumstances, Lemster entered the parlor bearing a silver tray. A sheet of sealed vellum lay on that tray. Lydia stared at it. It was nothing—an invitation, a letter from Papa or one of Mama's many friends. Just because it looked exactly like the letter of introduction from the mysterious Mr. Lang didn't mean it was anything sinister. Perhaps Lemster would carry it directly to Mama.

He carried it directly to her. "The gentleman asked me to bring this to you before I present him to you."

"Indeed." The hairs on the back of Lydia's neck rose with a shiver down her spine.

Not again. Not another gentleman with a letter of introduction. Not . . . not . . .

She picked up the letter with her thumb and forefinger. She'd already done Mr. Lang's dirty work, or at the least she'd begun it for him. Perhaps this was the man himself, showing himself to her in daylight instead of sneaking about in the dark or just out of her sight. Perhaps it was merely an acquaintance of her husband's.

She slit the seal with her thumbnail and unfolded the letter. *The honorable Elias Lang wishes for his dear friend Lady Gale . . .*

She was going to cast up her accounts. Right there in the middle of the drawing room and half a dozen ladies and gentlemen of the ton, she was going to be sick.

She took a deep, steadying breath and finished reading the missive. *Please welcome my associate, Monsieur le comte Christien de Meuse.*

Monsieur—a French affix. *Christien de Meuse*—a French name.

No. Her lips formed the word without a sound.

But the answer was yes. Movement in the doorway caught her eye. She glanced up in time to see him saunter into the drawing room—the man she knew as the chevalier Christophe Arnaud, now calling himself Christien de Meuse.

5

Christien's lips stiffened the instant he saw the horror on Lydia Gale's face. His morning bread and chocolate, which had been all the nourishment he'd consumed that day, roiled in his gut, and each breath made his chest feel as though he'd broken a rib or two on the way from Upper Brook Street to Cavendish Square.

This wasn't his first covert operation, but it surely had to be his worst. Face-to-face with the lady he had every reason to believe had given him her last valuable possession to provide him with food and shelter, he preferred betraying all those who trusted him to carry out his mission to betraying the lovely widow.

But he had a family too. His sisters needed marriage portions in the upcoming years. His mother deserved security, and his brother wanted an education so he could go into the church.

He fixed the faces of his loved ones in the back of his mind and made an elegant leg to Lady Lydia Gale. "Good afternoon, madame. I trust I do not intrude overmuch on your guests?"

Those guests continued their conversations while peering at him from around fans and teacups.

"You." Her straight, white teeth snapped together behind a smile that was more of a grimace. She dropped a slight curtsy.

When she rose, she met his gaze, and her dark eyes glowed with an inner fire that sent a radiance of heat swirling through him. "This is our afternoon for receiving callers, so you are not intruding, monsieur. But pray tell, what brings a Frenchman into our English midst?" Under her breath she added, "And one who has lost much of his accent in a matter of weeks."

"I have lived in England since I was ten years in 1792."

Except for the ten years he'd spent on the continent with Napoleon.

Ah, the lies, the games, the need for nightly repentance that never assuaged his burden of guilt.

"How fortunate you were to keep your head attached to your neck and away from the guillotine." Lady Gale tilted her head. As though a curl, like many of the guests smiling around them, believed her words flirtatious, it slipped from its moorings and brushed her cheek.

Christien wondered if he could keep his head around her. He raised his hand, nearly brushing that curl aside. He pictured himself lifting it to his lips, inhaling its honey-citrus fragrance, testing its silkiness against his cheek.

He shoved his hand into his coat pocket. "My family was most fortunate to keep our heads. And now I am even more fortunate that we have a mutual friend who has so graciously allowed me to make your acquaintance."

"Indeed." Lang's letter crunched in her hand, mangled beyond recognition. "A friend of my husband's, I presume?"

"*Biensur.*" At the sibilant French word, a few ladies waved their fans more vigorously.

Madame Gale gripped hers as though she would smack him with it or she wished it were a truncheon instead. "I suppose I need to introduce you to my guests."

"I would be most grateful. London is a lonely place without friends." He offered what he hoped was a charming smile.

She blinked, and a hint of pink rose in her cheeks, testimony to the fact that she was not as indifferent to him as she pretended.

His smile broadened. "And perhaps a drive in the park afterward? It is a fine day for the end of March in this cold country."

"Yes, it's likely raining in Tavistock, don't you think? Or have you never been to Tavistock?" As though discussing the weather under normal social conditions, she took his arm and nudged him forward.

He resisted the urge to cover her fingers with his and press them against his forearm, reassure her that her family would come to no harm through her actions or his. At least he would do his best to keep them all safe—by beginning with pretending that her comment about rain in Tavistock hadn't been uttered.

"Monsieur Lang has told me of the beauty of the Bainbridge ladies," he said. "Having met you, I believed him."

"Flattery will serve you nothing here, monsieur. Though my youngest sister is quite a beauty, she is barely out of the schoolroom. She isn't here. Cassandra is on the settee at the far end of the room, speaking with her fiancé and a friend. Mama is here." She made these announcements in a breathless rush and stopped a yard from a lovely middle-aged lady with silver-gilt curls and a gentle smile. "Lady Jersey, Mama, this is Monsieur le comte de Meuse."

Lady Jersey, one of the scions of Society. *Tres bien*. A step in the right direction. She was famous for her flirtatious ways. Even as he bowed over her extended hand, he caught the flutter of her lashes and felt the pressure of her fingers.

"An émigré?" she asked, holding his gaze too long.

"*Oui*, madame. My family lives in Shropshire." Conveniently far from London.

"What has kept you from us for so long?" Lady Bainbridge inquired. "And how do you know him, my dear?" she asked her eldest daughter.

"I have been serving my country," Christien responded automatically. At a start of movement beside him, he added, "My adopted country, *n'est-ce pas?*"

"His service is how I met him." Lady Gale took half a step away from him. "I see that Lady Melby is leaving. I should say goodbye."

Before Christien thought of a way to hold her beside him, she slipped away to a wispy lady old enough to be his great-grandmother.

"Are you a military man, monsieur?" Lady Jersey asked.

"An attaché to the foreign office only. But my uncle died last year, so I was graciously allowed to come home and have decided to spend this Season in London." He reminded himself to make himself sound as much like an English family patriarch as possible. "I have two younger sisters who will reach the age for their come-out next spring, and another sister who has resisted a Season thus far, but should no longer."

"Laying the groundwork for their success." Lady Bainbridge's smile was approving. "What a good brother."

"And thinking of setting up your nursery?" Lady Jersey gave him a slanted smile.

"With the will of *le bon dieu*."

If God honored men who had made a career of lies enough to provide a wife.

His gaze strayed across the drawing room to Lady Gale. She stood by the door, talking with a lovely young woman with the same dark hair and eyes, and a young man who gazed at the second lady as though she were a treasure for which he'd sought all his life. Christien flicked his gaze back to Lady Gale and wondered if his expression resembled that of the younger man.

"From all I hear," Lady Jersey said in an undertone that would reach no ears but his, "you'll catch cold in that direction. Lydia Bainbridge Gale is little more than a recluse with no interest in a second husband."

"A pity. She's beautiful." Christien glanced at the mother. She too watched her eldest daughter. Her face reflected sorrow.

"How did you meet Lydia?"

"I was able to perform some service for her husband many years ago." Christien's fingers curled into a fist before he could stop them. "Monsieur Lang and I, that is. I did not know his wife was such a beauty."

"I have been blessed with exceptional daughters." Lady Bainbridge began to rise.

Christien offered her his hand. She leaned on him for support, and he realized how frail she appeared, her skin translucent, her hand thin enough to show all the veins, her bones as fragile as a bird's wing. Quite a contrast to her robust eldest daughter.

"You do not object if I take your daughter for a drive in the park?" he asked.

"I'll wager she doesn't go." Lady Jersey trilled a laugh.

Lady Bainbridge clucked in disapproval. "No wagering in my household, Sally. And no, of course I don't object. But it's Lydia whom you will have to convince. She isn't inclined to allow herself to be courted in any way."

"I'll convince her." Christien smiled, bowed to the ladies, and wended his way through tables, sofas, and chairs to the door and Lydia.

Yes, she was Lydia. He'd thought of her as Lydia since reading her letters. He had to force himself to call her Lady Gale. Calling her Lydia would insult her. She was a lady, poised and elegant in her city finery. Poised and elegant in the shabby gown she'd worn to the prison. Both attested to breeding and manners.

He counted on those to get an opportunity to be alone with her.

"Are you departing so soon, monsieur?" she asked him at the door.

"Not unless you agree to join me." He smiled at her.

Her sister giggled. "Lydia, you didn't tell us you have a suitor."

"I don't." Lydia's knuckles whitened around her fan. "Monsieur le comte de Meuse, Cassandra, Whittaker."

A curtsy and bows were exchanged.

"Are you truly French?" Miss Bainbridge asked. "I would love to talk to you about life during the Terror. One day I want to write a history of the French Revolution and . . ." She trailed off, her face reddening. "I beg your pardon. Perhaps you do not wish to speak of it."

"I would not mind, but I was but a child at the time and my recollections may be corrupt. Perhaps one day you can meet my maman and get a better perspective. She is *une Americaine* and had revolutionary ideas, though married to my papa. I expect her to come to London next year."

"And we'll be in Lancashire." She gazed up at the young man beside her. "We're getting married in June."

"An excellent month is June." Christien turned to Lydia. "Can you leave now for our drive?"

"Our—" She compressed her lips. "I'll fetch my pelisse and hat."

"We're off for a drive too." Miss Bainbridge tucked her hand into the crook of Whittaker's arm. "One never knows when we will have sunshine again."

They exchanged polite farewells, and Christien slipped into the entryway behind the couple to wait for Lydia. And wait for Lydia. If she didn't hurry, the footman stationed beside the door would toss Christien into the street for loitering. Several guests gave him odd glances as they departed. The sun began to slant too far to the west.

Just when he wondered if she intended to remain above stairs and leave him to cool his heels until dark, footfalls sounded on the upper floor, died on the runner down the steps, and Lady Lydia Gale rounded the curve of the stairway.

A hat of white leghorn straw with a nosegay of pink roses on one side perched atop a cluster of curls that appeared a bit disheveled, with two curls dangling against her cheek instead of the one from earlier. Several long white hairs adorned her pink pelisse, and a scratch reddened an inch of fine skin beside her left ear.

"Is all well, madame?" Christien touched the scratch before he could stop himself.

She flinched and looked away. "My cat doesn't like being shut up in my bedchamber and finds ways to get revenge." She plucked several hairs from her pelisse. "What should I expect but trouble from a French cat?"

Christien laughed and offered his arm. "Come. We shall discuss the French felines along the way to Rotten Row. I have a fondness for cats."

"Right now I'd happily give you mine." She took his arm, and the footman sprang to open the front door. "My husband gave him to me for a betrothal gift. I think he knew—" She caught her breath.

"*Oui*, madame?" Christien welcomed the coolness of the outside air despite the odor of coal smoke strong enough to taste. "What did your husband know?"

"It's unimportant." She released his arm the instant they reached the bottom step and stood beside his curricle. "Your horses are lovely. The foreign service must be good to you."

"My family has prospered here, not the foreign service." Christien leaped aboard the open vehicle and leaned down to offer the lady his hand.

She grasped his fingers like a drowning woman, stepped onto the spoke, and swung aboard with the fluidity of a sunrise banishing darkness. Even if clouds had filled the sky, he would have rejoiced to be beside her, inhaling her perfume, hearing her voice, feeling the occasional touch of her arm against his.

A man could not fall in love at first sight. Not outside the pages of a romantic novel like those his sisters read, but a man could fall in love with an action that shouted of a lady's character. Christien had done so the instant she pressed her bracelet into his palm and promised him freedom.

If he didn't win her to his side, she would rob him of freedom just as quickly.

He unwound the reins from the whip box, called to the lad holding the horses to release their heads, and set the curricle surging forward to bounce over the cobbles of the square before glancing at his companion and launching into his prepared speech. "Thank you for not giving me away. I know you could have easily done so, and I would have found myself right back in Dartmoor Prison. Probably in the black hole there."

"I didn't do it to spare you the deprivations of prison. Right now I'd like to see you back there." She sighed. "No, that isn't true. I wouldn't wish any enemies to live like that, not even you."

"I am not your enemy, my lady."

"You are French, are you not? We are at war."

"You are at war with Napoleon's France, not Bourbon France. I am of Bourbon France."

"And a month ago, you were an officer in Napoleon's Army. Do please tell me which person is the true man—Christophe Arnaud or Christien de Meuse."

"Both."

She gave an unladylike snort.

"*Mais vraiment*. I am Christien Christophe Arnaud de Meuse."

"Please forgive me if I do not believe you." Her voice held no true request for grace.

He granted her forgiveness anyway. "I understand your doubts, your distrust, your skepticism, your—"

"Outrage? Why don't we begin with my outrage, monsieur." She glared up at him with such ferocity he feared passersby would think he had said something improper to her.

He sought for words to calm her. "*Oui*, you have reason for outrage. I took advantage of your kindness—"

"And now are taking advantage of my love for my family and my fear that something terrible will happen to them if I don't cooperate with whatever all of you want."

Christien started. The reins jerked. The team of bays reared and halted. "What all of us?"

"Mr. Lang and his other friends. Not that he seemed much of a friend of yours when he confronted me."

"What all of us?" Christien repeated. "Lang is my friend of many years and working with me alone."

"Don't ye be stoppin' in the middle of the road, you blithering idgit," a hackney driver shouted from behind them.

A few other drivers and small boys along the pavement began to pick up the chorus. They added some less savory comments to their catcalls.

Grinding his teeth, Christien snapped the reins to get the bays moving again and turned to Lydia. "Your statement implies that you have had other callers sent by Monsieur Lang."

"As if you don't know." She curled her upper lip.

Kissing it would be a fine way to wipe the sneer away from her lovely mouth. One day. Not yet. Not while she thought of him what she should.

Thought of him what she should . . .

He concentrated on navigating the curricle between pedestrians and carriages. "*Vraiment*, madame, I know of no others Monsieur Lang has sent for your assistance."

"Indeed. And do you know all of Mr. Lang's dealings?"

"Thank *le bon dieu*, no."

"No honor amongst spies . . . or traitors?" Her tone was mellifluous, her glance as sharp as a pickax.

Christien's lips twitched. "What we don't know, we cannot tell."

"You admit it?" She jerked beside him, rocking the vehicle.

"I admit nothing."

"But you said—"

"I have no secret that I am working with Monsieur Lang. That does not make me a traitor." Christien let her stew over that one for a few moments while he maneuvered the team through the crush at the entrance to Hyde Park. They entered the procession of phaetons, curricles, and barouches taking advantage of the rare fine weather to parade down Rotten Row.

Most of the vehicles held couples—early Season courtships, the newly wed, others who gave Society a less than good name at times. He wondered why a Christian lady like Lydia would bring her younger sisters to London to find them husbands. It seemed the worst place for courtship if they were to make connections with godly young men. Whittaker seemed a nice enough fellow, but Christien had heard talk of the younger man's escapades at university . . .

But men changed. He had through trial under fire.

Now to convince Lydia Gale of that fact. Or at least convince her of the facts he needed to tell her so she would work with him, not against him.

"I am not on the wrong side, Lady Gale." He turned his head so he could look at her. "I have lived in this country since I was ten years old. England gave my family shelter and protection when our own people tried to kill us. An Englishman got us out of France and to safety. We bought land and have prospered. Why would I turn against all this to work for the Corsican monster?"

"You were in Dartmoor because you were doing just that." She held his gaze without wavering. "You were with my husband at his death because of that—working with the Corsican monster."

"Or was I working with your husband for England?"

Christien posed the question, then focused his attention on turning the curve in the lane without hooking wheels with a youth showing more enthusiasm than skill at driving.

Lydia said nothing. He felt her stiffness beside him. A glance told him she looked straight ahead. Those curls bobbed against her cheek, and the silk petals on her hat's roses fluttered in the cool breeze. The rest of her remained still, motionless.

"You're too polite to call me a liar?" Christien asked, flashing her a smile.

"Perhaps I'm too frightened to call you a liar." The coolness of her voice evoked no hint of fear. Challenge, yes. Apprehension?

Christien slipped the reins into one hand and tucked her errant curls behind her ear. They were every bit as soft as he imagined they would be. "Then you'll accept the possibility that I tell you the truth?"

"I saw you in that prison. Surely our government wouldn't ask that kind of sacrifice, that kind of horror in prison, of you, of anyone working for them."

"Ha!" His laugh burst from him.

Several matrons in a nearby carriage glanced his way, then took a second look.

He smiled at them and bowed from his seat, then he returned his attention to the lovely widow. "Men suffer far worse for causes in which they believe. Your husband saw the men go aboard the transports before going himself, and when the horses panicked, he saved men's lives at the cost of his own, eventually. But it was a cause in which he believed—fighting Napoleon for his country."

"Which only tells me that you endured prison for the cause you believe in—fighting the English for your country."

Christien frowned at a pair of curricles ahead of them moving at an even slower pace than the sedate promenade that was normal in the park. A lady drove one and a gentleman drove the other. They appeared to be engaged in an intimate tête-à-tête and paying no attention at all to how they held up the progress of others.

"For a yard of tin to blow like the mail coaches," he murmured.

Lydia laughed. "You'd probably start a stampede."

"We'd be moving then, no?"

"Yes, we'd—"

A crunch of wood and iron colliding cut across her words.

Ahead, the two curricles stood motionless with their wheels locked. The lady began to yell at the gentleman for not steering straight. He in turn made some rude remarks about ladies driving.

"I believe," Christien drawled, "we will be here for a while."

"You won't go assist them?"

"Will you be here if I do?"

"You expect me to slip away from you and walk home the minute your back is turned?"

"I don't know what to expect from you, Madame Gale." Christien turned to face her. "You think I am up to no good. You do not like Monsieur Lang's methods of getting you to cooperate with us."

"Would you?"

"I don't. I asked him not to do what he is doing, not to bring you into this. He did not listen to me. So here we are, stranded together." He glanced toward the tangled vehicles.

Several young men had removed their coats and demonstrated their physical prowess by leading the horses out of the shafts and pulling the two curricles apart.

"They don't need your assistance after all," she said.

"No, but I need yours, *ma chère*." He tried to look into her eyes, but her hat brim frustrated his efforts. "Without entrée into London Society, I cannot succeed. I need to move freely around and through the ton to complete my mission. With you at my side—"

"Your mission." She gripped her reticule so hard he suspected her knuckles were white beneath her leather gloves. "The man who blackmailed me into helping you said nothing of me remaining at your side after I make introductions."

Guts twisting, Christien drew up on the side of the path so

he could face her. "What do you mean by the man who black-mailed you into helping me? Lang is from the Home Office."

"Don't play the innocent with me, monsieur." Her dark eyes flashed, and a white line formed around her mouth. "I am as well aware as you that our government doesn't need to meet ladies in dark gardens to force them—"

Christien grasped her wrist. "What dark garden?"

"As if you don't know." She wrinkled her nose as though smelling something revolting. "Now let us be gone before we make more of a spectacle of ourselves than we already have."

Carriages flowed past them, and many persons stared. They needed to move on, stop drawing so much attention, but Christien's innards told him something was terribly wrong, and he wasn't about to move until he got the truth from Lydia.

"Tell me what garden . . . *s'il vous plait*," he persisted.

"The one in Portsmouth, six days after you escaped from England against the terms of your parole." She spoke behind a stiff smile and clenched teeth. "You know that quite well."

"No, Madame Gale, I do not. Monsieur Lang was with me that night."

6

What ever had possessed her to purchase a red riding habit?

Lydia stared down at the deep wine-red jacket and skirt, then up at her reflection in the mirror. She didn't look like a widow. With the red bringing out the roses in her cheeks and somehow making her hair glow with blue highlights, she looked like a lady in search of a husband, and with two men vying for her attention, that was the last impression she wished to give.

Not that they wanted her attention for any honorable reason. Barnaby and de Meuse needed her for her connections in Society. Seen with her, a widow above reproach whose ancestor had signed the Magna Carta, whose husband had died in the service of his country, the men would find themselves welcomed anywhere she requested they be welcomed.

Except perhaps Almack's. No one told the patronesses whom to invite to those hallowed and—if Lydia remembered correctly—dull halls. But Lady Jersey had an eye for attractive men, and Christien de Meuse was certainly that—attractive, charming, treacherous.

If she could expose him first . . .

Yes, he should be the easiest man to be rid of, being French. Though émigrés dotted Great Britain—from kitchens as chefs, to dressing rooms as ladies' maids, to drawing rooms as honored guests—the men and women who were or had served the aristocracy of France were not entirely liked or trusted.

With good reason. No one should trust Christien de Meuse. A mere month ago, he had been in Dartmoor, taken when the ship on which his regiment had been sailing was captured by the English Navy. She was supposed to believe he was a double agent, with England the country in which he placed his primary loyalty. That's what he'd told her as they resumed their leisurely drive along Rotten Row and back. Mr. Lang was supposed to meet her in Plymouth and ask her to help. But a Mr. Lang had met her in Portsmouth and compelled her to help. No doubt, if asked, Mr. Barnaby and Mr. Frobisher would declare they were the loyal subjects of King George of Hanover and Christien de Meuse was the traitor, or the Frenchman in their midst would declare them traitors—Englishmen working for Napoleon.

"How to know the truth?" Lydia picked up her hat and perched it on her head at first one angle, then another.

Hodge leaped from the floor to a stool to the dressing table, then launched himself at the perky feather curling over the hat's narrow brim.

"Beast." Lydia jumped back in time to protect her hat and coiffure. "It's not attached to a bird, I promise. Not that you've ever caught anything that flies." Mice, on the other hand . . . Hodge earned his keep at the cottage. "Be a good kitty and I'll take you for a walk in the mews later. Maybe even the park." The idea sounded lovely even as she spoke it.

For now, she wasn't riding out with de Meuse alone. She doubted she should be alone with any of the gentlemen, not in a carriage, on horseback, or in a parlor, regardless of crowds around them.

She wanted to stay alone in her room or find a quiet corner of the park to paint and think. But the hands of her clock pointed to 10:30, and Whittaker and de Meuse were expected any minute. Barnaby wasn't expected for another half hour.

And there went the knocker. The banging of the brass ring echoed up the steps of the tall, narrow townhouse. Across the hall, Honore and Cassandra's bedchamber door opened.

"Lydia?" Honore called. "Are you ready? I believe the gentlemen are here."

Lydia joined her younger sister in the passageway. "You look lovely."

"Not as pretty as you. How I wish I could wear that color." Honore sighed.

"And I'm wishing I'd chosen your deep blue instead of red." Lydia smiled. "But the blue suits you. It matches your eyes."

"And Mr. Frobisher's." Honore's eyes grew dreamy. "Did you notice that we have the same coloring? Don't we make a nice picture?"

"If I say no, it would be a lie, but, Honore, you can't be thinking . . . I mean, you just met him. You know nothing of him."

"He's a friend of your friend. Isn't that enough? And in my novels—"

"Novels are called fiction for a reason, child." Lydia smoothed a curling strand of hair off Honore's face. "Life isn't like that at all."

"But you barely knew Sir Charles before you married him. Wasn't that love at first sight? Didn't you feel like your heart would just beat out of your chest when you looked at him, and get all warm—"

"That's not love." Lydia softened her tone. "Honore, love isn't a feeling. It's deeper. It's friendship and understanding and—"

What did she know about love? Charles had departed for his regiment before the first blush of marital bliss had faded. He'd departed and doused the flames with the chill of rejection.

"We didn't have friendship." Lydia blinked against a mist in her eyes. "Get to know the gentleman a little first, Honore. He mentioned going to Watier's. Men play a deep game there. You don't want a gamester for a husband. And we don't know if he's a man of property."

"I have a fine dowry."

"Honore, please don't toss your hat over the windmill for the first pretty face you see. Now, let's be on our way. Monsieur de Meuse and Lord Whittaker are waiting."

"Not Mr. Barnaby and Mr. Frobisher?" Honore's full lips dropped into a pout. "But I understood they would be."

"Perhaps later."

God had ignored her prayers to keep the men away, at least until de Meuse had departed for whatever occupied his time. She didn't want to pretend liking or even politeness with either man.

"Then perhaps I should wait." Honore half turned toward her bedchamber door.

"You're coming with us." Lydia curved her hand around Honore's elbow and steered her toward the steps.

"But there won't be a gentleman to accompany me. I'm like a carriage with five wheels. It would look unbalanced."

"My dear girl, if we don't attract a whole platoon of eligible young men, I'll be surprised. Now scoot."

Honore scooted with enough alacrity to give Lydia hope that her younger sister liked the idea of other young men swarming around her. And surely they would. She was so pretty and sweet, if a bit too dreamy. Those dreams—the belief that attraction could be instant and permanent—caused trouble for too many young women. If Honore was one of them . . .

But she wouldn't be. Lydia would make sure of it. That was one reason she'd asked de Meuse to come a half hour earlier than Barnaby and Frobisher planned to arrive.

With the time limit in mind, Lydia followed her youngest sister down the steps to the entryway. Honore stood talking to de Meuse and Whittaker, who poised beside them in a stance suggesting he intended to dash off somewhere at any moment.

"Where's Cassandra?" Lydia asked.

"She's not upstairs," Honore volunteered. "I haven't seen her for hours."

"Hours?" Lydia gripped the banister and took a deep breath to stop herself from screeching. "Why didn't you tell me she wasn't ready?"

"Perhaps she is." Honore shrugged. "I was in the music room playing the pianoforte and thought Cassandra had changed into riding dress before me."

"Could she have gone out on her own?" Whittaker's lips tightened. "She wouldn't, would she?"

"Not for a minute." Lydia finished descending the steps and patted his arm. "She's in the house somewhere."

"But did she not hear us knock?" De Meuse raised his brows. "I noticed she had the myopia, but—"

Lydia laid a finger across her lips. She couldn't believe Whittaker hadn't noticed that Cassandra barely saw more than a blur a yard from her face, but she thought he knew nothing and, for whatever reason, wished to keep it that way. It wasn't Lydia's or anyone else's secret to share.

The notion that de Meuse had noticed without even spending time with Cassandra sent a chill rippling along Lydia's arms, and she flashed a glance at Whittaker. He was speaking to Lemster and hadn't apparently heard de Meuse.

"I'll find her." Lydia gathered up her train and mounted the steps.

A glance into the sitting room warned her that the hour approached with rapidity. If they didn't find Cassandra and depart within the next few minutes, Barnaby and Frobisher would arrive.

She wished. She doubted.

Her heart as heavy as the extra long skirt of her woolen riding habit, Lydia pushed open the library door. She expected to see Cassandra bent over the desk with pen, ink, and half a dozen books in front of her. But the desk chair stood empty, the surface of the table clear of all but ink and quills. A quick glance hinted at an empty room. Lydia was about to close the door and search elsewhere when she caught the soft rustle of paper.

"Cassandra?"

A thud sounded from the far corner of the room, behind one of the long draperies that half covered the windows. "Who—? Oh." Cassandra's pale face showed from around the edge of the crimson velvet curtains that formed an alcove with a window seat. "I didn't hear you come in. Did you need me for something?"

"We were scheduled for a ride in the park fifteen minutes ago." Lydia spoke in an even tone with her jaw tight to stop herself from shouting.

"I thought we weren't going until—dear me." Cassandra rubbed her eyes. "I misread the clock. I'm sorry. Give me ten minutes more. I'll be ready."

Ten minutes more would take them too close to eleven o'clock.

"I'll see if Whittaker wishes to wait." Not daring to say more,

Lydia spun on her heel and marched down the steps to the waiting group.

The waiting group, and Frobisher and Barnaby just entering through the front door.

Lydia sagged against the banister. "Cassandra will be delayed. Do you wish to wait for her, Whittaker?"

"Of course I'll wait." Whittaker's smile was indulgent, his eyes patient. "She read the clock wrong, right?"

"Precisely. Good day, gentlemen." Lydia turned her attention to the newcomers, her smile fixed. "Monsieur de Meuse, allow me to present Mr. George Barnaby and Mr. Gerald Frobisher. Though I expect the three of you are already acquainted, are you not?"

"We are not." De Meuse's tone was cold, his posture stiff.

Barnaby gave her an equally frosty glare and didn't so much as nod to le comte. "We had an appointment, did we not, Lady Gale?"

"So did Madame Gale and I." De Meuse looked down his high-bridged nose at the shorter man.

"I tried to tell you, Mr. Barnaby . . . I prefer to ride with my sisters." Lydia glanced at her younger sister. "I couldn't allow Honore to ride out alone with anyone I don't know well enough to trust."

Honore might as well have been alone in the entryway with Mr. Frobisher. They stood half a dozen feet apart but gazed into one another's eyes as though breaking the contact would send them both crumpling to the floor.

Lydia felt sick.

"We need to be going." Her tone was sharp, an ax to cut the contact between the two young people. Or chop the ice crackling through the air between de Meuse and Barnaby.

Would they lock her up in Bedlam if she simply began to bang her head against the nearest wall?

"The horses have been standing long enough." De Meuse held out his arm to Lydia.

Before she could decide to take it, Mr. Barnaby stepped forward and took her hand. "I'm desolated not to have this opportunity to be alone, my lady. Surely we can ride ahead and talk."

"I will ride beside my sister." Lydia extricated her hand from his grasp and grabbed Honore's arm. "Come along if you want to go."

"What? Oh yes, of course." Honore's smile radiated enough light to break through a London fog.

The young lady showed to advantage atop her gray mare. She and Cassandra both excelled at horsemanship. Lydia had preferred a sedate trot to whatever site proved the best for her paintings or sketches.

Unbidden, an image floated into her head—an English bull mastiff facing a French boarhound across a frozen stream, with her stuck in the middle like some dinner table epergne. Her fingers itched to pick up her charcoal pencil and get to work.

She picked up her train instead and led the way to the door. Lemster, mouth grim, opened the portal for her, and she stalked down the steps to where several grooms held the horses.

"Lord Whittaker and Miss Bainbridge will be out in a few minutes," she told the men holding their mounts.

"I'll assist you in mounting, my lady." Barnaby stood beside Honore's mare.

"It is my honor, *non?*" De Meuse picked the right horse, a gentle roan gelding.

Roan indeed. Her wine-red habit would clash. All the better if she looked a fright. Perhaps she would embarrass the "gentlemen" so much they would choose to abandon her as their entrée into Society.

Barnaby's eyes narrowed as Honore approached her mare. "I thought Lady Gale would want a more spirited animal."

"Lady Gale is a gentle lady, an artiste, *n'est-ce pas?*" De Meuse cupped his hands together.

With the groom still holding the reins, Lydia had no choice but to accept le comte's offer of a leg up. But she approached him with caution, another image of her sketch spreading through her head—her arms as bones over which the dogs were struggling, each trying to drag her to their side of the frozen stream.

Every nerve ending tense, she approached de Meuse. Always before she'd used a mounting block. Cavendish Square didn't offer such a nicety, as did her family home in Devonshire. She knew how to mount with the assistance of a strong gentleman, and Christien de Meuse looked strong enough despite his prison stay—something that should have warned her then?—but she doubted her own strength, her own agility in gathering her skirts, holding onto the pommel, and launching herself high enough to land on the saddle and not fall short or go over the other side of the horse's back.

"I won't let any harm come to you, madame." De Meuse smiled into her eyes. "That I have promised."

"I 'ave 'er reins good an' tight, m'lady." The groom spoke up from the front of the gelding. "Nothin' to fear."

"Of course not." Lydia made herself smile, then inserted herself between de Meuse and the horse.

Lydia grasped the pommel of the saddle, thanking God she was on the tall side and didn't have to reach too far over her head. Then, bracing to keep her legs from shaking, she lifted her left foot and set it into the monsieur's hands.

"Ready, madame?" His blue eyes held hers. Against the smoky blue of the sky above him, those eyes looked intense. She'd need the old lapis-based paint to get the color right. "On the count of three?"

She nodded. Even through her boot, her foot felt oddly warm in his hands. It was such an improper thing to do, even though it was how ladies all over the city mounted.

"One. Two—"

On the count of three, she bounced off her right foot. Simultaneously, de Meuse lifted up, and she pulled with her right hand holding the pommel. With grace and dignity intact, she landed with her seat in the saddle.

And she'd forgotten to hold on to her skirt. The tiresome extra fabric, intended to preserve her modesty, draped too far beneath her, tugging the skirt too far down on her right side, tightening the waistband across her middle, and leaving precious little material for the freedom to securely loop her right knee around the pommel. She gasped. She pulled. Wedged beneath her, the skirt didn't move. She got her knee up, and the skirt pulled tighter.

She either had to dismount and try again, or suffer.

She chose to suffer. She didn't want to put her foot into de Meuse's hands again. She didn't want the odd yet accepted intimacy of him slipping her left foot into her stirrup. The morning held a chill. Her lower limb should not be warm and tingling through leather boot and silk stocking.

"Is that stirrup a good height?" de Meuse asked. "I can adjust it if it is not."

She would have endured the wrong height rather than allow him to brush aside the excess fabric of her habit skirt and adjust the straps.

"It's the right height." She spoke in a tight voice, not looking down, looking straight ahead where the others were already mounted and milling about the square on their horses to keep them from standing too long. "Do please mount, monsieur. I need to get this poor beast moving."

"But of course." He gave her a last look, lingering on her face, before striding to his own horse.

He mounted with the fluid grace of a man who had grown up riding horses and continued the practice regularly. Of course. He was an officer in Napoleon's Army.

Wasn't he?

Lydia nudged her gelding in the side and set the gentle mount stepping forward until they drew level with Honore and Frobisher. The couple rode along the square at a leisurely fashion that allowed them to gaze at one another without risking limb or life.

"I'm surprised to see you going so sedately," Lydia observed.

Honore glanced around. "We'll get a good gallop in at the park. Well, perhaps not a gallop, but at least a canter."

"Don't get too far ahead of me." Lydia shifted on her saddle, trying to readjust her skirt.

"Are you all right?" Honore whispered loudly enough for everyone to hear in the quiet residential neighborhood.

Lydia frowned at her. "But of course."

But of course not. Her right knee felt as though the weight of her heavy skirt would drag it off the pommel at any moment, and she could scarcely breathe with the waistband pressed into her middle.

Somehow she must tug some of the fabric out from under her. Now was the best time, before they left the square and headed into traffic, and certainly before they reached the park and everyone chose to ride faster.

As surreptitiously as she could manage, she gripped her reins in her left hand, raised herself a hair off the saddle with her weight on her stirrup foot, and pulled at her skirt with her right hand.

It didn't budge. Her mount, however, didn't seem to like the shift of balance and sidled, bumping Lydia into Honore's mount. The high-strung mare took offense and leaped forward, away from the offensive contact. Honore laughed and called out something that sounded like encouragement. Frobisher shouted back. The two of them disappeared into a parade of carriages, phaetons, and drays.

Lydia lost her balance and began to slide toward the cobblestone street.

7

"Catch her." Christien leaped from his mount and charged toward the widow. "Lydia."

Horses whinnied and stamped. Lydia's horse reared, hooves rearing at the air. Women shrieked. Men shouted. If Lydia's foot remained in the stirrup and that horse bolted . . .

Christien lunged forward. A horse bumped his shoulder. He dodged aside and ducked to avoid the flailing hooves of another mount. He could never reach her, could never stop her from landing on the cobblestones, from breaking something—like her neck.

"Ma chère!"

He arched his body forward and caught a flying handful of riding habit. The fabric held. Lydia's fall continued. Still gripping the habit skirt, Christien twisted. If he could get beneath her, break her fall—

A blow from a flying hoof slammed into his right shoulder. He landed on his back, the wind knocked from his lungs. Lydia sprawled across his chest, the hooves of a dappled gray gelding mere inches from his head.

"I am so sorry, de Meuse." Barnaby dismounted and squatted beside Christien and Lydia. "My horse was quite out of control there for a moment. Lady Gale, are you all right?"

"Yes." She pushed herself to a kneeling position beside Christien. "Everything feels intact . . . except my pride."

Her cheeks blazed nearly as red as her habit. Her hat had fallen away somewhere, and her hair tumbled down around her face in a silky black curtain.

She looked young and beautiful and oh so very kissable.

Christien tried to draw in a breath. Pain seared through his back, and he gasped.

"Monsieur de Meuse." Lydia laid her hand against his face. "You're not all right. You broke my fall and now—don't all you men just stare. Fetch some help. A litter. A physician."

"*Non, non.*" Christien shook his head. "Just winded." He got his left elbow under him. When he tried to move his right arm, it disobeyed. Pain screamed through his right shoulder, and he flopped back onto the cobbles like a landed trout.

"You're not all right." Lydia leaned forward and touched his shoulder. Her glorious hair caressed his face. Her scent filled his nostrils.

"Madame, please do not." He could hardly speak.

She seemed not to hear his plea for her to move away. Her fingers probed his shoulder. To his shame, a cry escaped his lips.

"Fetch a physician, now," Lydia commanded. "Mr. Barnaby, Mr. Frobi—where has everyone gone? This man is injured."

"The grooms have gone for help." Barnaby pushed back a strand of Lydia's hair from her face.

If she hadn't jerked away from the man's touch, Christien feared he himself would have knocked the interloper onto his posterior.

He chastised himself for the uncharitable thought. The man looked at Lydia with admiration blazing in his gray eyes. It was the same kind of puppy-dog adoration Christien feared he displayed. And Barnaby could be on Christien's side, a comrade in arms.

Just as long as he stayed out of Lydia's arms.

Barnaby rested his hand on Lydia's shoulder. It appeared as though he did no more than steady her or even himself as they crouched beside Christien. The only way to stop that contact, Christien figured, was to make his body obey and get up.

This time he tried to roll onto his left side. The instant his right arm left the pavement, agony rocketed through his body, and he collapsed yet again with an unmanly groan.

"Mr. Barnaby, do see what's taking so long." Lydia's face had turned white. "Something is seriously wrong."

"Indeed." Barnaby turned his face so the lady couldn't see it, but Christien caught the curl of the man's lip. "I've heard the French are weak."

"When struck from behind," Christien gasped out, "all men are weak."

"I don't like your meaning." Barnaby shot to his feet. "When you stop malingering to attract the lady—"

"There is only . . . one meaning in . . . truth." Christien closed his eyes. The pain increased with every word. He clutched at the air with his good hand, his operable hand, seeking something to grasp, to ease the pain turning the world black around the edges.

Long, strong fingers slipped between his. "Hang onto me, monsieur. The grooms are coming with a litter now."

"Where will they take him?" Barnaby demanded.

"Into our house, of course." Lydia spoke with calm strength, like her steady hand in Christien's. "If you would like to assist to make up for your discourtesy of a few moments ago, I doubt monsieur le comte will object."

He wouldn't, but only to please her.

"Yes, ma'am, of course it's the best option." Barnaby's booted feet tramped around to Christien's other side. He flinched as they passed his right ear, and braced for the "accidental" kick against his injured shoulder.

But that was nonsense. Barnaby wouldn't deliberately injure him. That was a madman's way. Or the way of a man assaulting an enemy he wanted weakened. Even if Barnaby were on the wrong side of matters, he wouldn't want Christien so injured he had to remain in the Bainbridge household for any length of time, in Lydia's company. No, Barnaby would want him well, not out of commission.

But that blow . . .

Christien's lips hardened. He opened his eyes and found Lydia peering down at him, her face tight with concern.

He managed a stiff-lipped smile. "My apologies for being so clumsy, madame."

"As though I blame you when it was for my sake." She dropped her thick, dark lashes over her eyes. "I am not a good horse-woman."

"We must remedy that, *non*?"

Feet crunched nearby, and something clunked onto the cobbles beside Christien. Instead of answering him, Lydia began to direct the men to move the litter to his other side.

"And be as gentle as you can. I believe his right shoulder is dislocated."

"*Biensur*," Christien grumbled.

The hoof that had barely missed his skull, that would have smacked his skull if he hadn't twisted to break Lydia's fall with his own body, had been powerful enough to dislocate his shoulder. The good news lay in that, once someone set it back into place, the pain would go away, but he wouldn't be riding for a while, at least not lifting a lady into her saddle. Dancing would be out of the question, as no lady deserved a one-armed partner. And driving in the park would prove difficult at best. All prospects led to the worst news of all—he wouldn't make his entrée into Society.

His reentry into Lydia's home, Bainbridge House, proved more than he could manage. Between the men lifting him onto the litter, carrying him back through the square and up the front steps, and depositing him on a sofa in the parlor, Christien faded in and out of consciousness. The final jolt onto the hard cushions proved more than his shoulder could bear, and the blackness took over until a man with a white mane of hair and a ruddy complexion leaned over him, poking and prodding him into enough pain to awaken him.

"Aye, 'tis the dislocation," the man said in a thick Scottish burr. "My lady, leave the room. This is no sight for your gentle spirit."

A snort that didn't sound in the least ladylike came from Lydia. "I'm a widow, not a green girl, Dr. McPherson. I will stay."

"Suit yourself. But don't you be fainting away on me. I have na the time for two patients." McPherson laid his hands on Christien's shoulder and elbow as though the physician were the one with the gentle spirit. "This will take but a—"

He twisted up and back in one fluid motion. Torture surely felt better than the sensation that shot through Christien from shoulder to toes. Then the pain ebbed to settle into a deep throbbing.

"That will set things right if you do na move it." McPherson stepped away from the sofa. "I'll affix a sling, but this sofa will ne'er do. 'Tis na wide enough."

"I have rooms on Upper Brook Street," Christien offered.

In comparison to how he'd been feeling before the doctor's ministrations, Christien now thought perhaps he could rise and perform a credible minuet.

"Nay, too far. The jostling will dislocate it again. My Lady Gale?"

"A room is being prepared at this moment." The cool response set Christien's heart racing.

Entrée into Society indeed! If the Bainbridges allowed him to remain in their house even for a day while he convalesced, no one would shun him for fear of offending them.

Unless they put him in the servants' quarters.

But of course they would not. The lady who would give a near stranger her last possession of value would never treat that man so shabbily, regardless of her suspicions against him.

"You are a true Christian, madame," Christien murmured.

"More like the good Samaritan," came the disgruntled tones of Mr. Barnaby. "It isn't necessary to discommode yourself so, my lady. The house Frobisher and I have leased is only around the corner from the square. We're happy to take—"

"Mr. Frobisher, Honore," Lydia cried. "Where are they? It's been an hour. They should have returned. And Whittaker and Cassandra. Oh my stars, I must go—" She wrenched open the door. "Lemster, send a groom for my horse. He'll have to accompany me. We must . . ."

"Be a gentleman and offer to fetch the errant couples." Christien spoke to Barnaby while Lydia continued to issue orders.

"I don't wish to leave her with you here." Barnaby, seated in a chair adjacent to the foot of the sofa on which Christien reclined, indeed appeared as though he held no intentions of leaving.

"But she can't ride out. She's distraught."

"Aye," the doctor agreed, "she'll be upsetting her nag and I'll

have two patients to attend to. Now gang on with you, man."
McPherson pointed from Barnaby to the door.

Muttering beneath his breath, Barnaby rose as though he
were a man twice his age with rheumatic joints, and stalked to
the door. He rested his hand on Lydia's shoulder in that too-
familiar fashion that set Christien's blood boiling, but whatever
he said had her nodding her head and rescinding her orders to
the butler. Barnaby raised Lydia's hand to his lips, then disappeared out the front door.

Lydia wiped her hand on her dusty riding skirt, then issued
different orders to the butler.

Christien grinned.

"I was going to be offering you a dose of laudanum," McPherson murmured, "but I think you're feeling little of the pain
right now."

"It's much improved, monsieur."

"Weel, just the same, I'll leave a bottle and instructions with
the lady. And now I'll be wrapping that shoulder."

The doctor closed the parlor door, removed Christien's coat
and shirt with the aid of a sharp knife, and wrapped his shoulder in lengths of white linen intended to keep the joint and
arm immobile. As he finished, McPherson poked a bony finger
at Christien's other shoulder. "Have you been engaging in the
duello, monsieur?"

"No, never." Christien tensed, knowing exactly to what the
physician referred. "I work for the Home Office."

"Balderdash." McPherson rolled his *r* to draw out the word.
"Gentlemen working for the Home Office do na get themselves
shot."

"They do if they're in the wrong place at the wrong time."

And if they recruited a man from the War Department.

Christien shrugged one shoulder. "It happens, *biensur.*"

McPherson snorted. "Depends on where is the wrong place for a Frenchman. But I'll be saying naught. If the lady chooses to trust you, 'tis no affair of mine." —

"She doesn't," Christien murmured to the physician's retreating back.

She neither trusted him nor chose to have anything to do with him. She wouldn't have chosen him to stay in her house. A lady like Lydia Gale, however, would never turn away an injured stranger or enemy.

His heart ached with longing to be other than what he was. Now the truth would serve nothing more than to drive a deeper wedge between them. He felt like a starving man sipping at drops of kindness for his nourishment.

Of course, simply because he resided in her house, her family's house, until the doctor said he could be moved didn't mean he would see the lady. She held a number of responsibilities, according to Christien's source that had instructed him on the family. Miss Cassandra Bainbridge wanted to get married but cared nothing for the preparations, and Miss Honore should be married off as quickly as possible to rein in her high spirits. Lady Bainbridge was a near invalid and scarcely lifted a finger to assist with anything. The brother took his studies at university seriously and was scarcely around, and the father would never do anything to help England other than serve his role in the House of Lords, as he fiercely protected his family from outside influences—or tried to.

Which was one reason why Lydia had been chosen. The family might bear a minor title as far as the rank of titles went, but in an age of said title, it was one of the oldest in the realm. When Lord Bainbridge spoke in Parliament or at a dinner party, others listened. Many disagreed.

Christien needed to know who did what—amongst other duties that should have him dancing attendance on half the hostesses in London. He was, after all, that valued commodity—a single, eligible, and well-off male. Even if his title was French, it was a title.

Though he would have preferred to drop it. It led to suspicions such as those Lydia had expressed. But he'd been told to flaunt it. And who was he, a minor player in the drama that was this lengthy war, to argue with those who presumably knew better? He'd followed orders for ten years.

Those orders never before involved a lady with beautiful dark eyes and a giving heart.

So giving a heart she did not leave him to the care of servants alone. He'd barely been settled into a room by two burly footmen carrying him up two flights of steps when she and another lady, the one who had accompanied Lydia to the prison, entered with trays.

"I've brought you refreshment." Her tone was brisk, her gaze cool. "It's just toast and chocolate, but if you need laudanum, it won't make you ill if you eat something."

"Your kindness exceeds your beauty." Christien smiled at her from his mound of pillows.

The companion sniffed, her nostril pinched as though he smelled as bad as he had in the prison. "Pretty words will get you nowhere, Mr. Meuse."

"Barbara, be respectful," Lydia chided her companion in a gentle voice. "He cannot change his birth any more than a cat can be a mouse."

"More like a rat." Barbara thunked her tray onto the bedside table. "I'll serve him."

He wasn't certain he wanted her to. She might be inclined to dose him with the sort of poison she might use to kill off a rat.

"Please do, Barbara." Lydia took up a position at the foot of the bed so she looked Christien full in the face. "I have to believe, monsieur, that this was all an accident. Surely not even your kind could plan such a debacle just to—what?"

"What indeed, madame?" He held her gaze without flinching, despite the sparks flickering in their velvety depths. "I am not in the habit of placing myself into such ignominy for any reason; thus, my imagination does not stretch to the lengths of yours. Pray, tell me, what you are thinking I am guilty of?"

"My sister was alone with Frobisher—" Lydia's eyes flicked to Barbara, who had poured his chocolate and now stood away from the bed but held her gaze on him, making no pretense of turning her attention anywhere else. Flexing her fingers around the rail at the foot of the bed, Lydia returned her concentration to his face. "The thought occurred to me that . . . Never you mind. If you can manage without further assistance, Barbara and I will leave you be." Without further ado, she spun on her heel and swept from the room, her now bedraggled riding habit dragging behind her.

The little companion scurried in Lydia's wake. Christien lay alone, hurting, but not enough to need the laudanum or to reason or speculate over what Lydia had decided not to tell him.

She'd told him enough for him to make some guesses. Her sister had been alone with the young man, the friend of Barnaby, because of the accident. No one had caused Lydia to fall from her horse. The rest, however, could appear contrived to a lady with reason to be suspicious.

She suspected he and Barnaby had cooked up the idea of him planning a delay so that the young couple would be alone. He would nip that notion in the bud as soon as he found the opportunity.

Which came far sooner than he thought. Within the hour, Lydia reappeared in his chamber, a book tucked under her arm. "I thought perhaps you could do some beneficial reading while you're stranded here." She set a Bible on the table beside him. "It's the smallest one I could find so you can hold it with one hand. If you cannot manage, I'll send Barbara in to read to you. She has a lovely reading manner."

"Thank you, I'll manage." He smiled at Lydia, trying to convey some of his feelings for her in his look. "Your thoughtfulness knows no bounds."

"I . . . well . . ." She glanced past him to the window, her face the same becoming pink as the rosebuds on the gown she'd changed into. "It's the least I can do, and you did claim to be a Christian."

"*Oui*, through my American maman." His heart ached with longing for his family, for his soft-spoken mother. "*Mon père* was with Lafayette fighting in the American war for independence and met her."

"Lafayette?" Her gaze snapped to his. "And the French revolutionaries wanted to kill him, all of you, anyway?"

He flinched, realizing his error, realizing how his family history enforced her suspicions. "Not everyone in the mob understood that nobility did not mean that we wanted France to remain as it was."

"And perhaps now you think England should change?" Her tone held as much curiosity as accusation.

"England is not France. We are all much better off here."

He didn't add that some things needed to change. She would brand him a revolutionary for certain if he mentioned one word of the machines putting men out of work—whole families out of work—or laws that kept food prices so high the poor went hungry.

"Not everyone thinks so." She backed toward the door. "I mustn't stay. Even as a widow, I must mind my reputation."

"But of course." He held up his hand. "But one matter very small . . ."

She paused, her hand on the door handle of the portal she hadn't quite closed, her eyebrows raised.

"I did not plot to have myself injured," he said, "in order to allow Monsieur Frobisher to press his attentions on your sister. Trust me in this, madame. I would have been more creative."

Her face remained expressionless for a moment, then she smiled. "I do believe you would, which is why I said nothing earlier. Still . . . it's all odd. Mr. Barnaby appeared to be a far better horseman than his loss of control demonstrated."

"*Biensur.* An excellent horseman is Mr. Barnaby, one who can make his horse do whatever he likes."

"I don't know about that. I didn't see him ride long enough—" She gasped. Her face paled. "Monsieur, are you implying—no."

"We can hope not." Christien bowed his head. "But the notion came to me that his horse was nowhere near where you fell. We were a dozen feet behind. But suddenly it reared up so much it kicked me? If I had not turned to take the fall instead of you, that hoof would have struck my head."

"And now you're all but accusing Mr. Barnaby of trying to kill you."

8

Loyal to the English Crown, or French revolutionary?

Meeting and holding Christien's gaze from across the bed-chamber, Lydia no longer believed she knew the answer with the certainty she'd felt since he sauntered into her mother's drawing room. Or perhaps earlier. More likely since the man in the garden informed her that the man from the prison had departed from England. She'd been ready then to send him to the Tower as a spy. Now . . .

"But Mr. Lang sent you both to me," she mused aloud.

"Did he?" Christien shifted on his pillows, a grimace twisting his features. "Had you seen his handwriting, madame?"

"No, but it proves nothing."

Except that she was not particularly bright when it came to in-trigue. Then again, she didn't want to be involved with intrigues.

"It disproves nothing either." He shrugged, paled, and closed his eyes. "Neither does it demonstrate any ill will Monsieur Barnaby may hold toward me. Please forgive me for any distress I may have caused you. I believe I will rest now."

"Yes, do so, and take some laudanum. You look in pain."

Indeed, beads of perspiration dotted his high, smooth brow. With an effort, she resisted the urge to cross the room and wipe a damp cloth across his forehead and face, to pour out the drops of medicine herself and ensure he swallowed all of it, to sit beside him and read until he slept, as she would for the children she'd never had.

Her head ached with the possibilities, the suspicions, the agony of knowing too much and too little at the same time. Leaving this man to take the medication for pain and sleep would do her good too.

"I'll bring you more books later," she offered. "Any sort you prefer?"

"Anything but a Richardson novel."

Laughing at the notion of the Frenchman reading Samuel Richardson's treacle-like tomes of *Pamela* or *Clarissa*, Lydia slipped from the room and closed the door all the way. She needed to find Honore and ring a peal over her head about riding off alone with Mr. Frobisher. She needed to find Cassandra and give her a dressing down about not being ready on time. After that, she would collect her paint box and pencils and Barbara, take advantage of the chilly but bright day to sit in the grassy circle at the center of Cavendish Square, and create the first picture she thought might gain her some attention with a printer.

She must work out who was the true Mr. Lang, find some key—

Of course!

She spun on her heel and darted up the flight of steps to her bedchamber. In her desk she would find the two letters from Mr. Lang. Though she had crumpled them, the handwriting should be clear and distinguishable. If they were two different men, even slight variations in the letter formations would give the game away.

She opened her bedchamber door. Hodge greeted her with a flash of green eyes before he pounced on a curl of paper and sent it flying across the room with the bat of one fluffy paw.

Smiling at his antics, Lydia paused to watch. With a crow of triumph, he pounced on the twist of vellum as though it were a fleeing mouse and proceeded to worry it between his claws.

"Silly creature." Lydia stooped to rub him between his pointy ears.

He spun and wrapped himself around her ankle. His purr rose like carriage wheels rumbling over cobbles.

"Are you lonely, my pet?" Lydia scooped him into her arms.

He butted his head against her chin, as though saying, "Yes, I'm all alone here."

"Do you like Frenchmen? You are French, after all."

"*Me-ow?*"

"Yes, I think I'll introduce the two of you. You can charm his secrets from him."

And speaking of secrets . . .

She set Hodge on the floor and picked up the curl of paper to toss for him. It nestled in her hand, unfurled enough for her to see writing slashing across the surface. Only a few letters, a partial word. No, part of a name—*de Meu*.

Sending the scrap sailing across the room like a misshapen sparrow, she leaped in the opposite direction and yanked open her desk drawer, where she kept her correspondences.

Where she *had* kept her correspondences.

The drawer wasn't empty. Indeed, it appeared fuller than it had when she'd slipped both Mr. Lang's letters of introduction there the day before to receive invitations to parties, and a letter from her mother-in-law pregnant with the same old refrain—she never came home.

As if the manor in the Yorkshire West Riding had ever been home. But now the letter from Charles's mother and the invitations—once gilded and leafed, embossed and engraved—lay in shreds. Sunlight caught a flash of gold here, of silver there. A word or number or curlicue design peeked out amidst the jumble of foolscap and vellum. Discovering which scraps belonged to Mr. Lang's letters of introduction, making comparison of handwriting between the two missives, was now impossible. Not a slip of paper large enough to use as a fire spill remained.

Someone had destroyed them all. The intruder hadn't just destroyed them, he had destroyed them in such an obvious way she couldn't doubt it was deliberate. She could never think she had simply misplaced the letters.

She dropped her face into her hands and rubbed her temples. None of it made sense. A floor below her, a man she suspected was working for the French claimed he was not the enemy, while the Englishmen made no claims for whom they worked. Christien declared he had been with Mr. Lang in Hastings the night Mr. Lang met her in a Portsmouth garden.

"Lord, I just want to get my sister married off and Honore at least through the Season without trouble. I can't manage my own life with any success. How can I end up in the middle of a spy network and not get hurt?"

Hodge meowed at her feet, as comprehensible as any responses she'd ever received from God. As a woman who called herself a Christian, she was supposed to serve God, yet God seemed like one more father wanting to control every aspect of her life, stopping her from the pastimes she enjoyed. She had a talent for painting, but her father disapproved of it so much she had crept around before marriage in order to paint or even draw beyond what was acceptable for a well-educated young lady. In the week she had lived with her husband after marriage, she had tried painting once, had begun the portrait of him. When he'd found her in the garden—

She slammed the door on that memory of the argument

between them, him yelling, her trying not to weep. "You will not—" He sounded like her father, ordering her as he had a right to by social custom, by law, caring nothing of what pleased her in any aspect of their time together.

She strode into the corridor. She still needed to find a book for Christien. She needed to get outside and draw. She needed to take the next step forward.

She headed down to the library, muttering, "What next? What next? What next?"

"Did you say something, my dear?" Mama called out as Lydia passed the sitting room.

"Just talking to myself." Lydia moved to stand in the doorway. "Do you know where Honore is?"

Mama set down her needlework. "She's out shopping with Lady Trainham and her daughters. Is our patient resting well, the dear man?"

"Dear man?"

"But of course, my dear." Mama gave Lydia her gentle smile. "He saved you from injury and was injured in the doing."

"Yes. Yes, he was."

Injured on purpose, perhaps.

A shudder raced through Lydia at the thought. If Christien was right, then they were on the same side. But which side was which?

How to know the truth?

"I'm going to the library to find some books for him," Lydia said. "He'll have a dull time of it up there otherwise."

"Indeed. If only your brother or father were here. But your father doesn't arrive until Saturday. At least that's when he plans."

"Wonderful. Is Cassandra in the library?"

Mama pursed her lips. "I can't recall if she's there or out shopping with Honore."

Lydia laughed. "She'd rather be in the library unless the shopping included a bookshop."

Lydia descended the steps and entered the library. The door stood open and no fire burned on the hearth. The room lay in shadow save for light ebbing through the windows that overlooked the mews and a branch of candles set atop the desk. Although Cassandra's Greek texts lay on the desk, the covers were closed and the stopper protruded from the top of the ink bottle.

That Cassandra would go shopping without a fuss raised Lydia's eyebrows, and she thought to hunt for her sister in her bedchamber after she found some books for de Meuse. If Cassandra had been awake late reading the night before, she could be taking a nap before the evening's outing to . . . Lydia couldn't remember in the hubbub of the day. She would look at her calendar, work out what to wear.

She trotted into the chamber and to a section of literature de Meuse might find entertaining. Sir Walter Scott? Tobias Smollett?

She tugged out a volume crammed into the crowded shelves. Its mates came with it, thudding to the floor.

Behind Lydia, behind the library door, a gasp sounded. Fabric rustled.

Lydia whirled, sending the book in her hand flying across the room in one direction and her gaze in the other.

Cassandra, her face red, her hair disheveled, stood in the circle of Whittaker's arms.

"For shame." It was an exclamation worthy of a matron twice Lydia's age, but it popped out of her mouth. Her own cheeks burned. An aching void opened inside her, a memory of being in love, a longing to experience the kind of wanting that compelled one to steal kisses from one's fiancé behind a door.

Yet this was her younger sister, sweet, bookish Cassandra, with swollen lips and a whisker burn on her chin.

"Don't go all missish on us, Lyd." Cassandra slipped from Whittaker's embrace and glided forward, her hands extended. "You know you did your share of kissing Charles before you were wed."

"Yes, but I—"

"Was a year younger than I am." Cassandra smiled.

"That doesn't mean it was right of me." Lydia glared at Whittaker.

He met the look with bold brown eyes. "I take complete responsibility, Lady Gale. I was annoyed with Cassandra over being late this morning. We exchanged some harsh words and . . ." He faltered, though when his gaze strayed to Cassandra, his expression softened to adoration. "We were expressing our regret."

"Express it in a more decorous fashion." Lydia spoke more harshly than she intended. "It's unseemly. It's indelicate. It's—"

"Don't say disgraceful," Cassandra interrupted, sounding bored. "Kissing is not wrong, and we . . . I . . . ." Her face flamed. "Oh, you know what I'm saying."

"No," Lydia said, "I don't."

"I would never dishonor her," Whittaker said.

"I should think not. But have a care." Lydia gentled her demeanor. "Others don't think being alone is proper, let alone any touching. So mind your manners. The wedding is in less than three months."

"And it's been postponed for a year." Cassandra's pretty mouth drooped.

"And that gives you reason to misbehave?" Lydia asked. "Truly, Cassie, with the way you try to avoid sessions at the dressmaker's, I'd think another year wouldn't be enough."

Whittaker's eyes twinkled down at Cassandra. "Be kind to

your sister and go to the appointments. I expect she spends enough time with you in bookstalls."

"No, but perhaps we can work out a deal?" Cassandra grinned at Lydia.

"If you can be on time for every appointment for a week, I'll take you to every bookshop or stall in London." Lydia retrieved the book she'd inadvertently thrown across the room. "Now go keep Mama company. I don't want you two alone any longer. No, wait, Cassandra, you go make yourself presentable. Mama wasn't born yesterday."

Singing some nonsense ditty about shopping for books, Cassandra darted out of the library and headed up the steps.

"I'll pay a visit to Lady Bainbridge, if you'll excuse me." Not waiting for Lydia to do so, Whittaker followed his fiancée out of the room.

Smoothing out the pages of the Smollett book, Lydia wondered if she'd been too harsh on the couple. Cassandra and Whittaker were responsible young persons, faithful to morality and the Lord. They wouldn't take things too far, would they?

Honore, on the other hand, needed a constant chaperone to keep her out of mischief, especially mischief involving that upstart Mr. Frobisher.

Another one of Lang's "friends."

Mr. Lang enjoyed far too many friends, or one powerful enemy. If they were all men he sent, likely they were supposed to look out for one another to remain true to the cause. If they came from separate sources, then Lang's secret was out and someone was using his tactics to find the enemy.

But whose enemy?

Lydia slammed the book onto the library table and gathered up the other two volumes that had fallen. She needed fresh air.

She needed her pencils and sunshine and the smell of grass to remind herself she was nothing more than a widow who had gotten herself into a muddle by being kind.

Books in her arms, she climbed the two flights to Christien's room without stopping to find Barbara as a chaperone. No one responded to her light tap on the door. Good. He must be sleeping. She would return later, probably with Barbara in tow for the sake of her own reputation.

Sometimes propriety was such a burden, especially when she knew her actions were above reproach.

Most of them.

She climbed the flight to her own room and set the books on her desk, then located her sketching materials. She should have an hour or two left of good light in the square.

Barbara grumbled about accompanying Lydia out to the circular patch of grass in the middle of Cavendish Square. Lydia ignored her companion and commenced producing sketches she later intended to turn into paintings—a street urchin grinning as he caught a coin tossed by a passerby, a group of boys bowling a hoop back and forth across the grass, an old man gazing into the window of the cabinetmaker near the corner. With a few deft strokes, she caught the essence of each moment. She could fill in the details later.

When the sun began to slip behind the houses, she rose, a little stiff from sitting in one position for so long, and returned to the house.

"Everyone was staring at you," Barbara complained.

Lydia merely laughed and entered the house. She needed to ready herself for the night's entertainment—a ball, the opera? Without her invitations, she didn't know.

"Is the opera tonight?" she asked.

"No, tonight is a soirée. The opera is in three days. But you know it's not truly an opera." Barbara looked smug. "The opera house burned down four years ago, and they haven't performed opera there since."

"Well of course they couldn't if it's burned down." Lydia couldn't help teasing a bit.

Barbara frowned. "I mean they haven't performed opera in the new one. It's a pantomime."

"Hmm." Lydia glanced at Christien's closed door. She must take him the books. The night would be long and tedious for him stranded there.

Stranded because someone wanted him out of the way, temporarily or permanently?

She really couldn't think of that. She needed to get ready, ensure Cassandra dragged herself from her books and Honore wasn't making more plans to ride off with Mr. Frobisher.

Christien smiled at her entrance with the books—a smile for the tomes, not her, of course. Still, it lit his eyes and twisted something inside her like a spill used to start a fire.

"You are kindness itself, my lady. But not kind enough to stay and talk?"

For a moment, she considered doing so, then shook her head and backed to the door. The less she knew of him, the better. "I have to go out tonight and tomorrow and—"

"In other words, you give me hospitality but will not give me company."

"I . . . cannot." As she hastened from his chamber, a tightness inside her gave fair warning that "I will not" might have been a better response. She would not spend time with him.

Avoiding him during the three days the doctor requested de Meuse remain immobile proved rather easy. Lydia kept herself and her sisters running from shops to social gatherings to long walks in the park. By the end of the third day, she wanted to do nothing but sleep. But they had a box at the Royal Opera House, and she had to chaperone the girls. Mama had gone to bed with one of her sick headaches and an alarming wheeze to her breathing.

"I'll call in the doctor," she told Mama. He could examine Monsieur de Meuse and send him home too.

The physician arrived while Lydia dressed for the evening. Caught up in his report on Mama's health and monsieur's healing injury, she completely forgot that one of the destroyed missives had come from Mr. Barnaby, promising he would accompany her to the opera house. He and Gerald Frobisher.

9

Seven of them slipped into the Whittaker family box at the Royal Opera House moments before the performance began. Candles blazed from the stage and chandeliers, reflecting in the jewels dripping from the ladies in the tiers and the paste gemstones on the females in the pit. The cheap perfume of those women rose on the heated air to mingle with the more expensive scents of the occupants of the boxes, and Lydia wrinkled her nose. She had to endure not only a form of entertainment she didn't care for but also the overwhelming odor of unwashed bodies masked with scent, the noise of people who never ceased talking, and the companionship of Messrs. Barnaby and Frobisher.

Gerald Frobisher lounged in one of the box's front-row chairs beside Honore. The young lady glowed in her white muslin gown trimmed in blue ribbons and embroidery that matched her satin evening cloak. More than half a dozen opera glasses flashed as they turned in Honore's direction. At the interval, the box would be crowded with young men—and older ones too, no doubt—wanting to make or further an acquaintance with Miss Honore Bainbridge. That was good. Frobisher would have less time to turn his charm on her.

With Barbara seated in the front also, between Honore and

Cassandra, Lydia seated herself in the back of the box. She intended to talk under cover of the chattering audience and actors onstage.

At least this wouldn't be an opera. Caterwauling, as Charles had always referred to it.

"I should have given my cloak to an attendant." Lydia plucked at the gold frog closure at the neck of her own blue satin wrap. "It's quite stifling in here."

Barnaby sat upright on his gilt chair, his gaze turned toward the drawn curtain. "You mustn't risk a chill, Lady Gale."

Lydia fanned herself. "If I never caught a chill living next to Dartmoor, I won't catch one here. Have you ever been to Tavistock, sir?"

"No, never. I've never been west of Lime Regis." A faint smile curved his lips, making him rather attractive. "For some reason, I think of Devonshire and Cornwall as being rather uncivilized."

"Then how do you know Elias Lang?"

Barnaby shrugged. "Lime Regis, I believe."

"Not Falmouth?"

"Falmouth, my lady, is in Cornwall."

Lydia glared at him. "I am quite aware of that, sir, but it's where Mr. Lang collected some information about a certain enemy of England, or so he claims."

"He is better traveled than I."

No comment on the enemy of England.

"All the way to Paris, perhaps?" Lydia pressed.

"My lady." Barnaby's hand clamped on her forearm. "Have a care."

"Why?" Lydia gave him a wide-eyed glance. "If you're the sp—"

"Shh." Barnaby's hiss to be quiet joined that of other

theatergoers. Whether he intended to quiet her for the sake of the performance or the words she spoke, she couldn't be sure.

On the stage, the curtain rose to a two-dimensional woodland. The character of Queen Mab, played by a middle-aged beauty, sailed across the stage, intoning the speech that announced the beginning of the pantomime. What the words actually were, Lydia couldn't hear above the shouts and cheers from the audience. Fortunately, pantomime relied on the antics of Harlequin, his consort and supporting cast, and the charm of the dancers to entertain the crowd. Words to speeches or lyrics to songs would have been impossible to hear over the audience. The air heated as the candles blazed and the audience clapped, stamped, and cheered, or paid no heed at all to the stage.

"I need some air," Lydia exclaimed.

Mr. Barnaby ignored her. He perched on the edge of his chair, his fingers moving as though he conducted a miniature orchestra, and a look of such beatific joy washed over his face he appeared ten years younger than his perhaps forty years.

The performance held all of his attention.

A little wobbly inside, Lydia slid back in her chair and focused her attention on the stage. Harlequin danced with Columbine. The actors appeared young, aglow with delight at their art, graceful in their antics. A reluctant smile tugged at the corners of Lydia's mouth and pulled a chord deep inside her. A chord of memory, of sitting at pantomime for the first time, wanting to enjoy it, to have something intelligent to say to the military officer beside her, another guest of—whom? She couldn't recall. She only remembered the handsome man in his regimentals, his profile a perfect etching of manliness, along with his broad shoulders and upright stance.

At the end of the first act, he'd turned to her, his upper lip curled. "Men dodging shells on a battlefield dance more gracefully than that. But it's better than the screeching of the opera."

She'd agreed. Of course she had. She'd been taught to never openly disagree with a man. But she lied. She found the entertainment lighthearted and delightful and wanted to clap and cheer with the uninhibited bucks in the pit.

She never attended a pantomime or an opera again. Charles had begun to court her that night and for the rest of the Season. He was on leave—the second son, but the family's best hope for a marriage and heirs because the eldest son seemed to produce only daughters. Charles had kept her from Covent Garden. He liked dancing. He liked riding. He liked boating on the river. He told her what she should like and so she convinced herself of it.

That behavior for a girl of nineteen, who had a father who told her what she could and could not do—including her art, which she believed was a gift from God—was understandable. Now, a woman of six and twenty, of poor but adequate means, should have more independence, more of an ability to choose her path like others who had gone before her. Women like Mary Wortley Montagu, who had lived there in Cavendish Square, or Lady Mary Cowper. Mary Wollstonecraft?

Not Mary Wollstonecraft. She'd been independent, but she'd lived an immoral life and tried to kill herself. And the other two were married to influential men, who surely smoothed their paths to social acceptance and appearance of independent thought.

But that wasn't proper for the widow of a knight of the realm or the daughter of a baron.

Lydia's hands hurt. She glanced down to find her fists clenched inside the white silk gloves. If she'd made too many mistakes in her life, compromising her reputation was not one of them. Yet being a model of propriety had gotten her nowhere but genteel poverty because she wouldn't live at home and let her father dictate her days.

Oh no, and now some man, who seemed to have two manifestations—as the Mr. Lang who was supposed to have requested that she help Christien de Meuse, and the Mr. Lang who had blackmailed her in Portsmouth—was dictating her days. She must shake him loose as she had shaken loose her father.

And her husband?

"I can't sit here." She shot to her feet. "Please," she murmured.

Mr. Barnaby jumped, glanced at her, lunged to his feet. "I beg your pardon, do you want past?"

"Please," she repeated.

She slipped past him. She expected him to follow. He returned to his chair instead.

Alone in the passage, she took several deep breaths of relatively fresh air. Music soared through the thin barricade of the curtain. The pantomime was nearly complete and would become a play after the interval. Before the corridor filled with people, she needed to walk, to breathe, to . . . do something.

But no respectable female could stride up and down alone in the passage behind the boxes. With a sigh, she returned to the box just as the curtain fell and the crowd's voices rose to a roar of conversation and flirtation. As though someone had pulled a cork from an upturned bottle, the passageway flooded with people. Men swarmed from one box to another like honeybees seeking the sweetest flowers.

At least six headed toward the Bainbridges' box. Lydia stepped inside to chaperone Honore and keep Frobisher entertained so Honore could talk to the other young men.

Those young men cut Frobisher out without any help from Lydia. They flocked around Honore with compliments and invitations, a poem to her blue eyes, and a nosegay of pansies. Honore glowed.

Frobisher scowled.

Lydia touched his arm. "You mustn't be selfish, young man. This is Honore's first Season. She hasn't even enjoyed her ball or court presentation yet."

"Does anyone enjoy a court presentation?" Frobisher's upper lip curled. "The king is mad and the queen—" He snapped his teeth together as though someone had smacked him beneath the chin.

"Indeed." Lydia smiled. "Watch your tongue, sir. You might be accused of sedition."

And so might she if she drew the picture running through her head, if viewers misunderstood her meaning—Frobisher sneering at the queen instead of taking his bow. Frobisher not on the right side of the law, not serving England if he felt that way about the royal family, evidencing enough contempt to speak against them in public.

Or was it an act?

Lydia wished she could produce the volume of an operatic soprano. She might shriek in a high A and shatter some of the paste jewels on the "ladies" in the pit.

And a few on the ladies in the boxes, no doubt.

"Why do you wish to enter Society if you hold us in such low regard, Mr. Frobisher?"

Lydia scanned the crowded box. More men had come to pay their respects to Honore. A few spoke with Cassandra. Two gentlemen in particular had cornered her, though her smile and vivacious motions with her hands hardly demonstrated distress on her part.

Whittaker was the distressed one. He had his back against the front of the box and his arms crossed over his broad chest.

His mouth was set in a grim line, and he stared at Cassandra's callers from between narrowed lids.

"I don't hold Society in low regard, my lady," Frobisher was saying. "Your family especially intrigues me. So much beauty and talent in one group of ladies is unusual."

"Not at all." Lydia turned abruptly and grasped his arm, holding him against the side of the box. "What do you want with all of us?"

For a heartbeat, his eyes widened and flared. Then his expression grew bland again, and he gave her his sweet smile. "Why, nothing more than I'm getting—a seat in a box at the opera house, invitations to several balls and soirées, an opportunity to play a little faro or whist and perhaps make my fortune."

"Your fortune." Lydia released his arm and stepped back as though he were a poisonous snake. "You're nothing more than a gamester wanting to play the high stakes of the wealthy. You're a Captain Sharp."

He blinked and shook his head. "My dear Lady Gale, I am wounded that you could think such a low thing of me."

Little did he know what relief she would feel if all he and Barnaby wanted was an introduction to the gaming set. She abhorred gambling so much that anyone who engaged in it deserved what fleecing he got.

Well, perhaps not. Their families didn't deserve to be impoverished by their carelessness, and she would hate to be the instrument of one of her peers losing an ancient family estate. Sadly, it happened on the turn of a card or a raindrop too slow to reach the windowsill during a storm, or whatever nonsense gamesters chose to stake their futures on.

"Then why were you . . . gentlemen so anxious for introductions?" Lydia pressed.

Out of the corner of her eye, she noticed Barnaby in earnest conversation with one of the young men who had entered the box with others of Honore's admirers, then remained on the fringes of the crowd. Their heads were rather too close together for casual conversation.

Or was she seeing spies around every corner?

Face stiff, she returned her attention to Frobisher, only to notice that he too watched Barnaby and the young man, and his eyes glowed like those of a little boy in a sweets shop. Lydia half expected him to start bouncing from foot to foot. Instead, he excused himself and joined the other two men.

Left to her own devices, Lydia edged her way around the box to Whittaker. On her way past Honore, she heard her younger sister laughing and chattering like a brook sparkling in sunlight. She waved her fan, tapped it on her chin, and rapped one young man's knuckles as he reached for her hand.

Surely Honore would forget her *tendre* for Frobisher now.

Lydia focused on Whittaker, who had drawn his dark brows together in the grim scowl of an angry man. Beyond him, Cassandra, like her younger sister, shimmered in her silvery pink gown.

"I've never considered balloon travel useful," she was saying. "I thought it merely a lark. But if you've made scientific calculations with wind velocity . . ."

"If she thinks she's going up in a balloon," Whittaker growled, "she'd best think again. I won't have her risking her neck like that."

Lydia opened her mouth to respond. A voice echoed so loudly in her head she couldn't think what to say. *If you think*, Charles had shouted, *that you're going to join me on campaign, you'd best think again.*

"It's too dangerous," Whittaker added.

It's too dangerous, Charles had claimed.

"Many people fly in balloons." Lydia tried to defend Cassandra's position, as she had tried—and failed—to defend hers. "I think it looks vastly entertaining."

"Lady Gale—Lydia, nothing that leaves the ground like that can be safe enough to be entertaining." Whittaker frowned at Cassandra. "She met those two in the park the other day and has been turning her attention from Homer to aerodynamics. The dead Greeks I can tolerate. Live aeronauts I cannot. It's not decent."

It's not decent, Charles had claimed, though thousands of officers' wives accompanied their husbands on campaign.

He didn't want her with him. After only a week of marriage, he wanted away from her.

"Don't be autocratic with her, Whittaker." Lydia injected as much urgency into her tone as she could manage. "Please."

"I'm not being autocratic. I want to keep her safe."

I want to keep you safe, Charles had insisted.

I want my girls to be safe, Father said every time he stopped them from enjoying some lark.

"If you will excuse me." Whittaker turned toward his fiancée and shouldered the other men aside. "I'd like to walk, Cassandra."

"But I'm talking to these—oh, all right." She flashed the gentlemen a brilliant smile. "Do call at our next at home. I'd like to know more about your plans." She took Whittaker's arm. "It's so fascinating, Whit. There's a Russian man trying to affix propellers to a balloon . . ."

Her voice faded into those of the crowd and the beginning of *Macbeth*, which no one seemed to notice. Not even Mr. Barnaby, who was still engaged in subdued conversation with Frobisher and the other man. The latter kept glancing across the opera house. Lydia followed his gaze but couldn't work out to which box it was directed. Not the royal box at any rate. That meant nothing. The royal box was empty.

Wishing theirs was too, Lydia strode to the curtain at the back of the box and glanced down the corridor toward Cassandra and Whittaker. He gripped her hands and gazed down at her, his brows still furrowed and dark. Cassandra blinked up at him with nearsighted vagueness, her lips pursed, her chin set, and a muscle jerking at the corner of her jaw.

Lydia took half a step forward, not certain whether or not she should intervene. She'd been so concerned about protecting her family from her own blackmailer, especially protecting Honore from Frobisher's attentions, that she hadn't considered needing to protect Cassandra from her fiancé. If he was just as domineering as Father, preventing a Bainbridge daughter from pursuing an interest that hinted of independent thought, something must be done about it. Cassandra mustn't end up feeling as inadequate as did her older sister, nor as lonely.

Lydia took a step forward.

A hand landed on her arm. She jumped and turned to see Mr. Barnaby standing beside her.

"I beg your pardon, my lady. I didn't mean to startle you."

"It's all right. How may I assist you?"

"We need to talk someplace where we will not be disturbed. Will you please ride with me in the park tomorrow without any interference from others?" His tone, his expression held an intensity that sent a frisson of apprehension down Lydia's spine.

She licked suddenly dry lips. "Could we take a carriage? I prefer that to riding, if I'm to talk."

"Of course." He released her arm and bowed. "Tomorrow at eleven o'clock."

"I'll be ready."

To hear what? Truths or lies?

"Now, if we may be so impolite, my lady," Barnaby said, "Gerald and I must take our leave. We are committed elsewhere."

"All right." Lydia stepped aside.

Barnaby, Frobisher, and the other man to whom they'd been speaking swept past her. The latter two engaged in dialogue still. The word *faro* drifted back to Lydia.

So they were off to a gaming party. She curled her lip and turned back to the box to chaperone Honore and the gentlemen remaining in her company.

"What do I have to say?" Cassandra's voice rang down the passageway. "Five words, Whittaker. We are not married yet." She wrenched her hands free of her fiancé's and dashed along the corridor.

"Cassandra, don't," Lydia and Whittaker called together.

Catching up with her, Whittaker reached out to grab hold of Cassandra.

Lydia stayed his hand. "Let me go after her. You're making a scene."

"She's making the scene. I only want—"

Lydia grasped his shoulder and turned him toward the box. "Look after Honore. I'll be right—"

A cry rang above the tumult inside the auditorium. Lydia swung around in time to see Cassandra miss her footing at the top of a flight of steps and begin to tumble to the bottom.

10

Christien's shoulder throbbed. The numbing effects of the laudanum had worn off, and now his head was clear, his memories sharp.

He lay half propped up in the big bed, listening to the sounds of the house. It ticked and creaked, as did most houses at night, but no one seemed to be about. He hadn't heard a single voice or footfall on corridor or step in the past half hour of wakefulness. Someone had been in his room, but long enough ago the fire burned low along with the candles on the mantel, and when he struggled to rise, he found the water in the pitcher tepid at best.

A bell pull dangled in one corner of the room, a thick rope decorated with gold embroidery. He stretched out his left hand with the intention of pulling it and requesting fresh candles so he could read, a pot of tea or coffee to drink, perhaps some food to eat.

He curled his fingers around the pull. Silken threads dangled halfway to the floor and twisted above to the ceiling and the mechanism that would ring in the kitchen below stairs. Long and soft like Lydia's hair. Or as he imagined her hair would be flowing down her back. The curls that perpetually escaped their pins and bounced against her cheek right in front of her ear charmed him, lured him. He'd longed to stroke it, even cut it off in that prison office when he feared he would never get released from the living death of Dartmoor. In the parlor, in the park as she attempted her less than graceful mounting of the gelding, that curl bounced and swayed, shimmering with blue-black lights.

He released the rope without tugging it and pressed a hand against his brow. He must think of something about Lydia other than his attraction to her—whether or not to take her into his confidence. He hoped it would compel her to leave London, as much as he wished for her to remain near, selfish man that he was. He wanted her to take her family and return to Devonshire, where the men who wanted him dead couldn't include her in the accident that would again befall him. The fatal accident, if they had their way.

Now that he'd been introduced to a few important hostesses, he didn't need Lydia's company. That he wanted it didn't matter. Her safety did. And if he told her the truth, she wouldn't betray him. The blackmail assured her silence.

"*Quel désastre!*" Christien pressed his left hand against the pounding pain in his right shoulder. The agony was beginning to seep up to his head the longer he stood.

He sank onto the edge of a chair and propped his chin in his hand. The shoulder would hold him back for more days, possibly weeks. He needed to move, to work. Lydia was his only hope.

Another reason to take her more deeply into his confidence and pray she believed him.

He feared his prayers would not be heard. His work had forced him to tell too many lies over the years, lies that sometimes caused harm to others. They were necessary. This was war. Yet righteous as his actions might be in the eyes of man, Christien feared they were not in the eyes of God. Telling the truth to someone would feel like a spring shower washing the grime of winter away from cobblestones, brick, and mortar.

But the other man calling himself Mr. Lang, the one who had blackmailed Lydia, would too likely stand in his way, having convinced Lydia that Christien was an enemy of England. His own Mr. Lang, the legitimate government agent who had directed Christien's path for a decade, hadn't made contact since reaching London. Christien's messages had gone unanswered.

Many explanations occurred to Christien as to why. Lang often got called away, had to slip into France to rescue an agent. With matters going badly between England and America, he could have been sent to the other side of the ocean, trusting Christien to follow instructions and work on his own, as he had so often managed over the years.

Lydia didn't trust easily. With a husband like Sir Charles Gale, Christien understood why. He had been a neglectful and selfish husband.

An unfaithful one.

Christien hadn't liked him, even while he helped him. He needed to help him. It made up for those he'd hurt in the performance of his duty to his country. But for a man with a beautiful, intelligent, and talented wife like Lydia to die with the name of another woman on his lips . . .

Christien's left hand curled into a fist. "How could he wrong her like that?"

Gale's behavior had opened the way for the second Mr. Lang, the wrong Mr. Lang. But how to convince Lydia that Christien knew the right one, or a different one, for that matter?

The letters of introduction, of course. Sometimes the

differences in handwriting could be difficult to detect, but it was worth a try.

He'd suggested she look and tell him what she found. She never had. She hadn't remained in his chamber long enough to say anything beyond courtesy and had never been alone long enough to give herself the opportunity to share a word with him.

Despite the pain, he must not let himself take medicine again. Despite the pain, he must learn what she had. He could wait and ask her the next time she deigned to visit him, or . . .

He glanced at the brass clock on the mantel. The hour was early by ton standards. The first act of the play would scarcely be over. No doubt the servants all lounged in their hall, enjoying their night off from tending to the family. He could go to her room and look for correspondences with no one the wiser.

He knew the location of her room. He'd heard her talking. He couldn't hear words, only the rich timbre of her voice. She'd been scolding the cat. He caught the meow responding as though they shared a dialogue. He'd smiled.

He didn't smile now. His face tightened with every step toward the door. Putting his foot down, however gently, sent fresh pain shooting through his shoulder. No matter. He must go, must find out, must make plans in the event the two handwritings were the same.

If they were the same, he must abort his mission and flee— with Lydia.

Awkward in a nightshirt, with one sleeve cut out to accommodate the sling, and a dressing gown only draped over the right shoulder, he haltingly made his way to the door and pulled it open. In the opening, he stood and waited, listening. Inside, the house lay quiet. Outside, carriages rumbled past, and some drunken-sounding young men stood in the square and sang off-key. He couldn't hear so much as a mouse creeping about, let alone a member of the family or staff. Not even the cat.

Reassured, his way lit by candles in sconces affixed at intervals to the walls, he painstakingly began his way up the steps. He needed to grip the banister and take one step at a time, setting first his left foot on the tread, then his right. One . . . two . . . three . . .

He reached the next landing. Two doors opened off it. More rooms ran through the house toward the front, but because of the window tax, they wouldn't have direct access to the outside. The notion of sleeping in one of those chambers made Christien shudder. It was too much like the black hole, the windowless chamber at Dartmoor where the guards tossed prisoners for punishment.

He'd gone there for two days when he'd insisted once too often he should be released.

Shivering in the chilly air of the stairwell, he turned to his left and gripped the door handle. It lifted under his fingers. The door swung inward. He stepped over the threshold to a soft Aubusson carpet in blues and lavenders, silk draperies and cushions, and that sweet, crisp scent of honey and citrus that Lydia wore.

He couldn't close the door or he would have no light. No matter. He could see her desk, the most likely place for correspondences to lie.

He also saw the cat. A ghostly image against the carpet, drifting toward him. "*Me-ow?*"

"I'm just intruding for a moment." He wanted to stoop and stroke the feline's fur but doubted his ability to rise again. "Perhaps we can get acquainted later."

He limped into the room and pulled open the top drawer of the desk.

And three floors below, the front door opened to a rush of excited female voices.

"I can walk." Cassandra pushed against Whittaker's shoulder. "Let me down."

"You shouldn't. Where should I take her?" He looked toward Lydia.

Cassandra clenched her fists. "You may ask me, sirrah. I am nearly one and twenty, quite old enough to make my own decisions."

"Up to her bedchamber," Lydia said.

"And have to endure Honore's sulks." Yet Cassandra was the sulky-sounding one at that moment.

"I'll take her to the library," Whittaker suggested. "I have a thing or two to say to her—"

"I won't endure you sounding like my father." Cassandra spoke through clenched teeth.

"Children." Lydia sighed. "But the library—"

"Just set me down and go away," Cassandra commanded.

"Take her into the library," Lydia said. "I'm not certain she needs a physician, but some cold compresses won't go amiss. Barbara?"

"I'm here." Barbara headed for the kitchen. "We should have ice enough to make a cold compress, and I'll get some tea going."

"You'll get a servant to get tea going." Lydia pursed her lips for a moment. "If you don't, our little cook will be outraged."

Barbara sniffed and pushed through the green baize door behind the staircase.

"Set me down or I'll be outraged." Cassandra struggled in Whittaker's hold.

"Go ahead and be outraged. It won't compare to how I feel right now." His mouth was grim, his eyes cold.

Cassandra shivered. "You needn't be. I—"

Two footmen appeared in the corridor. "Not here," Lydia said with a quick jerk of her head.

"Lady Bainbridge has gone to bed," one of the servants said. "Shall I light candles and lay the fire in her sitting room?"

"Yes," Lydia said.

"No," Cassandra said.

"I may as well go to my room and pack for the journey home." Honore flounced toward the steps. "My Season is ruined. I've never been so humiliated in my life, dragged away from all those young men. I'll never find a suitor . . ." Her voice grew fainter as she stomped up the steps.

Lydia sighed and pressed her fingertips against her temples. "How I wish we could go home. But there's Honore's coming-out ball and your wedding—"

"If Whittaker doesn't set me down," Cassandra blurted out, "there won't be that trouble."

"Cassie." Pain rang through Whittaker's voice.

Pain ricocheted through Lydia's head. She would leave them alone to finish their argument.

"I'll return in no more than a quarter hour." She started up the steps to soothe Honore's ruffled feathers.

The family had come home from the theater hours early. Christien stood frozen in the center of Lydia's bedchamber, listening to the voices, the patter of feet on steps, the bang of a door, for only moments. They were precious seconds lost. He couldn't get away, couldn't run, couldn't sprint down the steps and slip into his room, as innocent as a babe.

But he tried. Favoring his right side, he limped to the open door and started into the passageway. A voice on the lower landing sent him slipping backward and closing the door. It wasn't Lydia. It was one of her sisters, her voice lighter, a little petulant, growing closer with a rapidity that suggested she raced up the steps. Seconds after the latch clicked, leaving him in near total darkness, the top tread squeaked, then a skirt rustled on the other side of the panels. Finally, the door across the way slammed.

"So where is her ladyship?" Christien addressed the cat circling his ankles.

"*Ma-row?*" the feline responded. He rose on his back legs and pawed at Christien like a dog. "*Ma-row.*"

"Down, you. Those claws are sharp."

"*Ma-row.*"

"I can't pick you up with only one hand."

But if he could carry the cat, or persuade him to follow, he might be able to bluff his way out of trouble with his gracious, albeit reluctant, hostess.

"All right, come with me." Christien opened the door.

The cat began to knead his claws on Christien's dressing gown, right through the heavy silk and into his knee.

"*Arretez-vous.*"

Whether the French cat didn't speak French or chose to ignore the human, he continued to sharpen his claws on Christien.

"*S'il vous plait.*" Christien started to lean forward to detach the feline. The room began to spin and lights flashed before his eyes. "Lord, please help me." He leaned against the wall and waited for the world to settle down again. "At least keep her away."

No voices penetrated the door. Surely they had all gone into a room for tea or chocolate before retiring for the night, especially since they were hours early. If he got the cat to follow him, he could claim the creature had been crying and he wanted to shut it up.

A lie. Yet one more lie. One more necessary lie, but still a falsehood to add to his decade of falsehoods.

And he would be lying to Lydia.

Would he be better off telling her the truth and facing the consequences?

Before he decided on an answer to that question, the door flew open and slammed into his shoulder. Pain soared through his body, an explosion of white-hot agony that drove him to his knees with a groan escaping his lips.

"What are you doing in here?" Lydia demanded.

11

Candlestick solid in her hand, Lydia stared down at the crouching man. Her knees wobbled. She gripped the door to keep herself from sinking down beside him to make certain he wasn't about to expire on her. She didn't want a dead man in her bedchamber. That was the source of her concern.

She wanted him alive to answer for his deeds. For his misdeeds.

"The cat." He drew in a sharp breath that sounded like a cry in the quiet room.

"What about my cat?"

Hodge sat in the middle of the rug, a pale blur in the candlelight. His green eyes glowed as though he were up to mischief.

"Why would my cat bring you up to my bedchamber?" Lydia persisted.

"He—" Christien let out a breath on a long sigh. "I cannot lie to you, my lady. It wasn't *le petit chat*. My reasons—I cannot talk like this."

"You'll talk like that to me or the Watch. I don't appreciate thieves. Not that there's much to steal, since you already have my bracelet." She stepped farther into the room and pushed the door to, without latching it. "Or rather, you had my bracelet. It was sold to the jeweler in Tavistock, was it not?"

His face nearly as pale as Hodge's fur, Christien grasped the door handle, attempted to haul himself to his feet—and failed with a grunt of disgust. "Falmouth."

Lydia's hand jerked so hard her candle extinguished. "You don't deny it?"

"No, my lady, that much I cannot deny, as it is the truth. The rest . . ." His voice trailed off.

She couldn't see his face now, but every word he spoke declared his fatigue and pain. Her heart squeezed, melted.

"Let me help you back to your room, monsieur." She opened the door to let light into the room, then reached her hand out to him.

He grasped her proffered hand, his fingers long and smooth, as a gentleman's should be. So smooth that the lines of scars stood out in distinct ridges. She resisted the urge to stroke the marks, to ask him how he'd come by them.

Though he curled his fingers around hers as if she provided the only lifeline off a sinking ship, he didn't rise. "I need to talk to you." Crouched on the floor, gazing up at her through the dimness of candlelight a half dozen feet away, he resembled a supplicant, a man forced to be humble before a superior.

Her imagination, or a clever act on his part? Either way, it further softened her heart toward him.

"We can talk in the morning." In the morning, she had committed herself to a talk and a drive with Barnaby. A breakfast cose with the Frenchman would make no difference. "Right now," she added, "you are in no condition to talk."

"*Peut-être, non.*" He rose then. A low moan escaped from his lips, and he swayed.

"Let me help you." She laid his arm over her shoulder and left her room.

He didn't resist. He leaned upon her, silent save for an occasional grunt of pain.

"If you needed to talk to me," she said as they made their way down the steps, "you didn't need to skulk in my room."

"I wasn't skulking in your room to talk to you. I wasn't skulking in your room at all. You came home early."

Lydia missed the last step. He caught her shoulder, held her upright, turning her to face him.

For a heartbeat, they stood with nothing more between them than the layers of fabric of their garments. Lavender scent rose from his, the aroma of the leaves in which his borrowed dressing gown had been packed since the previous Season, too sweet for him. He should smell of sandalwood or bergamot, something heady and exotic.

Only a lightly sun-bronzed hue to his complexion kept the pallor of fatigue at bay. Dark shadows beneath heightened the blue of his eyes. And his mouth—firm, full lips set above a cleft chin . . .

She tore her gaze away from his mouth and licked her dry lips. "You were looking for something in my room." For her own sake as much as to taunt him, she added, "Because you're a French spy."

"*Oui*, Madame Gale, I am French and I am a spy. But matters are not what you think."

She jumped. She hadn't expected him to be so blunt, so honest. Too honest? A disarming action?

With her entire body tense from the effort, she managed a cool, "Indeed." She stepped away from him. "I'll send one of the footmen up to assist you further. Tomorrow I expect an explanation." She reached the third step of the next flight down, then tossed over her shoulder, "A truthful explanation."

"So you shall receive."

She would believe that when she heard it, and she didn't expect to hear it. Even blackmail couldn't guarantee her silence, surely, if she learned he intended to do something truly harmful for England.

Halfway down the steps, she paused to lean on the banister and stare into the well. Far below, a footman awaited orders for something. She should send him to bed. The family could manage without making a servant stay up half the night. They didn't have guests other than—

But they did!

Lydia sprinted down the last of the steps and eased open the sitting room door. Her first glance showed her empty chairs and sofa. Her second fell on the couple. She frowned and took a deep breath as much to relieve a heaviness in her chest as to calm herself before speaking.

"That's enough." She managed the words in an even tone.

The couple sprang apart. Their faces glowed with either embarrassment or passion. Cassandra's hair hung down her back with pins gleaming on the sofa and carpet around her, and Whittaker's hair stuck straight up in back. His cravat drooped, and Cassandra's gown . . .

"Go to your room, Cassandra." Lydia felt as though she hadn't slept in a week. "I'll be up to talk to you in a minute. No, better yet, go to my room."

Where the Frenchman had been up to no good, most likely, and distracted her from the couple in the sitting room. She'd delayed more than a quarter hour. From the look of the pair, it was good she hadn't delayed longer.

She fixed her gaze on Whittaker. "I'll talk to you down here."

"It's not your place to say anything, Lydia." Cassandra

scrambled to her feet without assistance, though Whittaker held out his hand to her.

"Someone has to."

"Father will be here tomorrow."

"And you'd rather we talk to him about your behavior with Whittaker?"

Cassandra dropped her gaze. "There's nothing to talk about."

"We differ on that, and I hold the winning hand here." Lydia stepped out of the doorway. "Wait for me."

Cassandra trudged past her, not saying a word to her sister or fiancé. The steps creaked in an uneven pattern, a wordless testimony to Cassandra's injured ankle.

"You should have let me carry her up," Whittaker said.

"I wouldn't let you near a bedchamber with my sister." Lydia closed the door and leaned against it, her arms crossed over her middle. "Whit, I don't want to do this. I'm only a year older than you are. And I'm a female, albeit a widow. But if I don't say this, no one will. You know as well as I do that Father would be likely to forbid Cassandra to see you until the wedding if he finds out you two can't be trusted alone together for five minutes."

"I know it looks bad." Whittaker mopped his brow with his limp cravat. "All right, Lydia, it was probably as unacceptable as it looked. And I have no excuse, not even the old one about how we're to be married soon."

"That makes it a bit more understandable, but no, it's not an excuse. After the wedding—"

"That's what I'm saying, Lydia." Whittaker rubbed his hands across his face and speared his fingers through his thick, dark hair. "I'm not sure there will be an 'after the wedding.' I'm not sure there will be a wedding."

"Whit—" Lydia sank onto the nearest chair, her legs no longer strong enough to support her. Between Cassandra's fall, finding Christien in her own bedroom, and finding her bookish sister in a fairly compromising position, the burden of the entire household landed on her shoulders.

She gazed up at her future brother-in-law—she hoped. "Why do you say that? You just had a little spat tonight."

"It wasn't that little." Whittaker shoved his hands into his coat pockets and paced to the window. "Something's terribly wrong if she believes I'd stop loving her because she wears spectacles. But what's worse is that I didn't notice she can't see a yard in front of her face. I didn't notice something so important. I only notice her—her gentleness, her sweetness, her beauty. Mostly her beauty."

"Attraction is important."

Whittaker's shoulders slumped. "That concerns me. Attraction might be all we share. That is to say, the other things about her, her intelligence and sweetness . . . I try to think about those instead, but I don't, as you can tell from our behavior. Attraction is a start, yes, but we've been betrothed for nearly a year. There should be more."

"And you fear there isn't?" Lydia brushed a hand over her own brow. "What does Cassandra say?"

"She doesn't believe I love her. And do I, if I'm persuading her to compromise her modesty? Willingly?" He let out a bark of humorless mirth. "I'm not certain anymore. It was so much easier before I inherited the earldom and the estates and mills. For some reason, Cassandra believed I loved her then."

Lydia stared at Whittaker's slouched posture and understood.

"But we haven't seen one another for nearly six months. I'm afraid . . . in that time . . ." Whittaker swung around so fast Lydia jumped. "I can't do it without hurting Cassandra, but I think perhaps we should postpone the wedding again."

"I think—" Lydia stopped. She couldn't support him in that. It was too self-serving. "I'll talk to Cassandra. If she thinks waiting is best, then we'll all talk to our father when he arrives tomorrow. Unless—" She narrowed her eyes at Whittaker but couldn't ask him the question. She would have to pose it to Cassandra.

But Cassandra wasn't in Lydia's room. Hodge perched on the dressing table grooming himself in the mirror. Otherwise, the room lay quiet and empty and smelling of lavender.

Lydia wrinkled her nose and crossed the hallway. No one responded to her tap. She pushed the door open. The room lay in silence too, save for Honore's even breathing from the bed. Cassandra wasn't there.

Grinding her teeth, Lydia descended the steps to the library. As she suspected, Cassandra sat in there, but she wasn't reading.

"My spectacles are in the sitting room." She rubbed her red-rimmed eyes. "I threw them across the room."

"A little childish, don't you think?"

"I wasn't thinking." Cassandra blinked several times. "I want to go home to Devonshire."

"So do I." Lydia slipped an arm around her sister. "But we have to stay for Honore and your wedding."

Cassandra shook her head. "Not my wedding. Whittaker needs someone better than I am now that he's the earl. I'll make a terrible countess."

"Would you marry him if he were still the second son?"

Cassandra nodded. "We used to talk then about interesting things like books. He never would have worried about me wanting to go up in a balloon. He'd have joined me. But he can't now because he's the last of his line and needs to produce an heir. I'm not certain I want to live that kind of restrictive life."

"You always have."

Cassandra grimaced. "I was looking forward to a little more freedom as a wife. You know, attending lectures and reading more extensively and now ballooning."

"You don't think you can bring Whittaker around once you're married?"

"Did you bring Charles around once you were married?"

Lydia winced, then decided to be completely honest with her sister. "No, I couldn't. I failed as a wife."

"Lydia, you never fail at anything. You're beautiful and you married well—"

"For all the good it did me."

"And you paint well."

"I can't get anyone to buy my work."

"Hmm." Cassandra looked down at her crumpled bodice. It hung askew. Lydia suspected she'd hooked it back together crooked.

The idea that her younger sister's gown had been unfastened at all, even a little, sent tension tightening Lydia's muscles. The urge to go out and smack Whittaker's face swept through her. How dare he behave so improperly.

Because he was young and not thinking with his head.

"I don't want you to call off the wedding, Cassandra. Wait a bit longer." Lydia cleared her throat. "Spend more time talking. Ask him if he'll attend lectures or go to the museum with you."

Cassandra's dark eyes twinkled. "A lecture on aeronautics?"

"That," Lydia agreed, "is highly likely to help you see his love over lust."

Cassandra blushed. "I'm so sorry."

"I'm not going to say it's all right. You know it isn't, but it's forgivable. Now then, let's not talk about canceling your wedding right now. You're both too overwrought to be logical about this. And too tired."

"I am." Cassandra yawned.

Lydia urged her toward the door. "Up to bed we go. Tomorrow is going to be a long day."

If she got through the long night.

Lydia tossed and turned so much Hodge retreated to the dressing room to sleep. At last, with dawn just breaking through the smoky air, Lydia rose, washed, and dressed as best as she could unaided. If she slipped to the kitchen, she might reach it before the Frenchwoman realized someone had invaded her domain. If she reached Christien before anyone else rose, they might have their talk with no one the wiser.

Unless she felt inclined to strangle him.

No, she would at least hear him out, then hear Barnaby out, and compare.

As quietly as she could manage, she slipped down the back stairs and stepped into the kitchen. It lay in darkness save for glowing embers on the hearth. She coaxed them into a blaze, added more coals, and swung the huge water pot over the flames. While the water heated, she prepared a tray of teapot, cups, and slices of bread and butter. More she dared not take.

She was just pouring steaming water over the leaves in the pot when she heard a footfall on the steps. With a sigh, she glanced up to see Barbara enter the kitchen.

"What are you doing here?" they asked simultaneously.

"I often make myself tea this early," Barbara answered first. "You should have called someone to get it for you."

"I've been making my own tea in the morning for seven years. Why should I do differently now?"

"Because the cook will be greatly offended. Let me help." Barbara reached for the tray and stopped, staring. "You have two cups here."

"I'm taking tea to our guest."

"Alone?" Barbara's eyes widened. "It's improper. It's bad enough that sister of yours acts like a tart—"

"Barbara."

"Well, truly, Lydia, I saw her come upstairs. Her gown was all askew."

"Yes, but that makes her an unwise young person with strong feelings for her fiancé, not a tart."

"Perhaps, but I won't have the servants talking about you too. I'll come in with you."

"You don't like him."

"He's not so bad, and he's a gentleman." Barbara took the tray from Lydia.

"We'll be talking in French." It was the best solution she could find.

"It's not what you say that matters." Barbara preceded Lydia up the steps.

Lydia tapped on the door.

"*Entrez*." The rich, dark voice rang strong and clear through the panels.

A frisson of awareness raced up Lydia's spine. She rubbed her arms, feeling gooseflesh beneath her thin sleeves, and glanced at Barbara. "Yes, stay if you like."

Then she opened the door to Christien and the truth he promised to tell her.

12

Christien heard Lydia coming long before she reached his room. China rattled, floorboards creaked, her voice flowed like hot chocolate along the corridor and beneath his door. Then she pushed the door open and glided in with all grace and elegance in a cream-colored gown and scarlet ribbons.

She didn't smile at him. Indeed, her mouth appeared tight, with a muscle bunched at the side of her jaw. She kept her lashes over her eyes, concealing the expression in the velvet-brown depths.

Her companion proved a different specimen. Blonde hair frizzing around her pale face, she shot a glance at him that held pure venom, antagonism beyond the usual for even an Englishman to demonstrate toward a Frenchman.

"I don't approve of my lady taking breakfast with you in your chamber," Barbara announced. "But she has a mind of her own. It doesn't bode well for her following the Lord's will, but that's between her and God."

"Indeed it is." Lydia shot her companion a frosty glare. "Monsieur de Meuse wishes to speak with me, and his injury precludes him from leaving his room."

It might have been his imagination, but Christien thought her eyes rolled upward, in the direction of her room. His injury hadn't prevented him from climbing the steps to spy.

To spy. He'd confessed to being a spy, and she all but ignored it. Almost as though she would believe nothing he told her, so he might as well talk if it made him feel better. As long as the blackmailing Mr. Lang's threats kept her working with Christien, things might work out. How much better if . . .

He drew the dressing gown more tightly around him. "You ladies are very kind."

"It's our Christian duty." The companion snatched the tray from Lydia and all but slammed it onto a low table. "Sit down, Lydia. I'll serve you."

"You needn't—" Lydia stopped, glanced around, and drew a chair closer to the one Christien had pulled as near to the hearth as he dared.

April or not, spring in England forever chilled him.

"Unless you wish Miss Bainbridge to hear what you have to say," Lydia said, "I recommend we talk in French."

"Of course." Christien glanced at the sour-faced spinster, and his heart pinched.

Her dislike of him should have curdled the milk in its Wedgwood pitcher. Yet she served with care, not spilling a drop of the tea or skimping on the butter for the bread. She might scowl at him, but she looked at Lydia with kindness and concern.

No doubt the basis for her animosity toward him. He was the enemy to Miss Barbara Bainbridge, apparently some poor relation to the family. She wouldn't know how much of an enemy Lydia thought him. He was simply French by birth, by the first ten years of his life spent in that country, by the part of him that longed to return to the verdant countryside and strong coffee for *le petit déjouner* instead of the endless English tea. The way Miss Bainbridge stood as far away from him as possible while still handing him his cup demonstrated her unwillingness to come near him. Yet she was near him, helping Lydia because it was the right thing to do.

He smiled at her. "Would you prefer we wait a day or two for this talk? *Peut-être* wait until I am whole enough to go down to a parlor or, better yet, my own home so you don't have to stay here?"

"I would stay by Lady Gale regardless of your location." Barbara took a cup of tea for herself and withdrew to the furthest seat in the room—the stool in front of the dressing table.

"It's all right." Lydia smiled, though it didn't reach her eyes. She switched to French. "I warned her ahead of time we would speak in French for your sake."

"I expect she thinks I'm too barbaric to speak King's English for more than a sentence or two."

"Something like that." Lydia's smile relaxed, and the corners of her eyes creased the tiniest bit.

"Would it help if she knew I attended Cambridge for three years?"

"Not particularly. Cambridge, you may remember, didn't support the king in the Civil War."

"You're jesting, *non*?"

Lydia shook her head. "Barbara is still uncertain of the Regency we have right now. To her, taking power from the king is akin to . . . cutting off his head."

Christien glanced at Barbara. Her face was set in such stony lines he wondered how she could open her mouth to drink her tea.

"My family came close to joining Louis, *vous comprenez*?" he reminded her.

"Indeed. And yet your father was a revolutionary from the American rebellion." Lydia gave him a sidelong glance.

"The American rebellion was nothing like what happened in France. If war can be polite, it was in comparison." Christien gazed into the now tepid brown liquid in his cup. "Papa loved adventure, and a war in the wilderness of the New World seemed exciting to him. He would have approved of me, if things had gone differently in eighteen three."

"In 1803?" Lydia straightened in her chair. "What happened then?"

"You British canceled the Treaty of Amiens. The little peace with Napoleon ended, and my father was caught inside France where he was suddenly no longer welcome." The sludge in his cup sloshed dangerously close to the rim, and he set the cup on the table. "He never reached home. Napoleon's men captured him and killed him. They said he was a spy, was an enemy to France. But he was simply there to see his lands, to see if he could salvage something . . ." He raised his head and looked into her big, dark eyes. Though his own eyes felt hot with the tears of grief, he knew better than to shed them. "That is why I am not working for Napoleon. His men killed my father."

She gazed right back at him without a flicker of emotion. "It is also why you could be working for Napoleon—because if England had not canceled the peace, none of that would have happened."

"Ah, my lady, it would have. We begged Papa not to go." From the corner of his eye, he caught movement from the companion and glanced her way. She smoothed out her features, but not before he caught her sneer.

So she disliked emotion.

Or she understood every word after all and thought him a liar?

His mouth tightened. "This is part of my story for you, my lady. At least hear me out before you say I don't speak the truth."

"Of course. I am sorry. You can understand my position, can you not?" For an instant, grief contorted Lydia's features.

Christien remained still. More than still. He clamped his good hand onto the arm of the chair to stop himself from going to her, drawing her to him. She shouldn't suffer because of the games despots played. Like his father, she was caught in the middle because she wanted to help her family, because she wanted to help him and repay an old debt.

Before this moment, he had admired her, cherished her, experienced some thoughts about her that perhaps a Christian man should not. Right then, with a yard of space and two cups of dreadful English tea between them, he accepted that he loved her, had probably loved her the moment she handed him her bracelet.

His heart expanded so that his chest could scarcely contain it, and it threatened to rip wide open and expose every feeling spilling through his lifeblood and yearning toward her.

Je t'aime. Je t'aime. Je t'aime.

I love you. I love you. I love you.

His heart pushed the words upward, choking his throat.

"My lady—" He swallowed, shook his head to send the foolishness away from his mind, if not his heart.

The love wouldn't leave his heart.

He swallowed again, tried to speak again. "Since my father died, weeks before I reached my majority, I have dedicated my life to bringing Napoleon to his end." Conviction rang in his tone. He couldn't have asked for better.

He could have asked for more reaction from Lydia. She sat so still with her English reserve that he almost believed she hadn't heard him. Likewise, her companion didn't move. She seemed to be examining her fingernails, clean but bitten to the quick.

Resisting the urge to squirm like a schoolboy instructed to explain toads in the schoolmaster's bed, Christien continued. "For nearly ten years, I have worked for your government inside

Napoleon's Army. I have posed as an émigré who wishes to serve the emperor to gain favor and have my family lands restored."

"And they believe you?" Lydia's nose pinched as though she smelled something distasteful.

"The British government gives me bits of information to feed the French." He sighed. "Gave me. The English won't let me go back. I have been discovered, I think. But I get ahead of myself."

And behind in time. The house was stirring. Maids trotted up steps with water jugs sloshing and coal scuttles rattling.

Without time to coat the truth in subterfuge, he blurted out, "Your husband, my lady, was my spy master."

She jumped. "Charles?" Her hand flew to her mouth, and her face paled.

The companion sprang to her feet so fast she knocked over the stool. "What is it?" she demanded in English. "Is he maligning your sainted husband?"

"If Charles was sainted," Lydia muttered, "then there is no hope for Christendom."

"Lydia." The companion's jaw dropped.

"Sit down, Barbara, please." Lydia clasped her hands in her lap, though they continued to tremble. "Monsieur de Meuse has succeeded in gaining my attention."

"*Tres bien*." Christien gave her a wry smile. "Very good indeed. Shall I continue?"

She nodded.

If he were closer, he would have taken her hands in his, warmed them, calmed them. He was not near enough, and the pain in his shoulder prevented him from moving. He settled for catching and holding her gaze. "Charles ended up left behind in Spain because he had paused to get a message to me. It was all chaos with the horses left on the beach and trying to swim out to their masters on the ships, and baggage left behind. Our men were looting and gleeful, and no one noticed me finding the chevalier and getting him to my quarters. We were able to talk before he succumbed to his wounds and before anyone would disrupt us. He gave me the names of other men. One was a Monsieur Lang—please, hear me out."

Lydia inclined her head. The errant curl bobbed against her cheek, a distraction. A temptation.

Christien heaved a silent sigh of relief and tried to proceed as quickly as he could, for now he heard one of the sisters talking in the corridor, the pretty blonde saying she intended to ride.

Lydia sprang to her feet. "Barbara, stop her. She can't go riding this early without someone going with her."

"I can't leave you here alone with a . . . gentleman." Barbara remained put.

"Monsieur de Meuse is a gentleman, whatever else we think of him. My virtue is safe, and so is my reputation if you don't go telling everyone I'm here." Lydia glanced toward the door, outside which Miss Honore now spoke in her trilling songbird of a voice.

"Mr. Frobisher is bringing the horses around from the mews in five minutes. I positively must be ready."

"Now, Barbara." Lydia's expression was fierce.

Mouth shut as tight as a miser's purse, Barbara rose and stalked to the door. She slammed it behind her.

"Why does she dislike me so?" Christien reverted back to English.

"It's not you personally." Lydia returned to her chair. "It's the French. She lost her fiancé in the early days of the war."

"I am sorry for her then. We've all lost too much in this war. And now we've this trouble with America too. More wars. More death. I've been trying for ten years to see it end." He fixed his gaze on her face, drawing her attention. "With England the victor. Without that, Napoleon will conquer the world, and we do not want his regime here."

"So you have worked to stop it. How then did our government let you get into our prison?" The question held curiosity, interest, not a sneer or speculation.

Christien relaxed for the first time since the night before. Even the pain in his shoulder diminished to a dull throb. "I was a French Army officer. Quite simply, I was on my way from Marseilles to Cadiz, as I'd been on leave, and my ship was taken by the British Navy. I couldn't divulge who I was without giving myself away to my fellow officers and risking the British not believing me at the same time, so I had to go to prison and trust that you would help, as Charles said you would. I did not have as great a faith in you as he did upon his deathbed, but he said something about favors you owed."

"Did he?" Her face contorted. Her eyes glistened.

"Does this distress you, my dear—my lady?"

"It doesn't matter. Continue." She nearly barked out the words. "You contacted me. With the intention of blackmailing me into getting you into Society?"

"No, I had nothing to do with blackmail. My Mr. Lang had nothing to do with blackmail. I fully intended to go to your house in Tavistock and await orders. But while on my way there, the guard slipped me a message that said I was in danger and must vanish, must get out of Devonshire immediately. He helped me escape, so I went to Falmouth and sold the bracelet for passage to somewhere. I planned to go to Guernsey."

"So how did you end up in—Exeter, was it?" She tilted her head to one side, a little smile on her lips.

"Hastings, my lady." He smiled back. "Lang. He caught up

with me there, in truth. He took me to Hastings because he said no one would look for me there. I have been there for a month at his home, eating well and resting. He has been with me, telling me of what he thinks may happen here in England, and we have been planning what to do."

She sat up straighter. "Happening here in England?"

"*Oui*. Unrest is here with the length of the war and the losses, the trouble with America, and the machines in the north. We think Napoleon has sent men to foment more trouble, incite riots and revolution here."

"No."

"Yes." He leaned forward, reaching out, but not quite able to touch her. "The countryside is ripe for revolutionaries to harvest. People are hungry and tired of losing their loved ones to war. The king has failed them in his madness, and the prince regent is a man led more by pleasure than—"

"Hush, you speak sedition." Her face whitened, her knuckles whitened.

Christien sighed. "*Peut-être* I do, but it is more the truth than not, and Napoleon is happy to bring France's oldest enemy down from inside."

"No, it can't happen here. I won't . . . I can't . . ." She raised her hand to her brow and closed her eyes. "If you are telling only a little of the truth, my family is in danger and I've failed so much, I—" She dropped her hand to her lap and stiffened her posture. "What am I saying to you? For all I know, what you tell me is balderdash. Why would France want to use Society? You'd think revolution would come from the lower classes."

"It didn't in America or, truth be told, France. The lower classes need someone to organize them, someone who is literate and used to leadership. And who is closer to the powers that be to do the leaders damage than those in the Upper Ten Thousand?"

Her fingers writhed on her lap. "I wish you didn't make sense. I wish I knew whom to believe. Mr. Lang waylaid me in the garden of an inn and blackmailed me into introducing you to Society."

"Me or Monsieurs Barnaby and Frobisher, one of whom tried running me down with his horse the other day."

"So you say."

"And what does Mr. Barnaby say?" Christien spoke through clenched teeth.

"I'll learn later this morning. At least he said he wished to speak with me."

"You won't meet him alone, will you?"

"A drive in the park. Not that that's any concern of yours."

"It is my concern. I drew you into this with my letter of introduction and request for further help."

"You—" She started. "There's the flaw in your story. The only Mr. Lang I could possibly know is the one who blackmailed me into taking his letters of introduction."

"But of course you know Lang. He's delivered two important messages to you. Two letters of introduction—Frobisher and Barnaby, and myself. Or so it appears."

She opened her mouth, then closed it again. Her brow puckered and her eyes flickered.

He grasped the moment of her uncertainty. "Was the man in the garden the same as the man who delivered my messages? Did you look at the handwriting?"

"I . . . can't be certain of the former or the latter." She pressed her fingertips to her temples and closed her eyes. "The letters were destroyed along with all my correspondences. I couldn't make a comparison."

"Destroyed?" Christien shot upright and choked on a groan of pain. "How?"

"You didn't reach my desk, monsieur?"

"You arrived home early." He smiled at her.

She smiled back, briefly, but enough to lighten his heart. Perhaps, just perhaps, she was beginning to believe a little of what he said.

"All the papers in my desk were ripped to shreds. But left behind so I'd know they'd done it."

"And done so from inside your household." A chill ran up Christien's spine. "My lady, this is too dangerous. You cannot remain in town."

"How can I leave? Mr. Lang has threatened my family through accusing me of helping you escape from England."

"He didn't—" He stopped, shook his head. "My dear lady, we have gone in a circle, *non*? Until you believe that someone is an impostor, we can never work to find the source of the danger to England."

"If there is danger to England. Oh my, I don't know." She rose and began to pace around the chamber, flipping the draperies back from the window to expose a slow drizzle of rain clouding the glass, then stooping to gather something up from the rug beneath the dressing table.

Her gown flowed around her, a swirl of gauzy muslin to emphasize her grace of movement. The errant curl bobbed between ear and cheek, a hint of rebellion amidst the proper—the modest dress and tightly pinned coiffure. Christien wished he were an artist so he could paint her. That way he would have a picture of her to cherish when he concluded this mission and returned to his family and relieved his maman of the burden of running the farm, capable though she was at doing so. He wouldn't even consider taking the flesh-and-blood Lydia back there. She wanted to run as soon as she dared. Only the blackmail held her in town now.

And loyalty to her family.

The family had taken him in without question, and he had possibly led them into danger if someone within the household worked against him already. He wanted to run too. Yet forces beyond his control held him in place, held him to the assignment, as they had too often, compelling him to undertake roles he didn't want to play.

Roles that built a wall of deception between him and his loved ones, between him and God.

Despite his throbbing shoulder, he rose and approached Lydia once again at the window. "I cannot make you believe me, not when others have done their best to muddy the waters. But please do not dismiss me out of hand."

In more ways than one.

"But I understand if you do," he added.

"Then you'll understand if I don't." She faced him, her eyes pinched at the corners. "If you're telling the truth, then your cause is just and you need my help. If you are lying, then I don't dare anger Mr. Lang, the blackmailer. So for now, monsieur le comte, I will remain at your side. Now, if you'll excuse me, I must speak with my sisters about their behavior."

And she was gone, slipping out the door with a last flutter of her pale skirt and a gentle click of the door latch.

His blessings always came with a barb inserted. He got to keep Lydia near him, perhaps persuade her to care for him, to believe him at the least, yet at a cost to her.

Non, he mustn't think that way. He hadn't created the difficulty unless he could blame his long-ago desire for revenge on the country that had killed his father and taken the smile from his mother's eyes.

He leaned his brow against the chilled window glass. Nearly ten years of his role was far too long. He should have stopped years ago, perhaps after Charles Gale had died. He should have stopped before he dragged Gale's widow into the debacle of this mission.

Then there was Barnaby and Frobisher and a man named Lang with connections that had to come from within the Home Office.

Christien couldn't think. He'd taken too much of the laudanum the day before. Despite continuing pain, he wouldn't make that mistake this day. If he could obtain some coffee, strong and black with a quantity of warm milk, his mind would function more clearly.

Some of his French habits would never change. They held such a grip on him he would have sworn he smelled coffee.

He turned from the window. He should try for more sleep. Once rested, he would return home. If someone intended to harm him, the last thing Christien wanted was to drag so much as a mouse from the Bainbridge pantry into danger.

He stepped toward the bed. His door opened and closed so quickly he thought perhaps a maid intended to enter then changed her mind. But a quick glance showed him a diminutive creature in white apron and cap, bearing that most blessed of kitchen utensils—a coffeepot.

"I knew you'd be wanting your morning *café au lait, mon frère*," she announced.

"Your brother, indeed." Christien staggered a step forward and gripped the bedpost. "What are you doing here, Lisette?"

She tossed her head. "What I do better than dancing or husband hunting. I'm the new Bainbridge cook."

13

Lydia wondered if banging her head against the wall would do any good. It might make her forget everything around her if she hit it hard enough. She could end up an invalid tucked up in bed with others waiting upon her and no responsibilities.

A pleasant dream despite the need for pain involved. Unfortunately, it was pains she need not endure because she could not become an invalid. Her family was crumpling without her adding the burden of being blackmailed.

As she left Honore's room and returned to her own chamber, she imagined her forthcoming interview with Father.

Yes, sir, Honore is riding out with an unsuitable young man and wanting to marry to get out from under your authority. Cassandra is a little too close to her fiancé, so she apparently thinks they shouldn't see one another and shouldn't get married. A Frenchman who may or may not be loyal to England is recovering from an accident or a deliberate attempt on his life in one of our bedchambers. Oh yes, and I'm being blackmailed, possibly by an associate of that Frenchman.

Her head began to throb as though she actually had been banging it against a wall. She headed down the steps and the knocker sounded, and she recalled her plan to drive with Mr.

Barnaby that morning. Cassandra would have to wait. Honore would have to wait. Father would have to wait.

She heard Father in Mama's sitting room, his booming voice rumbling through the door. As she headed back to her room for her pelisse, she caught her name and her sisters' and something about the cook.

Of course, the cook. He wasn't going to like that his precious French chef had defected to another family and sent his daughter to replace him. Yet she'd proven to cook as well as her parent, perhaps even better in the pastry department. But Father was likely to send her packing without a reference and no doubt expect Lydia to find another chef too soon before Honore's coming-out ball.

Perhaps this was the time to pray for something. Thus far, though, God hadn't gotten her out of her predicament with Mr. Lang, who was probably not Mr. Lang at all.

Two Mr. Langs? No. Only one had contacted her, whatever Christien claimed should have happened.

Lydia had no idea what to believe regarding Christien's tale. Part of her—too much of her—experienced an urge, a longing to believe him. He'd been direct in his looks, his blue eyes as limpid as a summer sky. His voice, as smooth and rich as velvet, flowed over her, around her, enveloping her like a warm cloak on a cold day. Not simply agreeing to go along with him because she accepted every word proved more difficult than she'd anticipated when she walked into the room.

Two Mr. Langs?

She hesitated outside his room. Her hand twitched to reach out and turn the handle, ask him questions, questions she hadn't formed in her mind as of yet. She made herself keep going around the corner and up the next flight of steps.

His voice rumbled through the door, and she stopped, her foot on the first tread. To whom could he be speaking? The words proved indistinct through the thick panels of the door. French or English? Surely someone hadn't sneaked into the house and met with him. Surely he wouldn't hold espionage assignations right under her roof.

In a heartbeat, she was across the landing with her ear to the door. Only a few seconds. Soon a footman would be coming up to find her, if the person at the door was Mr. Barnaby.

". . . Protection and peace." The voice was clear now. Clear and strong with a hint of tension. "Please, even if You'll do nothing for me, give her guidance to find the truth . . ."

Lydia shot away from the door as though someone had opened it. Someone might as well have. Christien's interlocutor knew she was listening.

He was praying. He was more than praying—he was praying for her.

Feeling lightheaded, she gripped the banister and climbed the final flight to her bedchamber. Her pelisse lay on the bed, ready for her to go out driving. But of course she couldn't drive today. Rain fell in earnest now, streaking the window and pinging against the glass.

She couldn't wear her pelisse either. Hodge lay in the middle of the scarlet silk, his pale fur a stunning contrast to the coquelicot color of the fabric, but not a particularly attractive decoration.

"You'd think I'd know better than to leave clothing lying around." She stroked Hodge's back.

He began to purr without lifting his head.

"It's a good day to stay in bed and sleep." She shivered in the chill and retrieved a shawl from her dressing room, then returned to Hodge.

His purr sounded like the velvety voice rumbling through the door of the room below hers. The voice of a man praying for her—for her safety, for her peace of mind, for her guidance into the future.

Surely no man who prayed thus could lie about his role in life, in the war. But Charles had prayed and he'd lied about staying with her and leaving his regiment. The lure of intrigue had been stronger than the love of his wife.

It could be the same with Christien. The thrill of espionage could outweigh the need for truth and faith and putting God first.

As if she put God first. Yes, one more thing at which she proved to possess too little skill.

Some things she mustn't fail at, though. Working out who was telling the truth was one of them. She mustn't let a pair of beautiful blue eyes and a black-velvet voice deceive her.

And how would Mr. Barnaby deceive her?

A knock sounded on her door. She opened it to find a footman waiting in the hallway.

"You have a caller, m'lady. Lemster has placed him in the parlor. There's a fire there, and everyone else is in Lady Bainbridge's sitting room with Lord Bainbridge."

And they hadn't called her down to join them?

Lydia squelched the twinge of pain. Father had been clear when she refused to live with them at Bainbridge Manor that his first daughter would be his last.

"I'll be right down. Will you see to it that tea is brought in, in about a quarter hour?"

"Yes, m'lady." The footman withdrew to descend the back steps behind their narrow, concealing door.

Lydia descended in the opposite direction, her footfalls

growing heavy with each flight. Second floor, where Christien's room lay silent now. First floor, where her father's voice rang loudly enough as if there were no door. Ground floor, where the chill dampness from outside penetrated one's bones and firelight from the parlor drew her as though she were a moth.

This man didn't draw her in the least. Christien tempted her to moments of yearning for other worlds behind them and different countries between them . . . For no good reason, George Barnaby didn't appeal to her. Unless perhaps it was because he came from Mr. Lang first without any previous acquaintance. She couldn't forget Christophe Arnaud in that prison, grateful for her help, speaking of his faith and his American mother.

Now Barnaby was in her family's house, speaking of Christien before making an attempt on his life.

Thinking perhaps she believed Christien, she pushed the parlor door the rest of the way open. George Barnaby stood with his back to the fire and his eyes on the door. Candlelight and illumination from the window brightened his face. Lines showed at the corners of his eyes, as though he'd spent a great deal of time squinting into the sun or smiling. The lines at the corners of his mouth suggested the latter.

He smiled now, the curve of his lips and flash of rather good teeth making him attractive. He bowed with grace. "My lady, so good of you to see me."

"Of course. I gave you my word and feel I should apologize for the rain that keeps us in." She swept forward, seated herself beside the fire, and gestured for him to sit. "We should go undisturbed here, however. My father has just arrived, and my mother and sisters are with him."

"And your companion? Will she join us?" Barnaby took the chair adjacent to hers, a little too close.

"I don't believe she will. I've left the door partly open and there's a footman in the hall, so no need for a chaperone."

"But I wish for this conversation to be private." He glanced toward the door. "Unheard by anyone."

"My father is speaking in the room at the top of the steps. I doubt the footman can hear you." Lydia smiled to take any sense of parental criticism from her words.

Barnaby rolled his eyes upward, where the rumbling voice penetrated the ceiling painting like continuous thunder. "Of course. A drive would have been preferable . . ." He shrugged. "My lady, any time in your lovely presence is welcome."

"You needn't flatter me to get me to hear you out, sir." Lydia sat as stiff as a fashion doll on the edge of her chair.

"It's not flattery." Barnaby looked into her eyes, and Lydia started with the realization that he spoke the truth.

Admiration gleamed in the dark gray depths. His gaze swept from her twisted-up hair to her shawl-clad shoulders to her scarlet slippers, and her blush rose in the opposite direction, climbing from those daring slippers to her middle to her cheeks.

No one had gazed upon her with such blatant interest, the type a man demonstrates to a woman, since her first Season. Soon those looks stopped, after Charles began to court her. No one wished to incur his wrathful glare in return. After that, she was married, then a widow poorly dressed, often with her hair in a rat's nest of unkempt curls, even more often with charcoal pencil or paint daubing her cheeks. Here, however, she was groomed and pampered, dressed well and with her hair reasonably neat. And her face was clean. For her efforts, two men—two gentlemen, whatever their purpose—had expressed interest in her just that morning.

"Thank you." She managed the two words through stiff lips, while struggling to think how to proceed.

The rattle of china in the hall gave her an idea, a reprieve. Sighing with relief, she jumped up to greet a footman with a tray of cups, teapot, milk pitcher, and tiny sweet biscuits.

"Thank you," she said to the servant. "Just set it on the table. I'll pour."

The footman did as bid and withdrew. Lydia poured, offered the plate of biscuits, and took her own cup of tea to her chair. The pallid liquid sloshed in its cup. She'd poured too much milk in it. She didn't even like milk in her tea. What had she been thinking?

She set the cup aside and clasped her hands together in her lap, much as she had done while listening to Christien's tale of wanting revenge on the country that had killed his father and robbed his family of their heritage. "So, Mr. Barnaby, tell me why I should believe your tale and why you are working with Mr. Lang."

"Mr. Lang works for the Home Office." Barnaby settled back on his chair as though about to smoke a cheroot in perfect ease at a gentlemen's club. "Helping me be accepted into Society is doing one's duty by the realm."

"Indeed." Lydia's lip curled, and she posed the same question she had to Christien. "Since when does the Crown have to resort to blackmail to get its subjects to do their duty?"

"Blackmail?" Barnaby's hand jerked. His eyebrows shot up toward a lock of hair now charmingly drooped over his forehead. "I know nothing of blackmail."

So clear was his gaze, so direct, he was either telling the truth or a consummate actor.

Lydia laced her fingers together. "You're telling me you know of no blackmail?"

"I know of no blackmail. If someone calling himself Lang blackmailed you into doing something, then it's the wrong Mr. Lang."

Nearly the same thing Christien had said.

"It's the only Mr. Lang I've met," she said.

Unless Christien was correct and Lang was the mysterious man, the one she'd presumed was a smuggler, who had made those two early-morning deliveries to her Tavistock cottage—one with the bracelet and news of Charles's death in Spain, the other with news of Christien de Meuse née Christophe Arnaud, in Dartmoor and needing her to fulfill her promise to help him, as he had helped her husband.

"Are you certain?" Barnaby had paled, and no man could make himself pale. "My lady, this is distressing."

"Indeed it is. I don't like my family being in danger."

"Oh no, your family isn't in danger. We would never endanger you or your family. I just need the introductions and will see to the rest of the . . . investigation."

Lydia slid even closer to the edge of her chair. She leaned toward Barnaby, her gaze intent upon his. "And what, sir, is that investigation?" She held her breath, waiting to see if he would say the same thing as Christien or something far different.

"You needn't know, my lady. It's best if you don't."

"Then I am free to go to the Home Office and tell them what has happened to me and ask about you? Or perhaps simply go upstairs and tell my father. He's a member of Parliament and sits in the House of Lords."

Barnaby's hand clamped down on her wrist, and his eyes turned to pure steel. "Don't do that, my lady. Please. The fate of Great Britain rests on your discretion and assistance and silence."

"Why?" Lydia whispered the word through gritted teeth, and she forced herself not to jerk away and smack him across the face for grabbing her.

"Because we have traitors in the highest echelons of Society, men who are to England what Lafayette proved to be to his class in France—revolutionaries." Barnaby released her and returned to his relaxed pose. "This I blame on the influence of French émigrés. Not all are here because they object to Napoleon's reign."

14

Christien accepted his host's invitation to join him for breakfast in the dining room early, before the ladies rose. Christien regretted his lordship rising earlier than the females. He hadn't seen Lydia since the previous morning. He hadn't even heard her voice in the corridor or on the steps. He'd caught a glimpse of her the previous afternoon, striding from the house as though setting out across the moors, a portfolio under her arm and a footman trailing behind, carrying a box. He couldn't see her face, but every rigid line of her spine and swirl of her muslin skirt pronounced agitation or anger.

What would she paint in such a temper?

He possessed some of her drawings. She'd sent them to her husband, sketches that spoke of quiet domestic life more than any number of words—the cat perched on a garden wall with a laden apple tree behind it, Barbara bent over some sewing, Lydia herself kneeling in the dirt of a vegetable garden and pulling up weeds.

Charles had crumpled that one and tossed it aside. "I told her to go to my family or her own, stubborn, stupid woman."

Stubborn, yes. Stupid? Not Lydia. Christien didn't know why she wouldn't go to the home of her husband, where she wouldn't need to toil in a garden for vegetables, but he guessed she had her reasons, and good ones at that.

Five minutes with Lord Bainbridge taught Christien that she also possessed good reasons for living in genteel poverty on the edge of Dartmoor instead of in luxury at Bainbridge Manor near Exeter.

"I don't like you French," Lord Bainbridge greeted Christien, "but I understand you saved my daughter from injury or worse, so hospitality is the least I can offer you."

"Thank you." Christien's tone was dry as he took the chair a footman drew out for him across from his lordship.

Whatever else she did not share with her father, Lydia had gained her looks from him. He was tall and finely built, with a figure still lean despite what must be at least fifty years. Gray streaked his black hair, which was abundant and waved back from a noble brow that ended in arched brows over brown eyes. A handsome man with wealth, power, and a wife and three daughters who were an asset he didn't seem to appreciate any more than Charles Gale had appreciated his wife.

"I would have preferred to grow up in France," Christien added, "though England has been kind to us."

"Yes, well, how do you know my daughter?" Bainbridge posed the question, then tucked into a beefsteak nearly the size of his plate. The man must have been doing considerable exercise to maintain his youthful physique.

Christien buttered a bite of bread roll, awkward with one hand. "I was a friend of her husband's."

"Gale. Humph. Fool, going off to the continent like that when he had a wife and home back here. But I hear he was a fine soldier."

"*Oui*, my lord, he was."

"And his mother was a harridan, which was probably what dragged him into the Army."

"Sir Charles was not overly fond of his mother, I know."

Except Charles and Bainbridge thought Lydia should live with the woman, though neither of them liked her. Surely God wanted more for a daughter and wife than a contentious mother-in-law.

Christien's wife wouldn't have to suffer mistreatment. Maman was the kindest lady who existed. She would probably not even scold Lisette for more than an hour or so for running off to play chef in the place of the man who now served the de Meuse family. And pretending to be the man's daughter.

Christien crumbled his bread roll. Lisette was fortunate he had the use of only one arm. A young lady of twenty-five years or not, he would be tempted to turn her over his knee for her antics, antics from which he hadn't yet worked out how to extricate her with grace.

"And your mother is an American," Bainbridge said. "Another unruly lot."

Christien laughed. "My mother is the most soft-spoken lady I know, lovely and gracious."

"And loved by everyone except those who wanted to cut off her head." Bainbridge's upper lip curled.

"Mobs turn the heads of even the most sensible of men and women." Christien kept his tone even.

Bainbridge smiled. His features relaxed, giving Christien a glimpse of a kindness beneath the brusque and rude surface. "And we fear mobs in this country doing the same things they did in France. If this were a more Christian nation, instead of one pretending to be, perhaps we'd have fewer fears. But we have little more than an endless pursuit of pleasure—too much like the French court for my liking."

Christien bit down on an urge to ask why he'd allowed his daughters to come to London for the Season.

"I can only hope and pray," Bainbridge continued, "that my daughters find Christian men with whom to share their lives. Cassandra is all right, but Honore . . . And Lydia is too young to remain a widow."

Too young and lovely and vital.

Christien sat still while his coffee cooled in its cup and his plate held nothing beyond the crumbled bread roll. The reason for the invitation to the meal seemed about to be revealed.

"I've made enquiries, de Meuse." Bainbridge leaned forward. "About you and this other man keeping company with my eldest daughter. There's a little too much secrecy about you and George Barnaby. But right now I'd welcome any suitor for her who is a gentleman and has a modicum of faith, so I can concentrate on keeping Honore on the straight and narrow."

A gasp from the doorway echoed Christien's silent inhalation of outrage. He glanced up to see Lydia standing framed by the dark wood lintel, tall and elegant in pale yellow muslin, save for that playful curl on her cheek. A cheek blazing with color.

His gut tightened, and he stumbled to his feet. "My lady."

"No," she said in her clear, crisp voice. "I am not and not likely to ever be."

Heat blazed in Lydia's face, in her belly, all the way to her toes. She shook with the surge of energy racing through her veins. Her hands curled, wanting to grip something and rend it so she wouldn't do something unspeakable like shake her father.

"So this is why you truly brought me to town?" She fixed her gaze on her father, ignoring Christien, who was still standing. "You intend to marry me off? To whom, the highest bidder?"

"Lydia, this is inappropriate." Father pointed a finger past her shoulder. "Leave us now. You and I can discuss this in the library later."

"No, we cannot. I have work to do later. Work that has to do with why I'm here in town, not why you want me in town—to get rid of me like—" She stopped before her voice broke on the sob rising in her throat and tears spilled past her lashes.

Always her father wanted her to be something she wasn't, wanted her to succeed where she failed in his eyes. Even her marital status, or lack thereof, was onerous to him, though she never asked a thing of him. He'd rather she marry a stranger he knew little about than remain a widow. But he wouldn't sell one of his horses to a person he knew little about.

She took a deep breath, seeking for something to say that would take the pity from Christien's eyes. "After church I'm off to Almack's to work on the arrangements for Honore's ball. All three of us will be gone most of the day, and tonight we have a soirée to attend. I may have time to talk to you tomorrow. Do please be seated, Monsieur de Meuse. You are still an invalid." That delivered, she spun on her heel and swept from the room.

"I apologize for that outburst." Father's voice trailed after Lydia as she raced up the steps to collect her pelisse and sisters.

This was why she'd married the first man who offered for her. She would have rather been the wife of a soldier than the daughter of a man who wanted her to be—what? He hadn't been pleased when she married Charles. Father wanted a title for her, a fortune, an estate in the country. He got none of these things and sought them again, apparently.

How Cassandra must have disappointed him when she

engaged herself to a younger son, and how pleased he must have been when Whittaker inherited the earldom so unexpectedly. But Cassandra had scarcely come out of her room in two days. She'd pleaded a headache and stayed home the night before and refused to see Whittaker when he called. Should Lydia warn her how much she would displease Father, that he might make her life unpleasant if she postponed or even canceled her wedding?

And Honore! Was Father driving her right into the arms of Gerald Frobisher? Lydia knew too little of Honore's life at home. Whether Frobisher was a good man or bad, Lydia herself wished for her sister to look elsewhere. He was attached to Barnaby, who was attached to Lang, who was . . .

The bane of Lydia's existence these days.

She entered her bedchamber and composed herself in front of the mirror. That one curl had come down again, bouncing in front of her ear like an exuberant caterpillar. She pinned it up again, retrieved her pelisse from the back of a chair, and crossed the hall to knock on her sisters' door.

No one answered.

"Cassandra? Honore?"

Nothing.

She opened the door. The room was empty. Cassandra's books lay strewn across the bed—a collection of Greek texts and a two-year-old copy of the *Monthly Magazine*, an odd contrast until Lydia flipped it open and found the well-marked pages on aeronauts.

"Oh, Cassandra, it's too dangerous."

And so was working with—or was it against?—the British government.

Blushing all over again at the notion her father thought

Barnaby and de Meuse were suitors, Lydia left her sisters' room and descended the steps to find them in their mother's sitting room.

"Come along, *mes soeurs*. We must settle the arrangements for the ball so we can get Honore married off and make Father happy." Hearing the bitterness in her own voice, Lydia wasn't surprised at the shock on her sisters' faces.

Mama looked sad. "If your father is pressuring you to wed again, Lydia, it's only to see you better settled than you are now."

"I'm quite content where I am right now, thank you." Lydia gentled her tone for her mother. "I have Barbara's companionship, my painting, and—but Father doesn't like my painting."

"Not selling it," Honore exclaimed. "That's so close to trade."

"No more so than writing a book, and many ladies write books." Lydia stepped back from the doorway. "We need to be on our way."

"Cassandra isn't going," Mama said. "Whittaker wrote to say he's calling."

"I'm going with my sisters." Cassandra glided past Lydia and onto the steps. "Are we taking a carriage or a hackney?"

"A carriage. It's waiting for us in the square. Come along, Honore." Lydia gestured to her youngest sister.

Honore paused long enough to kiss Mama on the cheek before skipping to the steps. "Do you think it's all right for a lady to write novels?"

"Of course." Lydia slipped her arm through Honore's and propelled her a bit faster to the carriage. "Do you plan to write one?"

"I do. Something set on Dartmoor, with smugglers and secret goings-on at night."

Like men in gardens calling themselves someone who should not have been there.

Lydia bustled the girls into the carriage, and they set out for Almack's Assembly Rooms on King Street. Any day they expected to receive the vouchers that would allow them to purchase tickets for the Wednesday night balls that only the best people were allowed to attend, but for now they would enter the hallowed halls through renting them out for Honore's coming-out ball, as their own townhouse didn't boast a ballroom. Their grandfather, who had purchased the Cavendish Square house, decided to use the space for bedchambers and drawing rooms used daily, rather than a ballroom used perhaps twice a year. Lydia appreciated the fact that having to rent a ballroom meant they wouldn't have strangers, or near strangers, traipsing through their house, going up to her bedchamber, and leaving cryptic messages.

No, the message wasn't cryptic. It clearly told her to trust no one.

Across the rough cobblestones of the city, Honore chattered about her novel. "It'll be far more intriguing than *The Mysteries of Udolpho*, which I found rather dull."

Lydia smiled at the girl's enthusiasm until she glanced at Cassandra, who had brought a copy of a magazine with her and sat reading in her corner of the carriage.

"What is it?" Lydia asked.

"*Gentleman's Magazine.*" Cassandra's voice sounded muffled behind the pages of the periodical. "An article on aeronauts."

"Not more balloons." Honore made a face.

Lydia frowned. "Why are you pursuing this interest when you know it distresses Whittaker?"

"Why does Whittaker pursue me, when he knows it distresses me?"

"You won't distract me that way, Cass. We'll talk about this. Why would you wish to distress Whittaker?" Lydia pressed.

Cassandra shrugged. "Machiavelli says to begin as you intend to go on. If I want Whittaker to let me read what I like, discuss what I like—within reason of the profane or vulgar, of course—then he will allow it. If he won't, then we share nothing."

"That's not what I've heard." Honore giggled.

"You've heard too much," Cassandra shot back. "It's not like—it's not like you think."

"I don't know what you're talking about," Lydia admitted. Both siblings turned to stare at her.

She laughed. "I've been a wee bit preoccupied."

"Who'd have thought you'd have so many suitors at your age?" Honore said.

"Yes, I'm so ancient, I had to pluck gray hairs from my head for an hour this morning." Lydia scowled at her youngest sister. "And I'll pluck all the blonde hairs from your head if you keep implying I'm old." She made a grab for Honore's hat.

Honore squealed and slid across the seat. They arrived laughing at the assembly rooms, where they spent a pleasant hour wandering around the ballroom and working out what decorations would best suit. Cassandra vanished after the first hour of planning, and Lydia found her examining the door between the ladies' and gentlemen's retiring rooms.

"Why do you suppose there's a door here?" she mused. "There isn't one between the ballroom and card room."

"I've always wondered about that. No one seems to know." Lydia approached her sister and laid a hand on her arm. "Cassie, now that I've got you cornered, tell me what's wrong. Why won't you see Whittaker?"

"Because—because—oh, Lydia, I'm so ashamed of myself, I can't look him in the eye." Cassandra burst into tears and buried

165

her head against Lydia's shoulder. "I know we're misbehaving, and I didn't tell him no."

"He has a responsibility too."

"I know, and that makes me angry. I'm so humiliated. If you hadn't come back when you had—" A shudder ran through Cassandra. "And he always starts kissing me when I won't go along with what he wants me to. Or when I won't stop what he doesn't want me to do. And I give in too—too much. How can I marry him if I can't bear the sight of him now?"

15

"She wants to call off the wedding." Lydia faced her father across his big desk in the library, her mouth dry, her pulse racing.

"Why?" Father posed the inevitable question. "I thought it an excellent match, a better match than I'd expected for Cassandra now that he came into the earldom so unexpectedly."

"It is. But—"

"Sit down, Lydia, and tell me what's happened these past six weeks."

More than she dared tell him.

She sat. "Sir, Cassandra never told Whittaker about needing spectacles. You know how sensitive she is about it."

"And rightly so. Men don't want a wife who looks like a freak."

Lydia ground her teeth and counted to ten before she managed to continue in a level voice. "She looks charming in her spectacles, much like a stu—"

"No female should look like a student. Now what does all this have to do with her wanting to call off the wedding? I'd think Whittaker would be the one doing the jilting if the spectacles are a bone of contention."

"No, sir, Whittaker adores Cassie." Lydia's heart squeezed

with the memory of the way Whittaker gazed at Cassandra, as though he expected the sun to rise at midnight just because she walked into the room. "She . . . He . . ." Her cheeks heated. "Father, this is difficult. Perhaps I should have Mama tell you."

"Except your mother doesn't know, does she?" Father's cocoa-colored eyes clashed with Lydia's.

She broke contact first, let her gaze drift toward the window and the sunlight that lured her out to the park to paint. "I try not to distress Mama."

"As do we all." Father's tone softened. "So you'll have to tell me. What has Whittaker done to persuade Cassandra she doesn't wish to marry him?"

"He's been too affectionate," Lydia blurted out.

"What has he done to my daughter?" Father's voice held an unnatural calm.

Lydia shivered, though her face, neck, and lower burned. "He, um—"

"Lydia, say it. You're a widow, not a schoolroom miss. What liberties has this man taken with my daughter? Do I need to call him out or merely horsewhip him?"

"Neither, I hope. That is, I only saw a few buttons—"

Father said a word Lydia had never heard him utter and sprang to his feet. "One or twenty, it's too much without the vows. Where does he live? I will see that this engagement is ended right here and now. The scoundrel, the—"

"Father, please—"

But he stormed past her, out of the library and down the steps. His shout calling for a horse and his coat and hat rang through the house.

Lydia dropped her head into her hands. "God, what have I done?" *Go after him.* She must go after him, stop him.

She started to rise, sensed rather than heard someone behind her. Christien stood beside her chair.

"I'm sorry to disturb you, my lady. I wanted to find my host and thank him for his hospitality." He smiled, the curve of his lips and the blue of his eyes soft and gentle. "And you, to thank you for your kindness."

She gathered her manners around her. "It was the least we could do after you saved me." She blinked hard to clear the blurriness from her eyes. "My father has departed the house just this minute."

And if God didn't think her too unworthy, He would protect the man from a quick temper that could get him killed. Surely Whittaker wouldn't take up a challenge to a duel. Surely he would understand that—

Lydia started.

"What is it, my lady?" Christien held out his good hand. "You look pale."

"I'm concerned about my father. Are you certain it's all right for you to be up and about?"

"More than all right. A little pain, is all. This is more an inconvenience to me, and I believe I may be an inconvenience to you, after our discussion." He held her gaze, the sea-blue of his eyes no longer soft. "Have you given that thought?"

"Yes, of course."

Too much, thoughts that drifted to the speaker and not the words, the timbre of his voice, the caress of his accent.

A shiver far different from the one of fear over her father with Whittaker ran through her, raising the fine hairs on her arms. Of its own volition, her hand reached out, touched his, warmed with the hard strength of the fingers that curled around hers.

"I don't know what to think yet," she managed to eke out of a tight throat. "Mr. Barnaby . . . he tells a good tale too. I'd rather have nothing to do with either of you. Surely I've fulfilled my promise to Mr. Lang. That is, surely he cannot blackmail me further."

"Since the man I work for never blackmailed you at all, you are free to go your way." He raised her fingers to his lips. "But we shall meet during the Season, *n'est-ce pas?*"

"Yes, it's so. And I shall afford you—both of you—all the courtesy any member of the ton deserves. Now, if you'll excuse me, I must go after my father before he does something foolish like challenge Lord Whittaker to a duel."

"A duel? Why—? But it is none of my concern. Forgive me for asking. But may I be of service?"

"No, thank you. I must call for a carriage at once."

"But mine is awaiting me in the square. Can I not take you?"

Lydia bit her lip, darting her glance around the room as though she could find an alternative. Nothing would be faster.

"Thank you."

Catching up with Father would be worth spending more time in Christien's company.

"*Allons-nous.*" He offered her his good arm and led her downstairs. "Let us go."

Not until she entered his carriage did she realize she wore neither pelisse nor hat. No matter. This was a closed vehicle. Another faux pas perhaps, to be in a closed carriage with him. And crossing town to the Albany, where Whittaker had rooms rather than residing in his family's townhouse as a bachelor.

"Father will get there faster on horseback." Lydia gripped the strap over her head for balance as the vehicle jounced across the cobbles. "If he does something foolish, it'll be my fault. I shouldn't have told him. I should have let him think Cassandra was simply frightened—" She stopped. She was babbling.

Christien took her hand in his, his fingers warm and strong, and she realized she wore no gloves either. "Calm yourself. Lord Bainbridge isn't likely to do anything foolish, as you seem to fear."

"I thought as much too, but he was angry, as though he cared—"

"But of course he cares about his daughters. If I'd stayed home and been more protective of my sisters, perhaps—but that is my concern, not yours."

"Of course. You needn't tell me anything you don't wish to." Lydia murmured the polite words while she watched the city speed past. "Your sisters are ready for their coming out, are they not?"

"They are past ready. But I've been away, and Maman did not feel comfortable bringing them to London on her own, not being English or French. Now the twins are nearly twenty and the eldest five and twenty and headstrong."

"Indeed?" Lydia flicked her gaze toward him. They approached the Albany, and she saw no sign of Father's horse amidst the other mounts and carriage teams in the street, with grooms or boys holding the horses' heads. "How distressing."

"To have one employed, *oui*."

Lydia swung around to face him. "What?"

"Ah, I wished to see if you were listening to me."

"I beg your pardon."

"No matter. We are here, *non*? Shall I go inside and look? I think this is not where a lady may go."

"No, it isn't, especially since—" She touched her hair, found the curl bobbing over her ear, and gave it a shove back toward its pins.

"But it is charming, my lady." He tugged the curl free from her fingers, then alighted from the carriage with a bit of stiffness.

The man was in pain. He had just bounced across town when she suspected he should still be resting. How selfish of her to forget his injury when it had happened to her benefit.

Or because of Barnaby?

If only Father challenging or even horsewhipping Whittaker was all she had to worry about, she would be thankful.

Lord, just let me get Cassandra married and Honore betrothed and sell a few paintings or prints and—

She asked a great deal of the Lord for a female who paid Him little attention. She didn't do any better as a practicing Christian than she did anything else.

Except paint. That she knew was good. Good but useless if she couldn't sell enough to return to Tavistock as a lady free of worry and with some money in the bank and the Funds.

But the Season was just beginning, and she couldn't leave yet.

She lifted the curtain on the carriage window and peered out. Christien was departing from the hotel. He caught her eye, and she jerked back in the event others might see her.

A moment later, he climbed back into the vehicle. "Lord Bainbridge has gone. Lord Whittaker isn't here."

"Gone where?"

"Lord Whittaker has gone back to Lancashire. He left a letter to be delivered to Miss Bainbridge, I was informed. Your father took it."

Lydia covered her face with her hands. "What will happen next?"

"Nothing, I think, but a notice to the papers that there will be no wedding."

"I wish I could say you're wrong. It's all so foolish. Cassandra needn't take this drastic step over—well, it's not an unforgivable situation. But to have Whittaker run off . . ."

"There is trouble in the north, you know. These men calling themselves Luddites are breaking looms and causing trouble. Perhaps he must protect his interests."

Lydia's hands fell to her lap, and she swung around on the seat to stare at him. "What do you know of Lord Whittaker's interests with looms?"

"We wouldn't have recruited you to assist us if we hadn't known a great deal about your family, my lady."

"Enough to know I'd do anything to protect them?"

"*Oui*, we know your loyalty to those close to you."

"Which gave you room for blackmail."

The carriage slowed to turn into Cavendish Square, and Christien sighed and leaned his head against the cushions. "*Vraiment*, truly possible, indeed. I know not how to convince you otherwise."

"You needn't, if I may go about my own way and get through this Season so I may return to the country knowing my siblings are happy and safe, and I have time to paint. That is all I ask of life."

"I am sorry for that, my lady." The carriage stopped in front of Number Thirty, and Christien laid his hand on her arm. "I hope today has taught you something about your father."

Lydia stared at him, her brain disrupted by the non sequitur. "I beg your pardon?"

"Your father cares about his daughters as much as you care about your siblings and mother. That is why he thinks you're wasted there on the moor living in genteel poverty, and I tend to agree. You have a great heart, and it is indeed wasted there."

Her nostrils flared. "I suppose helping French spies is a better use of my heart?"

"No, *ma chère*, we took advantage of your heart." He tucked her errant curl behind her ear, allowing his fingers to linger a heartbeat too long, then rose and opened the carriage door. "I will contact you only if I need your assistance, but seeing one another is inevitable. Be civil, *s'il vous plait.*"

"I will, though it doesn't please me."

Yet she lied. A hollowness had opened up inside her, a sense of loss, as she descended to the ground and entered her house. If she had a heart, it had just been wrenched from her by a near stranger telling her she had one.

"But I don't," she murmured to herself.

She'd been vicious to her husband in her letters. She'd said terrible things when he refused to come home to her, sell his commission, and take her to live in a real house. He'd been no different than her father, controlling her life—only worse, for he wasn't even providing her with glimpses of concern for her, of caring, as Father often did.

Like today with Cassandra.

And Cassandra was who mattered right now. If Whittaker had left her, he accepted the end of the betrothal, and Cassandra might be hurt. Even if she wasn't, Mama and Father would certainly have a great deal to say to her about it, badgering her. Father was likely to tell her to find another husband before the end of the Season.

"I won't pay for the expense of bringing you all to town again," his voice boomed from Mama's sitting room. "The money is better spent improving the lives of the tenants on the estate, getting children educated, aiding returning soldiers who've been wounded."

"Then give me my dowry and let me out on my own." Cassandra's airy voice sounded strong, vibrant. "I can go live with Lydia."

"Who will get herself a husband by the end of the Season too, if I have my say."

"Not if I have mine." Lydia charged into the room. "Cassandra, you are welcome to stay with me, with or without your marriage portion."

"Girls." Mama paled. "I don't know why you are so opposed to marriage."

Cassandra and Lydia glanced at their father.

"I don't object." Cassandra twisted her gown's sash between her fingers, fraying the ribbon. "I want a man who honors me, and Whittaker did not. And now he's deserted me, which proves he does not."

"He's trying to save his mills," Father bellowed. "Can't you understand that, girl? It's his livelihood."

"And he'd rather have that than me." Cassandra's ribbon tore up the middle.

"You—"

"Father, please." Lydia held up her hand and turned to Cassandra. "Cassie, don't you understand that dozens, perhaps hundreds, of people will be out of work if these men get to Lancashire and destroy the looms? Sometimes we have to put the good of many over—over the good of one person or a few."

She managed to finish the sentence—barely. Her mind had begun to race, spin, drag out a line of thinking she wasn't sure she wanted to follow.

"You sent him away," Father said with a bit more calm than earlier. "You can't expect the man to give up his pride after that. And over something for which you are equally responsible. Or did he force you to let him . . . er . . . take liberties?" He cleared his throat, and his face turned red.

Lydia's lips twitched.

Mama began to undo a bit of her embroidery she had apparently stitched incorrectly, and Cassandra wiped her streaming eyes with the ends of her ruined sash.

"Why don't you go upstairs, sweetheart." Lydia handed Cassandra a handkerchief. "Things will be all right in time. Time heals everything."

The kind of platitude she'd been told after she'd received word of Charles's death. But time hadn't healed her wounded spirit, her sense of inadequacy as a wife, as a woman. It might not heal Cassandra's shame and humiliation as quickly as they wished, or at all.

Will You listen if I pray for her, Lord?

Lydia took Cassandra's arm and urged her out of her chair.

"Yes, go rest a while, dear," Mama said.

Father drummed his fingers on his desk, his lips set in a hard, thin line.

Lydia got Cassandra to the door, then turned back to her parents. "Let her alone. She'll come to her senses sooner or later."

"As long as it isn't too much later." Father's lips hardly moved. "I thank the Lord my son isn't as much trouble as my daughters."

"Yet," Lydia muttered. "Now, if you'll excuse me, I have things I'd like to do. Do you know where Barbara is?"

"She's in the kitchen learning how to make brioche," Mama said. "Something about selling the buns at the fair back in Tavi—"

Father began to rant about his daughter's companion acting like a common baker, and Lydia fled. She decided to take a footman and maid with her to the park rather than disturb Barbara from her baking lessons.

The fashionable hour for driving along Rotten Row hadn't yet arrived, so Lydia shared the park with nursery maids and their charges. Rather than annoying her, the boisterous offspring of the *haut ton* inspired her. When they came to hang over her shoulder and watch, she told them to go around in front of her and made sketches of them. She allowed each subject to take his or her likeness with her. After a while, the novelty of a lady artist left the children, and Lydia began to draw on a canvas. Later she would paint in the colors for the picture, making her bedchamber smell of turpentine and oil. Barbara would complain a bit, but nowhere else in the house afforded her space to set up her easel now that Father had arrived.

She concentrated on her work, tried to think of nothing but the landscape she intended to create, something delicate and vibrant, lush and soothing. A picture a lady would want in her sitting room or boudoir. A picture that would sell. She did not let herself think of the revelation that had struck her in the library. She could think later, examine the good and bad of the odd notion that sometimes one's country, keeping one's nation and fellow subjects safe, came before family.

No, she wouldn't think about that, wouldn't consider it. Cassandra and Honore needed her love and guidance right now. Barnaby, Christien, Lang—whether they were on the side of right or wrong—could muddle along on their own.

But what if they were on the wrong side, had been sent to cause trouble in England as they had suffered in France? Shouldn't she try to stop them?

No, it wasn't her place to do so. Her father's will to simply marry his daughters off to anyone must be fought. Let those who knew about spies and sedition do the work. She must make money in the event Cassandra did join her household. She must paint while the sun shone, a rare enough occasion in London.

From the corner of her eye, she saw her maid speaking to

two of the nannies. The footman joined some older youths in skipping stones across the water. Neither paid attention to her.

Or the owner of the long shadow that fell across her shoulder and onto the canvas.

She jumped and started to turn.

A hand pressed on her shoulder, gentle but warning. "Don't move. I'm merely admiring your painting. Should I add it to my collection of Lady Gale pictures?" asked the man she now knew as Elias Lang.

16

The sling into which his valet tied Christien every morning, after a painful session dressing, gave him entrée into the drawing rooms of numerous ton matrons. A bachelor was always welcome to round out the numbers at dinner parties or small dancing parties. A bachelor with an arm wounded saving a lady from injury was pure gold.

"Even if he is French," he overheard one dowager in a purple turban remark.

"Because he is French," her interlocutor responded. She was a plump young wife with eyes like pansies. "I know we're at war with them, but we're not at war with the aristocracy. We're trying to save the aristocracy and bring back their king, are we not?"

"Of course. Kings are the natural order of things."

The young wife giggled. "Men who look and talk like he does are the natural order of other things."

Christien, resting behind a potted palm tree, slipped away before his heated face set the dry fronds on fire.

He spent a great deal of time ducking behind draperies, doorways, and decorative vegetation in an effort to catch snippets of conversation, avoid other interludes of dialogue, or simply give his aching shoulder a rest. So far, he had accomplished nothing from the first reason. If an agent was working amidst the upper classes of London Society, Christien had no idea who it could be after two full weeks of attending every gathering to which he gained an invitation.

He didn't even see George Barnaby. The man seemed to have vanished. Christien tried to find him, to confront him about the "accident" the day Lydia fell from her horse. None of the typical haunts for bachelors claimed he was in residence. None of his hosts or hostesses recalled who he was, with one or two exceptions, who said they hadn't encountered him. Not even young Gerald Frobisher knew where his mentor had gotten himself to.

Christien found Frobisher riding in the park early one bright morning in mid-April. His companion wore a blue riding habit and a loo mask, but Christien thought he recognized the mare and the lady's honey-blonde curls peeking out from beneath a perky hat. Surely Lydia didn't know what her younger sister was doing any more than he had known what his younger sister was doing.

He pretended not to recognize Honore Bainbridge and addressed Frobisher. "I haven't seen Barnaby in weeks. Has he taken himself off from London?"

"I have no idea." Frobisher shrugged. "I am much too preoccupied with my entertainments to worry about what that stick has gotten himself up to."

Honore giggled.

"I thought you were friends." Christien turned so he didn't accidentally glance at Honore, though he wanted to snatch her off her mare and carry her back to Cavendish Square for her father to deal with. Or Lydia.

But he tried not to think of Lydia these days.

"I wouldn't call us friends," Frobisher drawled. "We met at an inn on the Great North Road to London and merely traveled here together. Never saw him before. No need to see him since. He's quite, quite dull."

Unless he was an assassin.

Yet if he were, why had he simply vanished, leaving Christien wounded, but not particularly badly?

"Well, if you encounter him," Christien said, "please tell him I wish to speak with him."

"But of course." Frobisher yawned, then turned his mount away from Christien's curricle.

His companion followed, a small, erect figure on a stunning gray mare. A gray mare too recognizable.

The little fool. Why hadn't Lisette told him about Honore still riding out unaccompanied by anyone but Frobisher? She was supposed to be watching out for the Bainbridge ladies, the only reason he allowed her to carry on with her masquerade. If she would simply provide him with information about the ladies' whereabouts and activities and welfare, she could remain the cook until the end of the Season. Then she must go home and stay there until he and no one else found her a husband.

If he survived that long.

Apparently he would. He felt as dull as Frobisher claimed Barnaby was. London was as calm as any metropolis of its size and dense population could be. Despite riots in the north over mechanization of weaving and spinning, the capital remained free of any rebellious activity. No one made an attempt on Christien's life again, not even while he was vulnerable with his right arm still in a sling. Wars outside of England seemed to hold the gentlemen's conversation—would Wellington make progress in Spain during the summer campaign? Would the Americans dare go to war with England? Which horse would win the races at Newmarket? And who would win the hand of the lovely Miss Honore Bainbridge?

War, social intrigue, and games of chance and other pursuits of pleasure occupied the gentlemen of the haut ton. Sedition seemed the furthest thought from anyone's mind, and Christien began to think Lang, as representative from the Home Office, was mistaken in his information.

If only he could find the man and ask him. But Lang had proven as elusive as Lydia. Lang did not contact Christien as he claimed he would, and Lydia did not appear at any of the social gatherings he expected her to.

Neither did Cassandra, though word of her broken engagement traveled through the drawing rooms and assembly halls. Honore enjoyed as many entertainments as any one person could. Once or twice she arrived on the arm of Gerald Frobisher and always accompanied by friends and their mamas.

Finally, near the end of April, with his arm healed enough for Christien not to need the sling, Lisette sent word that all of the Bainbridge ladies would attend the Tarleton masquerade ball.

If she got through the Tarleton masquerade ball without a disaster, Lydia would consider herself blessed and sleep for a week. Even without Cassandra's wedding to plan, she found her days maddeningly occupied from too soon after dawn to too close to dawn. Her paint box and sketches lay idle, but would not, must not for long. She had work to do.

But first the ball.

She balked at wearing a costume, but her sisters insisted. They, of course, wore costumes—Cassandra as Athena, the goddess of wisdom, and Honore as Daphne, the nymph that the myth said turned into a laurel bush.

"You shall go as Hera," Cassandra told Lydia. "The mother goddess."

"I'm not that old. Nor am I cow-eyed." Lydia's protest landed on deaf ears, and the girls dressed her in a flowing white robe with peacock feathers sewn around the hem. They tried to make her wear a mask of peacock feathers, but Lydia put her foot down about that and chose a plain white silk. They did make her a crown and a peacock feather fan, which she agreed to sport, and they pronounced her well enough.

"Keep a close eye on your sisters," Father admonished her as they left the house. "You know what sort of trouble one can get into at a masquerade."

"In truth, Father, I don't know." Lydia paused on the threshold. "You didn't allow me to attend one."

"Humph. Perhaps I shouldn't—"

"Father," Cassandra and Honore cried together.

"Just make sure your sister knows where you are at all times." He vanished into the library.

"That will be difficult," Honore pointed out as they climbed into the carriage. "I know they will have at least five hundred people there."

"I'd like to say I trust you." Lydia fixed Honore with a steely glare.

Honore tossed her head, sending her silk laurel leaves rustling.

"You know you can trust me," Cassandra said. "I expect I'll sneak into Lord Tarleton's library. He has some original Greek texts—"

"Cassandra," Lydia and Honore protested together.

Cassandra pursed her lips. "I wouldn't want to go to this ball otherwise."

"You're hopeless." Honore shook her head.

"What's hopeless is this crush." Lydia glanced out the window at the line of vehicles disgorging passengers in front of the Tarleton townhouse in Grosvenor Square, and leaned back to rest for the long wait before their turn came.

"Do you plan to dance?" Honore asked.

"Me? No." Lydia didn't open her eyes. "I plan to slip about the sidelines with the matrons, chaperones, and young ladies without partners."

"But you're so pretty." Honore sounded dismayed. "Someone will wish to dance with you."

Christien's face flashed before Lydia's closed lids. She blinked it away. He couldn't dance with his arm not quite healed. And she doubted he would be there.

But of course he would. What better opportunity to work on ferreting out a troublemaker than at a ball with all the guests masked until midnight? Could she—should she—help him?

No, absolutely not. She was out of it. She'd done her duty by her country, however her country had compelled her to help.

The carriage rolled forward, stopped. A footman opened the door and let down the steps. Lydia followed her sisters inside the house and up the steps to greet the host and hostess dressed like King William III and Queen Mary II, an apt choice since Lord Tarleton stood shorter than his wife. More queens, kings, Roman emperors, and characters out of mythology surrounded them, with a few shepherds and goose girls scattered amongst them. One gentleman lurking near the ballroom door wore the sober garb of a solicitor, which made Honore exclaim in disgust and Lydia laugh. Then she realized Cassandra had already vanished, and sobered.

"She was serious about the library," she whispered to Honore.

Honore nodded. "She—ah, my first beau of the evening."

A tall, slender gentleman, wearing the powdered wig and satin breeches of half a century earlier, bowed before Honore. "May I have this dance, fair lady?" He led her into the ballroom ablaze with chandeliers, noisy with the small orchestra and loud voices, and redolent of perfume, pomade, and a few bodies that could have stood a wash.

"Madame, you are without escort?" A hand touched her arm, bare from her costume.

Lydia jumped and turned to find the solicitor beside her, his features indistinct behind his black silk mask, but his voice oddly familiar.

"I am the escort, sir." She smiled beneath her mask. "For my family."

"Ah, but that is no fun for you. Would you enjoy a dance?"

Lydia glanced at the crowded ballroom and shook her head. "I would enjoy a glass of lemonade and a chair."

"I think you are too young for that, but I can oblige. Wait here." He vanished into the throng.

Lydia stared after him. Was the man an apparition? One moment he'd been at her side, too close, and the next she couldn't find him amongst the other guests. He'd simply melted into the crowd—

Like a certain man had melted into the blackness of a Portsmouth garden.

The ballroom turned cold. At the same time, she couldn't catch her breath. The solicitor who could vanish amongst people as easily as he had vanished amongst the shrubbery of a Portsmouth garden, who had disappeared without showing his face after admiring her paintings, was the man who had called himself Mr. Lang.

Instinct told her to leave, to gather her sisters and disappear from the ball. A few calming breaths later steadied her into thinking better of running, though running was easier. Always easier. She could talk to him, quiz him, try to learn why he resorted to blackmail when Christien thought she would have been willing to help voluntarily.

She gripped her hands together, wishing her costume allowed for gloves to hide her sweating palms. Perhaps he wouldn't return.

He returned bearing two glasses of pale yellow liquid. A footman followed, carrying a gilded chair.

"Sit, Madame Hera," he commanded.

Lydia sat, a relief to her wobbly knees.

He handed her one of the glasses. "This will refresh you."

She thanked him and sipped. The lemonade tasted bitter, as though the Tarleton kitchen had skimped on sugar. But it was cold.

"You are enjoying the Season, madame?" the man asked.

"As much as a country woman can. I miss fresh air." Lydia held the glass to her lips without drinking. "Like gardens."

Not so much as a ripple in his drink gave away whether or not she had startled him. He merely nodded. "Perhaps you may return to the country soon. Or does business keep you in town?"

"Sisters to find husbands."

"And nothing else?"

"Nothing."

Nothing that should give her cause to see Christien's face again.

She sipped more of the lemonade. "And you, sir?"

"I am in the country as little as possible."

"You move from city to city, perhaps?" She sipped to wet her dry lips. "Like London to Portsmouth?"

"Indeed." He pressed his hand on her shoulder. "You understand me well."

"I've done what you asked." She started to rise.

His hand on her shoulder held her in place. Without creating a scene in the boisterous crowd, she couldn't break away.

"Not quite yet, madame." The pressure of his hand increased just a little. "You have neglected Mr. Barnaby."

"I haven't seen him about."

"That's the difficulty. I insist he be invited into your circle of friends." Something shimmered at the corner of her vision. She turned her head in time to see him slipping her bracelet into his pocket.

The message was clear—and more. This man was not Christien's Mr. Lang, who had never had the bracelet, and George Barnaby was not on the side of England. In no way would the Home Office blackmail her into helping, then renew the threat when their man failed to get the proper entrée into Society. She should have known that from the beginning, followed her instinct to trust Christien without question.

She shook the man's hand off her shoulder and rose. She stood half a head taller than he and stepped close to him to emphasize that fact. "Why does England need to blackmail its subjects into helping with the war, sirrah?"

"Would you have helped otherwise?" He maintained his cool, indifferent tone.

"Yes." The word spoken with more certainty than she felt, she spun on her heel and rushed away from him so fast she bumped her glass against a pillar. Its sticky contents splashed over her hand and over the silk flowers wound around the post to make it look like a trellis of roses. As soon as she found a place, she set the glass down and wiped her hand on a serviette, then fled the ballroom.

A mistake. She never should have run. She should have gone along with his intimidation, let him think she would do what she must. Through running off, she'd given herself away. A mistake.

Running was always a mistake. It was the only recourse for eluding the coil into which she'd gotten herself. But she wasn't prepared to engage in espionage, not even as an auxiliary to the real participants.

Stomach knotted, head spinning, she searched for and located a door leading to a miniscule balcony. Cool night air washed over her, clearing her head, calming her pulse. Below, the Tarletons' garden smelled of lilacs—sweet, pure, the promise of spring, a harbinger of summer beyond. She leaned on the balustrade to take in the sweet, spicy aroma—

And someone grabbed her legs, began to lift.

She shrieked. Her fingers scrabbled at the stone railing. No handhold. No way to stop. Her scream blended with the tumult inside the ballroom. She tried to kick. Strength poured from her assailant's hands into her ankles, lifting up and up until she flipped over the balustrade and tumbled toward the garden below.

17

The scream brought Christien running from library to garden. A blur of white shot past him from the overhanging balcony. He lunged to grab it, caught only white silk. The grate of tearing fabric ripped the night, then the crunch of breaking limbs and thud of something striking the earth.

Not something—someone.

He rushed outside, dropped to his knees beside the crushed lilac bushes, and reached for the wearer of the white silk costume. He touched an arm, silky black hair, a mask torn half off. "Madame, *vous tges*—" He took a deep breath of the air smelling of crushed flowers and grass and a honey-citrus scent. "Lydia—I mean, Lady Gale?"

No answer. Wrong woman? Others could wear that unusual fragrance. Or—

He ran his fingers along a smooth neck, found a pulse, breathed a sigh of relief. It beat strongly under the skin, fast and a little erratically, but a true sign of life. But she could suffer from many injuries after a fall like that—broken limbs, ribs tearing into vital organs, a crushed skull.

His own heart pounding out of his chest, he began to run his hands along her arms, up to her shoulders, into her mass of dark hair in search of breaks, blood, lumps. He must fetch a physician to examine the rest. He didn't want to leave her. A shout would bring someone from the library. Cassandra must still be in there, hiding behind the curtains with a thick Greek text.

"I'm going to call for help." Slowly, he began to remove his hands from her hair.

"No." Little more than a whisper, the touch a mere brush of fingers on his sleeve. "All . . . right."

"You need a physician."

"No. Please." Her grip grew stronger. "Winded."

"Something could be broken."

"Only the bush." A sound like a breathless laugh escaped her lips.

"*Vraiment*, madame?"

"*Vraiment*, monsieur." She raised her hand to his cheek, her touch light and cool, burning him like flame. "Please, help me up."

"Of course, if you're certain." He slipped one arm behind her shoulders. Still cradling her head in his other hand, he eased her to a sitting position. "Shall I find your sisters?"

"In a moment. I need to collect myself."

"Collect yourself? Madame Gale, you just fell off a balcony."

"No, monsieur, I didn't fall. I was pushed."

Christien caught his breath, waited for her to say more.

"My Mr. Lang is at this masquerade—" She broke off and ducked her head.

He cupped her chin in his hands and nudged her face up, then his nostrils flared. "Pardon me, madame, but have you been drinking gin?"

"What?" She sounded normal now, her breath restored along

with her strength, and she pushed him away. "I don't even know what gin tastes like, let alone drink it. How dare you accuse me. I say I was pushed, and you accuse me of drinking."

"I am sorry." His face burned in the darkness. "But I know the scent. Could someone have given it to you without you knowing?"

"I drank only lemon—is gin kind of bitter?"

"What will you think of me if I say yes?"

"More than I did not so long ago." She shifted, groaned. "No breaks. Lots of bruises. Will you help me stand?"

"*Oui*, but I fear your costume is ruined." He gathered her hands in his and rose, drawing her with him.

"Better my costume than my person, which was someone's intent." She gripped his forearms. "Or do you simply think I'm making up a tale because I've been drinking?"

"I believe someone could have played a May game with you and tried to get you to drink lemonade with spirits in it. But surely you'd notice. And who?"

"It was Mr. Lang. He even had my bracelet to remind me to cooperate. As for why . . ." She took a deep breath and winced.

"You are injured."

"I have bruising, but it's not important. Why I fell is."

"He thought to have people think you'd been drinking to give reason for your fall, *n'est-ce pas?*"

"Yes, I believe it is so. I implied I was weary of helping and—" Her voice shook. Her hands shook.

Christien drew her close to him, tucked her head against his shoulder, and stroked her hair. He murmured nonsense in French, so much softer and more soothing than English. He rested his cheek atop her head and, with great willpower, managed not to turn his face and brush his lips against the glossy curls. She needed comfort, not advances.

191

She acted like she trusted him.

He embraced her until her trembling ceased, then held her at arm's length and peered into her face, nothing more than a pale blur in the dark garden. "We must talk about this more, but I think you should go home now, take a bit of laudanum, and rest."

"My sisters. I must find them."

"You cannot go back to the ballroom, my lady. Your gown—"

She let out a little shriek of horror.

"Here." He enveloped her in his voluminous domino. "Come into the library. Miss Bainbridge was hiding there earlier."

He led Lydia into the house and a room not open for guests, as the garden was not. But Miss Cassandra Bainbridge still skulked on her window seat, as though a woman screaming in the garden meant nothing to her. She didn't even look up at their arrival.

No wonder Whittaker grew frustrated with her.

"Cassandra, we're leaving." Lydia's tone was sharp, showing no trace of her quiet hysterics of moments earlier.

Cassandra glanced up. "Lydia, what happened to you? Why are you wearing Monsieur de Meuse's domino?"

"I had an accident with my gown."

"Indeed?" Cassandra's eyes narrowed.

"Yes, an accident," Lydia snapped. "Now, go find Honore."

"I shall find her," Christien said. "She is more likely to come if I say so. You ladies remain here. I will have your carriage brought around to the mews." Christien slipped away.

Behind him the door latch clicked. Good. No one would disturb them. He should have told them to lock the windows too. Whoever had pushed Lydia—

She'd been pushed off a balcony!

Christien tamped down his own desire to shake at what could have happened to Lydia and pressed through the crowd that grew denser the closer to the ballroom he drew. He would think about the mishap later. He would wait and get more information from Lydia. He must find Honore.

He had spotted her earlier with her charming crown of laurel leaves, and found her again. The gentleman with whom she shared a glass of something that looked suspiciously like Madeira wore a domino and mask, but Christien never doubted for a moment he was Gerald Frobisher. And the youth held Honore close with an arm around her waist. A good tableau to end.

"Miss Honore," Christien clipped out, "your sisters need you immediately. Come with me."

"But I—"

"You can't drag her away, whoever you are," Frobisher protested.

"I can and I shall." Christien grasped Honore's elbow in a firm though gentle grip and turned her toward the library. "Do not make a scene, Miss Honore. Your sister has had an accident."

"Don't tell me that Cassandra fell down steps again."

"No, Lady Gale."

That got Honore moving, firing questions at him he didn't feel free to answer. Let Lydia tell her sisters whatever story she liked.

Once the sisters were united in the library, Christien slipped out through the miniscule garden to the mews and sent a stable hand around to fetch the Bainbridge carriage. As he stood in the French window awaiting the vehicle's arrival, Lydia slipped up beside him, now smelling of lilacs along with her own scent.

"I think our culprit is George Barnaby," she murmured.

"Why?"

"I cannot say here. Call on me tomorrow."

But when he called on her the following day, the butler informed him that Lady Gale was indisposed. "She said she will send for you when she is well."

But she did not. For another week, Christien waited for messages from her. He waited for messages from his sister. He sought out Miss Honore at balls. That young minx acted as though she neither knew nor wanted to know him and gave him the cut direct with her pert little nose in the air. When he saw her riding in the park with Gerald Frobisher again, Christien suspected why.

Not wanting to intrude upon Lydia if she were truly indisposed, and concerned about his sister's silence, Christien finally made an appearance at the Bainbridge back door, wearing the plain garb of a tradesman.

"I need to see the cook," he announced to the tiny scullion who opened the portal.

"Are you the tea merchant?" the lad asked, his green eyes twinkling. "If so, she's likely to take her biggest skillet to your skull for delivering bohea day before yesterday."

"My reasons are my own, young man." Christien tried to be stern, though the corners of his mouth twitched.

"Yes sir, guv. It's your head at stake." The lad nipped inside.

A volume of French spilled from the half-open door like peppercorns from a broken chest: She didn't need to talk to a merchant. She was too preoccupied to talk to a merchant. How could she prepare the special broth for Madame if the oh-so-inconsiderate tradesman thought he could interrupt her day?

Christien pushed the door the rest of the way open and stood on the threshold.

"And now you bring in the damp and cold that will make my soufflé—ah." She stopped speaking, and her cheeks paled. "I will speak to you then."

The kitchen staff, standing as far from her as they could, gave Christien looks of awe.

He smiled, bowed, and ushered the cook up the areaway steps.

"You missed our rendezvous," he began in French. "You know our agreement. If you don't report to me regularly, I will make you go home and keep you locked up there until I find a man fool enough to marry you."

"I am so sorry, *mon frère*, but I have been inundated with the work. Madame is ill—"

"Lydia—that is, Lady Gale?"

"No." Lisette tilted her head sideways, and a little smile curved her lips. "It is Madame Bainbridge. But it is *tres interessant* that you would think of Lady Gale first."

"Only that she hasn't been about of late." Christien shoved his hands into his coat pockets. "And neither have you."

"Madame Bainbridge had a relapse of her lung fever, and I am kept on my little toes preparing invalid fare to tempt her appetite. I tell you, Christien, I have not avoided you on purpose."

"You should have gotten a message to me to let me know."

"Why? They are all safe."

"Except for Miss Honore riding out with Gerald Frobisher."

"That one." Lisette swept her arm out as though throwing something disgusting away. "There is no stopping her when Madame Gale is busy with her maman and preparing this ball and painting and . . . She scarcely sleeps, and keeping after that youngest one to behave herself properly is *tres impossible*."

"You should have told me, gotten me a message. I'd have—"

What could he have done? Call on her when she made it clear that she wanted nothing to do with him? He couldn't even use the excuse that he needed her help with entrée into Society. His desk overflowed with invitations.

"And how was I to do this? Send a footman to your rooms?" Lisette wrinkled her nose. "A fine kettle of fish that would have me stewing in, the cook sending the *billet dou*, the love letters to a gentleman, or so it would appear. I could not—"

Above them, a window slammed.

"Now that does it." Lisette planted her hands on her non-existent hips. "We have disturbed someone in the family, and I will likely be dismissed without a reference for conducting an alliance with a man when I am to be working."

"Nothing would make me happier. In fact, I'm sending you back—"

Running feet clicked around the corner of the house. Lisette's eyes widened.

Christien swung around. "My lady."

"Monsieur de Meuse, do tell me where you plan to send my cook," demanded Lady Lydia Gale.

Her words sounded calm to her ears despite tremors racing through her body and a bit of shortness of breath from her headlong dash down the steps to catch Christien with her cook.

With her cook!

"I think it is time for me to go back to my kettles, *n'est-ce pas?*" The diminutive chef darted toward the area steps.

Lydia caught hold of her arm. "Not so quickly. Why are you discussing me and my family with this man?"

The young woman's gaze shot to Christien. *Do not*, she mouthed.

"I asked her to inform me if all was not well with you." Christien smiled at Lydia.

She blinked and her toes curled. Her mind raced. "Why would

my cook do this for you, a stranger?" She narrowed her eyes. "Unless it has something to do with—"

"It has something to do with her being my sister."

"Oh, you *bête*," the girl cried. "How could you? Now I am ruined, finished, an exile."

"And I am struck dumb." Lydia glanced from Christien to the cook and back to Christien.

She saw little resemblance. The girl was petite and dark. Although Christien's hair and complexion ran on the dark side, his blue eyes gave the impression of lightness, of sunshine and warmth. The cook was more like a banked fire smoldering on a hearth and awaiting the merest prod of the poker to fan it into flames.

From the way her tiny fists clenched, the flames had ignited.

"I think," Christien said, "we should retire to a more private venue. We're attracting attention, and my lady is not dressed for the street."

Lydia caught her breath and stared down at the paint-smeared smock she wore over her oldest gown. Swaths of dark hair fell on either side of her face, one strand bearing a streak of periwinkle blue paint. Perhaps, if God really did pay attention to her, the paving stones would part and swallow her up into the tunnels and streams beneath London before anyone noticed who she was.

But God wasn't paying attention to her that day any more than He did any other. The pavement remained firm. Traffic continued through the square, and sunlight burst through the clouds, depicting her flaws in even brighter light.

She started to cover her face with her hands.

"Have a care." Christien grasped her wrists and held her hands away from her. Paint daubed her fingers too.

"Oh, my lady, I am so sorry." The cook—Christien's sister

indeed?—grasped Lydia's elbow. "We shall descend to my room and be private. You would like some tea? And *café au lait* for you, Christien?"

If they weren't related, the cook was unforgivably familiar with a gentleman.

"Let us." Still grasping Lydia's wrist, Christien headed down the areaway steps.

She didn't protest. Going to the cook's room was preferable to standing on the pavement for the passing world to see her in her painting smock and tumbled hair she thought she'd pinned up that morning. Either all the pins had come out or she had removed them as she worked. She didn't recall. If asked at that moment, she couldn't tell anyone the day of the week.

She'd thought she was dreaming when she heard Christien's voice below her window, especially paired with that of the cook. Surely he would have no reason to speak to one of her servants. Yet his voice drifted to her like a rising tide of caramel—smooth and rich. And her name drifted right along with it.

She needed to confront him, to learn his business with the cook, but for him to see her in such disarray pushed her life beyond the pale.

"I need a basin first," she said. "Strong soap and lots of water."

"We have that in the kitchen, but of course." The cook ran ahead and began issuing orders for water, soap, towels.

Lydia glanced up at Christien. She fully intended to demand an explanation then and there.

"You're not wearing your sling now," she said.

"A good disguise not to wear it." He touched his injured shoulder. "It pains me little most of the time. I can even drive with one hand." One of his fingers caressed the inside of her wrist. "Your absence has been felt. Your maman is well now, I trust?"

"My mother has never been truly ill." Lydia snapped her teeth together, but the damage was done. Sea-blue eyes, smooth, arching eyebrows, and that gentle hand on her arm compelled her to continue. "She's so embarrassed about Cassandra calling off the wedding, then me taking a tumble at the ball—the best explanation I could give for my bruises—she can't face the world. Father has convinced her she's a failure as a wife and mother—but this is none of your concern."

"Of course it is." He removed his hand from her wrist and laid his palm against her cheek, turning her face fully toward his. "Everything about you concerns me, *ma chère*. It has since I met you in the prison, but especially since you gave me your bracelet."

"That bracelet was always intended for you, was it not?"

"No." His hand lay warm and gentle against her cheek, and she suddenly found breathing difficult. "The bracelet was intended for you. Charles was given it by a Spanish woman—ah, here is Lisette."

But Lisette—presumably the cook's Christian name—wasn't there. Christien had changed his mind about telling her more about a Spanish woman who gave away expensive jewelry. Lydia's brain teemed with the possibilities—an informant, a camp follower of the lower sort, one of the highborn sort, one Charles had rescued . . .

A reason why he had never even tried to come home.

"Who was this Spanish woman?" Lydia demanded.

Christien dropped his hand to hers, pressed her fingers, then gestured her forward without saying a word. The cook was coming now, beckoning them down to the back door and her rooms tucked behind the kitchen hearth—a sitting room and bedchamber not much larger than Lydia's dressing room. But the kitchen fire lent the chambers warmth, and bright chintz cushions made the small sofa and chairs comfortable.

"First the washing." Lisette led Lydia into her bedchamber, where she found warm water and soap so she could scrub paint off her hands.

"Why did you deceive us about who you are?" Lydia asked.

Lisette shrugged. "I wanted an adventure." She had lost her French accent and spoke with tones as British as Lydia's own. "My brother has spent ten years sneaking about the continent or pretending to be in the French Army, and I have been stranded in Shropshire with nothing to do but learn to cook because I am no good at sewing or reading."

"So you slipped off to London." Lydia cocked her head to one side and tried not to smile. "And acquired a French accent, I see."

"Well, yes." Lisette giggled. "I was only three years old when we came to England. And with maman being American and my governesses being English, I learned to speak the language well, unlike that brother of mine. He will never be English, however much he serves the king."

"That will do, Lisette," Christien called from the sitting room.

"*Oui*, monsieur. *Tout de suite*, monsieur." Lisette dropped a curtsy and scampered from the room.

"Minx." His glance, his tone reflected affection. "Ah, but she has managed me since she was born."

"Which is why you allowed her to stay here and didn't inform us that our chef is an impostor?" Lydia stood in the bedchamber doorway, finding Christien too close at his window post.

"I allowed her to stay here," he responded, "because I wanted to ensure nothing went wrong in your household that I did not know about. Though she has failed me."

"Why would you do that?"

"You tell me you get pushed off a balcony after someone tried serving you spirits, and you ask me why I would do that?" He made no apparent attempt to mask his impatience.

Lydia bowed her head in acknowledgment. "I should have told you I'm all right. I've been so preoccupied with my painting, as I've found a shop that will sell small ones, and with Mama being in her state of illness and Cassandra moping about, not to mention Honore's ball."

"Regarding Miss Honore . . ." Christien said.

"What about Honore?" Lydia demanded. Her hands shook.

"I saw her riding in the park with Gerald Frobisher. She was wearing a mask, but—"

For the first time since Charles had returned to his regiment, Lydia burst into tears.

18

Christien took the only option he saw open to him—he closed the short distance between them and slipped his arm around her. "There, there, *ma chère*. You're not alone. I'm here to help you. Ah, *mon pauvre, ma belle, mon amour*." And so he crooned while Lydia turned her face into his shoulder, hiccuped and sobbed, wiped her eyes on a sodden handkerchief, and tried to speak.

Sometime after the first few minutes, Lisette stepped into the chamber, then out again, closing the door. It wasn't the proper thing for her to do, but it was the right thing—leave Lydia to privately weep out everything that burdened her heart.

"I'm sorry. I'm so sorry." Those were the first coherent words Lydia spoke. She tried to pull away.

"No, don't." Christien stroked her loosened hair. "Let me be a friend to you, Lydia Gale, as I was to your husband." He took a deep breath. "And more. So much more."

"I can't." A shudder ran from her to him.

"You have to trust someone, Lydia." He pressed his advantage. "It may as well be me, the man whose life you saved, the man you helped."

"And I've had nothing but trouble since. That is—" She raised her head to show him eyes red-rimmed and awash in tears. "I've been hiding away because someone tried to kill me. Or at the least scare me badly. Why?"

"Because you have chosen to be friendly with me, I think."

She nodded.

"So you hid from me too."

"You spied on me."

"Only my sister. I left her here to watch over you, even though I should have sent her packing home with a flea in her ear and a dragon to guard her."

"And I'd have had more work and trouble trying to find another chef half as good."

"That too." He offered a smile. "We perhaps kept things as they are for that reason."

"I think I'd just pack up and run back to Tavistock if she left. I'm trying to make everything perfect for my family, please Father, get the girls married or at least engaged, keep the household orderly and Mama free of worry, and it's all gone wrong. It's just like—" She jerked away from him. "When did you plan on telling me about Frobisher and Honore?"

"As soon as I found you." He gazed at her, his chest aching. "I didn't know if I should call on you, and you were nowhere around town."

"Of course you should have called. I never said—" She gave him a wobbly smile. "I suppose I have given you the impression you aren't welcome here. I'm sorry. I think I've been wrong. I know I've been wrong. I know I've needed to take a risk." She rubbed her hands over her damp and blotchy cheeks. "Tell me about Frobisher, please."

Christien rose and stood before her, his hands shoved into his pockets to stop himself from reaching for her again. "I've been searching for Mr. Barnaby. He seems to have vanished from London. I hadn't seen Frobisher either but thought he might be riding in the park, so I went out there to find him."

"Surely you aren't riding with your arm not quite healed." The concern on her face warmed his heart.

"No, driving." He moved his hands to clasp them behind his back. "And I found him riding with a young woman in a mask. I recognized the mare."

"What is she thinking? What are the Tarletons thinking?" Lydia speared her fingers into her hair, and the mass of it tumbled around her shoulders. She gasped and let out a little moan. "What will go wrong next? No, no, don't say it." She held up her hand. "I can drive straight over to the Tarletons' and confront her."

"Or you could drive out with me tomorrow morning and catch her in the act."

She compressed her lips, and the corners of her eyes pinched. Then she nodded and her face relaxed. "Thank you. I don't know why you'd do this for me, but I'm grateful."

"I want to be your friend, my lady." He let himself touch her then, rest his palm against her cheek. "I'll say this until you believe me. I want to help you get through this time, as you helped me. I want—"

More than he would tell her then.

"I will call on you at seven o'clock," he concluded.

"That early? The wretched little hoyden. Why does she want to ruin herself?"

"I think little sisters are—in French we have the expression *infant terrible*."

Lydia laughed. It sounded hoarse, a bit like a rusty hinge. Nonetheless it was an unmistakable chuckle. Her whole face, tearstained and puffy around the eyes as it was, lit up for a moment. The entire subterranean room grew brighter. "So they are." She sobered. "What respectable man would encourage a young lady to ride out with him that early and unchaperoned?"

"That answer, *ma chère*, is simple—he wouldn't. Considering he arrived with Mr. Barnaby, I can only suspect he is up to no good where Honore is concerned."

Lydia caught her breath. "Of course. More blackmail against the family."

Because she could manage it without looking in the mirror, Lydia braided her hair and pinned the plait in a swirl atop her head. Rather than awaken Barbara to help her and be asked questions, she waylaid one of the chambermaids to button up the back of her deep rose carriage dress. Then, half boots in hand, she slipped down the steps.

And came face-to-face with Father.

"Where are you sneaking off to?" he demanded.

"Not sneaking off, sir, just ensuring I don't awaken Mama."

"Which doesn't answer my question."

"No, sir." Lydia dropped onto the next-to-last step and pulled on the ankle-high boots. "I'm taking an early drive with Monsieur de Meuse."

"Indeed. I thought you frightened him off like you do all men."

"Like I what?" Lydia shot to her feet, one booted, the other stockinged. She glared down at her father, half a head shorter than she from her elevated position. "What are you saying?"

"Seven years ago, you had a husband who stayed home for a week before leaving forever. When I arrived this Season, you had two suitors, now you have none. I expect no man wants to be around a female who smells like turpentine."

"And no woman wants to be around a man who—you know I'm painting?"

"Of course I do. I expect you think you'll support Cassandra and yourself with it." He curled his upper lip.

"I'd like to try."

"You have other things that need doing, like getting yourselves married off."

Only if she could find men who weren't like him.

But he cared about them. She must remember that. He wanted them married for their own security and comfort, their standing in Society, and, as he thought, their fulfillment as females.

"Will you approve of us if we wed, sir?" she asked in a small voice.

"What a ridiculous question. Approval has nothing to do with it." Turning his back on her, he snatched his hat from a stone-faced footman and marched to the door.

Another footman opened the portal, and he headed out to his waiting carriage. As he pulled away, an open vehicle drew up at the foot of the front steps. With a shriek of horror that she still held one boot in her hand, Lydia dropped onto the steps and began to buckle the footgear. Straps flew out of her fingers. A buckle slipped out of her hand and bounced to the entryway floor.

Christien entered the house in time to retrieve the silver clasp. "May I?"

Not waiting for permission, he knelt before her and slipped the straps through the rings of the buckle and pulled. He bent over his work, his hair falling across his brow in a blue-black wave, his fingers deft and swift and too close to her ankle.

"It's not proper," she whispered.

"Of course it is." He smiled up at her. "Do not the gentlemen help you on and off with your patens in the winter?"

"Yes, but—"

None of the handful of those gentlemen, who had assisted her in removing the shoes with their iron rings on the bottom from over her delicate slippers, left her feeling light-headed. She couldn't remember her husband performing such a duty and having any kind of effect on her because, by winter, he had no longer been around.

"It is but a moment," Christien assured her. He slipped the second buckle onto the straps, tightened it. "*Voilà*. Are you ready for our drive?"

"I am. And if I find—" She glanced at the footmen and clamped her mouth shut. If the servants learned what Honore was doing, she might as well announce it in the *Times*.

Christien held out his hands. "Let us go then."

She placed her hands in his and allowed him to lift her from the steps, then lead her out to his open carriage. A youth held the horses' heads. Once Lydia settled on the seat and Christien sat beside her, the reins in his uninjured hand, the young man let the horses go. Christien tossed him a sixpence. The lad bit it, then grinned and ran off across the square.

Lydia pulled on a loo mask and tucked her feet under the seat. Her heels connected with a wicker basket. She jerked them forward again. "Do you always carry provisions with you, monsieur?"

"It's waiting to be filled with provisions, my lady. Did you rest well?"

"Surprisingly, yes. And you?"

"Not long enough. I'm afraid my work leads me into some places and situations that require late nights and too much smoke."

"And you've gotten nowhere?"

"Other than your man at the masquerade, no. I can't find Barnaby anywhere."

"I'm supposed to help him. Apparently his entrée into Society hasn't been as grand as yours."

"But you've done nothing?"

"I can't perform a task without the man."

"But you told the man at the ball you wouldn't help."

"Foolishly, yes." Lydia shuddered. "And next thing I knew, I was tumbling into the shrubbery. What were you doing in the library?"

"Asking Miss Bainbridge where I might find you."

"Oh. I thought perhaps you were seeking information."

Christien sighed loudly enough to be heard over the rumble of the drays that trundled into London in the early morning to deliver goods to the markets and shops. "Yes, being a spy often leads one into suspecting everyone and sneaking about to investigate their personal domains. I think it is not *comme il faut*."

"Not the right thing, no, but does the end justify the means?"

"I never considered that until I saw you get hauled into this and in danger." He half turned toward her. "Will you leave London?"

"I cannot. Father wants us all married off, and finding husbands in Devonshire is not that easy."

"Alas." He slowed for the entrance to the park. "I saw Miss Honore here on Rotten Row."

That early in the morning, only a handful of serious riders populated the road, along with grooms exercising horses little used in town. A scan of the crowd in front of them showed no female in or out of a mask. The absence didn't ease Lydia's mind. If she didn't find Honore today, she would have to bring her home and watch over her.

Lydia tensed. She gripped the edge of the seat for fear she would simply rise off the cushion like one of Cassandra's hot air balloons if one more difficulty plowed into her life.

"There they are." Christien spoke softly.

Lydia jumped. "Where?"

"A hundred yards ahead, coming toward us."

Lydia squinted into the misty morning light. Yes, she saw them now, the mare, the blue habit, the mask. "I'm going to lock her to her bedpost," she ground between her teeth.

"She can join my sister." Though his mouth was grim, his eyes twinkled.

Some of the tension drained from Lydia. She faced a problem in Honore, but not alone for once.

The pair drew near, moving slowly. They leaned toward one another, talking, laughing, hands touching across the space between their mounts. Others glanced at them with indulgent smiles or disapproving frowns. No one appeared to recognize Honore. As the couple on horseback and the couple in the curricle came within a dozen feet, the former glanced up. Their mouths opened, then, as one, they kicked their horses, spun, and galloped in the direction from which they'd come.

"After them!" Lydia cried.

Unnecessarily. Christien had already snapped the reins over the backs of his team, sending them thundering after the fleeing pair.

Lydia gripped the seat. "What purpose does she think she'll serve in running?"

Around them, other riders darted out of the way or joined the chase, their laughter floating back to the open carriage. The lane turned. The curricle tilted onto its right wheel. Lydia's shoulder bumped against Christien's, then pressed against it.

She ducked her head. If someone recognized her, they would guess at Honore's identity.

Honore and Frobisher gained ground, getting too near the park gate and streets, where horsemen could weave in and out of traffic, but where a carriage, however light, could not.

A sob rose in her throat. "It's futile."

"We'll catch them at the house where she's staying," Christien said.

"As long as they go there."

He glanced at her. "Why would you think they wouldn't? Where else would they go?"

"Nowhere. That is—" Lydia shivered. "I think I should pray."

"Good, if God listens to you."

"I'm not sure He does these days."

Or any of the past seven years' worth of days.

Don't let him leave, she'd prayed.

And Charles had gone, not just for a time, but forever, with the harsh word of her last letter in his head.

She mustn't fail Honore.

At that moment, she thought she might be able to outrun the horses. Energy coursed through her, and her body strained forward, shouting, urging, not laughing like most everyone else.

Beside her, Christien sat with his mouth grim and his hand tight on the reins. He guided the flying team around a gaggle of staring grooms leading children's ponies, slowing him down. But ahead, grooms on fine, swift horses sped after the racing pair, flanked them, pulled ahead.

Lydia sat straighter, staring. "They've got them."

"By the grace of God they do." Christien's hold on the reins relaxed. The horses slowed so that they drove up to the surrounded pair with dignity.

"Stay up here so no one recognizes you. The mask doesn't seem to do that well." Christien leaped to the ground.

An urchin sprang from the very ground, or so it seemed, and grasped the reins.

"What do you think you're doing?" Honore cried.

"*Fermez la bouche.*" Christien directed Honore to keep her mouth shut. "She may listen to you, but I won't, you French spy," Frobisher shouted.

The laughter of moments earlier died. Silence reigned. Several pairs of eyes landed on Christien.

"It's true," Honore said. "I heard him talking to someone at a ball last week. They want to add England to Napoleon's empire by—"

"Quiet." Lydia employed the rough, deep tone she'd employed when Honore was a child who would never cease her chatter, regardless of the consequences to others.

At that moment, the harm pointed toward Christien. The faces, whether belonging to young Corinthian athletes of the haut ton or to grooms, registered hostility. A wave of muttering began.

Lydia glanced from man to man, to Frobisher's grinning countenance. A chill raced through her. If she spoke further, she would give herself away. Father's fury would know no bounds if he learned of this escapade. And he would learn of it.

But Christien had saved her on more than one occasion, and if he was an honest man . . .

She looked at his still and calm face and knew he was honest. Every word he'd told her was true.

Heart racing, she leaped from the carriage and slipped her arm through his.

19

Honore stared at her sister. "You're taking the part of a French-man?"

"I am." Lydia set her face. "If you get into the carriage, I won't tell Father of this little escapade."

"And I'll tell him you took the part of a Frenchman over good Englishmen." Honore tossed her head.

"Go ahead. Those good Englishmen were ready to assault a good man." Lydia gave Honore a gentle push forward. "Now go. Father will likely send you back to Devonshire and find you a husband if he hears of your behavior."

Boot heels dragging through the gravel, Honore headed for the curricle.

Lydia followed, grinding her teeth, while the other riders called out suggestions on what to do with the recalcitrant chit, then disbanded.

The curricle wasn't made for three people but boasted a seat in back for a groom. Lydia hauled herself into this ignominious perch and grasped Honore's shoulder as though expecting her to vanish off the moving vehicle.

"Take us home, monsieur, please," Lydia said.

"I want to go back to the Tarletons'." Honore pouted now.

"There's an excursion to Vauxhall tonight. You won't take me. You despise fireworks."

"I'll take you." Lydia glanced at the Frenchman. "*Merci bien.* You've been more than kind."

"I think it is quite the opposite." The smile he bestowed on Lydia sent butterflies fluttering in her middle. "You stood beside me against those Englishmen."

"He didn't need protecting." Honore's lower lip protruded in a childish sulk. "That sort of thing only happens in France."

"It's happening in the north right now." Lydia didn't hide the bite from her words. The curricle jostled over a broken cobblestone in the Mayfair street, and she grabbed for a better hold. "And what he means is that, because of your little excursion with Mr. Frobisher and protests against Monsieur de Meuse, those men were ready to do him bodily harm at best, possibly hang him at worst."

She'd chosen to stand by him. That fact was all Christien could think about as they headed back to Cavendish Square—that and the feel of Lydia close behind on the jump seat. The former made his heart sing, the latter made him restless. Restless and determined to suggest, insist—whatever was necessary—that she go along with his plans for the day.

"But Vauxhall tonight—"

"I'll escort you, of course." The gentleness of Lydia's tone warmed Christien.

Like him, she held a tender place in her heart for a wayward sister. Miss Honore had best watch her step or she'd find herself back in the country without a Season.

Thoughts of the day flashing through his head, Christien

drew the curricle up before Number Thirty. "May I escort you ladies to the gardens tonight?"

"We would be better off with a gentleman in tow," Lydia began.

"Mr. Frobisher is a fine escort." Honore scrambled to the ground and hurried inside.

"We will not go with that man." Lydia remained on her perch. "Thank you for your assistance. I do apologize for my countrymen and their behavior this morning. About tonight—" Her cheeks grew pink around her mask. "That is kind of you."

Christien tossed the reins to a waiting youth and climbed down. He looked up at Lydia. "My lady, I have it in mind not to assist you down but to keep you up there and take you for a drive into the country."

"The country? I couldn't. Cassandra, Honore—"

"Will survive a few hours without you." He offered her what he hoped was a persuasive smile. "Now that you've decided to trust me, take another step and trust me in this."

He read the longing on her face and pressed his advantage. "You can bring your painting things along."

"I promised Honore she can go to Vauxhall."

"We'll be back in time. While you gather up what you need, perhaps I can get that minx in the kitchen to prepare a picnic *déjeuner* for us. Bread rolls. Roast chicken? Surely you have some hothouse strawberries."

"I should see to Mama's well-being and details—"

"Will a few hours make a difference?" Christien held up his hands.

Lydia placed hers in them and jumped lightly to the ground. "All right, so I can paint. But not far."

"Only to Richmond. We'll be there in an hour and home in four or five at the most. Promise."

"Well." Lydia glanced around as though seeking guidance. "All right. I think it'll be all right." Then she picked up her skirt and dashed into the house.

Christien took his basket and descended to the kitchen. Lisette emerged at once, snatched the basket away, and returned with the hamper loaded. "You will feed an army with this, I think."

"Thank you." He resisted kissing her on the cheek so as not to shock the other servants. He returned to the curricle, stowed the basket under the seat, then headed up the steps. A footman opened the door with the news that Lady Gale would be with him shortly.

"You may go up to Lady Bainbridge's sitting room if you like."

"Thank you, I'll wait here." Christien couldn't face the lady of the house with the knowledge that he'd deceived her about her cook in order to have a spy in the household. His reasons were good. He wanted to ensure Lydia fared well. But one more deception now lay marking up his copybook.

One deception he did not perpetrate was how he felt about Lydia. The sound of footfalls on the steps drew his attention upward in time to see her rounding the banister, tall and erect in posture, her hair tucked beneath a white straw hat except for that single curl in front of her ear, a leather portfolio tucked beneath her arm. Her steps, though brusque, carried a hitch in them, a momentary pause before she took the next tread. Her lower lip protruded just a hair over the upper one, and a faint line showed between her eyes.

Worry. Uncertainty. Reluctance. All understandable. All something Christien intended to erase from her, if only for a day.

He held out his left hand. "I'll take the portfolio, my lady. It looks heavy."

"I'm used to carrying it, but if you like." She slid the scuffed and scratched leather folder into his hand. It smelled of charcoal and paint and the sweet citrus scent that floated around Lydia.

"Shall we be on our way?" he asked.

"We'll be home before four o'clock, will we not? Honore deigned to speak to me long enough to inform me that Frobisher intends to call for her then, and I want to ensure she doesn't take advantage of my absence to go with him." She glanced at the stone-faced footmen. "If Father isn't here, no one will stop her if I'm not back."

"We'll be back by then." Christien offered her his right arm. The shoulder still ached, but he could manage to escort a lady if she was gentle.

Lydia was gentle. Her fingers barely skimmed the sleeve of his coat. It was enough for now.

In the carriage, Christien took the reins from the street urchin, then headed south. "I thought you might be missing fresh air and some open land for sketching."

"More than anything. I really need to get some different kinds of paintings done to sell. There's a shop that will sell my pictures."

"You're selling your pictures?" Christien risked taking his eyes off the crowded streets long enough to stare at her. "Surely that isn't necessary."

"It is if Cassandra is to come live with me. She's determined to do so. Just keeping her supplied with books will eat away my pension, but how can I say no to her? She's so . . . sad."

"Over her broken engagement? You don't see any way to mend it?"

"Not with Whittaker in the north and Cassandra ready to head west any day I say so."

"And when will you say so, my lady?" He touched her hand with his.

"Not as soon as she'd like. If Honore doesn't secure a match this Season, Father will be angry, and her life at—" She jerked her hand away from his and tucked it beneath her elbow. "I apologize for discussing my family's business with you."

"Please don't. I want to know about your family. That is, I miss mine."

"Then you should stop your games of intrigue and go home."

"I will when I do this last service. But it's not going well. Nowhere do I find even a hint of someone stirring discontent, not amongst the nobles of this country."

"Could the Home Office be wrong?" She shifted on the seat to face him, her hands back in her lap.

Talk of her family distressed her. Talk of spies drew her interest. He would take what he could get for now.

"They've been known to be wrong, but not often. And with Barnaby and Frobisher arriving with letters from Lang too, and the blackmail . . ." He shook his head.

"You're right. It doesn't make sense that they're wrong. If only we knew what the true goal is, I'd be happy going home."

"Would you?" He tried to catch her eye.

She avoided his glance and faced forward again, her posture upright, stiff, until they left the city behind. As London traffic of carriages, hackneys, and drays thinned to farm carts and wagons, Lydia's posture, though properly upright, lost its rigidity. Her face softened. She glanced from houses more widely spaced than in town to the patches of green between, and inhaled deeply when they passed a garden bursting with lilacs in every hue from white to violet.

"I miss the moors." She spoke at last. "London air always smells of smoke and sewage. Do you miss Shropshire, or haven't you been there enough to know?"

"I miss my family, regardless of where they are. But yes, I think I miss the farmlands. And I miss walking. Do you like to walk?"

"For miles." She glanced at him from the corner of her eye, and her lips curved in a half smile. "Shall we climb the hill and see if we can spy out St. Paul's?"

"Yes, I think we should."

Christien unhitched the horses and led them into a meadow of grass, where he tethered them to ground stakes. Then he and Lydia headed deep into the ancient park. Through stands of oaks thick enough to shelter the red deer and hedgerows that would burst with brambleberries in the summer, they made their way up the highest hill in the park. They spoke little except to point out a thrush singing in a tree or the hint of a fawn through budding leaves. Fallen leaves cushioned their feet, quieting their footfalls. The freshness of growing plants scented the air. Sunlight spilled through branches like lemon custard, warm and sweet. Christien's shoulders relaxed even as his legs labored up and up and up, muscles stretching, blood flowing.

Beside him, Lydia kept pace. Color replaced the pallor in her cheeks. More curls escaped from beneath her hat brim, bouncing and bobbing with each step. She looked younger than her six and twenty years, too young to be burdened with the care of her family, with care for herself. She should be able to think of nothing but her painting and her comfort, and perhaps an occasional thought for her husband—

For him?

No, he was being ridiculous. She might like him more than she let on, but her feelings for him ran far from the directions his had taken for her. She didn't have years of letters and talk of him to fuel the connection with the real person, as did he from her husband's sharing of the letters, the pictures, the brief memories of the woman at home pining, raging, yearning for what Charles Gale could never give her—a life where her husband stayed put.

They reached the top of the hill. Puffing slightly, neither spoke for several minutes as they scanned the panorama spread out before them—the Thames River Valley with the river a winding ribbon of silver threaded through green fields and sprawling city, farmland and parkland. And above it all, the spire of St. Paul's Cathedral speared toward heaven.

"Ahhh." Lydia blew out a long, contented sigh, then smiled up at Christien. "Thank you."

"You're welcome." He gazed into her big, dark eyes, soft in the sunlight, then his glance dropped to her lips, parted, half smiling. His mouth went dry. She stood so close he smelled her perfume. The simplest of motions would close the gap.

He jerked away. "Would you like your painting things brought up here?"

"No, another trip up isn't necessary. I can hold this in my head." She tucked her hand into the crook of his elbow. "And I believe I would like that repast awaiting us."

"Nothing like a brisk walk to build up an appetite." Christien felt like running, not strolling, but he made himself maintain an even pace. "I suspect you haven't eaten much lately."

"No, I keep forgetting it's mealtime. There's been so much, and I've failed to look out for Honore . . ." She paused and looked up at him. "Am I being silly to dislike Frobisher so, even if he is friends with Barnaby?"

"No, he isn't actually. Barnaby said they met up at an inn on the way, and Frobisher attached himself to Barnaby. He said he knew Lang too." Christien stopped and faced her fully.

She frowned at him. "Why didn't you tell me?"

"I haven't seen you."

"You should have seen me—no matter about that now. I haven't trusted him either, but I have seen little of him."

"Should we perhaps follow him?"

"We?" Christien shuddered at the idea of Lydia doing anything so potentially dangerous. "Not you."

"But—" She started walking again, gripping his arm harder as they negotiated a patch of rough ground full of stones and protruding tree roots.

"No we," Christien emphasized.

"But, Monsieur de Meuse . . ."

They stepped into a patch of sunlight, and she paused to study his face. She rested her other hand on his left arm. An ache raged inside him so strongly he couldn't look directly at her for fear he would wrap his arms around her and draw her close against him.

Her face alight, she squeezed his arms. "Wouldn't you look less obtrusive following Gerald Frobisher or George Barnaby, or anyone else suspicious, if you were courting a lady?"

"You want me to pretend to court you?"

See her every day? His head felt light.

"Yes, it seems like—" Her hand flew to her mouth, that soft bow that curved upward even in repose. "That's it. That's why Lang compelled me to help you."

"He didn't compel you. But why is it you think he did?"

"To have a lady on your arm makes you less obviously in pursuit of anything but companionship."

"And since I knew your husband, the connection is natural." Christien laughed. "*Tres parfait, n'est-ce pas?*"

"I don't know if it's perfect, but it's logical and practical."

"Just like you—a logical, practical artist." He smiled at her and indulged in a brush of his fingertips across her cheek before he took her hand and headed back to the carriage.

He retrieved her portfolio and sent her off to sketch while he set up the picnic things and made certain the horses were all right. He returned to enjoy the peace of the tableau—Lydia beneath a tree, sunlight streaming between the new leaves, dappling her hat, drawing blue lights from her dark hair, caressing her cheek. The peace. The quiet. The vision of a future he could have if he left his work.

And failed to see his father avenged.

He shook off thoughts of France and its cruelty and unpacked the food.

"My lady." He held his hand out to Lydia. She slipped her fingers into his and rose with fluid grace. "I trust you're hungry. Your cook packed enough food for ten people."

"I believe I can eat enough for ten people. That walk and the fresh air have given me an appetite." She released his hand.

They retreated to their picnic. Silence lay between them as they ate. With trees and hedgerow separating them from the occasional passerby or vehicle on the lane, they'd never been so alone, more free to talk of whatever they liked. Yet words failed Christien. All his planned gambits about his family or places he'd seen on the continent, his experience at Dartmoor Prison or the discomfort of his brief voyage aboard the transport, fled from his brainbox. Unable to look at Lydia, as much as he might have liked to, he gazed at the pale blue sky, the pale green grass, the pale linen cloth, until his body felt so tense he jumped at the raucous cry of a rook. His glass of lemonade flew from his hand and smashed against a nearby tree trunk.

"I am so sorry." Christien leaped up before the sticky liquid reached his breeches. His plate tumbled onto the linen, sending greens, poultry, rolls, and hothouse strawberries skittering toward Lydia.

She let out a squawk not unlike the cry of the rook and jumped up. Her plate remained in her hand, its contents intact, but her lemonade glass toppled, splashing citrus yellow over the mess of food.

"*Quel désastre.*" Christien groaned and covered his face with his hands. "I am so sorry, my lady. I—"

A choking, gasping sound interrupted him. He lowered his hands and stared at Lydia. She stood two yards away, her hands pressed to her mouth, her eyes brimming with laughter.

"I'm sorry to laugh." Her words came out in gasps. "But your face . . . your voice . . . You look so elegant all the time, and you—oh, I must stop, but I haven't laughed in weeks." She wiped her eyes on the sleeve of her pelisse.

Christien closed the distance between them and produced a clean linen handkerchief. "I am glad I am so amusing."

He tried to sound severe. The corners of his mouth twitched. A chuckle rose from his chest with the slowness of a well bucket on a rusty chain, but rise it did until they both laughed over the absurdity of his clumsiness, the silliness of laughing at clumsiness, the pleasure of laughing.

And somewhere in the hilarity, they wound up holding hands. And gazing into one another's eyes.

"Why are you so nervous, monsieur?" Lydia asked in a whisper. "I've never meant you harm."

"No, but—" His face felt hot. "Lady Gale, I haven't been alone with a lady in too many years. Not a lady who isn't a sister."

She laughed, but ruefully this time. "Nor I with a man, except for my husband those brief days after our marriage and a few moments beforehand."

"And he took too little care of his precious gift." Christien gazed into her face, seeking the right words to say. "I know it is unforgivable for me to say this so bluntly, but he shared your letters with me and his—and with others."

Her eyes widened. Her face paled. "Even—even the shrewish ones, the ones that kept him away?" Her voice was barely audible above the sigh of the wind in the overhanging tree branches. "Tell me not those."

"I can't and not lie to you, my lady. But I can add that those letters didn't keep him away."

"Duty to country, I suppose?" Her upper lip curled.

"Mostly, *oui*." He released one of her hands to stroke his thumb along that sneering lip, softening it back to its gentle curve of a natural smile.

Not the mouth of a shrew. The mouth of a kindhearted lady. A mouth to be kissed into openness, into softness, into—

He cleared his throat. "Mostly it was fear. He thought you too perfect to his dying breath."

"Me?" She shook her head. "You must be mistaken."

"I don't like to argue with a lady, but no, I'm not mistaken."

"But I'm so . . . I didn't . . . I accomplished nothing as a wife that I should have. And I'm accomplishing nothing I intended to this Season. Cassandra's wedding plans are a disaster. Honore is sneaking out with a young man we have reason to suspect of sedition. And I haven't sold any of the paintings in the shop yet. Nor have I done anything but cause you trouble."

"You haven't caused me a bit of trouble and have given me great pleasure in your companionship, even when we disagree." He released her other hand and stepped back before he moved closer. "Now that you mention Miss Honore, shall we be on our way so she doesn't think we've abandoned her?"

"Oh, goodness, yes."

"Let me help with this . . . um . . ."

"*Désastre?*"

"*Oui*, I mean, yes."

Again they shared a companionable chuckle. Christien cleaned up the broken glass. Lydia scattered the bits of food over the ground for the birds and other wildlife to scavenge. Everything else went into the basket with the leftover food, and they headed back to the horses and curricle.

In moments, the horses were hitched, the basket and her portfolio stowed, and they headed out along the lane to the main road, where traffic greeted them like a deluge after drought. Three laden drays and a heavy traveling coach without a crest on the door crowded in around them, overpowering them with the odors of fish, ale, and stale wine from a leaking cask on the wagon directly ahead of them.

"I don't like the look of that." Christien frowned at the preceding dray. Barrels stood high over the sides of the carrier. Ropes secured them, but they still wobbled back and forth with the jouncing rhythm of the heavy iron wheels on the stone-littered road.

Beside Christien, Lydia tensed.

"I'm going to try to get out of this mess." He glanced from left to right and twisted around to look behind.

The coach lumbered on their tail, the horses practically breathing down their necks. Dray wagons pressed close on either side. Too close. Too many to be heading into town in the afternoon.

A chill raised hairs along Christien's neck and up his arms. Gripping the reins so hard his hands hurt, he took a long, steadying breath. "Lydia, get down on the floor." He braced, prepared to push Lydia behind the splash guard.

No need to fret. Lydia slipped off the seat and crammed herself into the well with one exception—she curled one hand around his knee.

Her warmth dissipating the chill, Christien hauled on the reins. His team stopped. The drays to the sides kept going. The coach behind and the dray ahead halted. But an opening grew. Christien snapped the reins. If he could slip into the space to the left side—

The blast of a horn rang from the pursuing coach. Christien's team lunged, surged forward. The curricle's right wheel collided with the dray's left rear wheel, locked, held. A rope snapped, its ends striking the backs of the curricle's team like a whip. They reared, locking the curricle to the wagon.

And a dozen barrels of wine rolled toward Christien and Lydia.

20

"*Allons.*" Christien's command to go rang above a rumble like thunder reverberating through the curricle. He grasped Lydia's hand and tugged. "*Maintenent.* Now, now, now!"

She scrambled after him. Her foot caught in her gown and tore the hem, tripping her. She fell against Christien's shoulder. They struck the road on hands and knees, scrambled to their feet, ran.

Behind them, the world exploded with crashes and creaks and the shriek of terrified horses.

Christien released Lydia's hand and spun. Lydia did likewise. Behind them, the casks of wine lay splintered or cracked. Their contents splashed curricle, horses, and road in streaks and pools like blood. The stench of fermented fruit rose on the air, overpowering the aroma of grass and wildflowers. Beyond the mess, the dray stood nearly empty. Even its seat held no driver, its shafts no horses. Behind, all that remained of the coach and its disastrous horn blast was a plume of dust drifting to the road. The otherwise empty road.

Beneath the tumbled casks, the curricle lay smashed like kindling.

"*Mon dieu precieux.*" Christien breathed out the words in a prayerful tone. "We could have been in that, smashed like—"

Lydia nodded, then feared she'd keep nodding from the

tremors in her body. "This was no accident. The drays and coach crowding us were no accident."

"They couldn't have known I'd try to pass."

"They didn't need to. If you hadn't, they'd have let the barrels fall anyway. They were ready for any move you made. Their horses and the drivers are gone."

"The horses." Christien surged forward. "I must attend the horses. If they're permanently harmed . . ."

They had to be injured. In no way could they have missed the onslaught of wine casks.

Lydia's hands balled into fists. A muscle bunched in her jaw, and she ground her teeth. What kind of monster, what kind of scoundrel perpetrated a crime like this?

And how were they going to get back home? The road lay empty. Too empty.

The nip in the early May air suddenly felt like a winter blast off the moor. Lydia shivered and wrapped her arms across her middle, where the cold settled in her gut.

If someone could perpetrate an accident with several drays and a coach, that same engineer could cause traffic to stop along the road to keep them isolated. But isolated for what reason? For how long?

They could walk to civilization, find a house or inn within an hour, probably less. An assassin with a rifle would take moments to shoot, kill, and disappear into the trees, join traffic that would suddenly flow again, and vanish into the London stews like coal smoke dissipating into the spring sunshine.

Shaking, Lydia ripped the rest of the flounce off the bottom of her skirt, then, with her ankles exposed in their sturdy walking boots, she headed for Christien.

He murmured to the horses. They no longer whinnied like

screaming women. Surely that, at least, was good. They seemed not to be in pain or as frightened, and were still alive if Christien was talking to them.

If he spoke to her in that tone of voice, would her trembling cease?

Lydia smiled in spite of herself and approached Christien at the head of the team. He smoothed back the horses' forelocks and spoke to them with gentle reassurance. Though their rear legs kicked out at random intervals and their eyes tended to roll more than normal, they submitted to their master's touch and voice.

"They're all right?" Lydia asked.

"Not quite." Christien smoothed one hand down the roan's glossy neck. "This one limped badly when I led him from the vehicle. I've checked his legs and think it's his left hip. Probably a cask struck it."

"How could they?" Lydia punched her palm. "They are so unkind to do this to poor horses."

"And us."

"Yes." She swallowed against her dry throat. "Us. The road is too empty."

"Is it?" He glanced up and down. "I didn't know. I don't know London."

"I don't know it well, but well enough to know this is unnatural and we're here like fish in a barrel. If we could ride the horses, doing something—"

"We cannot. They're too lame. We'll have to walk someplace for help."

Trees lined the road. Plumes of smoke over the crowns suggested habitation nearby, but they had to go through the woods first or continue on the road. Either way, someone could harm them.

"We'll go through the trees." Though he spoke as calmly

as Lydia had, Christien radiated tension, and his jaw looked like granite. "Let me disentangle this horse from the harness strap and we'll be off." He crouched to free the horse from the dangling harness.

And a musket cracked from the trees.

"Down, Lydia." Christien grasped her hand and dragged her to the road.

She landed on her knees beside him the instant another explosion of gunfire shattered the air.

"Can you run fast?" Christien asked.

Lydia nodded.

"Then we're going to run."

Another shot rang through the afternoon. The buzz of a bee sailed past Lydia's left ear. But not a bee—the musket ball.

She surged to her feet and began to run.

A barrage of shots followed. Not one gunman. At least two. No one could reload quickly enough to fire with so little space between. Shooting at Christien or Lydia or both.

Who? Who? Who? Lydia's breath sounded like the question, wheezing through her throat. She normally walked a great deal. She never ran. Ladies didn't run.

She ran now, feet skimming the road, the grassy verge, the carpet of pine needles and rotting oak leaves. Branches caught her hat, yanked it off. Her hair spilled down her back, flowed out behind. Roots and fallen logs threatened to catch hold of her feet. She jumped. She ducked. She never stopped moving.

She held Christien's hand, an anchor, a lifeline, a guide.

The woods closed around them, dark green and cool, smelling of leaf mold and rich earth, their own perspiration and the smoke from a nearby cooking fire. Peaceful. They stopped. Held their breath, listened.

"Nothing." Christien breathed no more loudly than the light breeze sighing through the upper branches.

"I don't hear the birds." Lydia stepped closer to him so her lips hovered near his ear. "Because of us or pursuit?"

They would have been easy to follow. They'd cared about speed, not stealth.

They remained silent now. Christien slipped his arm around Lydia's shoulders and held her tightly against his side. With one ear, she listened for the crack of a limb, the crunch of a footfall, the hiss of cloth against foliage. Her other ear took in the strong, steady rhythm of Christien's heart. The silk of his waistcoat caressed her cheek. His fingers tangled in her hair, stroked the back of her neck, curved around the back of her head.

"Lydia, *ma chère*." His other hand tucked beneath her chin, nudged it up.

The shade beneath the trees turned the blue of his eyes to midnight. She didn't have time to look or wonder further as he bent his head and kissed her.

His lips were soft and tasted of sweet lemon and sweeter strawberries. His mouth held hers captive, moving as though he spoke gentle words she could only understand through the contact of lips—love, longing, lust, perhaps mere relief that they were safe for the time being, a celebration of life sustained.

She sensed all of them, drank them in with an aching heart that she had tried too long to pretend wasn't longing for more in her life. Her legs lost their bones. She wrapped one arm around his waist to support herself and laid her other hand against his cheek—warm, smooth skin with a hint of whisker rasp.

Around them, the birds resumed their singing.

"We're safe," she whispered against his mouth.

"At least from pursuit." He released her insomuch as he shifted his hands so they curved around her face. He gazed into her eyes, and those deep blue orbs spoke the same language as his lips.

Her mouth went dry. She licked her lips, swallowed, found words stuck somewhere in the middle of her chest.

He smiled. "I think it's good I've been alone with a lady so little, if I behave in so ungentlemanly a fashion."

"Not ungentlemanly. That is, you didn't force your attentions on me, and I participated. I mean—" What did she mean? Her cheeks grew warm. "I'm not the first female you've kissed."

"No, but I want you to be the last."

"Monsieur."

"Christien, *peut-être*, after . . ." He rubbed the ball of his thumb along her lower lip.

A thrill ran through her, settling in her core. "Perhaps, yes. But the other, me being the last . . ." She drew away, growing colder with each inch of space she set between them. "We should get help."

"*Oui*, that we should. I believe there is a house nearby." His face suddenly bleak, he turned away from her, elbow extended in silent invitation for escort.

She didn't take it. If she touched him, she just might throw herself into his arms and beg him to hold her, kiss her again. It would be a mistake. She must succeed in her own right, let herself feel like she didn't always fail, before she allowed herself the luxury of love.

Love? No, surely not. Desire, hunger, yes. No one had held her in nearly seven years. Her body ached for the joy of strong arms around her. But not Christien, who had given up family for ten years to pursue a life of danger and intrigue. However great the cause, he had given up his family.

She could never give up her family for anything.

She followed Christien along a path that grew more well trodden the closer they drew to the cooking aromas. Burning mutton fat seared the air, sharp and gamey, softened with baking bread and roasting potatoes. Her stomach constricted. A bitter taste rose in her throat, where moments earlier the sweetness of Christien's kiss had lingered. Her head spun for a far different reason than the confusion over why he'd kissed her.

They had just run through the woods because someone had arranged an accident, then shot at them. Now they were about to approach a house of strangers with Christien in a torn coat, her in a torn, shortened gown, and her lips quite possibly puffy. And she mustn't forget her hair hanging down her back as though she'd just awakened in the morning, or . . .

The only kissing she was about to see was kissing farewell to her good reputation.

"And I was worried about my sisters," she muttered.

Christien paused. "I beg your pardon?"

"My reputation." She gestured to the farmhouse now in sight across a field of newly turned earth. "Will anyone believe us?"

"They will when they see the wreck."

"I hope so." She pulled as much of her hair as she could in front of her face, then tucked it back again. "I'd better do the talking. This close to the city, these people shouldn't be hostile to you, but they might despise all Frenchmen regardless of why you're here."

"But of course." He touched her arm. "After ten years facing the guillotine in France, I would dislike becoming a corpse at the hands of an angry English farmer."

"Shall we go this way?" She headed around the field.

As they approached the rear of the house, a woman straightened from hoeing a kitchen garden and shielded her eyes with a strong, well-shaped hand. "Where'd you come from?"

"The woods. There was an accident." Lydia didn't need to feign the tears that gushed into her eyes and spilled over. "We need help."

"Then you have it, madame. My husband and sons are in the barn. Your man can fetch them. You need to come in and sit down a bit."

"He's French." She may as well get it out. "But he's on our side."

"Indeed?" The woman fixed Christien with wide gray eyes. "Did you fight the Corsican monster, or just say you don't like him?"

"Both, madame." Christien bowed.

The woman blinked, and a hint of a blush darkened her rosy cheeks. "Then go on with you. I'll care for your lady before she falls down."

"I'm all right," Lydia insisted. She wanted to go with Christien.

"Go with this kind madame. You're looking pale," Christien said.

She didn't feel pale until the farm wife led her into the kitchen with its blazing fire and pot steaming on the hearth and nudged her onto a high-backed settee. Suddenly, she wanted to draw her legs up onto the seat, put her head down, and sleep for a decade or so.

She accepted a cup of hot, sweet tea instead, a slice of warm bread spread with bramble jelly, and a thick woolen shawl smelling strongly of lanolin. She rested her head against the back of the settee, closed her eyes.

And saw the wine casks tilting toward them, heard the rumble . . .

She jerked upright.

Christien stood near and held out his hands to her. "These gentlemen will take us back to fetch the horses and then drive us on to town."

"We only have the wagon," said the farmer, a burly man with

a face like a well-worn leather boot. "It's not comfortable, but it smells like apples, not the muck."

"Thank you." Lydia smiled.

The wagon did indeed smell like apples, and hay too. It wasn't comfortable. Perched on the seat beside the farmer, Lydia thought every tooth in her head would rattle loose before they reached the road and what was left of the curricle.

And a substantial crowd.

Traffic moved along the road now, but slowly, drivers cursing and complaining as the flow crept along around the curricle and dray. No fewer than two score people surrounded the wreckage.

"What is this?" Christien leaped from the back of the wagon and began to elbow his way through the throng. "Where are my horses?"

"This your carriage, frog?" A man in a blue coat with tin buttons down the front stepped forward.

The rest of the crowd fell silent, watching.

Lydia's heart skipped a beat, then took off running like a steed at Newmarket Races. *Don't tell him, Christien. Don't admit to ownership.*

But of course he must. He had already asked for his horses.

"It is mine. We went for help with these—"

"Then mebbe you can explain this." The man with the tin buttons stepped aside.

A clear path opened between the farmer's wagon and the curricle's remains.

Not just the curricle's remains. Human remains lay there amidst broken wheels and wine casks. A face shone waxen in the sunlight.

George Barnaby.

21

"Murdering frog." The shout rang from the back of the crowd around the smashed curricle and Barnaby's body. "Seize him, constable."

"Yeah, take him to Newgate."

Others picked up the cry. "Arrest the foreigner."

The tumult brought a halt to what little traffic managed to pass the wreckage. If a constable were in the crowd, he'd made himself scarce.

Lydia grasped Christien's arm and tried to pull him away. Perhaps someone would give them transport into town, preferably in a closed carriage. Or away from London. Right then, either sounded like a better prospect than staying.

But staying was what Christien did. His arm didn't budge. If anything, the muscles hardened under her fingers. His face grew stony and cold enough to freeze the spilled wine. "I have lived in this country since I had—since I was ten years old. I have served the king—"

"What? Frog legs?" The original heckler had moved closer, a man with a barrel for a belly. The belly rolled beneath his workman's smock. "It's all you Frenchies are good for—eatin' what isn't natural to eat."

"Which is why Napoleon's managed to keep the country at war for over a decade," Christien muttered.

Lydia gave his arm a warning squeeze.

He covered her hand with his. "Someone left that body there after we went for help. I had nothing to do with—"

Catcalls and jeers drowned his denial of guilt.

"Go back where you came from."

"Let them guillotine all you aristos."

"Kill him for killing an Englishman."

Those were amongst the most polite of the remarks. The others rained down like filth, like venom. Hostility toward the French. Hostility toward Christien in particular. The scene rang of the incident in Hyde Park, only magnified. Civil unrest as Lydia had never experienced.

Fomented by someone wanting a revolution in England, as in France.

For a moment, the sun blackened before her eyes. A pain like a knife wound stabbed through her middle. In that moment, she wished they were running away from a gunman rather than facing a mob.

"We've got to leave here," she told Christien. "Any minute now, they're going to—"

Her words broke off in a scream. Two men with arms like sides of beef lunged forward, grabbing for Christien. Lydia flung herself at the nearest one. With a flick of his wrist, he sent her sprawling. She snatched at his leg, wrapped her arms around it, yanked. With a roar, he toppled backward. Lydia kept hauling up, up, up. The man struck the road like a felled mainmast, and she stepped on his chest.

"Stay there," she shouted over the yells and cheers. "I am Lady Lydia Gale, widow of Major Sir Charles Gale. Christien de Meuse is my friend and more loyal to England than any of you with your seditious talk of killing aristocrats."

Beside her, Christien had sent his second attacker flat into the dirt, where he nursed a bloody nose.

Seeing others crowding close, Lydia plunged on. "Do you want this country to turn into France?"

"Frog lover," someone shouted.

Others took up the chant. The man on whom Lydia stood heaved her off.

Christien caught hold of her, lifted her over his shoulder, and headed for the line of vehicles. "You are either brave or foolhardy, *mon amour.*"

"Can I be both?" Lydia raised her head to see the crowd, disorganized around the fallen men and the corpse.

The corpse of a man who had flirted with her in her own parlor, who had talked of his work to stop dissension in England.

She dropped her head, let her hair obscure her vision, and concentrated on not being sick down Christien's back.

"This way!" someone shouted loudly enough to be heard over the bellowing throng. "De Meuse."

A friend, a savior.

Christien halted and set Lydia down on the step of a carriage. "*Merci bien.*"

Before she turned to see who their rescuer was, Christien headed back the way they'd come.

"Where are you going?" she called after him.

"The horses."

"You can't go alone." She leaped from the step.

Strong hands caught hold of her waist and lifted her into the vehicle. "I'll go, my lady."

The man stepped over her, then sprinted after Christien. His coat flapped open to reveal a short sword and a pistol. The latter he pulled free and pointed into the air. A single crack ricocheted around the road and vehicles and crowd. Like a slamming door, it subdued the rioters.

"Go home," the man shouted. "I'm a magistrate and will see to the Frenchman and the unfortunate man in the wreckage. If nothing else, have respect for him."

His speech worked. People released their missiles of small stones and dried manure and began to disperse. Traffic recommenced moving along the open part of the road.

Lydia leaned out the far window of the carriage and was horribly, embarrassingly sick. By the time the men returned, walking the horses, Lydia had seated herself, chewing a handful of pine needles, the only green thing she could reach from the vehicle. They tasted bitter and sharp but cleansed her mouth and cleared her head enough to feel as composed as a woman could in a ragged gown and loose hair.

"Are you a magistrate?" she asked Christien's friend, as if nothing untoward had brought her into his coach.

He smiled, showing her the most perfect teeth she'd ever seen. "In Sussex, yes."

"Mostly," Christien added, "he's my watchdog. Allow me to introduce Mr. Elias Lang."

Lydia had never been to Whitehall, that former palace of the Stewart kings now full of soldiers, sailors, and other government officials attached to the business of war. If she'd ever thought to go, she would have dressed appropriately. But she traversed the dank corridors looking like a waif from a shipwreck, not the widow of a respected military officer.

The mysterious Mr. Lang wasn't such a conundrum after all. He was a quietly dressed individual of early middle years, with sandy brown hair and no-colored eyes. In Sussex, he owned a small estate and sat as the local magistrate when he wasn't in London playing spy master.

Lydia learned all that on their way back to London, then on to Whitehall. She also learned he was not, in fact, the man in the garden in Portsmouth.

"The accent is all wrong. He was most definitely a London man or possibly Westmorland."

"Could he, in fact, be George Barnaby?" Lang asked her from behind a battered oak desk.

Lydia cradled the cup of tea he'd prepared for her and considered his question. "You'd think if he were, I would have recognized him straight off."

"Unless he disguised his voice," Lang suggested.

"You could have done the same."

"I could, which is why Christien didn't introduce you to me sooner to prove he was telling the truth." He slanted a glance at his colleague. "That, and perhaps he wanted his lady to believe him on his own merit."

Christien emitted a rumbling noise like a growl, then shrugged. *"Peut-être."*

The look he cast Lydia threatened to melt her bones. She sipped her lukewarm tea and fixed her gaze on Lang. "Being from Sussex, you have the sort of friends who can get you back and forth across the Channel without questions asked, I presume? Which is how you got those messages to me."

"Yes, some of my friends escape prison helping me." Lang shot a glance at Christien. "But when this reprobate Frenchman got himself captured by English sailors, I needed help getting him out of that prison without exposing myself or his role."

"You took a risk having him walk into my parlor that day."

"We didn't think it was a risk," Lang said.

"We thought you'd been fairly warned of further help needed," Christien added. "But someone interfered with the message and blackmailed you instead to muddy the waters, we presume."

"Barnaby?" Lydia posed the question, then shook her head. "But who would kill him?"

Lang sighed. "Whoever was using him."

"Frobisher seems obvious," Christien said. "Too ob—"

"Frobisher." Lydia sprang to her feet, adding tea stains to her bedraggled gown. "I can't stay here. I've got to get home and get ready for that ball. Honore has likely already gone off with Frobisher. And he could be a murderer." She slammed her thick earthenware mug onto the desk. "Please, someone take me home."

Christien and Lang were on their feet in an instant. "I'll take you," they said in unison.

"Of course, I'm not done questioning you about today," Lang added. "I could do so in the carriage."

"Unless you're detaining Chris—Monsieur de Meuse, I suggest you both take me." Lydia smiled at the gentlemen and led the way to the door.

If they didn't follow, she would never find her way out of the building. And she must reach Honore, wherever she was. And with Frobisher? A murderer?

Too obvious, as Christien said. He'd arrived with Barnaby, who claimed he didn't know Frobisher until they'd met at an inn. Barnaby claimed he worked for England's good.

"That has many connotations." Lydia spoke her next thought aloud.

"What do you mean?" Christien tucked his arm through hers, a possessive gesture. But then, the way she'd kissed him back gave him reason for possessiveness.

"Barnaby insisted he was working for England's good. But that could so easily mean that changing England is what's good."

"You accused me of something similar, did you not?" Holding her close to his side with their entwined arms, Christien headed down the narrow dark passageway without a flicker of hesitation, Lang behind them. "I could be working for France out of revenge for England canceling the Peace of Amiens that got my father killed."

"I'm a beast for doubting you, Christien."

"Christien, is it?" Lang sighed. "I should have known. I suppose I'm too old for you."

"Never, sir." Lydia flashed him a smile over her shoulder. "Shared danger simply makes formality seem obsolete."

Not to mention an interlude in one another's arms.

She touched her fingertips to her lips before she realized what she was doing. Her face went warm in the chilly, dank corridor. An empty place opened inside her, a longing, a wish that the idea of them being something more than comrades in arms—military arms—didn't make her want to run screaming as far from Christien as she could get.

She could remain at his side to help find the sort of person who would stir up a crowd like the one in the park, like the one on the road, like others who might turn things into outright revolution—mobs capturing the poor mad king or beheading the prince regent, looting Cavendish, Grosvenor, and Berkley Squares, or smashing up shops along Bond Street. But repeat that kiss and its implications of a deeper relationship? No, she wouldn't trade her current freedom, however poor, for the control of a man like her father again. She could keep the wolves of true poverty from the door with her painting.

"Oh, no." She halted in the center of the hall. "My portfolio is still in the curricle."

"I'm sorry." Christien sounded as though he meant it.

"I have men collecting Mr. Barnaby's remains." Lang spoke up from behind. "They'll bring anything else that was in the wreckage."

"I'd rather not have it after—after it was beneath . . . Barnaby." Lydia tamped down nausea and resumed their walk to the exit and the waiting closed carriage. She wanted to run. But because they passed men in regimental red, rifleman green, and naval blue, she maintained her sedate pace alongside Christien. The walk took mere minutes. It felt like an hour.

Outside, the sun was already dropping behind the buildings. Night was about to fall. Soon carriages would be lining up before the great houses of the haut ton, disgorging bejeweled men and women for a night of revelry.

And the person who wanted to bring it all to an end.

She opened her mouth to ask why bringing the frivolity of London Society to an end would be so awful, then closed it before the words escaped. She might find herself a guest of the Tower of London without her blackmailer if she spoke those words in this hotbed of men managing the war.

But her blackmailer might be dead. Even if he was not, she was free from the threat. She always had been. Nothing stopped her from abandoning Christien to his own devices.

Yet more than the warm strength of his arm held her to him. She wanted to help, make her mark on a fragment of history, beyond the pages of what would one day be written of her time.

Or perhaps she simply wanted to have an excuse to be with him.

A warning bell clanged in her head, resounded in her heart. She stopped up her inner ear against it. Not now. Now she needed to catch up with Honore.

The coachman drove them at breakneck speed through the streets of London. Torch lights and lanterns blinked on as they passed other vehicles and houses. Shops grew dark.

Number Thirty Cavendish Square glowed with its light above the front door and several candles blazing inside. The light beckoned Lydia. She leaped from the carriage the instant it stopped and raced up the steps.

Lemster himself opened the door. "My lady, whatever happened?"

"Never you mind that now. Where is Miss Honore? Please tell me she hasn't left for Vauxhall yet."

"I'm afraid she has. She was overset by you not coming home in time to take her." Lemster stepped back to allow Lydia access to the house.

"Then whom did she go with?" Lydia demanded.

"The Tarletons."

"That's all right then." Lydia sagged. If Honore was with the Tarletons, she was all right.

"And Miss Bainbridge went with her too," Lemster added.

"Cassandra?" Lydia straightened. "Why?"

Lemster glanced at Christien and Lang behind her and cleared his throat.

"It's all right," Lydia assured him. "These are my friends."

"Yes, my lady." Lemster bowed to the gentlemen. "Miss

Bainbridge said something about finding any husband was better than listening to . . . er . . ." He glanced toward the library.

"I understand." Lydia suppressed a grim smile, then turned to Christien and Lang. "We need to go after her."

"*Biensur.* But may I suggest, without offending . . ." Christien's eyes flicked down the length of her.

She laughed. "Yes, of course I'll change my dress. And I suggest you do much the same, monsieur."

"I will return for you in half an hour," Christien said. "Monsieur Lang?"

The men bowed and turned to the door. Lydia spun toward the steps, then raced up them. She heard someone call her name, a male someone. Father, of course. She continued up to her room.

Barbara perched on the window seat with a book. She leaped to her feet, and the book slammed to the floor. "Lydia, where have you been?"

"I need to get ready quickly. The yellow gauze, do you think? Is Vauxhall too common for all those gold spangles?"

"Lydia, you look terrible. Your gown, your hair."

"Will not do for the gardens, I know." Lydia began to struggle with the buttons down the back of her dress, gave up trying to reach them, and ripped them free. They flew across the room. Hodge streaked out from under the bed and gave chase.

Barbara shrieked and ran into the dressing room.

Lydia proceeded to change her clothes. She wished she were an old woman so she could wind a turban around her hair and not worry about pinning it up in a manner that would hold the mass in place for at least a few minutes. She compromised by plaiting it and winding the braids around her head in a coronet, then decorating it with a length of ribbon and jeweled pin she snatched from Honore's room. That would do. She wasn't trying to charm anyone with her looks.

She'd already charmed a gentleman with something.

Her breath caught in her throat, and she pressed her fingers to her lips, remembering, savoring Christien's kiss, though it shouldn't mean so much to her beyond physical contact. Maintaining her good reputation, she hadn't so much as allowed a man to hold her hand since her husband died. Sometimes that proved a difficult rule to follow after a week of the privileges of marriage. But she had succeeded until Christien walked into her life.

Because she loved him?

"Lydia Bainbridge Gale." Her father's voice rang up the stairwell like a warning bell. "Don't you ignore me when I call you."

And Christien could walk out of her life when they caught their traitor, regardless of how she felt about him. Men had done nothing but rule her life and cause more trouble. She didn't need to compound the experiences with another husband.

She opened her bedchamber door to find Father on the other side about to knock. "Yes, sir?"

"I want an explanation as to what you were up to today with that Frenchman." He settled his hands on his hips and scowled.

"We went for a drive, had an accident, and got tangled up with Whitehall." She set her lips so she didn't laugh at his thunderstruck expression. "Now I must go find Honore," she added.

"Lydia, you will not speak—"

She pushed past him. "Father, I know I am under your roof, but it is only as a courtesy to Mama. Please tell me to leave and I'll happily do so. You and Mama and the girls can then see to Honore's ball next week and to repairing Cassandra's wedding without me."

And Christien could catch his spy on his own and she could remove herself from temptation.

Behind her, Father said nothing. Footfalls light, Lydia skimmed down the steps and reached the front hall just as Christien returned.

"Are you all right?" He gave her that sweeping glance of his, a frown puckering his arched brows.

"Why would you ask if I am? Do I still appear disheveled?"

"You appear delightful, *ma chère*, but you have some extra color here." He ran his fingertips along her cheekbones.

"Ah, my father is being autocratic. That being nothing out of the ordinary, shall we go?" She tucked her hand into the crook of his elbow and steered him around to the door.

Heavy footfalls pounded on the steps, and she wanted to be outside and on her way before Father reached the entryway.

Christien glanced over his shoulder, then quickened his pace to the waiting carriage. It was closed. For a moment, Lydia hesitated, wondering at the propriety of riding alone with a man in a closed vehicle at night, then shrugged off the notion. She was a widow, not a green girl. It afforded her some privileges of behavior.

They spoke little on the ride down to the river. Because of the boatmen, they couldn't speak freely in the wherry that carried them to the water steps of Vauxhall Pleasure Gardens. Once there amidst the shimmering lanterns, the crushing throng, and the orchestra, Lydia felt as though she still rode on the riverboat, with it sinking to the bottom of the Thames.

"We'll never find anyone in this crowd," she called to Christien.

He tucked her arm close to his side and leaned toward her to be heard over the laughter and chatter of hundreds of persons from all walks of London life. "The Tarletons will be in one of the boxes, I'm certain. We will start there."

They started with the rows of cubicles that persons could rent for the tables and chairs and the meager suppers to be purchased. Beyond them lay the walks—winding paths through shrubbery that gave couples too much privacy. Surely Honore wouldn't go with Frobisher or any other young man through one of those paths.

Oh, but she would.

Head pounding from the noise and too much cheap perfume, Lydia didn't hear Christien's exclamation of triumph until he drew her on a trajectory through the milling, dancing pleasure seekers. Lydia stumbled after him, then paused, a sigh of relief catching in her throat.

Lady Tarleton and Miss Tarleton sat with a handful of gentlemen Lydia didn't know, but neither Honore nor Cassandra was with them.

"Good evening, my lady, Miss Tarleton, messieurs." Christien bowed. "We apologize for this intrusion. We were led to believe the Misses Bainbridge are with you."

The Tarleton ladies exchanged glances. The gentlemen pretended Christien hadn't spoken other than nodding to him.

"Cassandra said she was staying home," Miss Tarleton said.

"And Honore said she was attending a rout—or was it a soirée?—with Mr. Frobisher," Lady Tarleton added.

So Honore was with Frobisher at some unknown location. And where was Cassandra?

22

He would never catch a traitor if he spent his time racing about after Lydia's recalcitrant sisters. For a moment, standing beside Lydia, Christien strained at the bit like an intractable horse. Nothing but good manners stopped him from leaving Lydia to head out on her own to seek her sisters, or to go home and leave them to their father. If Bainbridge wanted good matches for his ladies, he should keep a better eye on them than he did, pay more attention to his family than his seat in the House of Lords. Christien had more important matters to tend to.

Matters in which Gerald Frobisher could be involved.

Christien closed his eyes for a moment. His face felt flushed in the warm spring night. He wanted to—needed to—hang his head for his uncharitable thoughts. Had he truly been considering putting duty before Lydia? And he wanted her to love him?

She should be on her own, all right, but not so he could be rid of her. More like so she could be rid of him. He needed to finish his mission before thinking about love and the future.

He bade good evening to the Tarleton party and drew Lydia out of sight of their box.

"How do we begin to find my sister?" she asked.

"To where else did she have invitations?" Christien matched his tone to her coolness.

"There was a rout, a soirée, and a play at Drury Lane. It could take us three hours to hunt for her in all those places."

"And you think she's with Frobisher?"

"I do, except that Cassandra went with her."

"One sister at a time."

If he could tuck them all up safely in their home, despite the father they didn't want to face, he might be able to get down to his traitor-hunting.

"We'll start with learning Frobisher's whereabouts."

"How?"

"I know where he lives."

The boat ride back and carriage ride to the edges of Mayfair took nearly an hour. Frobisher's establishment wasn't fine, merely an adequate place to sleep. Leaving Lydia in the carriage, Christien rapped on the door. If Frobisher hired a valet or other form of manservant, getting information might be difficult. His own man proved loyal time and again. He had to be. Quite possibly the same with Frobisher's. No amount of money bribed a good servant into revealing information.

No private servant opened the door. Instead, a rotund female somewhere past middle age yanked open the portal and scowled up at Christien. "What do you be wantin' this time of night?"

"Mr. Gerald Frobisher."

"Ain't here."

"Do you know where he is?"

"Mebbe." The woman shrugged. The fat on her shoulder rippled beneath the thin wrap she wore over her nightclothes. "Depends on what a frog is wanting with him."

"It's personal business."

Or possibly of national interest. For Honore's sake, he hoped not.

He slipped a shilling into the woman's pocket. "We have a debt to settle."

"He can settle the debt he has with me first. Ain't paid his rent in a fortnight, and I'm about to sell his fancy clothes, for all his pretty face pleases me."

Revulsion crept through Christien, but he maintained his smile. "How much does he owe you?"

"You willing to pay?"

"If it's reasonable."

"Two guineas."

The sum was exorbitant and probably exaggerated. Nonetheless, Christien gave her half and held the other coin in his hand. "His whereabouts?"

She told him. Christien groaned silently at the idea that Honore could be with him there. Most young ladies would demand to be taken home. Honore, however, sought adventure and excitement and probably would encourage her inclusion in such an excursion.

Christien thanked the woman, gave her the other guinea, and returned to the carriage.

"What did you learn?" Lydia demanded the instant he opened the door.

"Frobisher's favorite place is what is commonly known as a gaming hell."

Lydia grimaced. "Such a vulgar term. It makes me cringe when I hear it."

"*Oui*, but it aptly describes the condition into which it leads too many men, and women too—outcast and completely despairing." Christien dropped onto the seat beside her and knocked on the roof to signal for the coachman to get moving. "They're nearly the worst of the dens of iniquity in this town."

"What could be worse than a place called a—a hell?" Lydia choked on the word.

Christien touched her arm. "I don't know if he'd take Miss Honore there."

"She'd go."

"I'm afraid I agree."

Lydia covered her face with her hands. "Where did I go wrong? I've tried to tell her how to go on here in town, and she seems determined to ruin herself. And after Cassandra . . . I just want to get their futures safely established so I can go home and forget."

Forget what? Him?

He tamped down the selfish pain. "Lydia, you're not responsible for their futures. Their futures are in God's hands and the hands of God's caretakers on earth—your parents."

"Who have designated them to me this Season. Mama is too frail to manage, and Father—" She flung up her head. "I don't know why Father expects me to manage. He never thinks I do anything right. All my life he's criticized whatever I do. If I was obedient, I didn't succeed in what I did do. My painting, my marriage, my—" She paused. "I'm so sorry. I shouldn't tell you all of this."

"But you should." He took her hand in his and laced their fingers together as best as one could wearing gloves. "Tell me more. What did he do when he was displeased? Did he . . . beat you as children?"

"Sometimes I wish he had. That pain would have been easier than the coldness, the constant criticism, the reminders of our failures." She turned her face away from him, though the carriage lay in darkness. "I wish he weren't right about my failure to succeed at even the most basic of womanly duties."

"Oh, Lydia." Christien's throat closed. He swallowed and held himself rigid to stop himself from drawing her to him. She needed more than the physical comfort he could offer. "I want to tell you that God loves you whether or not you are what others think is a good wife or daughter or sister, but it's difficult for me to believe for myself."

"Was your father autocratic too?"

"No, my father was the kindest of parents. He disciplined us when we needed it and loved us the whole time." Warmth and the familiar ache of loss expanded in Christien's heart. "He brought us up to love God and be obedient to Him, but when Papa died at the hands of the French, I abandoned his teachings and set out on my current course. I don't think God approves, and until I've stopped my attempt to cripple Napoleon, I don't think God will have a great deal to do with me."

"But if He's all-loving, wouldn't He, regardless of what we do?"

"He loves us, but we do have to repent, and I can't do that yet."

"And I don't know how a loving God could give me the father I have and tell me to honor him."

"The father you have has made you strong and courageous and determined not to give up." Christien drew her hand to his cheek. "Your letters to your husband spoke of your ability to face adversity with a cheerfulness that helped me keep going when I sometimes wanted to let a French firing squad end my pain."

"Christien." She started to turn toward him.

The carriage stopped, and the coachman opened the hatch. "We're here, monsieur."

"*Tres bien*." Christien released Lydia's hand. "You wait here."

"I'm coming in."

"Do you have a mask? You can't be seen here."

"I'll use my shawl like a veil. The lace is fine enough." She proceeded to drape the gauzy wrap over her hair and face like a Spanish mantilla gone awry.

A dozen arguments on his tongue as to why she should remain in the coach, Christien climbed down and assisted Lydia to the pavement. In front of them a lantern displayed a plain white door. No brass plate beside the portal or swinging sign above gave an indication as to the nature of the establishment. Nor did its neighbors help. They lay in darkness despite the rules about burning a light outside at night. The stench of refuse strong enough to taste told its own tale of a less than savory neighborhood. Christien half expected to hear a scream.

Instead, he heard a meow.

A cat, half the size of Hodge and as black as Lydia's cat was white, slipped from the shadows and began to wind itself around her ankles.

"It's so thin." Lydia stooped to pet it.

"Don't. It probably has fleas."

"But it's so dear."

Indeed, the creature had begun to purr.

"Perhaps they have more than drink inside and we can bring something out to it." Christien raised his hand to knock.

"Yes, yes, of course. Inside. Honore. I feel like I should pray she isn't there, but I don't want to be disappointed with God if she is."

Before Christien could respond—if he had a response—the door opened. A man taller than and as wide as the opening stood before them. "What do you want? This is a private house."

"I don't know the password, and I don't want to cause trouble. I'm merely looking for a young lady."

"This ain't that kind of establishment."

"No, not for that." Christien's ears burned. "She may be gaming and doesn't have the money to do so. I'd like to take her home to her family."

"Willing to pay her debts first?" the behemoth asked.

Lydia gasped. "Debts? She's gaming?"

"Well?" The doorman pressed.

"Yes," Christien said.

"But—"

He raised a palm to stop Lydia's protest. "But not her companion's debts," Christien added.

"That one." The guard spat a hairbreadth from Christien's left shoe. "He can go hang for all I care." He stepped back. "Come in, but if you cause trouble for this house, I'll personally see you're sorry."

"We won't."

A moment later, Christien wished he hadn't made such a promise. They descended a stairway darker and tighter than the servants' stairs at a townhouse, pushed through an ironbound door, and entered a room so full of smoke and the stench of perspiration and cheap perfume he could scarcely breathe. Candlelight blazed with a lurid glow through the smoke, and faces appeared as mere blurs.

"No wonder they call it a hell." Lydia stood as close to him as she could, her arm locked up with his. "How will we find her?"

"Especially since all the females are wearing loo masks." Christien began to walk, seeking honey-blonde hair for Honore or guinea gold for Frobisher. Surely they would stand out.

They did. At the back of the room, past tables of faro and piquet, dicing and roulette, they found a table with three gentlemen and one female in card play, and several onlookers.

"Only one thing left to give up, sweeting," one of the latter shouted. "Your virtue."

Lydia gasped and gripped his arm harder, if possible. Christien clenched his fists. Planting the man a facer would do no good for anyone and would likely cause trouble.

"How much does she owe?" he asked.

All eyes turned toward him. Honore's hands flew to her mouth, and she sprang to her feet fast enough to knock her chair into the man behind her, the one who had suggested she offer up her virtue for debt payment. The heavy back struck him in the middle and he reeled into the man beside him. The two of them staggered in a weird dance and careened into a third observer, and the group went down like ninepins, taking a tray of glasses with them. The pungent odor of brandy added its stink to the room. People shouted, cursed, began to fight.

Christien scooped Honore into his arms, flung her over his shoulder, and headed for the exit at a trot, Lydia still clinging to his side. Hands flung out to grab them.

The guard from the door stepped into their path. "Payment," he shouted.

Christien veered to the side, knocked a table over between his group and the guard, and kept going.

He set Honore down at the steps. "Go." He gave her a nudge in the center of her back.

"But my reticule—"

"Go," Christien and Lydia commanded together.

The door behind them opened on billows of smoke and the roar of the tumult inside.

Honore went, running headlong up the steps. Christien and Lydia followed, the latter ahead. They burst into the night, the air sweet compared to the Hades belowground.

Door open, the carriage waited. Christien lifted Honore and then Lydia inside and leaped in after them. "Go!" he shouted to the coachman and slammed the door.

A fist pounded on the carriage. Shouts and the rumble of wheels rang out behind them.

"*Me-ow*," said a fourth passenger inside.

23

Lydia grabbed for the kitten. It shot through her reaching hands and landed on Christien, scrambled up the front of his shirt, and perched on his shoulder, swaying with the jostling of the carriage.

"A female, certainly." Lydia's lips twitched.

"An *infant terrible*." Christien grasped the feline around the middle. "Off."

It began to purr and rub its head against his chin.

"Hodge liked you too." Lydia stroked the kitten. "She's soft, but she looks like she has a wound."

"She's probably full of fleas." Christien's hand joined Lydia's on the cat's back.

The feline purred louder.

"A few drops of pennyroyal will take care of that." Lydia drew her hand free. "I can take her home to Hodge. He might stop attacking my hairpins if he has a companion."

"Miss Barbara will not be pleased. I don't think she—"

"Will you two stop talking about that stooopid cat?" Honore's voice rose like a portentous wind from the opposite corner of the coach. "It doesn't matter when my life is ruined."

Suppressing a sigh, Lydia turned to her sister. "Why would

you think your life is ruined? Were you more than gaming in that place?"

"No, but—"

"Did you ever take off your mask?"

"No, but—"

"Do you plan on repeating your actions of tonight?"

"Certainly not. I hate-ed it." A sob hitched her voice.

Lydia ground her teeth. "Then your life isn't ruined, thanks to our intervention and Monsieur de Meuse's quick wits in getting us out of there, not to mention his ability to find you in the first place. But if I ever see you with Gerald Frobisher again, I will tell Father, and then your life most definitely will be ruined."

"But I love Gerry," Honore wailed.

"*Me-ow*," the cat protested.

Christien muttered something that sounded suspiciously like, "My sentiments precisely, Noirette."

Little black one.

Lydia's heart squeezed with a sentiment she wasn't certain she wanted.

"You're too young to know what love is," Lydia snapped.

"But I'm expected to marry? That makes no sense to my mind." Honore sounded like nothing so much as a sulky child.

Too young indeed. She'd been the one Father had adored, lavished attention and approval upon, protected from his criticism until recently. Apparently, the sheltering had kept her younger than her years.

"No one should expect you to wed until you're ready." Lydia softened her tone and reached across the carriage to touch Honore's hand. "And that includes you continuing to see Frobisher. Believe me, out of sight, out of mind."

"Was that how it was with your husband?" Honore demanded

with a hint of belligerence. "Did you stop loving him just because he was on the continent?"

"After marriage is different. There are things . . . We'll discuss that later." Lydia felt too warm in her lace shawl and silk gown. "If you want to stay in London long enough for your ball next week, you will watch your p's and q's, and that includes sneaking around to see Gerald Frobisher."

"If I may say here," Christien inserted, "the man appears to be nothing more than a common gamester."

"A good one." Pride rang in Honore's voice, much to Lydia's horror. "He always wins."

"A regular Captain Sharp," Christien continued. "Dishonorable, but nothing more."

Lydia understood the message—Frobisher was the wrong sort of companion for Honore, certainly not husband material, but from all appearances he was neither a murderer nor a traitor. Appearances could be deceiving, but she suspected Christien could judge what was right. He had ten years' experience ferreting out spies, traitors, and others who would harm England. He was not infallible, yet Lydia's own instincts inclined her to agree with him.

Now to convince, bribe, or bully Honore into dropping the man before she caused real trouble for herself.

"Honore," Lydia began, "you are a lovely young lady, one of the prettiest I've seen here in town this Season. You are also intelligent and charming when you choose to be. You can reach much higher than a nobody from the provinces playing at man-about-town."

"There is nothing higher than the heart." Honore's words defied Lydia's remark about the girl's intelligence. "And you and Cassandra chose men you lo—"

"Cassandra." Lydia nearly leaped to her feet. "Where is Cassandra?"

"With her ballooning friends," Honore answered.

Lydia didn't like the fact that she missed Christien. More than missed him. She found herself waking in the middle of the night remembering being close to him, and an emptiness surrounded her like a void of darkness. She was not . . . hadn't been so foolish as to . . . wouldn't let herself be in love with him.

But for all her days beginning early and ending late, packed with preparations for the ball, painting whenever she could spare a moment, and attending one social gathering after another with her sisters in tow and never let out of her sight for a moment, the barrenness of her heart warned her she may have committed the second greatest error in her life.

She had failed to keep her heart free of entanglements.

Cassandra claimed she had too. "I take more pleasure in discussing aeronautics with my friends at the Chapter House coffee shop than in kissing Whittaker" had been her comment when Lydia, Christien, and Honore had tracked her down at that highly respectable establishment.

Respectable if accompanied by proper chaperonage, anyway. Alone with two gentlemen took Cassandra beyond the pale. Fortunately, no one who mattered had seen her there.

"But if I ever catch either of you behaving like worse than hoydens," Lydia lectured the two of them in their room, "I will pack your trunks myself and drive the carriage out of town if I have to."

"Just don't tell Father." A little pale, Cassandra worried a sketch of a balloon and basket in her hands. "I know I shouldn't have gone, but Honore wanted to go to Vauxhall, which I cannot abide. And the men and I began to talk, and one of them wanted to show me his new design, and . . . I shouldn't have done it. But if Father finds out, he'll worse than send us away."

"What could be worse than that?" Honore asked.

"Picking a husband for us," Cassandra grumbled.

Not even Honore argued with that. She knew Father was perfectly capable of doing so, someone he considered suitable—one of his political cronies, like an older man with five children to keep his wayward daughters too busy to get into mischief.

"I'd run off to America first," Honore said.

"Let's get your ball under way before we worry about that." Lydia managed to distract both girls.

They endured final fittings for their gowns and matched acceptances of invitations with the list of guests invited. They ordered the correct number of ices from Gunter's and then reordered them, as the guest list changed at the final moment.

That final moment approached with a rapidity that left Lydia drinking coffee instead of tea to keep her awake and wondering if she should have chosen a more matronly purple satin instead of the youthful silver gauze with pink embroidery for her ball gown. Too late to change it now. It hung in her armoire beneath a sheet of muslin to protect it from both white and black hairs and tiny claws.

The possessors of those hairs and claws ruled as king and queen over her bedchamber. After initial hissing on both parts, they decided to be friends, companions in mischief, and playmates. Chasing one another around the room at high speed, they managed to create havoc such as knocking over her easel, clearing her dressing table of ribbons and the rice powder box, and sending Barbara sprawling on her face.

"Either they go or I do," she declared, picking herself up.

"They need a garden to run in and lots of creatures to terrorize." Lydia smiled at the twin pairs of eyes peeking out from beneath the bed. "Perhaps I can send them back to Devonshire somehow."

But the idea of not having their furry bodies snuggled up with her at night left her aching. Still, it was only for a few weeks. A very few now that the wedding had been called off. Even if Honore snared a husband, she wouldn't get married until autumn at the earliest.

"Give me time to find a way to make everyone happy."

In a huff, Barbara stalked through the dressing room to her tiny chamber.

Lydia finished getting ready for that night's rout, the entertainment of choice—Honore's, not hers. She wore her plainest evening gown, one she'd worn twice already. No one noticed clothes at a rout. The crush of people, engaged in no more activity than strolling through the rooms of the house and returning outside again, tended to be too great for one to notice more than the face or waistcoat of the persons coming down the steps as one walked up. If someone didn't faint from the crowd or heat, the night was a failure.

Lydia tamped down her sarcasm about what she considered the most ridiculous of entertainments and called to Barbara to come hook up the back of her gown. "Are you certain you don't wish to come?"

"I'm going to read to your dear mama. She's had a headache all day."

Lydia compressed her lips and said nothing about Mama's increased number of headaches.

"I think it's her grief over losing her daughters," Barbara

continued. "She firmly believes Cassandra will marry Whittaker in the end, and Honore is sure to find someone soon."

"I don't think she should. She's too young in her behavior. No judgment."

"And since she is losing her daughters . . ." Barbara glanced past Lydia's shoulder and met her eyes in the dressing-table mirror. "She's asked me to come to Bainbridge Hall and be her companion, and I've accepted."

"Accepted." Lydia repeated the words like a sailor's parrot—hearing the word without comprehension of its meaning. "You can't. I mean, of course you can, but I count on you for respectability."

"You're respectable enough without me. Indeed, Sarah's household is far more to my liking, you know."

Sarah? Lydia started. She so rarely heard her mother's name she barely remembered it. Even Father called her Lady Bainbridge.

"Yes, she can pay you more than I can." Lydia glanced at her latest painting, only half finished and already sold. At last she was developing a tidy nest egg through the print shop buying her pictures, but she could never offer Barbara the luxury of Bainbridge, just mild comfort.

"And Sarah would never consort with Frenchmen who are enemies to this country," Barbara added like a slap.

"Chris—Monsieur de Meuse is not an enemy to this country."

"Then why was he in Dartmoor?"

"I've told you. It was a mistake, an accident."

"Humph. And don't think I missed your slip there, calling him by his Christian name."

"He's my friend. He—"

Voices in the corridor interrupted Lydia. A moment later,

Honore and Cassandra burst into her room on a cloud of white muslin and pastel ribbons, lilac scent and quiet giggles.

"Look what someone sent you." From behind her back, Honore whipped out a bouquet of lilies of the valley. Their fragrance overrode Lydia's own linden blossom scent and Honore's lilac with a sweetness that made her heart ache with longing for woodland meadows and fresh air.

The attached card said simply, "Until I can see you again."

No signature accompanied the card. She'd never seen Christien's handwriting to know for certain, but she knew the flowers came from him, wherever he was of late.

"You have a secret admirer." Honore clapped her hands.

"Perhaps not so secret." Cassandra winked. "*N'est-ce pas?*"

"No, it isn't so. Not that sort of admirer you wish I had." Lydia clipped out the denial even as she brushed the waxy, pale blossoms against her cheek. She told the truth. Christien's admiration wasn't secret at all, not to her. Not to her heart.

God help her—no, He hadn't helped her. If He had a plan for her life, as the Bible said He did, and He allowed this to happen—even perhaps made it happen—she rebelled against the Lord's will. She did not, must not, could not love Christien de Meuse.

The quivery warmth inside her chest at the sight of the flowers, the sorrow gripping her at the realization he must be away and wouldn't return for a while, and the way she couldn't get his kiss out of her too-frequent thoughts told her if she had failed at anything, this might be the worst of her shortcomings.

She was in love with Christien Christophe Arnaud, Comte de Meuse.

She needed to be finding a traitor instead, concentrating on the words, gestures, and actions of her fellow English aristocrats.

She should be helping Christien, not mooning over him like a schoolgirl.

But she tucked the flowers into the neckline of her gown, where their perfume rose as a constant reminder of his thoughtfulness. His thinking of her.

"So who is it?" Honore asked.

"Never you mind. We need to be on our way." She showed them toward the door but paused for a glance back at Barbara. "Perhaps Mama can find a more comfortable bedchamber for you than that box room. I'll hire a maid."

Barbara paled. Good if she found Lydia's dismissal uncomfortable. She was abandoning her in the middle of the Season.

Or perhaps she had simply failed her cousin.

No, she wouldn't accept that edict, not even from herself. Barbara had chosen to live with Lydia, knowing the conditions. If she'd chosen to ingratiate herself with Mama to gain a better position, it was on her head and good for her for going after something she wanted.

Especially her heart.

Lydia paused on the first floor landing to take a deep breath. The *lis de vallée* scent permeated her senses, heady, enticing. So French for a man who had called England his home for more years than France.

A tingle of uneasiness rippled up her spine. She decided to trust him, believed him because someone had tried to harm her when it could not have been him, had tried to harm both of them. She shook off the frisson of suspicion and set her foot on the top tread down to the entryway and her waiting sisters.

"Where are you off to tonight?" Father stepped out of Mama's sitting room.

"A rout. And you?" She tried to smile at him.

"My club. I don't hold with being crushed half to death."
He glanced down the steps, then fixed his cold gaze on Lydia.
"There are wagers in the betting book at White's as to which
of you girls will marry first. Right now, the odds are none of
you for being stubborn minxes. I can scarce hold my head up
in there anymore for the shame of it."

"The ones wagering should be the ones who are shamed."
Lydia's nails pressed into the carved banister. "Such gaming
is disgraceful. We won't ruin our lives to suit some people's
penchant for gambling."

"You'll ruin your lives for not marrying. It's a woman's only
rightful place."

Lydia's jaw bunched, and she spoke through stiff lips. "Then
let us be on our way so we can find these men worthy of us."

"I doubt you'll find them at a rout. I'd rather you found country men, not these city bucks and Corinthians who care more
about their cravat ties and how many bottles of wine they can
drink in a night than the people who grant them the income to
do so. But your mother wanted you all to have a Season. I thank
the good Lord Honore is the last of you."

Lydia stared at him, her heart softening. "You know, Father,
I agree with you. But there are some of those in town seeking
wives. Whittaker is one, which is why he isn't here trying to
woo Cassandra back."

"Indeed. Well, I think I'll be sending you all back to the
country shortly. London grows less acceptable every year." He
looked so tired all of a sudden that Lydia reached out a hand
and touched his arm.

"I think we all might enjoy a relief from this constant activity. Even Honore. Let us first see how things go with her ball.
She has so many admirers, one or two are surely acceptable."

"I hope as much." Without another word, he brushed past her and entered his bedchamber.

Footfalls slow, Lydia descended the steps to her sisters. They didn't say anything until the three of them were settled in the carriage and the vehicle was on its way to Bedford Square.

"What did Father want?" Honore demanded.

"Us to be married in a week or so." Lydia grimaced. "Preferably to men like Whittaker who aren't afraid to get their cravats dirty."

"Whittaker is a lecher. I mean—" Cassandra clapped her hand over her mouth.

Honore giggled. "Don't be the pot calling the kettle black."

"I know. I'm as bad as he was. Perhaps we should have simply eloped sooner and put an end to all the temptations. That is— Lydia, I miss him terribly and think I made a mistake sending him away over something so easily fixed." Cassandra gulped.

"Don't cry, now," Honore admonished.

"I won't." Cassandra sniffed. "I was just so ashamed and thought getting rid of him was the only way to redeem myself, but that's silly. God redeems me just for the asking. If He can forgive me, I should forgive myself for giving in to the flesh. But now it's too late."

"I don't think so, my dear." Lydia's mind raced. "A well-penned letter telling Whittaker exactly what you've told me just might change things."

And Cassandra would be settled. If Lydia managed to repair that relationship, she would have succeeded at something. A good something. Even more so, Cassandra seemed to have a better understanding of God than Lydia did. He forgave human shortcomings, so one should forgive oneself for them too.

She would talk to Cassandra about it further. At the moment, the carriage was slowing to enter the line of vehicles disgorging passengers into the Square. Serious discussions could be interrupted at any moment.

"I've tried to write," Cassandra said, "but we have other matters between us too, like him wanting to curtail my translating because he thinks that's why my eyes are bad, and he wants to stop me from studying aeronautics. I know a husband has a right to stop all these things, but I've had a lifetime of sneaking behind Father's back. I don't want a lifetime of sneaking behind my husband's back."

"And Father is easier to bamboozle than a husband would be. Father is so often away and meeting with his friends all locked away in his study." Honore leaned toward the window and lifted the curtain. "Oh, look, there's Mr. Glendenning. I wonder if we'll see him inside."

"From the look of this line of vehicles," Cassandra said on a sigh, "I don't think we'll see anyone."

"Nonsense." Lydia laughed. "We'll see everyone."

They were both right. Squeezing up the steps of the house and walking on a circuit through all the rooms set up for the guests, they saw scores of persons, most of whom they had encountered somewhere else during the Season. They managed nothing more than a lifted hand, a smile, perhaps a polite word. But they didn't see anyone who interested them long enough to bear the crush for any longer than necessary.

Necessary proved to be two hours, by the time they jammed their way into the overflowing house and managed to return down the steps and then await their carriage.

"Has there ever been a more ridiculous form of entertainment?" Lydia stared down at her crumpled gown, its Vandyke hem torn from where someone had stepped on it coming down the steps.

Her shawl was missing, and two curls bobbed against her cheek, their mooring pin lost somewhere after she'd caught it on the waistcoat buttons of a gentleman who had reeled into her, apparently having imbibed too freely before attending the rout. The only part of her ensemble that appeared unharmed remained her nosegay of lily of the valley. It nestled at her throat, warm and fragrant, each breath of the perfume a reminder of her foolish heart.

"Shall we do something sensible now?" Lydia continued.

"Like go home?" Cassandra asked.

"Yes." Lydia slipped her arm through her sister's. "Honore?"

"Yes, I want to go home. Perhaps all the way home to Bainbridge."

Lydia glanced at Honore. "What—oh, my dear."

Tears glistened on Honore's lashes.

"What is it, child?" Lydia tucked Honore against her with her other arm.

"Him." Honore shook her head, blinking hard. "Gerry is there with another female. With Olivia Tarleton, my dearest friend. I thought . . ."

And the wealthiest heiress of the Season. Probably more proof that he was nothing more than a fortune-hunting gamester. Yet he still bore watching because of his connection to Barnaby. The gambling, the heiress-wooing might be a cover for other activities.

"He's not good enough for you, but I know that doesn't help." Lydia spotted their carriage and guided her sisters toward it. "Let us go home and enjoy hot chocolate and Shrewsbury biscuits and a good cry if we like."

They went home to find the house quiet. Lemster informed them that Lady Bainbridge had retired to her room. Miss

Barbara was reading in the sitting room, and Lord Bainbridge was still out.

Lydia ordered the chocolate and sweets, then directed her sisters up to their rooms to don wraps and night rails and meet her in her chamber. There amidst the antics of the cats, Lydia's paintings, and reams of foolscap as Cassandra tried to compose a letter to Whittaker, they feasted on cakes and biscuits and laughed together as they hadn't done since Lydia had left home to marry. They went to their beds at midnight, early for the Season in town, but the next day was May 11, the date set for Honore's ball.

As much as she wished to, Lydia didn't sleep late. She woke at eight o'clock and began her work of inspecting last-minute details. Before the ball, the Bainbridges would entertain thirty guests for dinner. Christien wasn't one of them. She had considered placing his name on an invitation, but Mama said no, it would displease Father to have the Frenchman at the table.

"He doesn't trust him, you understand," Mama said.

Mama made so few requests that Lydia complied. Finding eligible and unattached gentlemen was no difficulty. Making certain they were worthy of the exclusive dinner, and therefore being first arrivals at the ball without having to wait in long lines before enjoying the entertainment, proved more of a challenge. Lydia had managed, though, and rather looked forward to the event. And afterward, Christien would be at the ball . . .

At five o'clock, all of them went to their rooms to rest for a while before they began to dress. Lydia lay down for five minutes, found the cats deciding to use her for a battleground for territory, and rose again to begin brushing out her hair before pinning it up again. A hundred strokes with the boar's bristle brush would make it gleam like black satin. She'd never cared much about her looks before, but now—

The pounding on the front door of the townhouse reverberated loud enough to reach her third-floor room. She sprang to her feet, brush in one hand, other hand clutching her dressing gown to her neck, and raced from her room.

"What is it?" Honore burst from her chamber, Cassandra on her heels. "Why the racket?"

The three of them leaned over the railing, peering down the stairwell thirty feet to the entryway. Lemster unlatched the door. Before he turned the handle, the portal flew open and a young man without a hat and with his cravat askew tumbled into the hall.

"Where's Lord Bainbridge?" he shouted.

"Young man," Lemster began, "that is no way—"

"Out of my way, man. I need his lordship." Announcement made, he charged down the corridor, calling to Father.

Lydia gripped the balustrade, expecting her face had gone as white as her sisters'. "Something terrible has happened," she whispered.

Below, the young man pounded on the library door. "Lord Bainbridge, come quick. Perceval is dead."

"Perceval?" The corridor and steps began to spin around Lydia. "The prime minister is dead?"

The young man's voice rang out like a funeral bell. "Assassinated."

24

So they had failed.

Christien's hands fell from the ends of the cravat he was tying, and he stared at his valet in the mirror. "Who shot him?"

"Too many rumors to be certain right now," the man said. "I just heard it in the street and came up straightaway."

"Of course you did. Thank you." With hands that shook a bit, Christien finished the intricate knot of the cravat. "I'll learn more while I'm out."

A Frenchman risking his life to cause havoc in Britain? An American wanting the same? An Englishman treacherous to his country? Any were disastrous to Christien's mission. It meant failure, possibly worse trouble to come.

And Lydia, with her belief she proved unsuccessful in too many things in her life, would take the news like a blow.

He wanted to be with her. Given his way, he would rush straight over to Bainbridge House and reassure her that she had been as much help as anyone. More so than he had been. He was trained to ferret out assassins, not let them get away with their deeds.

And the prime minister. Who'd have thought even a traitor or agent of the French would be so bold? Fomenting discord amongst the common people was one thing—not that difficult in the depressed economy and lengthening war that wasn't going so well for England, and with a prince regent who cared more about his pleasure than his kingdom. But the most important man in the country, the man running the country . . .

If only Christien had been in town that week, he might have prevented the disaster. But Lang had sent him on what turned out to be a wild goose chase. All the way to Portsmouth to see if anyone could identify the man in the garden.

Of course no one had. Lydia herself had said it was so dark she saw nothing. In a busy and centrally located city like Portsmouth, too many persons came and went without notice. Christien and Lang and Lydia remained stranded, suspecting it had been Barnaby.

If only Christien believed Barnaby was more than another pawn in the game governments made of war, he would have peace of mind about Lydia's safety. He would believe her blackmail threat had died with the gentleman. But a tension in Christien's gut told him otherwise. He'd survived in his occupation as long as he had because of those internal premonitions.

"I must go to Bainbridge House," he announced.

"But you weren't invited to their dinner." His English valet frowned in disapproval.

"Everything is going to be chaos with this news. I wouldn't be surprised if dinners and balls are canceled."

From the look of the streets, however, London was going on about its business. He saw a few more groups of men than usual clustered at street corners, talking. Voices remained subdued, as though fearing being overheard. Carriages trundled past at no great haste to be home or anywhere else. Open vehicles showed beautifully dressed ladies and gentlemen talking, even laughing. Perhaps they didn't know. Perhaps they didn't care. Perhaps the opposing party, the Whigs, would even celebrate this evening.

Celebrate over the death of a man who had served his country long and well.

Christien sighed to relieve the tension in his middle as the carriage drew up in front of Bainbridge House. No other carriages crowded the street, and he realized the time was too early for their dinner party to have begun. He would interrupt their preparations.

He got out of the carriage and trudged up the steps to the front door.

"Monsieur de Meuse." The butler looked confused upon opening the door to Christien's knock. "You weren't—I didn't realize—"

"No, I was not invited to the dinner, Lemster; however, I wish to see Lady Gale."

Wanted to. Needed to, ached to.

Lemster wrung his gloved hands. "I—I don't know if she's available. The family is quite overwrought with the news."

"Of course they are. But will you please ask her if she'll see me?" Christien glanced to his right. "I will wait in the drawing room."

Not waiting to be shown to the chamber, he strode across the entryway and opened the pocket door to a chamber readied for guests. Fresh candles stood in their sconces, awaiting a taper to light them. Fresh roses perfumed the air with a warm scent. Every bit of brass, wood, or glass shone with a recent cleaning.

Christien strode to the window and drew back the edge of the blue velvet drapery. The square remained subdued by way of traffic and pedestrians, save for a handful of boys playing with a ball in the grassy center circle. In the distance, a seller of news sheets cried the news of the shooting in Parliament itself.

A prime minister dead in front of dozens of others—members of Parliament, guards, British subjects.

The house lay in unusual stillness for a residence with six

family members present and three times as many servants. Everyone subdued, contemplating, waiting for news. He should send a message to Lisette. She should be gone. If this had been a French plot, none of them, émigrés or not, would be safe. He should have sent Lisette packing the instant he knew of her game.

Games. Everyone played them, from him with his double agent work, to Lisette playing informant, to Frobisher and his gambling. Lang played chess master, moving his retinue of agents around like pawns.

Christien wanted out of the game so he could clear his conscience and live his life for Christ. What that entailed besides being involved with his land and family, he didn't yet know.

He glanced down at his hands. Encased in gray kid gloves, they bore fewer signs of labor than they had a few weeks ago, turning the smooth whiteness required of a gentleman. To Christien, they felt sticky with blood. Like Lady Macbeth, he couldn't scrub them clean. But he tried. He removed the gloves, shoved them into his coat pockets, and rubbed his left hand over the back of his right.

"Are you all right, *mon ami*?" Lydia asked from close behind him.

He spun, nearly drew her to him. "*Cherie*. I didn't hear you approach."

No wonder she slipped up on him. In silvery gauze embellished with pale pink ribbon rosettes, she resembled a drift of smoke or mist off the sea.

"The door was open and you seemed engaged." Her glance dropped to his hands. "Did you injure yourself?"

"No, I simply feel—" He looked to the still-open door and lowered his voice. "Unclean sometimes. The things my work has called upon me to execute." He shuddered. "A poor choice of words. Forgive me."

"I think there's no need to forgive." She didn't quite meet his eyes. "You, of course, didn't commit this heinous crime against Perceval."

"I?" Christien jerked back a step. "That would be acting against . . . England. I have never—" He felt ill. He yanked his gloves from his pockets. "It was a mistake for me to come, if you think for a moment I knew of this assassination. I'd have stopped it if I had."

"But you weren't even in London."

"I had business." He turned toward the door, caught the rustle of fabric, the whisper of leather soles on wood flooring.

Servants moving away from their eavesdropping position.

"If you still don't trust me to be on the same side as you, I have nothing more to say." The ache in his chest would prevent speech in another half a minute. "I have failed England," he added, his voice thick and dry.

"We have failed England." Lydia's hand was on his shoulder, the other one on his face, turning him toward her to read the pain in her eyes. "I'm sorry. I—" She ran her tongue along her lower lip.

And he kissed her there in her father's drawing room. With the door wide open to any passersby, he bent his head and drank in the sweetness of her mouth. For a full minute, he forgot about assassinations and intrigue, traitors and spies, in the taste of an herbal tisane, her sweet and aromatic scent, the smoothness of her face beneath his caressing fingers.

"*Cherie*," he breathed against her mouth. "*Mon coeur, ma vie, je t'aime.*"

There, he'd said it, called her his dear, his heart, his life, and admitted his love. For a heartbeat he dared not breathe. He didn't feel her warm breath against his lips, as though she too suspended taking in life's oxygen. Even the rustling and sliding feet in the corridor ceased.

Then the door knocker sounded. Lydia gasped, flung herself away from him, and raced to the drawing room door like the silver lining of a cloud. She stopped in the opening, her hand to her mouth, either rubbing memory of his closeness away from her or holding it near.

Christien joined her in time to see Lemster admit a youth in sweat-stained livery.

"He's from Parliament," Lydia whispered.

Christien followed her into the corridor.

"Lord Bainbridge?" the messenger asked.

"Here." His lordship appeared on the steps, attired in black evening dress. "News?"

"Yes. Yes." The youth took a few quick breaths. "The assassin is a man named John Bellingham." He began to recite as though he had said the same thing many times. "He has a grievance against the government, but we have no reason to believe he is anything but a private subject who perpetrated this crime out of personal anger, not for the sake of any foreign power or attempt to foment revolution in this kingdom." Speech delivered, he slumped against the front door.

Lydia swayed back against Christien. He wrapped one arm around her waist, feeling his own tension escape like acrid smoke from burning refuse.

"Thank you for this news." Above them on the steps, Lord Bainbridge tossed the messenger a coin. Silver glinted in the dim light of the entryway and disappeared in the boy's hand. "It's not welcome. We'd rather Perceval be alive, but we're relieved it's not part of a greater plot by our enemies."

"Indeed." Lydia sighed. "I owe you an apology, Christien. I never should have thought even for a moment that you—I wasn't thinking."

"None of us is." He released her before someone noticed them and moved away a foot, no more. "But I am thinking now, and we—I need to work harder on finding our traitor. I wouldn't be surprised if this John Bellingham was encouraged to his action by someone wanting to create chaos in the government."

"Christien." Lydia faced him, but heavy footfalls on the steps sounded, and her face grew still and cold. "Thank you for coming, monsieur. We are all well here. I will see you at the ball?"

"Indeed." Christien managed not to flinch. He saw her father rounding the staircase and understood her sudden coolness. "I won't disrupt your dinner."

"You may as well stay." Lord Bainbridge loomed in the doorway. "I'm going out, Lydia, and that will disrupt your numbers. I expect a number of others will be gone too."

"But, Father, you must at least come to Honore's ball. You should lead her in the first dance."

"The affairs of this country are far more important than a silly dance." Bainbridge turned away.

"But what about you wanting Honore to find a husband immediately?" Lydia asked.

Bainbridge paused a moment, then shrugged. "Right now, I want you girls out of London. It's safer with the way—" Without finishing his sentence, he strode away, snatched his cloak and hat from a footman, and vanished out the front door on the heels of the Parliamentary messenger.

And someone else, a glimpse of a passerby caught like a will-o-the-wisp—eavesdropping or following?

Lydia raised her hands to her face. They shook. "No matter what I do, he disapproves."

"He is right, *peut-être*." Christien did not—could not—move. He continued to stare at the blank panel of the front door as though he could bore a hole through it and pursue Bainbridge through the square. His mind spun like a child's hoop trundling downhill.

He was mad. Never should he think what he was thinking. He had no evidence other than that glimpse and a father wanting to look out for his daughters.

Except . . .

"I shall return," Christien told Lydia and slipped out the door before she could ask him questions.

He could never answer her, tell her what he was thinking or doing. He was chasing the wild goose, nothing more.

But he followed Lord Bainbridge anyway.

Lydia thought packing and heading for the country immediately sounded like a wonderful idea. It was one of the few times she agreed with her father. But she still expected many guests to attend dinner and must make arrangements to reorganize the table in the event that several—those who were members of Parliament in either the House of Commons or the House of Lords—decided not to come. Some ladies wouldn't come either. They, like her own mama, would be so distraught by the news of the prime minister's assassination that they would be prostrate upon their beds and not wish to remain in the street.

She didn't want to be in the street even to travel to Almack's Assembly Rooms for Honore's ball, fearing riots as she did. But surely matters would settle as news spread of the assassin being nothing more than a man with a disturbed mind who had committed the crime. People would wish to gather, to talk about where they were when they heard the news, how they felt about it.

Lydia still felt sick. She'd made herself dress and bullied the girls into dressing. She still needed to persuade Mama that she must attend Honore's ball. Tomorrow they could leave for the country. Lydia was of no use there in town. She couldn't hunt a traitor. That lay in Christien's hands.

And Christien had sped out of the house as though a man announcing himself as disloyal to the crown had walked past the window. He'd said he would return. She mustn't fret if he didn't. England mattered more than a party, indeed.

Yet Father had been so determined they all marry this Season. Why the sudden change in plans or opinion?

Stomach roiling, head spinning, Lydia climbed the steps to Mama's bedchamber. She didn't knock. Mama had told her to go away the past two times she'd done that. Lydia simply turned the handle and entered the chamber.

Mama reclined on a chaise longue. Barbara hovered on a stool beside her, waving a fan in one hand and smelling salts in the other. The stench of ammonia permeated the chamber.

"Open the windows." Lydia trotted across the Wilton carpet to do so for herself. Though smelling of coal smoke and a faint whiff of horses from the stables in the mews, the breeze sweeping into the chamber surpassed the vinaigrette for freshness.

"Night air." Mama pressed a hand to her brow. "I simply cannot breathe night air."

"You should have a care for your mother's health, Lydia," Barbara scolded.

"I do." Lydia set her hands on her hips. "But I care for Cassandra and Honore more right now. Mama, this is your youngest daughter. She deserves to have you at her side on this important night. You can drift away after the guests have arrived, but right now you need to be with your daughters."

"I cannot." Mama moved her hand to her chest. "My heart."

Lydia softened her tone. "We all suffered a shock tonight. But it was nothing more than a madman with a private vengeance to settle." She hoped. "Honore cannot have her coming-out ball with neither parent present." Lydia spoke with determination and a hint of anger. "What gentleman will wish to court her if he thinks neither of her parents cares enough to be at her side on this important night? Do you wish her to marry? Or would you prefer she join me in Tavistock?"

"Heaven forfend." Mama struggled to sit up.

Barbara glared. "She wouldn't."

"Rather than live with an autocratic father and a mother who apparently doesn't care with whom she sneaks out of the house, yes, she would, I think." Not waiting to observe the response for that, Lydia spun on the heel of her silver slipper and stalked from the room.

She hesitated in the corridor, waiting for guilt to slam into her. It didn't. Instead, a sense of peace washed over her, as though at last she'd done something right.

Yet was it? She'd been raised to honor her mother and father. Wasn't speaking her mind like that dishonoring them? If she wasn't to completely fail as a Christian woman, shouldn't she apologize, beg forgiveness of them, let them have their way in all things? She'd been told that all her life and transferred that belief to her role with a husband. Obedience without question. So she'd let him go without a fight and harbored the bitterness against him for seven years to the extent that marriage seemed like the cruelest state for a woman. Speaking her mind to her mother hadn't been disobedience. Mama hadn't told her to do something she hadn't. Nor had she dishonored her. She'd honored her in knowing the importance of her presence with her daughter.

At that moment, Lydia wanted no part of Mama, Father, or Honore's ball. She wanted to be rushing through the streets on whatever errand had drawn Christien away with little word. She could forget about family coils then.

But the good of the family came first. So she climbed another flight of steps to Cassandra and Honore's room to make certain they were ready.

They stood at the window, one fair, one dark, one in white muslin and silver spangles, the other in primrose yellow silk and lavender embroidery, both so pretty and young that shoving them into marriage under any circumstances felt like the real sin.

"What are you looking at?" Lydia asked.

They both jumped and spun around as though guilty.

"I thought I saw Whittaker." Cassandra blushed. "But my spectacles are in the library, and I couldn't see that far."

"I didn't see anyone that could have been him." Honore cast Cassandra a sympathetic glance. "But I think I saw Gerald."

"You mean Mr. Frobisher." Lydia's tone gently reproved.

Honore stuck her pert nose in the air. "He was Gerald to me, and I want him at my ball."

"He will be refused admittance after what he did the other night. Taking you to a gaming hell indeed, not to mention attending the rout with Miss Tarleton." Lydia gritted her teeth. "Come along. We must persuade Mama to get herself out of bed and into her ball gown."

"Mama isn't coming?" Tears flooded Honore's eyes, and she rushed past Lydia.

"Well, that should work to get Mama ready." Lydia offered Cassandra her own sympathetic glance. "I'm sorry Whittaker isn't here, but he hasn't had time to get your letter yet and reach London."

Cassandra plucked at a lavender petal on her bodice. "I haven't sent him a letter."

"Why not?"

"Too many reasons. All the same reasons. Mostly I don't want a marriage like yours."

"You wouldn't have a marriage like mine. Whittaker isn't a soldier."

"No, he engages in that ungentlemanly occupation of running his own mills, and now he has the estate. He hates town. I'll go mad in the country without bookshops and other scholars."

"The country is better for ballooning." Lydia offered Cassandra an encouraging smile.

She merely grimaced. "Which Whittaker disapproves of too. So how can I still love him?"

"I don't know what makes us love." The words slipped out unbidden.

Cassandra's head shot up. "Do you still love Charles? Or— Lydia." Her eyes widened. "Monsieur de Meuse."

"I hear the front door knocker. Guests must be arriving."

That being the truth, Lydia sped toward the steps, slowing only on the final flight in time to see Lemster ushering several guests into the drawing room. Lydia joined them. Soon Cassandra, Honore, Mama, and Barbara followed. Between greeting everyone, listening to people's repeated exclamations over the assassination of Lord Perceval, and sending new messages to the kitchen over how many guests would grace the dinner table, Lydia found no time to wonder about Father's whereabouts, whether or not Whittaker had been in the square, or whether or not Christien would keep his word and return for dinner.

The latter came just as Lydia and an elderly earl led the way into the dining room. Other than a brief apology for his tardiness, Christien said nothing more to Lydia before slipping into his assigned place halfway down the table.

More guests than Lydia thought likely had arrived.

"No sense in running about. We all know the next prime minister will be Liverpool," one peer announced. "No one else makes sense."

The presence of other noblemen set Father's absence under a glaring light. If anyone thought it odd that the father of the guest of honor was absent, good breeding led them to keep their opinions to themselves. They expressed it more indirectly through lavish compliments on the dinner, which was excellent, through praising Honore's looks—stunning—through keeping the conversation light, even amusing.

Except for Christien. He spoke to the ladies on either side of him, served himself and his dinner companions from the dishes at hand, and sipped from the glass in front of him, but his thick lashes veiled his blue eyes more often than not, and he smiled little. Twice, Lydia caught him gazing at her with his mouth set, as though he were annoyed or even angry.

The food everyone declared superb might as well have been lumps of colored clay and congealed oil paints on her plate, for all she tasted them.

At last the meal ended. Instead of the ladies withdrawing while the gentlemen enjoyed their time alone, everyone left together, gathering up wraps and calling up carriages to proceed to Almack's for the ball.

"My lady?" Christien moved to the side of the steps, where Lydia stood directing everyone's departure.

She leaned toward him, gripping the banister so she didn't touch him. "Yes?"

"Will you ride in my carriage with me? Please."

"I can, yes." She allowed him to hand her into the carriage, though she knew it was a declaration that they were courting.

But they were. They stood up together twice for dances at Honore's ball and went into the midnight supper together. Christien drove her home with Cassandra in the carriage, and he held Lydia's hand beneath the fold of her gauzy skirt as though he never intended to let her go.

Of course he must. "We can't live in one another's pockets," Lydia murmured to him at the door. "I don't want . . . I can't . . ."

"Not yet?" He tucked his forefinger beneath her chin, tilted her face up, and brushed his lips across hers.

The contact proved enough to send Lydia to her room on wobbly knees as she attempted not to smile. She must give nothing away, show little emotion. This was merely playacting, a ruse to persuade whomever they must that they were focused on one another, not French agents.

If any existed. Lydia wasn't convinced any longer. Yet she couldn't forget the blackmail, the fear, nor Barnaby's dead body. They haunted her dreams as much as did Christien—

And Charles.

Sometimes, after a drive in the park through sparkling May sunshine, or an afternoon of rain spent near the library fire, talking, reading, or playing a game with Honore and Cassandra, Lydia looked at Christien and pictured a future together, sitting by the fire in his Shropshire home, a mere cottage with only fifteen rooms, he'd told her, set amidst a mere five thousand acres. Not much of a house or lands for a nobleman, but they had prospered in other ways, thanks to his mother's business sense and good management. The girls would have good dowries, and his life would be comfortable.

But Charles had promised her much the same. They would live in his family home in Lancashire, cozy amidst the rolling hills and meadows of sheep. And nothing came of it. He left.

He stayed away. He died without once taking her to his family home, and the home that should have been theirs went to a distant cousin by the laws of inheritance.

"I can't do it," she told Christien near the end of May. "I can't continue with seeing you or I'll care too much."

"You don't care too much now?" His smile was gentle, his fingers caressing her hand gentler still. "I believe you love me."

"Perhaps I do." Not perhaps. She knew she did. "But, Christien, you work for the government too. It's not the Army, but it takes you away. It puts you in danger. It put me in danger. What's next? My family?"

"It'll be done with soon."

"Will it? Nothing has happened since the prime minister was assassinated. You have no clues and no evidence other than someone trying to harm both of us twice."

"These things take time—months, even years. I've told you about—"

"Yes, some of your missions, as though that should comfort me." She feared she would weep right there in the middle of Hyde Park. "Do I have to wait until this mission is done, or be in fear for your life and mine too? Would you, unlike Charles, resign and settle for being nothing more than a gentleman farmer, husband, and—and father?"

He said nothing in response. His gaze had strayed across a line of open carriages to two persons riding.

"*Tres interessant*," he murmured. "I haven't seen Gerald Frobisher in weeks, and he's keeping august company."

Lydia suppressed a shriek and managed a calm, "Please take me home. I have my answer. And you may have yours—no future together."

"Lydia, *je regrette*—"

"Please take me home so you may go about your business unencumbered."

With a sigh, Christien turned the horses out of the park gate and returned Lydia to Cavendish Square. Head aching, she retreated to her room, where her easel stood empty and her paints dried.

She'd neglected her art for a man.

For the first time, she truly understood why Cassandra questioned the wisdom of marrying Whittaker. Cassandra didn't want to neglect her interests to have a husband. Father had suppressed their interests enough, and he'd kept Honore from developing any at all so that she appeared to have nothing more to offer the world than her pretty face and form and lively chatter about nothing important.

From his perspective, Father had been doing right by his daughters. Apparently, men wanted an escort, a companion when convenient to them, someone to bear their children and run their homes and nothing more. Christien was no different. His allowing Lisette to remain as the Bainbridge chef for weeks after discovering her presence in their household had given Lydia hope, but when she was no more useful as an informant, he had sent her packing, bundled her onto a coach bound for Shropshire with a dragon of a chaperone to ensure she arrived.

But none of that took away the pain, nor the hope that something would change. The way Lydia's heart leaped at the announcement that Christien had come to call the next day told her that. He had changed his mind. He was going to resign his position.

Footfalls light, Lydia skimmed down the steps, paused for a moment to tuck a stray curl into its pins and straighten her silk shawl on her shoulders, and glided into the drawing room as though all day would be too soon to arrive.

"*Ma chère.*" Christien turned from the window and held his hands out to her. He didn't smile.

Lydia gave him her hands and didn't smile either. "What's amiss?"

"Ah, you know me well." Christien indicated the rain streaking down the glass. "The weather is too foul to go out, so let us sit here together and talk very low so no one can hear what I have to say."

Now a little sick, Lydia followed Christien to a sofa as far from the door and listening servants as possible, and waited.

"Have you seen your father of late?" Christien began.

Lydia stared at him. "Of course."

"Has he seemed preoccupied?" he asked. "Perhaps not paying attention to his daughters as much?"

"Perhaps. I think he's resigned himself to our failed Season, but—"

"Lydia, listen." Christien's hands fisted on the thighs of his biscuit-colored breeches. "The night of Honore's ball, your father walked out of this house. He didn't take a carriage, he walked." He paused.

Lydia remained motionless except for her heart, which beat double time.

"I thought it odd," Christien continued, "so I followed him."

"What—what did you see?" Lydia could barely squeeze out the words.

"The same thing I've seen twice since—him getting into a carriage several blocks from this house or Parliament."

"That's not terribly odd."

"With Gerald Frobisher."

25

She was running away again, yet Lydia couldn't face another minute in London amidst the suspicions and apprehensions, the disappointments and the failures. She needed clean and sweet air, long walks and open moors.

"It isn't possible," she'd told Christien in the drawing room. "There is some explanation."

She repeated the words to herself again and again throughout the evening, then the night, when she couldn't sleep. She ended up packing instead. Father had an explanation. She must ask him, confront him, do something before they left town.

Running. Running. Running. Running from fear of the truth. Running from the disaster the Season had turned out to be. Running from her desire to cling to Christien and beg him to run with her.

By the time the Watch called the hour of six o'clock a.m., Lydia's clothes and paintings resided in trunks and bags. All that remained were two felines that had vanished beneath the bed. They, at least, would find the country more enjoyable.

She herself found the country more enjoyable, so why the reluctance now? The country didn't show her errors in brilliant light as did the city, where Cassandra's engagement ended,

Honore came too close to disgracing herself, and Lydia fell in love.

Her heart compelled her to stay. Her head said that was the best reason of all to leave. Run. Yes, she admitted, run away to the shelter of aloneness.

Aloneness that suddenly felt like loneliness.

Hearing Father leaving his bedchamber one floor below, Lydia slipped out of hers and followed. She caught up with him in the dining room. Lemster was pouring coffee into a fragile china cup, and Father seated himself at the long table, a newspaper in hand.

He glanced up at Lydia's entrance. "You're awake early."

"I didn't sleep." Lydia drew out a chair before a footman could reach her and dropped onto it. "I was packing, but I want to talk to you before you go. Will you send the servants away?" She couldn't give the order with Father present.

"If this is about Honore—"

"Not yet." Lydia glanced toward Lemster. He had just poured coffee over the sides of the cup and onto the saucer.

"If you must." Father gave the command, then scowled at the ruined cup of coffee. "You can take care of that for me."

Lydia obeyed, pouring coffee, selecting bread rolls and strawberries for both of them.

Once the food was served and she sat adjacent to her father, she gripped the edge of the table, leaned toward him, and asked in an undertone, "Why did you get into a carriage with Gerald Frobisher three blocks from this house?"

Father dropped his coffee cup. It hit the table and shattered. Coffee splattered across his plate, his paper, his pristine shirtfront and cravat. Swearing, he snatched up a serviette and began to dab. "Look what you've done, girl. I never make messes like this. It's you who make a mess of everything, including not keeping control over that youngest sister of yours."

"You mean your youngest daughter?" Lydia rose, found more serviettes in the sideboard, and brought them to the table. "Or is she only that when she's being a biddable darling?"

"Something you wouldn't understand. If you'd listened to me, you wouldn't have married Charles Gale. But you had to have him. And Cassandra wanted that younger son. Now she doesn't have that much, even if he is the earl." Father scooped the broken fragments of china onto the sodden newspaper. "And you came here to see to your sisters, and we've had naught but trouble, the least of which being Gerald Frobisher."

Lydia slapped the pile of serviettes onto the spilled coffee. "A gamester and, at least in attempt, debaucher of young ladies. So what were you doing with him?"

"That, young lady, is none of your concern."

"It is if you're involved in treason."

"Treason." The newspaper balled between Father's hands. His face reddened, and he opened and closed his mouth like a fish out of water. For a moment, he appeared to be suffering an apoplexy. Then he sank onto his chair, grabbed up Lydia's coffee cup, and drained its contents. "How dare you?" His voice, though soft, held the razor edge of broken ice. "How dare you even suggest, even think—get out of my sight. Get out of my house. And take your troublemaking sisters with you."

As though the coldness of his tone had frozen her, Lydia remained standing beside the table, scarcely able to breathe, let alone move.

"Get . . . out." Still with frigid control, Father drew back his hand.

Lydia fled before he struck her. The front door, open to receive

290

the mail, beckoned her. She should run to Christien, tell him of Father's reaction to her enquiries.

No, no, she should not. She was free of masculine control, of their power to order her out of the house, to strike her, to leave her penniless in a tiny cottage on the moors. Now she held a nest egg with her paintings and a shop that would sell all she completed. She could support herself, help her sisters if need be. She would not run into the arms of another man and lose that power over her own life.

Which includes You too, God.

She raced up the steps and into her sisters' room. They both slept, looking as innocent as they had when Lydia left home seven years ago, Cassandra with her hair a tangle upon the pillow, Honore's hair neatly plaited.

Lydia backed from the chamber. She would find a footman to haul down their trunks and begin to pack for them. If Lisette were still there, Lydia would have used her to send a message to Christien. But no, he could manage things on his own. That his sister had been the Bainbridge cook for so long stood against him. He'd left her there to spy on the Bainbridge family. He'd always suspected them. Lang must have always suspected them, especially once he knew about the blackmail and her acquiescence to it without a fight.

How could she have fought it? It threatened her family. Never could she threaten the welfare of her family, no matter the cost to herself.

Yet in compliance, hadn't she harmed her family? She'd introduced Gerald Frobisher to her sister. She'd been so intent upon Mr. Barnaby at the theater that she hadn't paid attention to the tension growing between Cassandra and Whittaker that led to their fight and the breaking of the engagement. And she'd been paying attention to Christien while Cassandra and Whittaker had been left alone in the library.

Halfway down the back stairs, Lydia paused and leaned against the wall, her eyes closed, her breath catching in her throat.

Perhaps she did need a keeper. Or at least an adviser, a wise counselor. Her own decisions in life, the choices she'd made, led to little success. On the contrary, they led to near disaster, from her marriage to confronting her father about meeting with Frobisher.

To running away from God?

You've never helped me, Lord. You let me go my own way and make mistakes, and I'll just fix them myself too.

Decision made, she continued to the servants' hall, where she found one footman to bring the rest of the trunks out of the box room, another one to order up the traveling coach, and a maid to assist in the packing. Lydia hurried back up to her sisters' bedchamber and woke them.

"We're leaving," she announced.

"Why?" Honore sounded like a petulant child as she sat up and rubbed her eyes. "I'm as much of a success as any lady can be without a betrothal. Even my ball was a success despite the assassination and everyone mourning."

"The Whigs weren't mourning." Yawning, Cassandra slipped out of bed. "But I can't leave today. I have books to return to Hookham's and an order to collect—"

"A footman can return the books and the order can be posted."

"But I'll never catch a husband if we leave London now." Honore remained in bed.

"From what I've seen of London gentlemen," Lydia said, "you will do better elsewhere."

"What? Some manure-caked farmer like a man Father wants for me?" Honore's face twisted with disgust. "You think I'll find someone civilized in Devonshire?"

"It's far more civilized than a London gaming hell." Lydia went to the door. "You have half an hour to get dressed before I have the servants bring in the trunks for packing."

"I won't go." Honore gripped her bedclothes as though they would hold her in town.

Lydia sighed. "You will if you don't want Father's wrath as I received it this morning." She touched the cheek he had intended to slap, and tears welled in her eyes. "Please, I want to be away from here this morning."

"Lydia, what happened?" Honore and Cassandra stared at her.

She shook her head. "Nothing. We had a row. It's always the same. He wants us wed and off his hands."

Because unmarried daughters embarrassed him, or because wed, he needn't worry about them if something happened to him?

The former, of course. Nothing would happen to her father. He wasn't any more guilty of treason than Mama was.

Mama was still sleeping, and Barbara refused to wake her. "She isn't well enough to travel today. You'll have to wait."

"Father says we cannot. Mama will have to follow later."

"Disgraceful, running away like this, like you've something to hide." Barbara sniffed.

Lydia wished she didn't agree.

"We'll be gone before noon."

They were, in fact, gone before eleven o'clock. Despite being dismissed from the dining room, Lemster must have listened at the keyhole and overheard Lydia's conversation with her father, for he sent up every footman and maid to assist in the removal. If Cassandra and Honore hadn't hastened to dress, they might have found themselves bustled out the door in their night rails. They did hurry, however, and once Lydia and Cassandra managed to coax Hodge and Noirette out from under the bed, with the assistance of two footmen moving the heavy piece of furniture to make the refuge less appealing, the three Bainbridge sisters and two cats crowded into the traveling coach and headed south, another carriage following behind with their luggage.

"Why," Honore asked for perhaps the hundredth time, "do we have to go?"

"Because Father told us to," Lydia responded for as many times.

"But why?" Honore persisted. "We've done nothing wrong."

But perhaps Father had.

The idea of that set Lydia's stomach to roiling. Perhaps Mama knew, and that was why she kept to her bed or sitting room when she should have been chaperoning Honore.

No, not even her father would she believe of committing treason. Even if he found liking his daughters difficult, he wouldn't harm his family, see them disgraced and dishonored, shunned from Society, perhaps forced penniless into exile. As his title and estates were attainder by the Crown, he would be declared to have a corruption of the blood, and all his family, his heirs included, would be made a pariah in England.

So why, Lydia asked herself, feeling like Honore, did he want them gone from town so suddenly, when getting them husbands had been his reason for allowing them all to go to London in the first place?

No answers came from her own head, from her sisters, from the city or farms or daunting edifice of Butser Hill, with its peak ominously titled the Devil's Cleft. None of them wishing for the steep descent to the downs of Hampshire inside the coach, they chose to stretch their legs and walk along the chalky out-croppings. Rolling hills dotted with sheep and copses of trees spread out below, all the way to the sparkling expanse of the English Channel.

Once again inside the trundling vehicle, they dozed. Cassandra even read or stared out the window. Only ten hours to Portsmouth from London with fine teams along the posting road. They reached the coastal city by dusk, dusty, quiet, too weary to eat.

"I have to walk the cats," Lydia said once they were settled into a room at the George. Neither sister offered to accompany her.

She clipped leashes onto the collars of each feline and carried them downstairs. At the door, she hesitated, remembering the last time she'd walked cats in that garden. One cat in the rain after dark. But Barnaby was dead. She need not fear anyone pouncing on her.

Shivering despite the mild night, she slipped out the side door of the inn and hesitated beneath the lantern hung over the entrance. Its yellow glow created a pool of light that reached the head of the path, an illusion of warmth. Lydia waited there, inhaling the aroma of lilacs and thyme, rosemary and recently mown grass. She listened to the whisper of the breeze passing through the shrubbery, the singing of passing sailors—

And the crunch of gravel just beyond the pool of lantern flame.

"Good evening, Lady Gale. I see we meet again."

26

"No post today?" Christien glanced at his valet's empty hands and away before the man read his expression.

"No, monsieur. I'm sorry." The man wasn't fooled, not when Christien sent him to the receiving office daily. "Perhaps tomorrow."

"Perhaps."

Christien left his rooms for a long walk through Green Park. He could be attending half a dozen entertainments, even that late in the Season, but the pain of hearing nothing from Lydia ran too deeply for him to share it with anyone. Lydia's silence spoke volumes. She wanted nothing to do with a man who would be so attached to the work he had taken to gain revenge on France that he would accuse her own father of treason. He should have known better than to say anything. He and Lydia thought, after all, that Gerald Frobisher was nothing more than a gamester. He did frequent the worst of the gaming establishments. But three times now, Christien saw Frobisher rendezvousing with Bainbridge, a man everyone knew never picked up a die or a playing card. Something odd was afoot there.

So Christien concentrated his efforts on keeping a record of both gentlemen's movements. Unfortunately, after the third time he saw Bainbridge and Frobisher together, the time that prompted him to say something to Lydia—the action that drove her away—both men ignored one another, even when they came face-to-face at a soirée Christien attended. Bainbridge left town the next day.

Christien longed to follow him. If Lydia wouldn't write, he would go to her. But Lang said no.

"Your work is here, *mon ami*. I cannot spare you."

"We've made no progress," Christien objected. "I'm wondering if we've been mistaken about someone attempting to provoke trouble, even revolt. My first suspect turns up dead, and the second one spends his time playing cards."

"And what is discussed over a game and a glass, eh?" Lang gave Christien a half smile, a knowing smile. "Have you tried?"

"I don't gamble."

Lang laughed, a low, throaty chuckle. "Of course you do. You've been gambling for ten years. What is worse? Your life or a game of chance?"

Christien wished Lang weren't correct. "I'll give it some thought."

He thought about it while having his valet teach him how to play whist. In the meantime, London simmered in the rising heat of summer, like a steam engine getting ready to blow off the top of its stack. During his long walks through Green Park or Hyde Park, Christien caught the huddled groups of people on street corners, murmuring about the mismanagement of the war, the laziness of the prince regent, the Luddites creating havoc in the north.

"They've sent in soldiers to kill good Englishmen," more than one man protested. "Killed us like dogs for fearin' for our jobs 'cause of them power looms. We're goin' t' have ourselves a civil war if this continues."

Which was exactly what Christien did not want to hear. Added to concern over soldiers going up to the northern counties to fight the men breaking up looms came talk of Wellington doing badly in Spain, increasing the threat of France and starting rumors of invasion once again. As though that weren't enough to bring the country to its knees, more rumors of Americans declaring war began to circulate around the middle of June. Official word hadn't reached town yet, but people had heard that the American president, Mr. Madison, had requested their government—Congress, they called it—to make the declaration.

Three wars and a staggering economy left the nation ripe for an explosion. All some Englishmen needed was another man like the one in the north calling himself Captain Ludd to send Londoners racing for the palace to seize the king or storming the walls of Parliament.

But that man couldn't be Lord Bainbridge. He had departed for his estate, along with his wife. If Frobisher was the guilty party, he was trying to accomplish his task over a stack of playing cards.

And why not? Christien watched the young man dealing and betting, along with three other men scarcely out of university, and felt a tugging in his gut at their grim faces. If they enjoyed play, their frowns and hooded eyes spoke otherwise. They could be playing too deeply and have concerns only for their ability to meet their debts, but Frobisher was worth watching. Christien couldn't forget that the young man had come to town with Barnaby, who'd held what had to be forged letters of introduction from Elias Lang. And Barnaby was now dead.

But two months of following Frobisher had gotten Christien nothing but Lydia's contempt for accusing her father of involvement in treasonous activities, and the knowledge that

Miss Honore was easily led astray by a handsome face and charming manners. And Frobisher supported himself with a shocking number of wins at deep play.

Wondering if tonight would find him good enough to deal himself into a game, Christien returned to the parlor, where a young lady with protruding front teeth and mousy hair played the pianoforte with the skill and heart of a true virtuoso. He slipped to the back of the room and leaned against the wall to absorb the liquid notes flying, floating, or thundering from the instrument.

He'd chosen his position badly. Several young ladies with bobbing curls and waving fans wagged their tongues on both ends. He started to move away from the hissing whispers, then caught what they were saying.

"Now we know why her sister whisked her out of town so fast." The speaker shook her head. A black curl bobbed against her cheek so much like Lydia's that Christien's heart twisted like hemp on a rope walk.

"She might be the prettiest girl who came out this Season," another dark-haired beauty declared, "but she was no better than she should be with her wild ways. Imagine going to a gaming . . . you know what they call those places."

Christien stood motionless. Could they possibly be discussing—?

"Honore Bainbridge seemed so sweet and kind." A third young lady, with just enough freckles to lend her face charm, stuck her tip-tilted nose in the air. "But we now know she was consorting with those kind of females."

"Perhaps that's why Lord Whittaker wouldn't marry Cassandra Bainbridge. I heard she was at a coffeehouse late at night with two men, of all things."

"And Lady Gale spent all her time with a Frenchman."

The girls squealed as though they'd just spoken the name of the evil one aloud.

Christien slipped away amidst a storm of applause for the talented musician. He scarcely heard the praise heaped upon the young lady. The other females' gossip rang in his ears— talk against the Bainbridge ladies. He knew of only one person outside of his coachman and the Bainbridge family who knew Honore had been to the gaming hell, and that same person, along with Cassandra's ballooning friends, was aware she had gone to the coffeehouse that same night.

Gerald Frobisher.

Across the corridor, that young man still played whist with his friends. Christien glided up behind one of the friends. "I'd like to take the next hand with Frobisher alone."

The men stared.

"I've never seen you play," Frobisher said. "Heinous, iniquitous, I believe you called that place you found me."

Christien shrugged. "That was for the benefit of the ladies. Can't have them thinking I can play, *n'est-ce pas?*"

And lose another piece of his soul.

He dropped onto the chair one of the friends vacated. "In for a penny, in for a pound."

"Guineas." Frobisher's upper lip curled. "I only play for guineas."

Christien stared at the cards and the gold coins glittering against the green baize of the tabletop, and a prayer formed in his head. He shoved it away. He couldn't pray to win a game like this.

But he did win. Every card he chose, every bit of pasteboard he slapped down proved correct. He took hand after hand until

Frobisher turned pale and thin-lipped, until the clock struck midnight, until Christien wanted to throw the gold coins worth a pound plus a shilling into Frobisher's face and run out of London, to Lydia, if she would have him. Home if she would not.

He'd never run away from anything in his life, so he stayed until Frobisher called for pen, paper, and ink and wrote out a vowel for money he couldn't afford to pay and Christien didn't need.

Lord, I don't want to keep winning. He did pray.

And he won again.

Frobisher's friends drifted away. The music ceased across the corridor. The card room emptied.

Christien finally folded his cards and lay them on the table. "Enough. You've lost enough."

"Just give me one more chance to win." Frobisher's eyes pleaded.

"I will, but not now. Not here." Christien rose, collected his winnings and the slips of paper with the simple vowels *IOU* and Frobisher's signature, and led the way out of the house.

Frobisher followed, pleading like a puppy begging for a denied meal. Christien felt like he'd kicked the puppy as well as starved it.

"Join me in my carriage," he told the younger man. "I'll take you home."

"No, I need to recover my losses." Frobisher hung on the carriage door. "There's a place—"

"Get in." Christien gave him a gentle shove.

Frobisher climbed in. Christien followed. A footman slammed the door behind them, and the carriage trundled off across the cobbles.

Christien took the bag of coins and slips of paper from his

pockets and held them out to Frobisher. "You may have these back if you give me information."

"I haven't any information to give." He was sulky again.

"Why did you start rumors about Miss Honore Bainbridge?"

"You'll tear up my vowels for that?" Frobisher laughed. "You're a fool, Frog. It's simple. Her father wouldn't pay for my silence."

"You're telling me that you tried to blackmail Lord Bainbridge in exchange for keeping your mouth shut about Miss Honore?" Christien felt as though someone had slammed him between the shoulder blades with a sledgehammer. "That's why you met with him?"

"Would I need another reason? If I couldn't get money by marrying her, then I tried to get it another way. Now she's ruined and will be pleased to marry me."

His valet would think him mad, but Christien would want a bath when he reached home after spending so much time with this man.

"Now may I have my money back?" Frobisher held out his hands.

"I'm not certain I believe you."

"You've got to." Panic tinged Frobisher's voice now. "I was counting on my wins tonight to—"

"To what?" Christien let the coins chink together.

Frobisher made a grab for them. "Please. I'm ruined if I don't pay."

"Ruined by whom?" Christien tucked the bag behind him.

Surely more lay in this than simple blackmail for an advantageous marriage.

"It doesn't matter to you. Just me. My life. Please." Frobisher breathed hard through his nose, sniffed. "Please. I'll tell you anything necessary if you just give me my money back."

"Who killed Barnaby?" Christien demanded.

"Barnaby? How should I know?" A note of hysteria entered the younger man's tone. "Not me. He was an acquaintance, nothing more. I swear it. I beg of you."

And he did beg. He slipped to his knees on the floor of the carriage and raised beseeching hands.

Christien felt sick. He didn't like Gerald Frobisher, thought him despicable for his gaming and the way he'd led Honore into imprudent behavior. But to see any man humbled like this—on his knees in a cramped well of space, raising his hands in supplication as though Christien were some sort of deity—released a veil, a black curtain from inside his head, and shone light as bright as day upon himself, his actions, his behavior.

He knocked on the roof of the coach. "Halt, *s'il vous plait*." The carriage slowed, stopped.

"Please," Frobisher cried, "don't put me out here penniless."

"I won't." Christien leaned forward and unlatched the door. "I won't even tell you to stop gaming. It won't do any good."

As though it were a live grenade that would blow up himself and the carriage, he tossed the bag of coins into the gutter, tore the vowels in half and threw them out to join the other refuse.

Frobisher scrambled after it, muttering thanks and gasping for breath.

"Drive on," Christien called to the coachman.

Not waiting for anyone to close the door, the carriage rumbled on, leaving Frobisher scrabbling for his money and vowels in the gutter.

"Sixty-five Curzon Street," Christien called to the driver.

They turned to skirt Hyde Park. In moments, the carriage drew up before the narrow house in the street, only fashionable because it lay in Mayfair, a respectable if not prestigious address.

A lantern hung over the green-painted door and gleamed off the horseshoe-shaped knocker.

Christien leaped out of the carriage and used the knocker to pound on the door. When nothing happened for several minutes, he repeated the action, and then again until a voice penetrated the wood of the portal, telling him to try not to wake the dead.

"But that's exactly what I have done."

At least, he'd awakened part of him that had been dead, dead to everything except for revenge against France and Napoleon specifically. He'd risen from the death of his soul being smothered into compromise and giving up everything in which he once believed—taking steps according to God's Word, the safety of his family, his own integrity. He'd awakened to the realization that he had put his revenge work above all, allowing Lisette to stay in town as a cook so she could inform for him, accusing his love's father of treason so that she ran from him, bringing another man to his knees so that he begged for mercy over gambling money. He possessed no more integrity, but perhaps if he repented now, God could see fit to restore his soul.

The door opened. Elias Lang stood in the doorway, a candle in one hand, a pistol in the other. He wore a velvet dressing gown over a pair of breeches and a shirt with its placket unbuttoned, and his graying hair stood straight up. "De Meuse, what do you want at this hour?"

Christien took a deep breath. "I want to resign my position."

27

Before the Bainbridge Manor butler slipped the news sheet onto the table beside her plate instead of Father's, Lydia knew something was wrong. The man's face, smooth from years of keeping his expression bland, showed a crease between his salt-and-pepper eyebrows, a sure sign of distress.

"Why are you giving that to her?" Father demanded from behind his copy of the *Times*.

"Forgive me, my lord," Dobbins intoned. "It is nothing but a sheet dedicated to the sort of gossip that interests females, not someone with the weight of the country on his shoulders."

Lydia's upper lip curled until she caught the man's wink from behind Father's back.

Father grunted in disinterest, as the aging retainer must have known he would. Dobbins had obviously looked at the sheets before delivering the mail to the table. Ladies' tattletales meant nothing to a peer of the realm.

Lydia wished they meant nothing to her. If a fire had burned on the hearth, she might have tossed the news sheets onto the flames without a second glance, without a first look. But this was mid-June, and the breeze wafting through the open windows smelled of freshly scythed grass, roses, and flagstones from the terrace already baking under the south Devonshire sun, and held little in the way of coolness, let alone a chill.

She opened the rolled paper.

What little breakfast she'd consumed rose in her throat, bitter and hot. Her eyes burned. Her ears rang with words murmured through a garden with the impact of a scream. *You'll regret running away.*

She'd known then she would. She knew now she did. She'd chosen to go her own way and failed her family in the worst way possible.

Honore was utterly ruined. The drawing and caption said it all. Though the female in the sketch wore a loo mask and the black-and-white print said nothing to hair color, anyone who knew Honore's pure oval face, her lush mouth and smoothly rounded chin, not to mention the graceful set of her long neck and slim shoulders, would recognize the maiden seated at a card table with three gentlemen of questionable repute. And the words beneath clarified those who might prove uncertain.

Did the Honorable Miss H. truly attend a certain gaming establishment with a Mr. G. F.?

Certain she was about to cast up her accounts, Lydia started to rip the news sheet in half. An unseen hand seemed to stop her. Or perhaps the sound of Father clearing his throat. He would wonder why she chose to shred a mere gossip sheet.

"If you'll excuse me, sir, I should see to the—the—" What household task would she need to see to right then? "The menu for the day. If we leave Cook to her own devices, we'll get mutton again, I do declare, and none of us is fond of mutton." She made herself laugh.

Father grunted, deep in concentration in a letter with a crested seal. "All we need is another war."

"Another war?" Lydia paused halfway to her feet. "Not the Americans. They wouldn't be so foolish."

"Of course they would. England's might didn't stop them thirty-five years ago, and it isn't stopping them now. The difference is, we're fighting the French and our resources are stretched thin."

Lydia flopped back onto her chair. "Yes, but they can't have many resources at all."

"They seem to think they do. Perhaps we can take them back." He flashed her a rare smile. "We could use all that forest for new ships and masts."

"I doubt they'll go down easily, though, and I hate the thought of more killing."

So much more important than her sister's reputation. And yet a war with America lay thousands of miles away. The war with France rested close to home, perhaps lay at home, in England, in her very family.

The blackmailer would stop at nothing to get what he wanted, not even ruining the future of a wayward but kindhearted and lovely young lady.

She should have given in. Once again she should have succumbed to blackmail for the sake of her family. But this was different. This man wasn't the same one as before with threats of accusing her of treason. He threatened to expose Honore's escapade at the gaming hell if Lydia didn't do as he requested.

She hadn't waited to find out. She refused to let herself succumb to blackmail again. Blackmail had ended up forcing her to introduce Gerald Frobisher to Honore for no reason, because the blackmailer was now dead. Since few men knew of Honore's folly, Lydia presumed it was Frobisher wanting money Lydia couldn't afford to pay him. Nor would she go to Father, Christien, or anyone else of her acquaintance.

But he had divulged Honore's shame, and now, unless some other scandal superseded this one, Honore was ruined for London Society until at least the next year.

Lydia left the sunny breakfast room before the smell of coffee and kippers made her ill. She made her way to the garden. Seeing two of the gardener's assistants pruning the lavender bushes, she continued through the gate and into the trees of the park. Coolness washed over her. She inhaled a lungful of the freshness beneath the trees and remembered Christien, running through the woods with him, pausing to listen for pursuit, kissing him.

A pain so profound it brought her up short stabbed through her heart. She stopped and leaned against the rough bark of an oak, her hand to her chest, the other hand still clutching the news sheets. She was running away again. She loved Christien but ran from him because she was determined to control her own life. She ran from God because she was determined to control her own life. She ran from a blackmailer because she was determined to control her own life. Now she faced an empty and aching heart and a ruined sister because she had done a poor job of managing her life and everyone else's.

"God, I don't know what to do."

As if God would listen to her when she had rejected His help for years because—why?

He had plans for her life, and she was weary of others with their plans for her life, from her father to her husband to her mother-in-law to a now-dead blackmailer. She had her own plans.

The crumpled news sheets, her aching heart, her very presence at Bainbridge Manor instead of her cottage on the moors told their own tale of how well she managed her own life. But she wasn't about to turn it over to Father or Christien.

Or God?

"I don't know about that yet. I have to accomplish something right on my own."

Spoken aloud, the thought sounded arrogant, self-centered. She snorted and headed back to the house. Repairing Honore's reputation lay at the top of her list of things to correct. Reuniting Cassandra and Whittaker came next. Both seemed impossible.

Cassandra greeted Lydia from her seat on the terrace. A book lay on the table before her, but she wasn't reading it. Creased as though it had been folded inside a letter lay the same news sheet Lydia clutched in her hand.

"Who would do this?" Cassandra asked. "Frobisher?"

"I think so. How did you get a copy?"

"Someone sent it to me." Cassandra held up a sheet of vellum with a blank seal, and color tinged her cheeks. "But I recognize the handwriting."

"And you blush?" Lydia took the paper and examined the address. "This was franked by a member of Parliament. And—ah."

Cassandra ducked her head. "He's been sending me news sheets and some scientific articles without actually writing to me. I'm not certain why."

"May I guess?" Lydia knelt beside her sister and rested a hand on her shoulder. "Have any of those articles been about ballooning, by any chance?"

Cassandra nodded, and her eyes shone behind her spectacles.

"He regrets what happened between you two and wishes to make amends," Lydia said.

Cassandra nodded again but kept her lips tight.

"Would you like to travel to Lancashire to see him?"

"He—he's in London, and we can't go there because of Honore."

And Lydia couldn't go there because of Christien. "What's he doing in London?" she asked.

"I think he wants to be there in the event the lords need to discuss matters pertaining to the Americans likely to declare war."

"You know about that?"

"He sent me a copy of the *Times* too."

Lydia grimaced. "Don't let Father know. He doesn't approve of females reading anything but—" She stopped at the crunch of masculine footfalls on the flagstones. "Father, what is it?"

"News sheets." His complexion was high, his brows thunderous. "You should have told me what was in that nonsense you females like to read." He held up a third copy of Honore's condemnation in print.

Lydia dropped her brow onto the edge of the table and groaned.

"Sit up, Lydia." Father's voice rang out above her. "You look a fool."

"I am a fool." She remained as she was.

"You don't think I should have known about my daughter's behavior in London?" Father demanded.

"We thought it was all right once we got her out of there," Cassandra said.

"Not 'we,' miss." A chair creaked, and Father sighed. "You were at the Chapter House coffee shop, I understand."

Lydia wondered if she could dash her brains out on the edge of the marble tabletop.

"How did you find out?" She straightened to confront him, his wrath.

Except sadness clouded his face instead of anger. "Gerald Frobisher tried blackmailing me on three separate occasions. The eleventh of May, the twentieth of May, and the first of June."

"The first of June?" Lydia scrambled to her feet, her mouth open, her eyes wide. "Father, are you certain it was him?"

"Of course I'm certain it was him. We met face-to-face at the Cocoa Tree."

"But—but—" Lydia tried to breathe, to think, to get her voice to emerge as something besides a squeak. "He tried blackmailing me at the George in Portsmouth on the first of June."

"Impossible." Father surged to his feet. "Someone thinks he can play May games with the Bainbridges. You didn't pay him, did you?"

"No, not a farthing. Did you?"

Father's face flushed again. "The first time. Couldn't have him ruining Honore's ball. But the second time . . . I should have. Put an end to this. I tried the third time."

"Or just go on forever." Lydia rested her hand on his arm. "But if he has an accomplice . . . We need to get to London and find him straightaway, do we not?"

"I'll go. You stay with your sisters or come later by carriage. I'm going by sea."

Lydia swallowed. She'd never been to sea. "I'll go with you. Sea will be faster. But isn't it dangerous?"

"Not along the coast," Father said. "But—"

"The others don't need to come."

"I'd like to," Cassandra said.

"Then be ready within the hour." Father strode away toward the stables.

Lydia exchanged glances with Cassandra.

"There's more to this than you're saying," Cassandra said.

"Perhaps. I don't know."

Christien would know. Lydia couldn't wait to find him and talk about . . . everything.

"We'd best change and get a valise or something small packed." Lydia spun on her heel and raced for the French window leading into the library, ran through it to the entry hall, up the grand staircase, and down the corridor to her bedchamber.

Where she skidded to a halt.

Honore's door stood open. Lydia glanced in. She should tell her youngest sister they were leaving. She deserved to know why and choose whether or not to come with them.

But Honore already knew. A fourth copy of the news sheet lay on her dressing table. Below the caption, she had scrawled, *I've gone to make things right the only way I know how. I'll elope with Gerald Frobisher.*

"Only a harebrained chit like my youngest daughter would think an elopement will solve this problem." Father exploded with the declaration for perhaps the tenth time since they had departed from Bainbridge Manor, sailing aboard a packet with little room and fewer comforts. "How can one scandal eliminate another?"

"A hasty wedding is preferable to attending a gaming establishment with women of questionable virtue," Cassandra said.

Lydia clung to the rail and concentrated on not succumbing to mal de mer. "I wonder if she knows about the blackmail and figures it's one way to stop it. If Frobisher gets her marriage portion, he won't have need to blackmail us into giving him money."

"But he couldn't have blackmailed both of you." Cassandra leaned to one side and flipped the flounce back into place at the bottom of Lydia's skirt. She maintained her balance on the heaving deck without holding the railing.

Just looking at her sister gave Lydia vertigo.

"Who could be the other extortioner?" Cassandra persisted.

"I don't know." Lydia closed her eyes, felt as though she were sliding to one side, and popped them open again.

"That Frenchman?" Father demanded from her other side. "He seemed a bit too involved in our family affairs."

"With good reason." Lydia's stays felt too tightly laced. "He was my friend."

"I'd say he was more than a friend to you." Cassandra's smile was sly.

Lydia's face heated, and she stared at the bobbing horizon and the distant shoreline in silence.

On her other side, Father cleared his throat. "I suspected as much. I couldn't scare him off for anything."

"You couldn't what?" Lydia's hands slipped on the spray-wet rail.

Cassandra slipped her arm, sturdy and strong, around Lydia's waist to steady her.

"I didn't think he was good enough for you." Father turned his back on them and gazed at the ranks of canvas flapping above them.

Lydia and Cassandra moved as one to stand on the other side of him.

"What do you mean, not good enough for me?" Lydia demanded. "He's a kind, Christian man who has sacrificed a comfortable life to serve this country. Just because he's French doesn't mean—why are you two laughing?"

Cassandra's low chortle blended with Father's rough chuckle, a laugh with a rusty edge.

"I knew it." Cassandra managed to clap her hands. "Didn't you, Father?"

"I suspected as much." Father nodded.

"Knew what?" Lydia asked the question, though a burning from her middle to her hat brim told her the answer.

"You're in love with him," Cassandra declared. "And it's obvious he loves you. If Whittaker looked at me like Monsieur de Meuse looks at you, I'd never have doubted he loved me."

"If a gentleman looked at me like I've seen Whittaker looking at you," Lydia returned, "I'd marry him."

"Then you'd better prepare yourself for a wedding." Cassandra patted Lydia's hand. "That man adores you. Has he never said so?"

"Yes, but—" Lydia ducked her head. Guarding her tongue was easy. She had managed to say little for so long that doing so now was no hardship. But she couldn't stop her mind from the memories, the sound of his voice calling her his dear, his heart, declaring his love. From recalling the feather touch of his fingertips on her face, the heat of his lips on her mouth.

Emptiness ripped open inside her, and her throat closed.

"We'll discuss this later, daughter." Father's voice held a gentleness Lydia had heard too rarely.

She shook her head, scattering a few tears to sparkle in the sunlight, much to her horror. "There's nothing to discuss. I won't remarry and let my life be controlled by someone else."

"That's silly if you love him," Cassandra said. "As a Christian, you let God guide your path."

"Did you let God guide your path when you broke your engagement?" Lydia shot back.

Cassandra dashed one hand over her eyes. "No, that's why I want to make amends, if he'll take me back. If God wills it, it will happen."

Lydia bit her lip and said nothing. She couldn't see God wanting to play matchmaker or healer of broken betrothals, giving a young woman what she wanted. God, like Father, gave some people poor marriages and unhappy lives.

Or was that the person making that choice for herself? Cassandra had ended the engagement. Honore had chosen to be wayward. Christien had chosen to fight for revenge against Napoleon.

And she had determined to marry Major Sir Charles Gale. No one but she and Charles had thought it a wise idea with him in the Army. He had promised to leave his commission, so Lydia had said yes and Father had given his consent. Father had given Lydia her own way, and she had made amok of her life. Oh, she had her cottage and her painting and a bit more income now, but if Cassandra didn't join her in the moorland cottage, Lydia faced days of loneliness now that Barbara had begun to work for Mama as her companion. Yes, Lydia managed her own days, but what good was rejecting love, friendship, and God in exchange for days she ordered only to find them as bleak as Dartmoor itself?

Had God brought Christien into her life for more than a way to help England in these bleak days of war?

"I don't know what to think, God," she murmured.

Three days aboard the packet from Plymouth to Portsmouth didn't enlighten her further. It felt like three weeks, but it took them half the time that riding or a carriage would have. No storms or French privateers annoyed them, and they sailed into the Portsmouth Harbor in late afternoon. A carriage smelling of fish and damp straw carried them to the George, the inn where twice someone had made blackmail threats against Lydia, the first for treason she hadn't committed, the second against Honore. The first had led her to help Christien without question, the second might have ruined her youngest sister for the rest of her life.

"Lord, can you make any of this right?" She glanced toward the garden as though it were Eden and God walked there, ready to vanquish the serpent of her blackmailers. "If you make this right—" She flopped without grace onto a chair in the private parlor Father had demanded and received at once.

She was in no position to demand things of God. She knew her Bible. She'd been raised going to church and listening to the vicar talk about one's relationship with God. He wanted that most precious of commodities Lydia refused to give—surrender, the death of her will.

"God, I don't know how to do that." She cradled her aching head in her hands.

Around her, Father and Cassandra engaged in talk of dinner, of the quality of mounts available at the inn to convey them the rest of their journey up to London, of what time to start in the morning, what to do if Honore had, by some miracle of travel, reached town before them.

Lydia saw her control of her family's future and her life slipping away from her into terrifying darkness. "Lord, how can Cassandra be so calm, so accepting of Your will for her future with Whittaker?"

A knock sounded on the parlor door. Father called for the person to come in. Lydia straightened, expecting the servants to march in with laden trays of food.

The man who strolled into the parlor was most definitely not a servant.

It was Lord Geoffrey Whittaker.

28

The last person Christien expected to see at his door was Lydia. Yet there she stood in a dark blue riding habit, the feather on her perky hat bent in the middle so it caressed her cheek, a pallid cheek emphasized by the purple shadows beneath her eyes.

"It's only ten o'clock in the morning." Inane words with which to greet a lady on one's doorstep, but the first ones that emerged from his lips.

"We rode all night." She swayed, and he caught her upper arms.

"It's improper, but I think I should invite you in."

"I don't care about my reputation. We need your help. Honore is missing, and we think she's run off with Gerald Frobisher. Everyone we've asked says he was last seen getting into your carriage last week."

"I didn't do away with him, if that's what you're thinking." Christien drew Lydia toward him. "Come, sit. I'll fetch you coffee while you tell me what's afoot."

"I know I shouldn't." She went into his parlor with little resistance.

He left her at a comfortable armchair with a winged back and found his manservant to bring coffee up from the bakery around the corner. "And some pastries too, I think. I doubt she's eaten." When he returned to Lydia, he found her dozing with her head tucked into the curve of the chair back.

She jerked upright at his entrance. "I'm so sorry. We left Devonshire four days ago and have sailed or ridden nonstop to get here. I'm such a poor horsewoman I may never walk again." She managed a credible smile, then glanced around and her eyes grew wide. "You're packing."

"Yes, I'm going home." He started to sit in the tiny parlor's other chair, then found the yard of distance too far to be away from her and perched on the arm of her chair. "I've left my post."

"You caught the traitor?" Her eyes widened, showed more life than earlier. "Christien, congratu—"

He held up a staying hand. "No, I didn't catch him. I'm not convinced anyone exists, at least not as I was directed to find. In three months, no one has shown any signs of starting a disruption, and there have been no disruptions."

"But why would anyone send you on this mission if no one existed?"

"Poor intelligence. It happens."

"But you're leaving before you know for certain?" She looked appalled. "Do you truly not care what happens to England after all, if France wins this war? I suppose you can simply go home and not care that Englishmen will suffer—"

"*Silencez.*" Realizing his harshness as soon as the word exploded from his lips, he moderated his tone. "*S'il vous plait.*"

"I thought better of you. I thought you were a man to be counted upon." She struggled to rise. "I apologize for interrupting your flight from duty."

"My flight? Mine?" Christien helped her rise, then gripped her fingers and held her gaze. "I did not hide away for seven

318

years when my spouse abandoned me. I did not hide away when my sister misbehaved herself. I did not run away from a person who loves me more than a life's work—"

"Work you're abandoning unfinished."

"Because it made me compromise my self-respect and what matters."

Her hands relaxed in his grip, and she gazed up at him, her eyes like pansies. "What are you saying?"

"I was sitting at a gaming table taking every penny Gerald Frobisher possessed and then some, because I wanted information from a man who didn't have any." Christien raised one hand to her face and stroked the fine lines of fatigue at the corner of her lips. "I lost the lady I love because I made an accusation against her father with little proof. And I let my quest for revenge lie between me and my relationship with the God I knew as a young man."

"Oh, Christien." His name sighed from her lips. For a glorious heartbeat, he thought she intended to kiss him.

Then his valet entered with a tray of coffee and rolls, and she broke away.

"I don't have time for refreshment. Honore—"

"Ten minutes will make no difference in what is amiss with Miss Honore, but it will greatly improve you." He grinned. "If any improvement is necessary."

She laughed at that, albeit feebly, and accepted the coffee.

Once the valet departed, Christien prompted, "What's wrong, *ma chère*?"

"You know about news of Honore and the gaming establishment reaching the news sheets?" Lydia took a deep drink of coffee, and a blissful expression crossed her face. "We all received copies. So she left without telling any of us except a note saying she would elope with Frobisher to set things right. She didn't get that much of a head start, but we haven't caught up with her except to learn she was on the mail coach."

"Is it possible you passed her?"

"We have to find Frobisher, if he hasn't left town after telling everyone of Honore's disgraceful behavior." She set her cup aside. "I know about his trying to blackmail my father. Do you?"

"Yes, I know. It was one of the things that shamed me into resigning my position. To accuse your father of treason spoke of my desperation and not the quality of my work."

"Father paid, but then Frobisher came back and wanted more. And there's something else, Christien." She leaned toward him, gripped his arm. "Someone tried to blackmail me again, the very night Frobisher was trying to blackmail my father."

Christien set his coffee cup down with extra care. "Who?"

"I thought it was Frobisher. He spoke of Honore's disgrace, and if I didn't do what he wanted, he'd tell everyone about it."

Christien struggled to keep his voice calm. "And what did he want?"

"I don't know." Lydia blushed and bowed her head so that charming curl bobbed against her cheek. "I ran away. I gambled with my sister's reputation and lost because I turned coward and ran."

"But you didn't know—"

"No, and I didn't stay to find out. I never do. That's the worst of it." Tears stood in her eyes. "Christien, I thought it was Frobisher, but it wasn't. It couldn't have been. This man was blackmailing me at the same time Frobisher was blackmailing my father. And if Barnaby is dead—"

"It couldn't have been him," Christien concluded with her.

"Ah, *ma chère*, we have something afoot that is more serious than your sister's running off, *n'est-ce pas?*"

Lydia's face worked for a moment, then she took a deep breath and nodded. "Yes. As bad as it is to let Honore find her own way home or—or let someone else see to her rescue, we need to find out who met me at Portsmouth."

"*C'est ma belle dame.*" He caressed her cheek, wiping away the traces of spilled tears. "My beautiful lady. Beautiful and brave. You're not running now."

"I want to run toward whoever has made havoc of my life for the past four months." Her hands clenched into fists.

Christien took them in his and raised her to her feet. "We will go."

"Where?"

"We will start with the only quantity we know—Gerald Frobisher. Now, did you wear a veil to that charming chapeau so you don't ruin your reputation coming into my rooms?"

"This is more important than my reputation."

"Then we shall go." He offered her his arm.

She slipped her hand into the crook of his elbow and followed him onto the street. They didn't wait for his carriage to be brought around but hailed a hackney instead. Christien gave the jarvey directions to Frobisher's rooms, not so far from Christien's.

Few members of London's Society walked or rode about the streets of Mayfair that early, if half past ten o'clock was early. To the haut ton it usually was. Frobisher would likely be in his rooms. They might find Honore there too. Or neither of them.

"Did you come to town alone?" Christien asked Lydia.

"My father and Cassandra came too. And Whittaker now." She smiled at that.

"*Vraiment?* Lord Whittaker?"

"Yes. We encountered him on his way west to see Cassandra. I think he intended to abduct her back to Lancashire if she wouldn't agree to marry him after all." Her eyes shone.

Christien's heart twisted. "It is true then that absence makes the heart fonder?" He looked into her eyes, wouldn't let her glance away.

She swallowed. "I think we've arrived at Mr. Frobisher's rooms."

So they had.

With a sigh, Christien left the hackney and approached the door. The same slatternly landlady answered his knock.

"I haven't seen him since last week," she claimed and slammed the door in Christien's face.

His skin crawled from the odor of garbage from a nearby alley, from the smell of fear emanating from the landlady.

Last week. Possibly the night disgust with himself had prompted him to remove Frobisher from the carriage without concern for where he set the young man down or how much money he was carrying. If he'd gotten Frobisher killed because of his self-centered actions—

He gave the jarvey directions to the gaming hell, where they'd found Frobisher with Honore, and climbed back into the vehicle. Just as he pulled the door shut, a thought occurred to him, and he leaped down again and pounded on the door.

"Go away," the landlady cried.

"I need information. I'll pay for it." Christien glanced back at Lydia, then up and down the street, where several young men stopped to stare, quizzing glasses raised to red-rimmed eyes. If any belonged to Society, what Christien said next would ruin Honore Bainbridge for certain.

"Go ahead," Lydia said from within the hackney.

Christien rapped on the door again. "Madame, has a young lady been here? Blonde hair?"

"Aye." The door burst open. "The little troll."

Lydia's sharp intake of breath hissed from the open hackney doorway.

"I'm weary of people pounding on my door wanting that no-good. He ain't worth the rent."

"It's paid up then?" Christien stuck his foot in the door so she couldn't slam it in his face again.

"Yeah, t' other one paid it."

"What other one?" Christien and Lydia asked together.

"Dunno. Man who looks like nothing." With surprising strength, she kicked Christien's foot free and slammed the door. A bar dropped into place with a thud on the other side.

Christien sprinted for the hackney and yanked the door shut. "*Allons*," he shouted.

"Let us be going," Lydia said in English.

The vehicle jerked, then trundled forward.

Christien stared at Lydia. "Who looks like nothing?"

But he knew the answer. Why he would be in search of Gerald Frobisher, Christien didn't know. Nor did he like the notion. He had been the one who declared Frobisher was nothing more than a gamester.

And Christien had believed him.

"We believed him." Lydia met his gaze from across the carriage. "We've always believed him."

"We may be mistaken."

"Honore will be wherever she's found one of them." Lydia reached out.

Christien took her hand in both of his. "We will do what we can."

"I should have sent for Father. He has authority. He's off making enquiries along the roads north. He should have stayed home. I should have stayed home. I thought I was running toward something for once . . ." She trailed off.

If only she were running toward him.

Christien moved across the carriage so he sat beside her. "We will find them. London is not so large."

"It's too big. I want Tavistock, where no one can hide, where I'm safe in my cottage with no one to concern me—" She shook her head. "I'm simply wanting to run away from the messes I help create. What I need to do is—is—" She gulped. "I need to ask God to take care of this."

"We both do."

As the vehicle rumbled over the cobblestone streets, Christien and Lydia squeezed themselves onto their knees in the narrow well between the seats. Hands clasped, heads bowed, neither of them said a word for several moments.

"I don't remember how to pray," Lydia whispered, as though God wouldn't hear her.

"I'm still accepting that I have a right to. But if this is drawing me back into my work, it is of His will, not mine. I left it behind and have asked forgiveness for my desire for revenge."

"Then you pray."

Christien started to do so, then shook his head. "It's your turn to surrender."

"My sister's reputation, perhaps even her life, may depend on this prayer. It has to be right."

"And come from you to be right."

Her face twisted as though she were in pain. Christien ached to help her, to speak the words for her. He knew he could not, he must not. Lydia needed to surrender to the Lord herself.

She dropped her head onto his shoulder. Her tremors raced through him. "Father. Heavenly Father, I—I don't know what to say except I cannot succeed in life without You. The more I try, the worse it gets. Like now. Please help us—no, please save Honore from whatever trouble she's in. I—" She took a long, shuddering breath. "I can't do it on my own."

The carriage stopped in front of the gaming hell. Christien and Lydia struggled to their feet. He opened the door and leaped to the pavement, then offered her his hands. Around them, the street lay in silence, as though holding its breath.

"Wait for us," Christien directed the jarvey.

The man grunted. "It'll cost you."

"I know fares are regulated. It'll cost me what's right, and you'll not get work here this time of day."

"Will this place be open this time of day?" Lydia asked.

"It's open every time of day. Some men—and women too— don't know when to stop." Christien turned the handle.

It didn't move. He knocked. Knocked again.

"Go away," a smoky voice called through the panels.

Christien kept knocking. Beside him, Lydia wrung her hands until the portal sprang open and a burly man in a stained smock stood in the entryway.

"*Pardonez-nous, s'il vous plait.*" Not waiting for the man to step aside, Christien shoved his shoulder into the man's chest, grabbed Lydia's hand, and ran down the steps.

"Hey, you can't do that," the man shouted after them, but he made no move to follow. Made no move to stop them.

"That was simpler than I expected," Lydia said.

"Too simple." Christien drew up short at the bottom of the steps. "Lydia, go back."

"Too late," a familiar voice spoke from the shadows.

Above them, the door slammed. A key turned in the lock.

Before them, Gerald Frobisher stepped out of the darkness broken only by a half dozen candles, his blond hair gleaming like its own candle flame. Beside him, Honore didn't fair so well. Her honey tresses hung in limp hanks on either side of her face, a wan face white to the lips and sporting shadows like bruises beneath her blue eyes. Her gown hung about her thin frame, limp and smeared with dirt, as though she hadn't seen a change of clothes or a hairbrush for days.

"How did you get here ahead of us?" Lydia started forward.

"Stay there." Frobisher held up his hand. A knife gleamed in the dimness of the subterranean room, sparkled as he bent his elbow and pressed the point to Honore's throat.

A scratch on the delicate skin told a tale of the knife having been there before.

Lydia let out a whimper, then murmured, "This is what comes of surrendering my life to You, God?"

Christien's own heart, his miniscule faith, shook inside him. If ever he needed wisdom, needed strength beyond his own, it was now.

"What do you want?" Christien asked.

"To kill you," Frobisher said, and smiled.

"It's always been our intention to kill you." Another voice spoke in the gloom.

Lydia gasped.

Christien grasped her arm to steady himself as much as to hold her close to him.

"The blackmailer." Lydia merely breathed the words. "But Barnaby—"

"Died for his failures." Into a circle of candlelight stepped Elias Lang. "But I did well convincing you he must have been the man who stole my message to you, my lady, and forced your hand." The latter part of his speech reverted to his native Sussex accent, the one Christien knew.

"How?" was all Christien could manage. "You were in the same house with me that night."

"You only thought I was with you." Lang propped a hip on the edge of a gaming table. "Indeed, you were sleeping the sleep of the . . . er . . . drugged. Not that that was necessary. I am rather good at slipping in and out of houses unnoticed. Those destroyed invitations, Lady Gale?"

Christien flinched, bile rising in his throat. "I'd rather you have killed me then than carry on this deception and bring Lady Gale into it."

Beside him, Lydia tensed, drew a little away from him.

Christien loosened his hold. If she wanted to retreat from him, he wouldn't force her to stay. He held his attention tightly on Lang. "Why the charade, Elias?"

"There was no charade. The Home Office did request that we find a French agent." Lang shoved his hands into the capacious pockets of his coat. "So I sent George Barnaby and young Gerry here after you."

Christien stared at Lang. *Pardonez-moi?* You sent them after me instead of the real culprit?"

"Oh, I caught him months ago." Lang removed one hand from his pocket and waved it in the air. "An émigré chef no one will miss."

Like Lisette.

Christien shuddered at what he had done to his sister in the name of revenge against France.

"Then why me?" Christien felt too numb to speak in anything but measured tones.

"You were useless to me once you got yourself released from Dartmoor." Lang removed his other hand from his coat pocket and leaned his weight on his palms behind him. He appeared to carry no weapon on his person.

He didn't need a weapon with Frobisher holding a knife to Honore's throat. Neither Christien nor Lydia would make a move to attack, guaranteeing the young lady's death.

"The French wouldn't trust you, knowing you had English connections in high places," Lang continued.

"Then why did you help me get out?" Christien tried to nudge Lydia behind him, the best way he could protect her. She wouldn't budge.

Lang smiled, a bland curve of lips in his bland face, surrounded by graying hair so fine it appeared to have no color.

A man who looked like nothing. A perfect spy. He blended into shadows and sunlight alike.

Or dark inn gardens after disguising his voice.

"Getting you killed in London would raise fewer questions than in the country," Lang said. "An accident while riding, a wrecked curricle, shot or mauled by a mob angry with the French." Lang shrugged. "So many possibilities that would have merely had people shaking their heads over the violence of the country or the misfortune of just one more Frenchman."

"Who has served his country well for ten years." The merest tremor marred Lydia's indignant tone. "You should have let him retire."

"I tried to leave." Christien fixed his gaze on Lang but watched Frobisher from the corner of his eye. "And now that I've mentioned leaving, we have a hackney—"

"Gone by now," Lang drawled. "My henchman sent him away. He's rather angry I wouldn't let him near Miss Honore here."

Lydia's teeth grinding sounded like a mortar and pestle.

Christien's own jaw tensed with an effort to remain calm, quiet. Only an arm's length away, Honore was so white and still Christien wondered if she had fainted and Frobisher was holding her upright.

"But you knew too much about me." Lang sighed. "A pity. You did a great deal of good, but I always get rid of my agents when they've served out their usefulness."

"Then why not kill him outright?" Lydia took a step forward.

"Back." Lang threw up his hand.

Honore screamed. Frobisher's knife had drawn a bead of blood from her throat.

"If you kill my sister," Lydia said through her teeth, "no place on this earth will be safe for you, Elias Lang and Gerald Frobisher. I will hunt you down—"

"Not if you're dead too." Lang yawned. "I'm quite bored with all of this. The explosion and fire in the spirits storage room will be much more entertaining. But you want to know about the charade. I suppose I should tell you. Always nice to die with one's questions answered." He yawned again. "Excuse me. It's been a long night. I didn't want you to trust de Meuse here, and I honestly needed to get George and Gerry invited into Society. Your husband always talked about how you were too responsible to your family, that he always felt he came second to them, so I thought threatening them would work."

"And your second blackmail attempt?" Christien asked.

"I wanted Lady Gale back in London."

"But you made a mistake." Christien allowed all his contempt to ring in his voice, show in his curled lip and pinched nostrils. "You should have gotten your timing correct with Frobisher and his game."

"Indeed." Lang shot Frobisher a glare. "He'll pay for that mistake."

"Will he?" Christien smiled. "Are you listening, Monsieur Frobisher? He intends to kill you too."

"Of course he won't." Frobisher smiled back. "He's my uncle. He wouldn't dare harm me. He's just been a bit slow on paying my gaming debts, so I had to get money on my own."

No hope of turning Frobisher against Lang?

"How will you make him pay then?" Christien asked.

"None of your concern." Lang whipped a pistol from beneath the gaming table. "Now get moving. Into the back room."

Christien didn't move. Neither did Lydia.

"Move." Lang pressed the barrel of the pistol against Lydia's temple.

Her face whitened. Her expression remained impassive, calm.

An ache settled in Christien's chest. Two men with weapons against him, an unarmed man. Impossible odds.

But not for God. Surely God wouldn't allow these men to win.

He set his lips in a thin line and led the way to the back of the gaming room. Honore's quiet whimper and the brush of feet and skirts against the carpet proved the only sound in the room. No noise of passersby infiltrated from the street, testimony to the notion that no screams would penetrate to the street from that subterranean room.

A cold subterranean room. Gooseflesh rose on Christien's arms despite his coat and shirt. No way to free them presented itself. Only the heavy brocade curtain separated the gaming room from service and storage rooms beyond. Storage rooms with spirits. One spark would set the chamber exploding into flames.

He hesitated at the curtain.

330

Lang cocked his pistol. Lydia drew in her breath with a quick, sharp gasp. Honore screamed, a scream cut off in the middle.

Christien whirled, lashing out with his foot. His boot heel caught Frobisher on the side of the knee. He staggered back, groaning, and fell, taking Honore with him.

And Lang fired.

Lydia cried out. Christien spun toward her, caught her as she fell. No blood. He saw, felt, smelled no blood.

"Where, *ma chère*?"

"A warning shot only." Lang proceeded to reload his pistol. He could afford the time. Frobisher had Honore at knifepoint again.

"You try to attack one of us again," Lang continued, ramming the ball down the barrel, "and I'll shoot for real next time."

Christien laughed. Lydia snorted.

"What difference does it make when you're going to kill us anyway?" Lydia drawled as though bored.

"*C'est vrai.*" Christien tightened his hold on her.

She drew away. "If you're finished reloading, sirrah, I'll go peacefully . . . if you let my sister go."

"You'll go peacefully even if I don't let your sister go." Lang laughed this time. "Gerry, take the child first."

"No." Honore stuck out her lower lip like a child. She grasped the edge of a table. "N-no, you can't b-burn me up."

"I can. My uncle is paying me." Frobisher held up the knife, and the candlelight flickered in a silver ribbon down the blade. "Steel. And I have flint in my pocket. One spark in an open cask of spirits and—poof!"

"No, please." Honore dropped to her knees.

Lydia opened her mouth. Christien locked eyes with her,

flicked a glance toward Lang, then to Frobisher, then back to Lang. If she understood—

She too dropped to her knees, then lunged for Lang's legs to throw him off balance, ruin his aim if he tried to fire again.

Christien grasped Frobisher's wrist, twisted. He grunted. Christien kicked his knee again. Frobisher went down. Christien remained standing in possession of the knife.

He turned toward Lydia, to Elias Lang. She lay in a heap of tangled skirts on the rug, her hands locked around Lang's ankle. He kicked out with his other foot, swung it toward her face.

Christien lunged, knife before him like a bayonet. The blade slid into Lang's chest. Momentum carried them back, across a gaming table, onto the floor. Christien scrambled to his feet. Lang remained motionless, the knife still buried in his chest.

"He's dead." Christien spoke in a flat voice. Numbness flowed through him like a waking sleep.

"It's over?" Honore whimpered from beneath a table.

"No," Lydia and Christien said together.

Frobisher had vanished from the gaming chamber, and a tendril of smoke drifted through a gap in the brocade curtain.

"Out." Christien grasped Lydia's hands and hauled her to her feet.

Honore surged up and raced ahead of them between the tables, up the stairs, to the street door.

The locked street door with no key in sight.

"No." Honore began to beat on the door with both fists.

"Other door." Lydia breathed hard. "There must be another door."

"Honore, come." Christien drew her away from the door.

The three of them charged back down the steps, through the gaming room, past the brocade curtain. Smoke blinded them, thick, pungent, filling their eyes and mouths. At one end of the corridor, flames flicked toward a line of barrels. The stench of spilled spirits stung Christien's nostrils, caught in the back of his throat.

They fled in the other direction. A stairway rose steep and dark. Light flared at the top. Sunlight broken by the shadow of a man.

"Frobisher," Christien shouted.

In seconds Frobisher would be out the door, slam it, lock it from the outside.

Christien took the steps two at a time. With a flying leap, he tackled Frobisher and brought him down atop a pile of refuse.

Behind them, one of the barrels exploded.

29

The blast sent a wave of heat and flame sweeping down the corridor. Lydia raised her skirts above her knees and fled up the steps. Seconds later, a second barrel exploded.

Honore screamed. Lydia whirled around. Her sister sat on the bottom step, staring at the encroaching flames with her hands raised as though she could ward them off.

"Honore, get up here," Lydia cried.

Honore didn't move. "He was going to burn me alive."

"Yes, now come along or he still will." Lydia ran back down, grabbed Honore's shoulders, and tugged her up.

Honore didn't run. She stumbled, she fell, she crawled out of the dark stairwell with flames at the bottom and sunlight at the top. With nudges, tugs, and a slap to stop her from screaming further, Lydia got Honore into the alley moments before a third barrel exploded. Her body said collapse onto the fouled cobbles. No more strength to go on. Instinct said to keep running away from the blazing building.

Toward Christien, who came to take her hands in his.

"*Je regrette*—" Christien said. "You shouldn't have had to see this or endure this."

"I was as much a part of this as you. But you're wounded. Let me help you."

He glanced down at his arm. "Just a scratch. We need to be away from this building before everything inside explodes."

"Frobisher?"

"He's dead." Honore crawled through the muck to reach his side. "Like he wanted me."

"Not dead," Christien said. "Just stunned. I'll carry him away if you will get your sister," he said to Lydia.

Lydia bent down to take Honore's hands. "We need to get out of here."

"I know." Honore wiped her sleeve across her face, leaving behind a streak of dirt turning to mud with her tears, then scrambled to her feet and charged down the alley.

Lydia ran after her. By the time she reached the corner, Honore had vanished. Poised on one foot, Lydia swiveled a moment between seeking Honore and returning to Christien. Honore was distraught and alone in a seedy part of London. Christien was wounded and in charge of Gerald Frobisher. Honore was her little sister.

Christien was her future.

With one last scan up and down the street and the alley, Lydia turned and ran past the burning building, past piles of garbage, toward the man at the far end of the alleyway. "We need to see if a fire service will come here." She was panting. "And a magistrate. And—"

A bell began to clang in the distance, growing closer and closer. A throng materialized seemingly from the broken cobblestones.

"They'll come." Christien glanced down at Frobisher lying in the street, his hands tied behind him with Christien's cravat. "Someone will—"

The clang of the fire wagon drowned out the rest of his words. Apparently whoever owned the gaming establishment had paid a fire company to protect his property. Watching flames leap toward the hazy blue sky, Lydia doubted the firefighters would get more accomplished than keeping the blaze from spreading to other buildings.

Bystanders began to help with that, carrying water from a public well. And in the midst of it, a constable arrived with Honore in tow.

"You've some explaining to do," the officer said.

"We will, mon—sir." Christien grasped Frobisher's tied hands and pulled him to his feet. "We need to get this one to a magistrate."

"Is that so, man?" the constable asked.

Soiled and smelling of refuse, Frobisher stared at the cobbles and said nothing.

The constable escorted them several blocks to the magistrate's office. Inside a chamber scarcely large enough to hold the six of them and smelling of pickled herring, Christien told his story of working for the War Department and then the special assignment for the Home Office. He told of Lang's treachery and his intention to kill them all.

"He's the murderer," Frobisher burst out from his corner. "He murdered my uncle, the French traitor."

"Indeed." The magistrate's gaze flicked to Lydia. "Lady Gale, what do you have to say regarding this?"

"She'll lie for him," Frobisher called out again. "She's his—"

"Quiet," the constable commanded.

"I'm his—" Lydia worried her lower lip between her teeth. "He was a friend of my husband's, is all."

Beside her, Christien flinched away.

"He is without question loyal to Great Britain," Lydia continued. "You can trust his word and the word of the daughters of Lord Bainbridge."

"Of course, my lady." The magistrate smiled at her and Honore. "I believe you, but I need to ask him more questions."

"Perhaps you'll allow me to take the ladies home first, sir?" Beneath the grime of smoke and dried blood, Christien's face gleamed a sickly gray. He held his arm, the one he'd injured while saving her from a fall in March, taut to his side.

"He needs to see a physician first," Lydia said.

"He will in good time." The magistrate nodded, sending his old-fashioned queue sliding over his shoulder. "And I'll send you ladies home in my carriage now."

"But—" Lydia began.

"Go." Christien's voice cracked like a whip. "You look like you're about to fall down."

She felt like she was about to fall down, but she wasn't comfortable leaving Christien with Frobisher and the magistrate. Without her and Honore there as reminders of who their father was, the magistrate just might choose to believe an Englishman. "If you'll take Miss Honore home," Lydia addressed the magistrate, "I'll stay."

"But, Lydia," Honore protested, "I need you to talk to Father for me."

"You can talk to him yourself. Right now, Monsieur de Meuse needs me more."

Honore burst into tears. Lydia remained at Christien's side. He gazed at her with his eyes bright and color returning to his skin.

In the end, Honore departed in the car of the constable's

spinster daughter. The magistrate sent a servant riding for the War Department to verify Christien's employment with them, and after Frobisher became sick on the magistrate's floor, the constable took him to a cell beyond a heavy door.

Once they were alone, the magistrate turned to Christien. "I believe you, sir, but must observe the formalities. There will be an inquest, of course, if they find the remains of Elias Lang. Such a pity."

"I thought he was my friend and a loyal subject." Christien sounded as though he spoke from inside a well. "I thought—it's good I already resigned. I can't have been a very good agent."

"Nor I a sister," Lydia said.

"But perhaps—"

The arrival of a colonel from the War Department interrupted Christien. They greeted one another with a firm handshake, obvious acquaintances or even good colleagues.

Christien turned to Lydia. "Lady Gale, allow me to present Colonel Jonathan Timmons."

"Gale?" Timmons's pale blue eyes widened. "Any relation to Sir Charles Gale?"

"His wife," Lydia said.

"Wife? But I thought—" Timmons glanced at Christien. "Quite a sense of humor good ol' Charles had. Saying you're a petite thing indeed. Ha-ha."

"Indeed." Lydia injected as much frost as she could into her tone. Frost to counteract the heat flushing through her. Frost to steady her suddenly trembling hands.

"If you please," Christien said, "I'd like to take Lady Gale home."

"But we need to know about Lang," Timmons objected.

"Later." Christien offered Lydia his arm.

"It's your duty to this country," Timmons insisted.

"Lang is dead. Enquiries into his death and what he told me beforehand can wait. My lady comes first." Leaving Timmons spluttering, Christien swept out of the magistrate's office, Lydia on his arm.

"You put me before duty." Not so much as a crystal remained of Lydia's frost.

"If I had weeks ago, none of this would have happened." Christien raised one hand to hail a passing hackney. "I should have resigned the instant you told me of the blackmail. I should have seen what Lang was doing. But my quest for revenge against Napoleon got in my way."

"I could have stayed and listened to you about my father. But I was so determined to be loyal to him, to my family." She swallowed.

The hackney stopped, and Christien handed Lydia inside. Once seated, she turned to him and demanded, "Was Charles unfaithful to me?"

"*Ma chère*, it does no one any good to rake up the past."

"Which is as good as a yes." Lydia stared down at her hands. They trembled. Her lower lip quivered. She clamped it to the upper, but the tears still came, hot, steady, unchecked in their twin paths down her cheeks. "I think I've always known, but I couldn't believe it. I didn't want to think he wasn't a gentleman or wasn't thinking of me while away—at least partly a good husband. But he lied and cheated and—" She pounded the seat with her fists until the leather cracked open and moldy stuffing oozed onto the floor.

Christien caught hold of her hands and began to caress them. "Lydia, this does you no good. You mustn't let his bad behavior destroy you. It . . . I . . ." He pried her fingers open. "If I can forgive Napoleon, surely you can forgive Charles for his *amour*."

"Charles, yes. Myself?" Lydia dashed her tears away on her sleeve. "I thought I was so clever marrying Charles, even though Father didn't quite approve. He signed the marriage license, as I wasn't of age yet, but he didn't like it."

"So he isn't always an autocrat." Christien smiled at her.

Lydia looked away, her face hot. "No, I suppose not. And he was right in the end. Oh, that hurts to admit."

"But you did it." Christien nudged her chin up with his fingertips. His eyes, bluer than a summer sky, gazed into hers. "Not all men are fools, liars, and cheats. And sometimes we have wisdom to impart."

"A great deal more than sometimes." Lydia ran her tongue along her parched lips. "I blamed Charles for leaving me in favor of his regiment. I blamed my father for trying to dictate my life. And you—" Her throat closed. She swallowed. "And you for—"

"For loving you?" He rubbed the ball of his thumb along her lower lip. "Or perhaps because you love me too?"

The power of speech eluded her, so she nodded, and he kissed her. He kissed her until they reached Cavendish Square. He kissed her after they stopped.

When the jarvey shouted for them to get down and pay, Christien stopped kissing her and drew away. "I believe after that, a proposal is in order. But I'd rather not ask on the heels of your learning your husband was unfaithful."

"Thank you. It's not that I think you will be. I simply fear—"

The hackney shifted, and the door wrenched open. "Get out and pay or I'll have the Watch on ye," the jarvey commanded.

"Of course." Lydia slipped past him and headed toward the house and the now-open front door. In a moment, she could be alone in her room to think, to ponder, to decide whether or not marrying Christien was wise after Charles. He would give her as much time as she demanded, not because he didn't love her enough to pursue her, but because . . .

Because he understood she needed to stop running and do some pursuing of her own.

Behind her, the hackney door slammed. Wheels began to rumble.

"Wait." Lydia sped down the steps and into the square. "Wait."

The hackney stopped. Lydia ran up to the door, making herself the entertainment of several dozen members of the haut ton. She yanked open the door. "Yes, I'll marry you on one condition."

Several onlookers, including the loitering hackney driver, applauded. Others called advice, from telling Christien to keep driving away to suggesting he get down immediately.

He took the latter advice. "What's that?"

She told him and he laughed. Hand in hand, they retraced her steps to the house. Lydia's cheeks burned at the audience, but she kept her head high and a smile fixed to her lips.

"We'll enjoy the news sheets tomorrow," Christien observed.

"Enough to eclipse Honore's behavior?"

"Along with Lang's disgrace, yes."

They climbed the front steps together. Lemster stood at the top, his grin broad. "The family is in the drawing room, my lady, except for Miss Barbara. She's in Lady Bainbridge's sitting room. But the library is empty."

"Thank you. We want the drawing room." Lydia turned toward the ground floor chamber door. Too little sound emerged from behind it, and her heart began to thud.

Was she making another terrible mistake?

She glanced at Christien, thought of their conversation that felt like a lifetime ago, and whispered a prayer. "Thy will be done, Lord."

Christien squeezed her hand and pushed open the door. A quiet conversation ceased. Father and Whittaker rose.

"What took you so long?" Honore demanded. She had washed away the dirt and changed her dress, but redness around her eyes told of her earlier tears.

"We had further business," Lydia said.

"You should have come home with your sister," Father said.

Lydia took a deep breath to keep her feathers flat. "Honore was taken care of, and I wasn't certain a magistrate from the East End would treat Christien fairly."

"Christien, is it?" Father grunted. "Rather familiar, don't you think?"

"She's agreed to marry me, sir," Christien said, "with your permission."

"My permission?" Father's jaw dropped. "Lydia, what do you say about that?"

"I said I'd marry him if you approved."

"Oh, Lydia," Honore and Cassandra squealed.

Mama started to speak.

A glance from Father quieted all of them. "Why would you suddenly want my permission for one of your starts? You've never wanted it before."

"I made a mistake with Charles. Not," she added with an upward tilt of her chin, "living in Tavistock, but marrying Charles. I should have listened to your objections."

"Yes, you should have. He was a lying, cheating—ahem." Father's face reddened.

"I know." Lydia sighed against a lingering pain in her chest. "In my heart I've always known. I thought I was just not a good enough wife. But really I wasn't a good enough daughter, rejecting your counsel."

Father cleared his throat and blinked. "I didn't want you to get hurt, but for all my efforts, I'm no good at denying you girls anything."

"Except me." Honore jumped up and embraced him. "You never have to concern yourself about me falling in love with the wrong man again. I'm done with falling in love."

Everyone laughed.

"It's true," Honore insisted. "I've learned my lesson."

The laughter continued.

Pouting, she dropped back into her chair.

Dabbing at the corners of his eyes, Father strode forward and clasped Lydia's and Christien's hands in his. "I never thought I'd want a foreigner marrying one of my daughters, de Meuse, but you'll do. You'll do nicely, though if you are ever unfaithful, you'd better run back to the continent. Do you understand me?"

"Perfectly, sir." Christien bowed. "Do be assured that I've waited for Lydia too long to not keep loving her forever, now that I know her in person and find her better in reality than in her letters."

Mama began to cry, though she smiled. Honore and Cassandra sighed.

Lydia's heart turned to melted wax. "I never realized that opening my door to a stranger would end up opening my heart to God, to my family even more, and to loving you." She turned to Christien and kissed him. "Now, can we get married by special license so we can run off to—"

She stopped and laughed and joined Father and Christien in their resounding, "No."

Acknowledgments

Without the ladies and gentleman of the Beau Monde, I doubt I would have made it through this novel with any accuracy at all. No matter how miniscule or silly my question, someone was there to give me the answer, from what was really wrong with Napoleon's regime to how I would manage to get three people into a curricle. And thank you for the ideas on disasters that can befall a lady in a riding habit and mounting sidesaddle. Any errors are mine, not theirs. Their assistance was beyond measure.

And to my husband, who put up with a lot of prepackaged food while I worked on this until—oops!—it's time for supper. Thank you for your understanding.

And speaking of understanding, I appreciate my editor's patience with my propensity for forgetting to turn off italics, my homophone-challenged spelling, and my lapses in logical thinking.

No one has put up with more angst from me than my agent, except some really special writing friends, amidst all the special writing friends who, no matter how busy, always took the time to smooth my ruffled feathers when I was being a birdbrain. Especially Debbie Lynne, whose last-minute assistance is a true example of blessings overflowing, shaken down, and spilling over.

More than I can express in a few words do I appreciate the prayer support I received from the His Writers group, the Finish the Book group, and CAN Inc. members.

And last, but far from least, I mustn't forget the special furry, purry support I received from my cats, who seemed to know when I was struggling and came to cuddle, and my golden retriever, who sacrificed playtime but remained at my side anyway—when he wasn't getting into mischief.

Award-winning author **Laurie Alice Eakes** wanted to be a writer since knowing what one was. Her first book won the National Readers Choice Award in 2007, and her third book was a Carol Award finalist in 2010. Between December 2008 and January 2010, she sold thirteen books to Barbour Publishing, Avalon Books, and Revell, making her total sales fifteen. Recently, she added two novella sales to that collection. Her first book with Revell, *Lady in the Mist*, was picked up by Crossings Book Club, and three of her books were chosen for large-print editions by Thorndike Press. She has been a public speaker for as long as she can remember; thus, she suffers just enough stage fright to keep her sharp.

In 2002, while in graduate school for writing fiction, Laurie Alice began to teach fiction in person and online. She lives in Texas with her husband, two dogs, and probably too many cats.

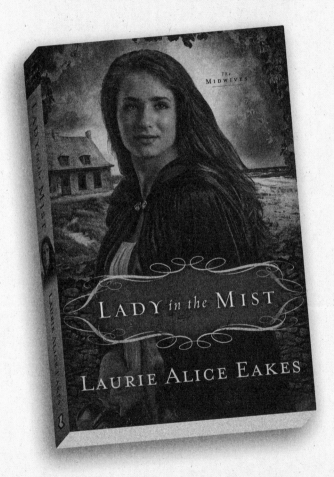